FIREWORK

T0155097

Tyrant Books
USA
9 Clinton Street
Upper north store
NYC 10002

Europe
Giancarlo DiTrapano
Via Flavia 72
Rome 00187
Italy

www.NYTyrant.com

Copyright © Eugene Marten 2017
ISBN 13: 978-0-9913608-6-4
Second Edition

This is a work of fiction. All of the characters and organizations
portrayed herein are products of the author's imagination or are used
fictitiously.

All rights reserved, including the right to reproduce this book or
portions thereof in any manner whatsoever without written permission
except in the case of brief quotations in critical reviews and articles.

Cover design by Erik Carter
Interior design by Adam Robinson

FIREWORK

a novel

Eugene Marten

To Gian

But always for Kelly

JELONNEK

The anchorman says, "A public employee." Then there is no sound. There is a woman on a corner, wearing white boots and waving at traffic. A station wagon pulls over. We don't know what color it was but can tell by the front plate it is property of the city, state, or federal government. We can't see his face. The woman leans in the window, moving her mouth.

There is no color, there is no sound. Then the anchorman says, "Trying to buy sex with your tax dollars." She slaps the top twice and steps back. A light flashes down the street. Because the lens through which we are looking is of the kind that compresses space, the unmarked car barreling toward us seems to get bigger without getting closer. (We don't know the light was blue.) Two men get out in a hurry, approach the wagon from either side. One of them talks to the driver. He opens the door and hauls the driver out by his shirt, forces him facedown onto the street and kneels on his back while his partner applies the handcuffs, helps himself to a wallet.

His lips move—the reading of the rights, we assume.

We don't know where the woman went but the driver's face is bloody. We don't know his name. We don't know that the unmarked car was green, that inside it smelled like fast food, that when they shoved Jelonnek into the ridiculous plaid of the backseat there was a metal bucket on the floor by his feet. That the cop pressing down on the top of his head said, "You spill em you swallow every last one," and the other cop said, "Like it matters," and the one pressing down said, "Like you know," and the other one said, "I know if they don't shine you can't see em," and his partner said, "They don't see em they smell em. I kill with those little black bastards." Then they got back up front and ate their lunch.

When they were done they wrote him a ticket for impeding the flow of traffic. A tow truck came for the wagon. The one who was going fishing jerked the gearshift, water sloshed in the bucket. They ran a light and turned, drove past a boarded-up gas station with weeds sprouting where they'd pulled the pumps, a check-cashing establishment (ten percent off the top), a modest brick building purporting to be the Refuge of Last Days; pulled up in the driveway of an old warehouse housing nothing now but dust in the dark. A paddy wagon like a black metal box on wheels, half-hidden in weed trees. Jelonnek was extracted gently from the backseat. One of the cops put his wallet back in his pocket. On his way to the back of the truck he looked into the lens of a camera perched on a man's shoulder like a rocket launcher. Because he was still too numb to just turn away or duck, his eyes bulge into your living room in living color, hands behind his back like he's got some terrible surprise.

In the wagon there were metal ledges on either side to sit on and only a couple of spaces left. It reminded Jelonnek of his paper route, of the truck that had brought the bundles—except for the partitions on the sides like stalls in a public lavatory. All you saw were everyone's knees. When you sat you had to bend over while they took off one of the cuffs, looped it through a shackle and put it back on your wrist. Then they rolled down the dark and the only light came through two small windows in the back.

"Why did the john cross the road?" someone asked him. The punchline had something to do with a social disease; Jelonnek was barely listening. Someone else laughed for him but it was an old joke the first time you heard it. Everything was: the way they called each other John, the fart you kept not hearing, the guy who would once in a while bang his head against the inside of the wagon. He would bang the back of his head against the metal and at the same time mutter, "Shit" or "Fuck" or "God" like some kind of hierarchic chant. The claustrophobe was even worse.

They'd written him a ticket for impeding the flow, for not wearing a seatbelt. He still felt the street on his face.

You got used to the dimness and when they opened the door the light started everything over again. The new guy looked like some sort of businessman, had silver hair and wore a nice suit.

"Put this man in first class," someone said. "Why did the pimp cross the road?"

Two or three guys said everything. You could feel someone's knees shaking. If you kept your back straight your arms didn't hurt as much.

"I wanna say no contest," a voice said, addressing the matter of pleas. The speaker sat across from Jelonnek. You couldn't quite make out his face but he was apparently something of an old hand, someone with a working knowledge of local jurisprudence, familiar with the statutes, the degree of misdemeanor, the names and temperaments of judges. The maximum penalties and alternative sentences.

"I wanna say diversion," he said.

"Da virgin."

"John school." You spent eight hours in a classroom, getting lectured by former hookers, watching footage of AIDS patients sloughing off their skin like snakes.

"And you got to pay for that?" someone said.

"Six of one, half a dozen of the other."

The engine idled. "The laws were made for kings and merchants."

Jelonnek felt himself nodding. He wanted to say something clever or useful, contribute—it seemed to provide a sort of status—but nothing occurred to him and then the claustrophobe started up again. He told whoever was listening how he'd spent an afternoon trapped in an elevator, how his rescuers had found him soiled, naked, curled into the fetal position.

"Well don't start that shit here," one of them said and Jelonnek said, "You should carry a card or something."

Another burst of quiet. The guy who'd been banging his head had stopped banging it and started worrying about his wife. Laid up in a maternity ward with an eight-pound boy. They loaded up one more john before they left. You could see the condition his face was in just before they rolled down the door again. There was no more room to sit so he lay on the floor between the ledges and said, "I thought this was America."

"Ah damn," the voice across the dark said.

"Always room for one more." Someone outside hit the truck twice.

"This is entrapment," the man on the floor said, his voice muffled, injured.

"Why *did* the john cross the road?" They lurched forward. Everyone swayed and banged their shoulders and someone swore. The old hand hummed "The Ride of the Valkyrie." Someone farted again and Jelonnek giggled. Time had resumed like the play clock in a sporting event and he was giddy with it. You were moving on to something new and next, even if it meant being swallowed. Tree branches scraping the sides of the wagon.

At the booking window they took his wallet again and didn't give it back. They took his watch, his shoelaces, keys, comb, and change, and itemized all denominations. The cop who stood him there was the one who wasn't going fishing. He seemed different now, bored and distant, and didn't call him John anymore. The fun part must have been over. The woman in the window asked Jelonnek for the information that wasn't on his driver's license. She didn't look at him till she took his picture. She kept having trouble with the computer, a support guy would have to come and help her. There was always trouble with the computer, it seemed, whenever you went some place that used them.

"Now press Enter," the support guy said.

"Jell-O neck?" the woman in the window said.

Someone laughed in the holding cell. Behind him. A guy in the holding cell had kept pacing, though there was hardly room for it. He was short and stocky and had red hair. He would get too close. He would almost brush Jelonnek's chest, almost step on his feet, though not quite. If they hadn't come and got him Jelonnek was sure he would have said something. There must have been fifteen of them in there.

"Jelonnek," Jelonnek said.

"Mother's maiden name," the woman said. "Influenza. Diabetes. Venereal disease." She said it like a single word.

There was a booking fee of twenty-five dollars. If you didn't have it on you they would bill you.

He wore his cuffs in front now. The cop next to him held his hand like a manicurist and told him to relax, rolled his thumb off the card. The woman in the window said, "Look up" and a Polaroid camera flashed in his face. He signed a form that absolved the city of all blame, though for what he wasn't sure. "Forever hold harmless," it said. Blue spots in front of his eyes. A red sticker meant suicide watch. The woman in the window looked up the bail schedule. If he couldn't make bail, they would hold him till his arraignment in the morning, or the morning after that. The word triggered a voltage of panic. Serious criminals were arraigned, murderers and molesters. He asked if he could make a phone call.

"You can make as many as you want for ten minutes," she said. "Collect."

They locked him in the phone cell. The phone was metal and looked indestructible but not for lack of effort. It was still warm. Jelonnek dialed O. A man asked if he could help him and Jelonnek gave him the number of the bank, her three-digit extension. She picked up halfway through the second ring and said, "Can you hold, please?" It wasn't the first time. Jelonnek heard music, a popular song. He didn't like it but was suddenly aware of nuances in it he'd never noticed before and didn't want to be; Jelonnek thought of himself as a rock-and-roller.

The song ended and a new one came on, one he'd never heard before. The operator said, "She doesn't seem to be answering, sir. Would you like to try again later?" Jelonnek said it was an emergency. He would have liked to hear the rest of the song, but the operator hung up. He hadn't heard it before, and he would like to have heard it till he came to like it, till it became the only thing he'd called for. Till it was like remembering something you never knew.

The guy at the booking window was explaining his tattoos in Spanish.

Jelonnek dialed the bank again direct. Another operator came on and offered assistance. Jelonnek recited the extension again but when he heard her voice it was recorded.

This happened sometimes as well. She invited him to leave a message but the operator wouldn't let him.

"It's chargeable," she said. "You can try again later." He heard a dial tone. The dial tone was replaced by another recording. It advised Jelonnek to hang up and try again. Or, it suggested, he could call the operator.

The phone smelled like spit.

The recording repeated itself. The line went dead. They were bringing someone else to the phone cell. Jelonnek recognized the last guy they'd brought to the paddy wagon. His eyes were swollen shut and as big as plums.

"Hello," he said into the void. "It's me." He pressed the receiver to his ear as if the silence might leak out. "I'm at the Justice Center."

The phone made a harsh sound, a loud broken buzzing.

Someone was always shouting something. On the way to his cell some kind of Muslim called Jelonnek an Amorite. He said the Amorites had pale skin because their father, Canaan, was cursed with leprosy. He said they had sexual intercourse with dogs and jackals in the mountains of the Caucasus. Dogs became man's best friend, he said, because they would lick his leprous sores.

"He say that to all y'all," the IG said.

The cell was empty. One of the IG's dropped his mattress on the bed, a metal plank fastened to the wall with angle iron. Then they slid the gate shut and took his cuffs off through the food slot. His arms floated, the best thing that had happened to him all day. His left hand was slightly purple. He tried to pee. The toilet had no seat and jutted low from the wall like a stainless steel jaw. For some reason he couldn't pee and tried to wash the ink off his fingers in the stainless steel sink. The water was cold, there was no soap. He sat on the middle of the bed and cleared his throat. A terse echo like the twang of a recoiling spring; he wondered what the walls were made of. They were smooth and painted and one had a piece of toilet paper stuck to it. Someone had drawn a window.

There was always shouting. At first all you could make out were the same two or three words. From the bed all you could see was the polished beige cinderblock across the hall. Part of a fire extinguisher. Jelonnek thought about counting the bricks but decided he could save that for later.

"Everything is everything," someone shouted.

But he was sure he would have said something to the guy with red hair.

They'd taken the businessman's tie but let him keep his jacket. He looked like some kind of vice-president or maybe a corporate

lawyer. He kicked his mattress to the wall opposite the toilet and said, "I'd flip you for the bunk but I won't be here long." He washed his hands, then paced in front of the gate for a while. Every time someone came down the hall he stopped and faced the bars as if at the approach of his liberators. Finally, he sat down on his mattress and said, "So what do you do?"

Jelonnek didn't like being asked this. He was bad at summing things up, but he tried anyway.

"I'd go crazy," the businessman said.

"That's what they say," Jelonnek said. "What about you?"

"Consulting." The businessman went inside his jacket like he was reaching for his card.

"Married?" he said.

Jelonnek shook his head. "You?"

"Thirty years."

"What do you think she'll say?"

"About what?"

"About what do you think?"

"I was just asking directions." The businessman looked where his watch had been. "Forty minutes, an hour tops." He went to the bars and demanded soap. He went back to the sink and washed his hands again, scraping the ink with his nails.

The young ones called each other out from their cells. Set to set, block to block, nation to nation. They called each other soldier. Six pop, five drop, nines and gats and gauges. Greetings and threats indistinguishable in the voices of monster children.

The IG's let them talk. The IG's were little more than civilians in uniform—pale blue shirts and dark blue pants. They had no weapons, just keys and radios. Some engaged the inmates freely in conversation, and even if you could make out these exchanges it was hard to tell on which sides of the gate the conversants stood.

◆ ◆ ◆

They rolled it down the hall on a cart and passed it through the slot in plastic trays, still warm. You got a paper towel and a spork. If the sporks weren't returned each inmate in the cell would be subject to a strip search.

"Any excuse!" someone yelled, and someone else in falsetto, "Me first!"

Meatloaf, mashed potatoes and gravy, peas and carrots, fruit cocktail. Someone down the row asked if they had to eat their vegetables.

"Beats airline food," the businessman said.

Jelonnek drank his apple juice.

Jelonnek didn't like the businessman but in a way was sorry to see him go. Before he left he reached inside his jacket again. He didn't say goodbye. Someone down the row said, "Thanks for the head." Any time anyone left, that was what he said.

Jelonnek stood over the toilet and pissed for forty seconds. He'd barely finished when he heard them opening the gate. He didn't turn around.

"I miss supper?" he heard someone say. "Can you make me a plate?"

"Is that for here to go?" Jelonnek pushed the button on the wall with his toe. The water vortexed weakly but didn't go all the way down. Then he turned around. The new arrival had his arms in the food slot. His flesh a calendar of scars.

"Let me smoke with you one time," he said to the IG, and the IG handed him a cigarette through the bars. He left his mattress on the floor and sat on the bed.

"I'm there," Jelonnek said.

The man on the bed tore the filter off and put the rest in his pocket. "You look like you over there to me."

"I mean I have the bed."

"I mean you did. Looks like I got it now—unless you plan to get it back."

Jelonnek looked at the toilet, then at the mattress in the corner.

"You look a little light in the ass to me," the man on the bed said, "but we can work." He stretched out to take a nap.

"We good then," he decided with his eyes closed.

Jelonnek sat on the mattress and tried to convey strong silence. A movement caught his eye, something scurrying out of sight in the hall, but he wasn't sure. He heard the new guy's stomach rumble.

"Three years ain't shit," he said in his sleep.

There were seventeen bricks from floor to ceiling.

"Tried to play me—big as I am."

"Is you big?"

"Bigger than you."

"You fat but you ain't big."

"Yeah I'm fat. You wanna hurt me call me skinny."

"They keep women here?"

"First District."

"I want to kick it over there."

"That figures—I thought I smelled pussy."

"That's just Puerto Rican." And everyone laughed who was in a position to.

Apparently they'd run out of mattresses but the next new guy said the floor was fine. His t-shirt said KILL 'EM ALL AND LET GOD SORT 'EM OUT, but he was friendly in his way. As soon as they closed the gate he started doing one-handed push-ups. Then he did sit-ups, squats, lunges, touch-your-toes. By the hundred. "You need to break off with that," the guy on the bunk said. "Ain't no room here

18

for all that." But he didn't make a move to stop it, and Jelonnek kept silent. The guy with the t-shirt switched hands.

He was friendly in his way. He talked on the toilet, defecating forthrightly as though it were a part of conversation. He kept winking but Jelonnek didn't know if it was a nervous tic or We Have To Stick Together.

The guy who'd stolen the bunk rolled over to the wall, muttering into his hand.

"It'll be better in Corrections," the guy with the t-shirt assured Jelonnek. He sat knock-kneed, made a noxious sound like an amateur trumpet. "After you get arraigned. They got dorms, no bars—this sheet of plastic just comes down from the ceiling. In the pods you get your own cell. If someone comes after your ass you can lock yourself in and only the guard can open it. *Noli me tangere.*"

"What's that?" Jelonnek said.

"Delta Company. First Battalion, Third Infantry."

"I think I can make bail," Jelonnek said.

The new guy rapped the wall with his knuckles. "Steel plate," he said and rapped his skull as if referring to both surfaces. Then he wiped himself and inspected the darkened swatch intently like a seer reading entrails. He pushed the button and stood and watched the contents of the toilet spin slowly without going down.

"Someone should've told you," Jelonnek said.

The Muslim or whatever he was who'd called Jelonnek an Amorite was shouting over everyone. "A trillion years ago the human race was all niggers living on the moon," he shouted. "The tribe of the Shabazz." Then they'd come down to earth, built the city of Mecca and wrote the Koran. Among them was a mad scientist who was eventually banished to a remote island along with 59,999 of his followers. In exile he plotted revenge, performing genetic experiments on his disciples toward the end of creating a race of super-warriors. As his work progressed, so did the aptitude of his subjects for violence and cruelty develop, so did their eyes turn blue and their skin become paler. Accompanied by this devilish new race, the outcasts eventually escaped exile and conquered the world.

"We the last descendants of the ancient Shabazz!" the Muslim yelled.

"You here that, Superman?" someone said.

"Public nuisance," the guy on the bunk said.

The guy with the t-shirt shook his head.

"Domestic violence," Jelonnek said.

The guy with the t-shirt shook his head again and got up. He stood over the toilet and unzipped his pants. Jelonnek felt another one coming on, too, but he thought he'd wait. See if this guy ever went to sleep.

The guy with the t-shirt finished and said, "They say I shot my neighbor's dog." He kicked the button.

"I shouldn't have done that," he said, and they watched it overflow.

He took off all his clothes and started to karate the walls, shouting with each kick and punch.

"Delta!" he kicked and punched. "Third Infantry!" He was sobbing. "Old Guard..."

The IG's came and told him he had a visitor. They had backup.

"What about his mess on the floor?" the guy on the bunk demanded, not for the first time.

"We put in a work order," the IG said.

"It stank."

"Hold your nose."

"We still breathin it."

The gate clanked shut. "He ain't comin back," the guy on the bunk said. He stood on it and pissed with great accuracy into the sink. A knuckle-shaped patch of red on the wall.

"Where's he going?"

"Safety cell. Butt naked, too." He lay back down. "Delta my ass."

"How do you know?"

"You see me tryin to sleep?"

The last new guy was small and slender and had a ponytail. He was dressed all in denim.

"That ain't no janitor," the guy on the bunk said.

"Watch where you step," the IG advised. He sprayed air freshener through the bars.

"Now it smell like strawberry shit," the guy on the bunk said.

The new guy asked Jelonnek if he could sit on the mattress with him. Jelonnek thought about it. Then he pointed to a spot by the bars and said, "It's almost dry over there."

Seventeen bricks from floor to ceiling. Thirty-five bars: eleven in the gate, twelve each in the stationary panels.

The guy on the bunk snored. The kid with the ponytail didn't say much, just squatted on the damp floor with his back to the bars, deflected Jelonnek's only attempt at conversation. He seemed to be singing to himself. Jelonnek had to piss again but he could wait till the kid with the ponytail was asleep; he didn't want to have to carry his mattress to the sink, didn't want to go near the toilet. He could wait for the janitor.

The lights in the ceiling were recessed and covered with wire screens. The screens were divided into little squares, fourteen by fourteen. It was still Monday.

A rat crawled into the cell and nibbled on a turd. Jelonnek put down his six and carried the one. He lost his place and started over.

The lights in the cell went out. The ones in the hallway stayed on.

The gate opened. He lay sideways, curled up with his back to the wall. His shirt bunched under his head. His eyes were closed but he wasn't sleeping. He had to go, he couldn't go. Like a metal rod in there trying to force its way out the tip of him.

The gate opened but he kept his eyes shut. Someone came in.

"Like he waitin on us."

"The fuck is this?"

"It ain't meatloaf."

"Used to be."

Frantic breathing, flesh in motion. He thought of the guy in the t-shirt doing his squats and lunges, but the guy in the t-shirt was gone.

"It's just a bad dream," one of them said.

"Goldilocks and the Three Dogs."

"Who been sleepin in *my* shit?" And whoever said it was pleased with himself and kept saying it.

Giggles. Blows like someone beating a rug. Muffled grunts.

"Open him up."

"Gimme the spoon then."

"You just havin a bad dream," one of them said.

He had to go. He could wait. He felt it in his back and front but he could wait as long as he had to. If you tried to straighten something would break. He didn't move or open his eyes.

When Jelonnek was a boy on the Fourth of July he lit fuses all day long. He launched bottle rockets from his hand, held a sparkler in his mouth and six in each fist, trying to write his name in light— the first letter always fades before the last one is done. Jumped through the Fountain of Flame like it was a lawn sprinkler. When the old man was too drunk to care, Jelonnek would reach for the big ones. The big ones had waterproof wicks and he'd toss them in the swimming pool next door: blue flash, muted thump, a column of water you couldn't see in the dark, but you'd hear it collapse. He'd light a quarter-stick with a mosquito chaser, cock his arm, wait till the fuse was just about gone. It drove everyone crazy but he still had all his fingers.

He wasn't sure why this came to him now, but it was as brave as he'd ever been.

The janitor came in the morning. The stench filled the cell but Jelonnek was glad; it might disguise the one he hoped no one would notice. He tied his shirt around his waist and was glad he wore dark pants. The kid with the ponytail was gone. The janitor waited with his mop and bucket and wet-vac while Jelonnek and the guy on the bunk were cuffed and taken out of the cell. They had Jelonnek's Polaroid. They took him around the corner where a dozen other inmates waited in single file. A common chain was threaded through the cuffs and they were led like a beast of many legs through a vestibule and down a long corridor with no windows. No talking, there was just the rumbling of the floor and the clink of the chain and Jelonnek thought he heard street traffic passing below them. Through another vestibule with a guard in a plexiglass booth like a cell of his own, into a stainless steel elevator the size of someone's living room. Right off the elevator they were taken into a long narrow chamber with benches along the walls. One side was already occupied by men wearing orange scrub suits and rubber slippers. One of them was standing in the corner and Jelonnek thought he looked familiar. Paul someone, someone he hadn't seen since the third grade. He'd stood in the corner then too, rehearsing his future. When Mrs. Bailey faced the choir with her back to him, he would turn around and expose himself. "Now let me see yours," he demanded later, in the cloakroom, at recess, of boy or girl. That was probably why Jelonnek remembered him. He even had the same silly grin, only higher off the floor. Their eyes met briefly.

His pants were no longer soaked but they were still very damp. The guy next to him looked hard at him, got up as though to move until the chain reminded him he couldn't. He started to say something and the door opened.

The chain was removed and an officer in another kind of uniform came in and led them through another door into the courtroom. It was filled with people and noise but not the same kind of noise as the other part of the Justice Center, where every sound you made rang and never quite died away. Thick carpet and wood-paneled walls, no windows in here either. The seats like pews, the first three rows empty. The scrubs sat up front. The women came in from the other side. They put them in the rows across the aisle and they looked worse off than the men because they'd fallen further and harder. Suits and briefcases standing up front and to the side. The judge had not yet arrived, the nameplate on the bench said magistrate. Everyone in uniform was a bailiff or a sheriff. The one with the loudest voice took the aisle between the seats and told everyone to be quiet, that you couldn't eat or drink in the courtroom. Then a woman in a black robe entered and sat the bench. All rose. The bailiff pronounced her name.

The judge explained the proceedings, the pleas available to them. The bailiff told someone to take his hat off. Another announced the time and date. It was still early.

They started with the last letter of the alphabet. An assistant stood next to the judge with his arms full of folders. You went up one at a time and stood at a lectern in front of the bench. There was a microphone but it wasn't on. If you pled not guilty you were taken out of the room and made to wait somewhere while they assigned a trial date. Some people were joined by attorneys. Some were found to have other charges and warrants outstanding, and these were usually returned to their seats, futures relegated to the back of the docket.

Drunk driving, simple assault, fourth degree assault, criminal mischief. The assistant would do something with the folder, then place it before the judge. But every other case was soliciting and she, the court, wondered aloud at such disproportion.

"Were they running a special?" she said, and the laughter was so boisterous she banged her gavel for order.

The guy who'd been roughed up stood. He still couldn't open his eyes and had to be led up the aisle. The only woman with a suit and briefcase met him at the bench, court-appointed, prematurely gray. After considerable whispering counsel and client left the room entirely, diverted to some unknown tributary of the system.

He bumped a chair on his way out, muttered something about kings and merchants.

Another day set aside, a new file opened, the next offender summoned to the bench.

The guy next to Jelonnek kept raising his arm, hand over his nose. He whispered to the bailiff.

"If she don't smell it," the bailiff said, "it don't smell."

Resisting arrest, endangering a child. The judge and her assistant moved them along, doled out due process with admirable rhythm and efficiency like servers in a public cafeteria. Menacing, menacing, criminal trespass. The right to a speedy trial waived. By the time Jelonnek heard his name, he'd heard enough to know that no contest was the only call to make. The court would reserve a day for sentencing and the whole circuit, without all those rights in the way, would complete itself that much sooner. And because he was a first offender, a working man who held a responsible job, he knew he would be released on his own recognizance, and on the way out he glanced at the man he'd been a boy with in the third grade, who glanced back as if he still might ask Jelonnek to reciprocate.

Finally it was Tuesday.

They gave back almost everything they'd taken from him. They gave him his car keys but his car was at the warehouse and he no longer had any way of getting there. He took the visitors' exit. The bus stop was around the corner and up two blocks, the Justice Center turning and looming the whole time like he couldn't escape its gravitational pull. He heard the sound of basketball coming faintly from the squat, fortified buildings beneath the court tower. Jelonnek hated basketball; football was his game, though he'd never played.

Tuesday was sunny, and warmer than the day before. At first the bus was almost empty. Jelonnek sat in the middle of it so the driver wouldn't talk to him, but the driver just raised his voice and asked Jelonnek if he fished.

Jelonnek hadn't been fishing since he was a kid. He opened the window.

"Too bad," the driver said. "Perch are spawning."

Jelonnek asked what day it was, just to make sure.

They crossed the river to the old market on the west side, yellow brick clocktower and windows like a church. The bus filled with shoppers, plastic bags and butcher paper. Jelonnek smelled meat and fresh greens. Himself. He moved to another seat but people kept looking at him so he got off two stops before his building.

They shared one bedroom near the edge of the city line. After he made sure she wasn't there he took a hot shower. Dozed on his feet. When he got out the phone was ringing, and he grabbed it in time to hear someone hang up. Her, or his job. He would call his job later.

He put on a robe and lay on the couch. He managed to doze off again, but something kept waking him up. It was the voice in the wagon, the old hand, but what if the old hand was wrong? He looked around for the phone book. Some of them gave free advice over the phone.

He heard the guy downstairs baby-talking his dog.

He couldn't find the Yellow Pages but there was a crack in the TV screen. He hadn't noticed it before (but he'd looked right into the camera). Then he couldn't find the stereo, then other things; a lamp, the hassock, small things. Clean spots shone on surfaces like gaps in his life.

He was thirsty. He went to the kitchen. The coffeemaker was missing and a note was pressed to the refrigerator with a magnet. A little plastic flower. He read the note and opened the refrigerator. There was one left. *I liked our story, I thought you did too.* Jelonnek wasn't sure what that meant, except that he was in some way free. He drained the can in one tilt of his head. He wondered if he should get more, or call a lawyer. 7-Eleven was four blocks away but he remembered the car was at the warehouse, and there was now the danger of being recognized. He should call Forms.

He started getting dressed. There were railroad tracks behind the building; they crossed the street in front of the store. He stepped into his pants. He would buy some beer, come back and make phone calls. He would take the tracks. He would not make eye contact. He would wear a suit ten days later in court, where there would be an audience but no jury. No lawyer. Before sentencing he would be instructed to turn and face the face of the community, their indignation, their signs, some of which would be carefully and persuasively worded, the products of some passion and wit. Ten days from now Jelonnek would turn around with nothing to say for himself, and in response to his silence would come a wave of outrage aimed at his conscience like a volley from a firing squad. Jelonnek would swear the john next to him was crying and would feel the sniggering come over him again like sickness when you're drunk. He would have to lower his head and put a fist to his mouth.

A big one was coming but he didn't know it. He didn't know anything at this point, not even that his fishing rod, the line hopelessly tangled, had already slipped into the water and sunk out of sight, along with his tackle box and the bottle with the black label, the amber liquid inside dissipating in the green depth. Nor was he aware that the wind had risen and the waves gotten rougher, first lapping the flat rock he sat on, then washing over it and soaking the seat of his pants. He didn't even know that both his legs now hung over the edge and were immersed almost to the knee, his chin resting on his chest, his shoulders tilting further and further forward in the manner of someone about to pitch headlong into a body of water.

Then he felt something. Someone had him by the hair.

"Gotchyou," someone said. Thunder, a slow rumble. This woke Jelonnek further and he struggled to rise, if only to escape the voice and its grip.

"Come on," whoever had him said, "It's fixin to throw down." Jelonnek felt himself fairly dragged up the rocks. Even when he was let go he continued to follow the man along the top of the breakwall as though he weren't, heading inland toward the parking lot, the lake on both sides.

He still didn't really know anything, only that he was running along the narrow flat top of the breakwall and part of him didn't mind this at all. This part of him didn't need to get anywhere, it just wanted to keep running with the waves breaking to either side of him and the wind pushing solid at his back. The further they went, the darker it got.

The Luminaires in the parking lot flickered on just before they got there. "God damn," the man ahead of him yelled. Then there was lightning and the lights, fooled again, flickered out.

God damn. Thunder made the other man jump but Jelonnek was still immune. They seemed to be heading for one of the cars. The rain started, you could smell the dust it kicked up. The man was yelling something but Jelonnek couldn't hear what it was. The rain fell so hard it roared.

The car was a four-door sedan. "In the back," the man said. It was spacious and warm inside, the air filled with incense and what it was trying to cover up. Two men sat up front in work clothes. The engine ran, a beat thumped from the speakers in back.

"Who the fuck," the man behind the wheel said. He was looking in the mirror.

"He was fixin to fall in," the man who'd had him by the hair said.

The driver turned around. "You sure you got the right car?" Jelonnek didn't say anything. He wasn't sure he could, hadn't anticipated this requirement.

"Can't speak?"

"He like to drown."

"Maybe he wanted to," the man next to the driver said.

"Then let him," the driver said. "Gettin my shit all wet not speakin."

"Biggest sheephead I ever saw," the man next to him said. The driver laughed and told him to shut up. Wind rocked the car. When there was lightning you could see sheets of water moving sideways across the windshield. The voice from the speakers rhymed murderously over the beat.

"That nigger ain't about nothing," Jelonnek heard in his ear. "He always got his ass on his shoulder."

"It don't make me deaf," the driver said, and Jelonnek tried to say something then. He pulled a sound up out of his throat, then another. He tried to shape them with his mouth but his lips and tongue couldn't seem to get a grip, and what came out was as raw and unformed as the croak of a catfish.

He wanted to say he was grateful. He was trying to say he'd been fishing. He was willing to offer money, though his wallet was in his tackle box.

The man next to the driver giggled. "He buttered."

"Through," the driver agreed and sounded almost appeased, though nothing would placate the voice behind them.

"Turn it up for we can dry off," the man next to Jelonnek said. The driver ignored him. He turned down the music instead and ran the wipers intermittently. Every few seconds they could see the skyline downtown, the lights in the buildings. Lightning struck the tallest one and the man next to the driver said, "Alright, where that fith?"

"Pass the Bird," the driver said to the man who'd brought Jelonnek.

"I ain't got it."

"You ain't bring it?" the driver said.

"Where the bottle?" the man next to the driver said.

"Still on the rocks, I guess."

"He brought this wet motherfucker," the driver said, "but he ain't bring the wine."

"Ain't life a bitch?"

"Why you ain't bring the Bird? It ain't the kind that fly."

"Why you don't keep up with your own shit?" the man who'd had Jelonnek by the hair said.

"You had it last."

"That don't put me in charge of it."

"You was drinkin it like you was."

"You damn straight."

"So go get it."

"Go call the L.A.P.D."

"I wish I would."

"I get it it's mine."

31

"You was turnin it up like it was."

"Hell yeah I was. Now walk your ass to the store for I can drink up the resta your check."

The driver laughed.

"Fuck some Bird, though. Make it the Dog this time."

"I'm partial to the Train myself," the driver said.

"And play my Pick 4." The man next to Jelonnek recited some numbers. "Straight up and box."

"Y'all shut up talkin to me. Y'all need to fish with y'all mouth."

"Can't nobody fish in this shit," the man next to Jelonnek said. "You called the day."

"It ain't the day," the driver said. "It's them netters. Canadian motherfuckers. They raised they limit."

"Ain't no limit."

The rain softened.

"I think it's fittin to let up," the driver said. "Then one a y'all can go get the bottle.

Ya heard, pale rider?"

"Maybe we just in the eye."

For a while it seemed the driver was right. The guy next to him turned on his side, opened the door, and relieved himself without leaving his seat. Nobody said anything and then the storm came back harder than before. The music stopped. The wipers cycled and they could see the skyline for a moment. Something was wrong downtown. The wipers waved again and showed them that the lights in all the buildings were out.

"God damn," the man who'd pulled Jelonnek out of the water said.

"Y'all done did it now," the driver said. "Any beer left?"

"It's hot," the man next to him said.

"If it's wet give it up."

"Back here," the man next to Jelonnek said. The one in front of him reached between his legs. You could hear a grocery bag. "Your boy want one too?"

"Yeah he do."

"I ain't hear him."

"He a man of few words—you don't need to speak to drink."

The driver laughed in disbelief but made no move to stop it. Jelonnek hadn't yet remembered how to refuse. The can was warm, his fingers cold. He opened it but didn't drink, didn't seem to have room. That was one of several things he now knew, the others being that he must have driven here, that he had to piss, and that this was not L.A.

The man with the beer asked him his name. He called him cousin. Jelonnek grunted.

"You can get back to me."

The driver chuckled. "What was he doin on them rocks?"

"I ain't see a rod," the man next to Jelonnek said. "Saw a bottle in the water, though."

"Maybe he fish with his hands."

"Maybe you just simple."

"Then just sittin on the rocks then."

"…havin a religious experience."

For a while they pursued the subject and Jelonnek listened to this conjecture in earnest, as if they might provide some clue as to his origins.

The man next to him drank with his hand on his groin. He crushed the can with it still at his lips.

The driver turned his head. "Too bad you ain't killin them perch like that."

"Ain't that a bitch?"

"He can't catch a cold," the man next to the driver said.

"You just mad I drank up your shit."

"Every time this fool throw out his tackle come aloose."

"I saw," the driver said. "Had me rollin."

The man next to Jelonnek turned his head and said in confidence, "That ain't happen but one time." Jelonnek had the feeling he and the man next to the driver were related.

"Nigger almost snagged a gull."

"You a damn lie."

"My woman fish better than your sorry ass."

"She do all kinda shit."

It sounded like it was letting up again. Jelonnek hoped it would last.

"Least I got a woman. Go on out and see can you bring one a them back."

The man next to Jelonnek was quiet. Then he said, "Let's fire one up then" and the two men in front laughed harder than Jelonnek had ever laughed at anything in his life. He didn't get it but he envied them; to laugh like that could put the lights back on downtown. He had no place there.

"Fire *what* up?" the driver said, barely able to. Jelonnek didn't hear the reply because he was already opening the door, already stepping out.

The driver yelled, "Bring back the Bird!" like some kind of motto and Jelonnek shut the door. The parking lot was almost empty. It was raining lightly now, the wind steady but milder. The half-dark the storm had brought seemed permanent. The Luminaires flickered weakly, but Jelonnek didn't need them to see the public restroom was closed—till Memorial Day, the sign said, and it was barely spring. Like people didn't piss before June. He heard muffled music in the car, another beat. He headed for the breakwall. When he looked at the city all he saw was its jagged silhouette. It scared him a little, made it harder to stay drunk, like the wind that blew through his skin. He kept looking.

He stopped and turned back. He could hear the waves. He was sure they were watching him from the car so he walked out onto the breakwall. A heaving grayness breaking white at the corner of his eye. He wondered if he would ever be out of sight. The water was calmer on one side than the other, and he climbed down on the rocks to his left. He stumbled only once, hit his knee so hard the pain would have stopped him had he been sober. He lost the beer. He spread his feet apart on a wide flat boulder and pissed into the crack of darkness right in front of him.

Other things came back now, like he was making room for them. He felt a light spray on his face and didn't know if it came from the sky or the lake or himself. Gurgling and sucking in the rocks under his feet. He zipped his pants, went further down. It was easier going without the beer but he was already starting to miss it. If he could find the wine he would bring it back to them. Might even have a taste first.

His foot kicked something that was not a bottle but the cork handle of a fishing rod. Nearby was a tackle box, wedged on its side between two boulders, and a bait bucket tipped over and empty. Jelonnek couldn't see the line. He picked up the rod and started reeling in. He reeled it in till he saw the sinker swinging before him. He reached out to steady it and felt the hook embed itself in the palm of his hand. He remembered where his car was.

Jelonnek didn't hurt anyone driving home, but he veered too close to a Mustang parked around the corner from his apartment and clipped off the mirror. He pulled straight into the angled slot behind the building, climbed the stairs and listened at the back door as he had all week. He entered carefully, a trespasser with a key. He took off his shoes. In the living room the light on the machine was blinking. No blackout here. He went into the kitchen and opened the fridge. There wasn't much left but there never was, and Jelonnek sometimes resorted to cheap wine like the kind the colored guys had been arguing about, Irish Rose or Thunderbird, but if you drank too much of it you'd end up like the zombies on Central Avenue, carrying your soul around in a bottle like some lab specimen in formaldehyde. And he tried to avoid the hard stuff; it made things happen too fast. Like today.

The living room was cluttered. Jelonnek did the dishes almost every day, but picking up was another matter and he had yet to do laundry. His pants were still wet. He lit a cigarette and sat on the couch. The crack in the TV screen was longer, but she'd left the Nintendo and the VCR and he slipped *Big Tit Harem* into the slot. The First Harem Girl crawls down on the flaccid Great White Tit Hunter. She is just getting results when the Sultan rings a bell or claps his hands. "My master calls me," she says each time, and each time the Great White Tit Hunter is left just short of a finish. Jelonnek wasn't doing any better; maybe it was the Black Velvet, or the tape had gotten old, but he sat there watching the movie as if for plot and character, holding himself like some detachable member not quite threaded in place. His arm rested on a pillow, the stuffed likeness of a barnyard pig she'd sewn from a pattern of her own design. She'd made other things, cushions and dolls, shirts for him, dresses for herself, the bedroom curtains, the big throw rug on the bare wood floor, woven on the hooplike contraption she'd thank God taken with her. She sewed, knitted, crocheted, macramed, beaded, took classes in batik and origami, replaced the float in the toilet tank and could do things with the car. Jelonnek could kill a six-pack by halftime. He did the dishes. She had a cleft palate and when she spoke certain consonants were drowned in spit, a sound that had made him laugh when they were strangers.

He thought he had room for one more. His legs were barely there and these were usually the first to go. He turned on the machine on his way back from the kitchen.

"Hi, it's me...just calling to say hi...see how you were doing," and he passed out reaching for a game control.

Woke to the gentle roar of white noise, the TV screen swarming with random particles like the initial state. His hand was on his chest, the cigarette a cold husk with an ash two inches high. Had the phone rung? He got up, planted his feet in the beer he'd spilled. He thought maybe the phone had rung but he had other priorities. He made it to the bathroom—he didn't always make it—retched up the last ten hours of his life in two proficient spasms, then came and lay back down in a soothing blue hiss of radiation. When he woke up again he could smell the beer he'd spilled and he was thirsty. It was fully dark. He switched off the VCR and one chaos coalesced into another: news of the world. There'd been a demonstration, a riot. Yugoslavia, or Bosnia, or Serbia, wherever it was; Serbs, Croats, Muslims, you didn't know who to root for. A man lay supine in the street, his head bloody. Another marcher goose-stepped toward him. He held a sign on a stick, and whatever was said in that inverted alphabet must have expressed an opposing opinion, because when the bearer reached the body he planted the sign in its groin like a flag in a conquered island.

The light was blinking. Jelonnek pushed the button.

"Hi," she said, "it's me. Hi." Reticent, like she didn't want to be overheard, but the tinny speaker of the machine amplified her defect. It made him thirsty. In the kitchen he took down the biggest glass they owned and filled it lukewarm, drank it down and filled it again. There was nothing to eat. He took the water into the living room and changed the channel.

"I've been thinking," she said. The pig was on the floor. The water tasted old somehow but Jelonnek finished it and started picking up beer cans. He wondered if she was reading from something. He turned the TV off, stuffed dirty clothes into a pillowcase.

She hoped, she knew, she understood, or tried to.

"We need to talk," she said, and Jelonnek kicked the pig across the room. He hated the words she used, *issue* and *communicate*, the vocabulary of talk shows and self-help, and he hated that she didn't hate him. He was emptying the ashtrays when she gave him her sister's phone number, as if he hadn't known.

He picked it up and put it back on the sofa. Drowned her out with the vacuum cleaner and made the bed. Changed the liners. Cleaned the toilet.

Then Jelonnek, Forms officer, ten years with the state, nine in Forms, took his copy of

Big Tit Harem out of the VCR and threw it in the dumpster outside. It was wet but it wasn't raining. Upstairs he reconsidered, went back down and retrieved the tape, hid it in a shoebox in the bedroom closet. He found some stale crackers and poured another glass of water. There were two more messages on the machine. The first was his brother, just calling to say he was getting married. Jelonnek had met her once. Jewish girl.

The last message was a wrong number, someone asking for Phil.

I f you worked for the state.

If you worked for the state in the State Office building downtown, also known as District, named for a late governor no one seemed to remember, in the Department of Commerce or the Department of Mental Health, the Department of Public Safety or the Board of Cosmetology, or in one of the offices not housed in the building but still within the boundaries of the district, like the Bureau of Motor Vehicles or the Office of Professional Standards; if you worked in one of these offices or departments and you needed a form and needed it in short order, you would be advised to go to the Forms warehouse, and you would be advised to take Eagle Street to the Eagle Street bridge, which is a vertical lift bridge, and if the center span wasn't closed for repairs or raised to allow for the passage of a tugboat or barge or freighter, you would cross the bridge and at the other end take a steep and winding road down to the west bank of the river. If you turned right at the bottom of the road you would soon find yourself in that part of town called the Flats, where the transformation of standing property into venues of entertainment was what passed for an urban renaissance, and you would pass the bars and dance clubs and comedy clubs and restaurants selling nine-dollar hamburgers and be reminded that you lived not only in the self-proclaimed Comeback City, but also in a four-time All-America City, and you would also know you had taken the wrong turn, because the road you should have been on would be cracked and potholed and sutured with railroad tracks, the buildings on either side devoted not to the nightlife of young professionals but to the manufacture of cap and set screws, wood and metal products, products of limestone and asphalt; to welding, grinding, folding, dry ice-cleaning—however that worked—stripping, casting, corrugating, stamping, powder-coating, to recycling glass of all colors in a place where the clamor of breaking bottles never stopped.

Company names stenciled on ancient brick and sometimes faded to cipher or revised with graffiti, what they did there now anyone's guess. CAL'S DINER just a sign now. PRIVATE PROPERTY, AUTHORIZED PERSONNEL, MUST VACATE, NO HELP WANTED. RECEIVING what? More dogs than people. Barbed wire, chain-link, crumbling brick where only a smokestack and a loading dock remained, a wide weedy stretch where someone had built a lean-to, a shopping cart parked next to it like a mini-van in a suburban driveway. Barges weighted to the waterline with shiny bales of crushed metal, Impound Lot Number Nine, a marooned cabin cruiser with a hole in the hull in a field nowhere near the water. Then an intersection under another bridge, a flashing red light regulating traffic that might consist only of you. Down that road would be steel, or what was left of it, but you wouldn't be going to steel. You would turn away from the river here, the road sloping down again and on your right in a man-made pit a cluster of outbuildings and blue storage tanks you would take to be empty and without function unless the weather was cold and you saw hanging over them clouds of white vapor that looked too thick and heavy to be steam. Then another intersection and then, on your right again, the Forms warehouse, a bend in the road hiding it from view till you were almost there.

You would pull into a gravel lot and back up to the dock. The door was always locked so you would have to ring the bell. You would wait. The warehouse was a big cinderblock building half-covered with ivy, wild rhubarb growing along a fence. You would not actually have driven very far but it would seem so, and you would understand why coworkers referred to this location as Moonbase Alpha or Bumfuck, Egypt or just BFE. Then, with a great rumbling and grinding, the big dock door would rise slowly, in jerky increments, and you would see a pair of legs, Jelonnek's, then the rest of Jelonnek, wearing his blue uniform or just regular clothes, or maybe the uniform shirt with blue jeans, or a football jersey bearing the number nineteen, the numerals cracked and faded like some of the company names you'd seen on the way down. He didn't look like an officer.

The door weighed well over half a ton and had once been manually operated. The previous Forms officer would raise and lower it with a chain, most of the actual work being done by a system of pulleys and counterweights, until that day, that hour, that moment, when one of the lift cables, apparently frayed and rusted to the breaking point, finally gave way. Unable to bear the load by itself, the other cable also snapped and the door crashed down on the previous Forms officer's wrist, all but severing his hand. The previous Forms officer had cinched his belt around his arm and dialed the emergency number, then went out to the gravel lot where he lit a cigarette (there was no smoking in the warehouse) and waited. He survived the accident but his hand did not. The insurance company mounted a thorough investigation and, although certain doubts were never fully dispelled, nothing actionable could be demonstrated and the previous Forms officer, debt-ridden in middle-age, had collected on his claim and moved to Reno, where he lived off disability and issued a dwindling number of postcards, the last, cryptic: "Wish I were here." The position was open.

Once it was posted, Jelonnek, who for the past year had been working the floor crew at District, part-time, graveyard, stuck around after punching out and waited for Human Resources to open. He was the first to apply but knew that this didn't guarantee him the job, that this being the state it was about seniority and minority, about being a veteran or physically-impaired, ideally some combination of disadvantages lined up like fruit on the the wheels of a slot machine. But one month after a perfunctory interview (the wheels turned slowly at District), having assumed he'd been passed over and having all but forgotten about it, Jelonnek was offered the job. Later he found out there was only one other candidate, that around the district the Forms warehouse was referred to as BFE and Timbuktu, that the other applicant, a guy from the mailroom with eight years' seniority and one leg longer than the other, had changed his mind, preferring the relative freedom of driving around in the mailroom van making pickups and deliveries, visiting the other offices and the secretaries who worked there. When he saw Jelonnek, though, he would often remind him of how things might otherwise have gone.

Jelonnek, for his part, shrugged. He had not taken the job because he desired advancement or even needed the money, but had done so at someone else's suggestion, and now was no longer sure who had whispered in his ear, nor what had been said. Unrequited, the mailroom guy limped away.

When he arrived in the morning Jelonnek would unlock the gate, park in the gravel lot, enter through the side door and disable the alarm. The side door had to be kept locked at all times. Inside the warehouse the ceiling was high and when it rained hard it was like being in a cave under a waterfall. There were no windows and Jelonnek entered primeval darkness. He used a penlight attached to his key ring to find the breaker box. He would throw twelve switches, and because it takes sodium-vapor lamps several minutes to fully incandesce, for that time there would be only a precursive grayish glow that showed nothing but itself. What light might have been before it was light.

The shelves gradually revealed.

The shelves were green metal, three tiers high. Row upon row mazed the warehouse, vast galleries of steel and paper. Aisle, section, tier, letter-number-letter. So if you worked for the state and you needed a particular form, a General Requistion for the Department of Administrative Services, or a Bank Affidavit for the Department of Insurance, an Asset Transfer Input or a Request for Release and Permit, a State Employee Suggestion Award, a Supplemental Nepotism Statement, a Bargaining Unit Teachers, a Merit Step Recommendation, a Calendar of Wages Paid, an Affidavit of Common Law Marriage, a Crash Report External or an Application for Crash Report HP90, a Fifty Hour Affidavit, a Consumer Complaint, Cemetery Complaint, Fraud Complaint, Multi-Purpose Complaint, Fire Drill Instructions, an Application for Tanning Facility Permit, a Surety Bond, a Blanket Bond to Cover All Agents, a Boating Accident Report, an Objection to Request for Recognition, an Application for Religious Exemption, a Time Report, Receiving Report, Route Slip, Batch Slip, Delinquent Claim, Allegation of Misconduct by a State Trooper, Declaration of Understanding, Certificate of Need, Application for Certification, Authorization, Agreement, Approval, Notice, Notification, Blank, Letter, Petition, Review, Release, a Radiation Accident Patient Tag, a Literature/Forms Requisition in the dust and sodium light, a Report of Convictions, a License Surrender, Vendor Master Input Document, License by Reciprocity, a Commitment, Grievance, Exhibit A, an Exemption from Rule, an Irrevocable Letter of Credit, a Request for Letter of Good Standing, a Request for Change of Location, a Statement of Preceptor, a Record, Receipt, Disclosure, Determination, Waiver, Citation, Transmittal, Suspension, Long Form, Survey, List, Change, Removal, Reversal, Inactivation, Short Form, Reactivation, a Stop, an Action, a Schedule, Conversion, Clarification, Warrant, Compliance, or a Major Unusual Incident Report for the Department of Mental Health, you would tell Jelonnek the name of the form and he would look it up in the catalog, where they were listed both alphabetically and by department, and a corresponding entry indicated the aisle, the bay,

43

the tier, A-1-A or Q-7-B. After nine years Jelonnek knew where all the most commonly used forms were, and many of the others not so popular, and each form had a Document ID including the initials of the department to which it belonged, a four-digit number, and the date of its most recent revision, and some of them consisted of a single white sheet, while a two-part form had a yellow copy, and there were three-, four-, five-, and six-part forms, with pink and green and blue and goldenrod iterations, and at one time there'd been a seven-part form but this was before Jelonnek's tenure and he did not know what the seventh color was.

For a couple of years now they'd been telling Jelonnek the entire inventory was to be uploaded to the computer. It would flag shortages, they said, generate random spot counts. The computer sat in the warehouse office, unconnected, the screen dark and gray with dust. There was also a typewriter in the office and it was this Jelonnek used for *Armageddon Zero*. Sometimes he took it home.

Notice of Appearance. Application for Grandfathered First Responder. They were stacked on the shelves in shrinkwrapped packages, by themselves or in boxes, the boxes stacked on wooden pallets. If Jelonnek had to retrieve a form from an upper tier he would wheel the slope ladder into place. It was twenty feet high. If the order was large and required several boxes, he would have to bring down the entire pallet with the forklift. Jelonnek liked driving the forklift. It was clean and electric and made a smooth whirring sound, and you drove it standing, there was no seat, and the feeling of motion was more emphatic and intimate when you rode it upright, down the aisles and cross-aisles, around corners, spinning in tight spots. Jelonnek charged it once a week, and put water in the batteries as needed.

He was paid twice a month. Like all government employees, he did not pay into Social Security, but contributed a sum from each check into a Personal Retirement Fund. Upon retirement or

Termination of Employment, you could either roll the fund over into another account, or cash it out in a lump sum. There were forms for this as well in the warehouse. There was a penalty for Early Disbursement, and then the IRS. After nine years Jelonnek's fund was in the lower five-figures.

Because of the amounts of paper involved there was a sprinkler system, and Jelonnek was required to observe strict regulations and preventive measures. He took his cigarette breaks outside. He took them at the same time every day, for exactly fifteen minutes, like someone was watching. He had not set a fire since he was eight years old. Outside there was a high fence along the far side of the building, so overgrown with rhubarb and weed trees and briers and vines you could barely see the railroad tracks on the other side, but you could hear the trains—always going, it seemed, in the same direction. Inside the shelves vibrated with their passing.

He didn't feel like an officer. He'd taken a class called The Life Cycle of a Form.

A bathroom. Two phones, one in the office. In the office a poster of Number Nineteen, and Jelonnek rubbed one off twice a day in the bathroom. There was heat but no air conditioning. There were no windows but metal shutters high on the walls and in the summer Jelonnek opened them with a long hooked pole. Once a year the warehouse was closed three days for a general physical inventory, but Jelonnek was required to track quantities at all times, and when a supply ran low he would put in an order. Print shops under contract delivered them by truck or van and Jelonnek would unload them by hand or with the forklift. Sometimes the drivers would ask him if he worked out here alone but it wasn't like you never saw anyone else. The mailroom delivery guy brought the interoffice mail every morning, mail consisting mainly of the requisitions people used to order forms. The pest control guy came once a month, and once he'd helped Jelonnek snare and release a barn swallow that had flown in through the shutters. Jelonnek also saw the Maintenance man when the toilet wouldn't flush, the Fire Inspector, the inventory team once a year, his supervisor on one of his random visits, the guy who picked up obsolete forms for recycling, or someone from the district who'd come to pick up an order, like the girl from the Bureau of Motor Vehicles.

Only once had he seen someone at the warehouse who wasn't supposed to be there. He was taking a break outside, leaning against the station wagon—the department vehicle. He looked up in the middle of a cigarette and a car was coming at him, a big loud car with no color but rust and primer, a vinyl roof rotting in patches like a disease of the scalp. It pulled up so close he would have jumped back if the station wagon hadn't been there. A woman came out already talking, saying thank God for a white face. It seemed to Jelonnek the car was still in gear. He leaned back in his shoes.

"Can I say something?" she said. A wire of a woman with all her hair tucked under a scarf. Her hood chained shut, a clothes hanger for an antenna. Jelonnek would have bet there was one holding up the tailpipe.

"I never thought I'd see my own kind again." Fast and through her nose. "Don't tell me you work around here. Meanwhile back in the jungle, I stop to ask one of the natives how to get back on the freeway? Man his lips kept getting in the way, I couldn't make him out. *You fo to go, you uppo to go.* Ha! I had to hurt his feelings. *Aw baby, why you come so cold?* Never again. I ran the light just like they do."

Her teeth moved independently of her lips. You could see a chain hanging from her rearview mirror, some tarnished bit of religion for luck. A few yellow strands escaped her scarf and Jelonnek wondered if that was all there was. If there was a condition. The exhaust was loud but it was hers he smelled.

"You're trying to get back on the freeway," he said.

"Ha! Would you believe I come up here from Akron? *Akorn*. I just come up to visit him in the workhouse. Not a bad kid, just dumb. I get off the interstate and hello! who turned out the lights? Couldn't see nothing but teeth. It was his rifle, you know. He only stole it back from his stepdad, goddamn Indian giver." She almost sighed, but she seemed to talk without breathing. "A gal can't be too careful, gotta lock it or lose it. They smell what they want, goddamn apes. Thank God the door don't open even for me. Got a Hefty bag for a window, thank God for duck tape. Only you can't keep out those jungle drums, *boom, boom, de-boom!* Tell me you don't work around here. How do you hear yourself think?"

Jelonnek said, "I don't hear anything."

"You don't would you believe I give him my last six bucks? Keep him in cigarettes, keep him in some decent food? Not a bad kid, just grabbed his sister's boob. Like she never. They used to be like this." Her fingers wouldn't do what she wanted them to. "I don't know what happened. Next thing you know I'm so lost I'm found. Go figure this zoo. Why did the boo cross the road? You know what they want, they can smell it. I ask this one for directions you should see how he come at me. In his dreams. *You need to get up offa that wet thang*—that's all I could make out. Ha. Where's the L.A.P.D. when you need em?"

"Lady," Jelonnek said. He knew where the freeway was, he just had to put it together for her. The signs, the turns, the lights.

He knew this was not L.A.

"Miss," he said.

"I ask you," she said.

"I'm trying to tell you."

"Can I say something here? My last six bucks is all I'm saying. Goddamn porch monkeys. You see how they cross the street? Like bowling pins—hey don't tempt me, my brakes are down to the rivets as it is. I forget what they call that thing on the passenger side I don't have, goddamn thing turns like a semi. Needs the whole road. No radio, but I got a hole in the tank bigger than your mama's. Thirteen dollars is all it can take, anything more it's piss on the freeway." She blew a raspberry and Jelonnek felt it on his his cheek. "That tank is bigger than I don't know, ten might do it. I'd be taking a chance but at least on a nice round number. It'll learn me my lesson, you'll never see me around what are you kidding? I only got a few drops left, just a corner. *Ain't but a cownuh, bruh.* Ha! Gimme a puff?"

Jelonnek's break was almost over. He handed her what was left of his cigarette. She dragged hard, looked at the filter. It was dark brown, pinched and wet. "Aw I niggerlipped it," she said. "You don't want that back."

Her car chugged, rattled, idled like a bad heart. Her muffler tapped the gravel. Jelonnek looked around like someone was watching. He looked in his wallet.

"Just make it five then," she said. "I got people in Kent."

He had three dollars. He had that kind of face, and she the other kind.

"Don't sound so happy about it." But she seemed to have to consider. "Mighty white of you partner, give a dog a bone. Hey, it just gets me back to the interchange I'll walk the rest of the way—away from you-know-who...What are you? I'm dying as we speak here."

When she drove away Jelonnek saw he'd been wrong about the tailpipe, but there was a bungee cord holding up the bumper. His break was over.

Sometimes it was three times.

Jelonnek usually shipped the orders he pulled through inter-office mail, but if someone needed a form right away, or just didn't want to wait, they would send someone from the office to pick it up. The girl from the BMV came no more than twice a month, and she usually wasn't alone. That was how Jelonnek knew her name. Her name consisted of three syllables, three sounds so arranged that whenever Jelonnek said them he felt like he was singing, and Jelonnek, who thought of himself as a rock-and-roller, couldn't sing or dance. She was as dark as an open door in the uncounted hours of night, and to look at her was to walk out of yourself and pass through it. She didn't say much. She wasn't unfriendly. She always said thank you and goodbye in her strong clear voice, and Jelonnek watched her mouth form the words the way he watched her body curve the colors she wore. Other times he talked to her eyes, so that she would be held by his. There was a scent. He'd offer her a chair in the office and she politely refused, lingering in the dock bay like some exquisite shadow. Light avoided her, it could not do her justice.

He wanted to ask her but he hadn't. He wasn't sure if he hadn't asked her because he lacked the nerve, because he savored the anticipation of the question, or because of the guy who usually came with her from the Bureau of Motor Vehicles. He was squat and sullen, had bad skin and filmy eyes, and his wardrobe apparently consisted of a single gray sweatsuit. Jelonnek wan't sure what purpose he served. You could tell by things he said that he was temporary or part-time, and in his silence you could hear exactly what was on Jelonnek's mind.

Jelonnek would try and make small talk. Jelonnek never made small talk and this was another effect the girl from the BMV had on him. He would ask if the bridge was out, if they were compensated for mileage. He would pretend he was asking both of them. The guy who came with her would grunt or exhale loudly or ask where the bathroom was. Once Jelonnek called him bro and the guy said, "I ain't got but one brother, and he at home watching cartoons," and Jelonnek chuckled and said, "No problem" in what he took to be a display of good nature and reasonable temperament. He didn't recognize himself around her; he was more than Jelonnek.

"We know it ain't," the guy had probably muttered and, pulling the order in the depths of the warehouse, Jelonnek could hear them talking. He couldn't hear what was said but he imagined the girl from the BMV defending him, rebuking the guy who'd come with her for his hostility and lack of cooperation. He imagined what she didn't say. The effect he had on her.

Power of Attorney. Application for Hearing Impaired Drivers.

If there was a box to load into the trunk, the guy who accompanied the girl from the BMV would do it, but only after Jelonnek had started to, grabbing the box roughly and muttering, "You gotta hire me before you can fire me." When they were getting back in the car, whosever car it was, Jelonnek told him to have a good one and he said, "I ain't, and don't tell me what to do," and spat in the gravel, and Jelonnek said he was talking to *her* and made a point of saying goodbye to the girl from the BMV. He would sing her name.

When she left she was still there, the way a light flashed in your eyes stays in them like a ghost. He stood in the space she'd occupied, her scent containing him. He couldn't even touch himself. He remembered a segment of *60 Minutes*, or *20/20*, one of those, devoted to the origins of the human race. We are all out of Africa, the scientist said, like every living thing. She was always there, always had been. She was The First Woman.

If, on the other hand, the office or department in need couldn't spare anyone and couldn't wait for the mailroom to pick up its order, Jelonnek would be required to deliver it personally. The station wagon parked in the warehouse lot had been provided for this purpose. It was beige, and Jelonnek hadn't driven it since they'd taken the keys.

◆　◆　◆

The Forms Coordinator was Jelonnek's supervisor. He came to the warehouse just before two o'clock. Jelonnek had told him they could just meet at District but his supervisor had insisted, said it would look better, and Jelonnek supposed he should know. The Forms Coordinator had been renowned for stretching his lunch hour into two or three, cashing his paycheck at a topless steakhouse downtown and leaving half of it there, coming back with a bloody lip, broken taillight, mouth full of vodka fumes and slurred speech. After his second DUI he was officially reprimanded, suspended, forced to use sick leave for rehab and weekends in jail, all but terminated because they didn't just fire you anymore, they intervened, diverted, gave you a second chance, or a third. You seemed to have no choice but to recover.

The State Office Building was the third tallest building in town and consisted of three walls, the front one curved so the structure resembled a wedge of pie forty stories high. A Japanese conceptual artist had been paid a large sum of money to install a giant mock bus stop out front, complete with statues of people sitting in a shelter and pigeons six-feet tall. Jelonnek didn't get it, nobody did. The Forms Coordinator shrugged and suggested they must be waiting on a giant bus, that the bus was in fact the state. Jelonnek was skeptical but had no better idea of his own.

Jelonnek's union steward hated the statues. He hated a building that didn't have four walls. He was a Boiler Operator II and he hated the Japs and probably would have hated them had his father not lost his head at Bataan. He was waiting in the lobby, holding a copy of the handbook. He was the tallest person at the hearing by a half-foot and you couldn't tell him anything, he already knew what you wanted: You wanted to work for the government, you wanted a house with two cars, domestic (but no Fords unless one of them was a truck), you wanted a beer gut, you wanted your wife not to work. You only thought you wanted anything different.

He pulled Jelonnek aside as soon as they arrived and glanced suspiciously at the Forms Coordinator. "What're you doing with him?"

"He thought we should come together," Jelonnek said.

"Hello, he's on their side. Did he say anything?"

They had talked about Chuck Norris films.

"Listen," the union steward said. "This is where you stand." Jelonnek listened to where he stood. The arraignment had seemed simpler.

The hearing was conducted at a round table in a round room, the chief interior motif at District being the circle; walls, stairs, hallways, the whole place a cluster of rotundas. There was no prospect of resolution. "Like a merry-go-round," Jelonnek's union steward said. "All we need is a fucking calliope." The District Coordinator entered. He was Jelonnek's boss's boss, white-haired and so close to retirement he wore a Hawaiian shirt and deck shoes.

The Director of Human Resources was also present. "We got your ass," he told Jelonnek, like he'd been waiting all these years.

"Well *Sieg heil*," Jelonnek's union steward said.

"The question is what do we do with it."

"Hold the phone," Jelonnek's union steward said, but all he came up with were delaying tactics. He leafed vigorously through the union handbook but the Director of Human Resources already seemed to know it by heart, like an atheist who knows the Bible.

"It is what it is," Jelonnek's union steward said. He sounded a little resigned. The Forms Coordinator nodded his head to everything and never said a word, not even "Close enough for government work," which he normally used at every opportunity. The District Coordinator said the new receptionist had legs like a grand piano. He was curious about Jelonnek's name.

"What is that, Hungarian?"

It was not Hungarian.

"You like baseball?"

"I don't know much about it," Jelonnek said.

"What do you like?"

"Football."

"What's wrong with baseball?"

Jelonnek shrugged.

"Slovenian." He was usually good with names.

"Married?"

"No."

"Girlfriend."

"We live together."

"How long?"

Jelonnek told him, though not how long they'd known each other before that.

"Jesus, what are you waiting for?"

"I don't know."

"What's not to know?"

"Same old, same old," Jelonnek's union steward said. He made a recommendation.

"Only piece of ass I ever paid for," the District Coordinator said, "I'm still paying on."

"The question is what kind of statement do we want to make?" the Director of Human Resources said, and placed a counterrecommendation before the District Coordinator, a sheet of letterhead dense with typing. The District Coordinator looked as though a waiter had served him someone else's meal.

"I got married when I was nineteen," he said. "Bought my first house. Four hundred bucks down, seventy-five bucks a month."

Jelonnek's union steward countered the counter. He clicked his pen on his teeth.

The Director of Human Resources asked Jelonnek if he had anything to say. He asked Jelonnek what he would do in their place. Jelonnek saw the Director down in the control room, at the panel, his union steward, Boiler Operator II, standing behind him, whispering in his ear, unbuttoning the Director's shirt while the gauge needle entered the red zone. Jelonnek saw things like that sometimes.

He didn't laugh but said he had nothing to say. The District Coordinator told a Polish joke.

While they deliberated Jelonnek found himself sitting next to a water fountain in a rare square niche in the round. Outside the stream of things. Magazines on a low table, another chair unoccupied. Jelonnek looked at the carpet. It was blue and made a sound, the sound of the fibers rising back into place after the District staff walked by. Jelonnek knew some of them, and he wondered if they thought they knew him now. If the women. He listened to the carpet, a faint crackling hiss like dissolving foam. It seemed to be the sound of waiting, of time, which does not pass but erases itself. Was this what the statues heard?

Someone else was coming. It was his union steward, and Jelonnek could tell by the look on his face that he'd been forgiven again.

The girl Jelonnek lived with could keep a car running. She could tune the ignition, change the oil, bleed the brakes, flush a radiator, replace a water pump, starter, clutch fan, or alternator. Her father had taught her how. It all came down to three things, he'd taught her: gas, air, spark. She could perform other repairs and adjustments as well, but not the real hard stuff, like pull the transmission or replace a timing belt, and Jelonnek took some satisfaction in that.

She asked him to hand her a box wrench.

Once he'd changed the front tire. A couple of weeks later, alerted by a rattle from the front end, the girl Jelonnek lived with had asked her father to take a look. He'd pried off the hubcap and found that the nuts had been put on backward and two had walked off the lugs completely. He never let Jelonnek forget it, wouldn't let him live it down up until the day his jack gave and a Cutlass Supreme dropped on his chest, rupturing his aorta.

Jelonnek handed her the box wrench; she'd taught him what one was. She'd taught him torque wrench, crescent, offset, the names of things and their uses. She'd taught him how to drive. He hadn't wanted to, hadn't felt the need; even in high school it had seemed wrong for him in some way he could barely define. Premature. He would have put it off indefinitely until the Forms warehouse position opened (possession of a valid state driver's license was a requirement). He'd passed the test on the second try and now sometimes even wondered what all the fuss had been about.

She asked for the ratchet handle and he gave it to her, handed her whatever she asked for, or at least looked, but sometimes she had to find it herself. She had him loosen the last plug, but usually her own was strength enough. It wasn't about muscle, her father would say, it was how you focused what you had. How you held the tool. Her hair was pinned up under a scarf. She took off her glasses and cleaned them with Jelonnek's flannel shirt. One thick lens smudged with grease, but she'd tried contacts and couldn't get used to them. She wasn't much on laundry but she could clean a carburetor, and Jelonnek didn't mind her wearing his shirt unless it bore the number nineteen. He didn't mind standing there watching her work on the car unless someone was coming (the guy downstairs who baby-talked his dog, the girl upstairs with the shouting bed), in which case he would reach for whatever tool or part was at hand, or just lean in under the hood as if he were giving instruction. As if people didn't know. He sometimes wished they could have done this somewhere else, but the manager was tolerant of people cracking their hoods in the parking lot as long as they knew what they were doing and didn't spill oil, and mostly Jelonnek was content to hand her tools and hand himself beer, the one not interfering with the other, on a late Saturday morning that was sunny and exactly as warm as it should be near the end of the first half of spring.

The girl he lived with looked at the spark plug. The firing end. She asked for the wire gauge and Jelonnek gave it to her. He opened another one and she asked how many that made.

"Today or in my whole life?"

Was he on the Titanic? she asked—she equated drunkenness with the deck of a foundering ship.

"I was watching the news," he said. He didn't usually watch the news, but it had appeared on the screen while he was sitting in front of it. Bosnia. Was that a city or was there a city in Bosnia? It always seems to start in the middle, without introduction, a word you watch on TV. There was shelling. Concentration camps. A voice saying, "If there are children in the room," and Jelonnek struggling not to get up for another beer. He'd never heard of a rape camp before. Slogans in those assbackward letters, not just on signs but carved into people's bodies. Maybe he'd dreamed it, but if he had, the dream didn't tell you who the bad guys were.

Sometimes when he woke up next to her his fingers were swollen like they'd been wrenched, twisted. Small concentrated aches in his back, bruises you could feel but not see. Once he thought he'd heard her crying and turned up the TV. He hadn't heard it again but just once was enough, like seeing a roach and knowing that meant you had them.

Gas. Air. Spark.

The girl Jelonnek lived with gapped the plugs with the wire gauge. If they were still good she put them in an egg carton, and in this same order she would return them to the engine block. Jelonnek swallowed and watched her fingers. They were pale and stubby and didn't seem designed to do the things they did anyway. She was talking about work.

She'd started as a teller. From the teller's window she'd gone to Asset Recovery, but she wasn't an officer. The officers were pricks, even the women—one of them once made a guy write a check for twelve cents when his company was just that shy on a payment. Jelonnek had heard this story before, but not the next one: the branch in Brookpark had been robbed by a woman who was eight months pregnant. They'd seen the tape. The woman wore maternity clothes, handed a note to the teller.

She sighed like she was in over her head.

It was the third car they'd had. They hadn't paid a dime for it, just like they hadn't paid anything for the other two. One of her father's hobbies had been buying cars that wouldn't run for next to nothing, then fixing them up and selling them. Or giving them to his daughter. His only condition was that she put her name alone on the title. Now he was dead and it was as though the efficacy of his repairs had expired with him: it leaked oil, needed a carburetor, brakes, the struts were going. The timing chain had never been replaced, and if it went while you were driving it could bend valves and maybe more and strand you at the roadside for good, dwindling in everyone's rear view mirror.

They could use her bonus for a down. Payments wouldn't be a problem; they both worked.

"Let me do it," Jelonnek said. He gave her his beer and took the socket wrench. Not too tight, she told him, he'd crack the insulator like before. She sipped his beer. He hoped she didn't finish it because there weren't many left—he'd counted. She wouldn't gulp, she took a sip at a time and you couldn't see her swallow. He heard the sound she made and he dropped the plug, heard it land somewhere under the car. He swore and crawled under the oil pan, and when he came back up with it she asked him if he was on the Titanic yet.

"Fuck it," he said, and traded the spark plug for his can. It was blackened from her fingers and her face was pink. Her fingers stained but clean...her voice moving through the trees...somebody watching cartoons loud...church bells singing the eleventh hour... the leaves making her voice, asking for the universal extension. A new guy in Commercial Loans, it said, a nice guy, and Jelonnek started listening again.

"What about him?" he said. She ran the engine.

It wasn't what he'd hoped to hear. The new guy in Commercial Loans was just out of college. He was also some kind of deejay, and he worked weekends at this new club on the east bank. She couldn't think of the name but it had been converted from an abandoned powerhouse into a multilevel entertaintainment complex. Dance floor, restaurant, game room, comedy club, lounge. The state of the art.

He could get them on the guest list.

"He plays records," Jelonnek said. She listened to the fan belt. If the belt sang, her father had taught her, it wanted you to replace it.

Jelonnek tilted the rest of the can into his mouth but didn't swallow. He didn't want to be on anyone's guest list, did not want a place being made for him, certain behavior expected of him in return. He didn't want to have to have fun. He'd hoped she would say something else.

Just needed tightening. The girl Jelonnek lived with loosened a bracket, had him wedge the hammer handle under the alternator, pulling it away from the block till the belt was taut. She tightened two bolts and he thought they were done, but she said they should replace the hoses. People kept walking by.

"Let's save it for later," he said. He said there was a section in the Classifieds, used cars for a thousand dollars or less.

Jelonnek waited for the bus with the shoplifter. All the glass in the shelter was broken, and a cool wind blew through it while they waited. The shoplifter stood close. Jelonnek wondered why he just hadn't gone in the van.

"I didn't see you at all today," the shoplifter said, sounding all stood up about it. He'd had to mow a whole lawn with a Weed Wacker. Then he was picking up glass around the swimming pool fence. He'd just finished, he said, he'd filled a whole bag, and some punk drained his quart and smashed the bottle a yard from his feet.

A bus approached. The sign above the windshield said NOT IN SERVICE, and it kept going.

"Guess you weren't finished after all," Jelonnek said.

"I was just thinking that in my head," the shoplifter said. He hit Jelonnek's arm and pointed through the shelter at the schoolyard across the street. Jelonnek wished he wouldn't point. "We're cleaning hopscotch, right?" He said there was a strawberry hanging around the fence.

"Strawberry," Jelonnek said.

"That's how they say." She'd looked like one of those starving African refugees, all bones and flies, right? but no shit, someone had managed to sneak her into the breezeway for five minutes. Jelonnek wondered if it was anyone he'd remember from the paddy wagon, the holding tank. He'd expected to see a familiar face, the old hand or the claustrophobe, like some kind of class reunion, but he didn't see anyone. He didn't remember the shoplifter, though the shoplifter claimed to remember Jelonnek from court.

There were two supervisors. They said if anyone spoke to you, just tell them you're working. They said not to pick up needles, just let them know.

Diversion was for second offenders. Some people just paid their fines.

The shoplifter was a small man who huddled like someone in need of a big brother. He almost made Jelonnek feel worldly and wise; it was usually the other way around. The only thing he seemed to know about were the buses. Another one pulled up but the shoplifter waved it on.

"What was wrong with that one?"

"It goes to the mall, right?" the shoplifter said. "We want downtown." He asked Jelonnek once again if he had a job. He asked Jelonnek what he'd done to wind up doing this.

"I was asking directions."

A bunch of kids made a point of walking through the shelter instead of around it, roughly single-file. Smiling but not looking, coming close but not touching.

Jelonnek could only work weekends. He'd sat in a cubicle across the street from the Justice Center, picking from a list. The first one was the best. They'd ridden the white van with red letters, were dropped off on the shoulder of the highway. They were given Day-Glo vests and plastic bags and worked the embankments, cars blurring past and sometimes people yelling things. The day had been cool and the work kept you just warm enough. The trees had blossoms. Some of the referrals had grabbers and some had pointed sticks, and Jelonnek and one of the DUI's kept goofing off with theirs, sword-fighting and playing lawn darts, lobbing roadkill at each other. Finally the guy from the city had made Jelonnek sit in a chair at the bottom of an exit ramp, counting cars and writing numbers on a clipboard.

The grass, the sky, the black and white of the road, the brilliant orange on their backs. The stunted skyline like a row of broken teeth, the buckled freeway bridges, flattened houses, the stillness of the desert...most of all the vast black crater in the center of everything.

"Easy money," the shoplifter said. "Gravy. First thing I took?"

Facades of buildings torn away, pigeonhole cross-sections of rooms, single walls standing alone like unmarked gravestones. The Survivor wanders what used to be downtown, calling out, pieces of auto rubber lashed to his feet. Vegas? Phoenix? Cars overturned, crushed, half-melted, shadows of pedestrians photographed onto walls as of some great flash of light and heat. Anyway, a desert city. The Survivor shouts himself hoarse to no purpose, till his shout becomes a chant that would conjure another voice where there is silence.

Cut to the Hunter. His crossbow, his goggles, his suit of human skin. His face seen only from oblique angles but its utter disfigurement apparent. He whistles a simple song, an anthem of the unspeakable. Cut to the setting sun.

The shoplifter had first picked a nursing home. "It wasn't as bad as all that," though nobody had said it was. " I dealt cards for four hours in the day room. Blackjack, baccarat, the old girls can't get enough. I even taught them blind hooky, right?" He made a face. "I couldn't do it every day, though. I'd leave out of there smelling like piss."

Jelonnek was starting to wonder if the shoplifter knew the buses as well as he claimed to. He was starting to wish he'd taken the van. But the van took you back to the Justice Center, and Jelonnek didn't want to go there.

She'd replaced the alternator. Now it needed something else.

The next time the girl from the Bureau of Motor Vehicles came to the Forms warehouse she needed a Financial Responsibility Notice and she was alone. It was a small order and she didn't need the help, or maybe they'd let him go, or he'd just stopped showing up. Or he'd been found in a vacant lot with a plastic bag over his head. Someone like that it's just a matter of time. Jelonnek didn't ask, but before she left, he was sure he would ask her something else.

She wore jeans and a tank top, her shoulders bare in the dust and sodium light. It was a one-part form. She only needed a package but it was on Tier 3. Jelonnek climbed onto the forklift and said he'd be right back.

"Are you afraid of heights?" She pointed at the slope ladder. "Or just lazy?"

"This is faster."

"I hope so."

He asked if she was in a hurry.

"Only if the rumors are true."

He looked at her.

"Those furry things with long tails….don't have me say it." She couldn't so she laughed instead, but you couldn't tell if she was nervous.

"Not so little," he said. He'd only seen them outside, but he didn't say so and didn't smile.

"Either you're playing or you should keep a cat."

He was quiet. Then he became someone who said, "You can always come along for the ride."

"Two people can get on that thing?"

"If they have to." He wasn't really sure and expected her to say no, but she stepped up behind him and held on to the frame. There was barely room and she had to stand close. Jelonnek took it slow. He couldn't tell if their bodies were touching but it was enough for now. He knew where not to go, patches of sheet iron riveted over holes in the floor.

They didn't speak. The motor hummed. Jelonnek felt something on the back of his neck, a warmth from inside her. They turned a corner, glided past the eyewash station, past the bay where inactive forms were stored, yellowing, curling, awaiting final dispostion in the dust and sodium light.

When they got to the aisle, the section, Jelonnek slowed and stopped as carefully as he could. There was just enough momentum left to press her gently against him and something passed from her into him as she entered his apocalypse.

"This my stop?"

"No," he said. "It'll just take a minute."

It took several. Twice he bumped the shelving with the forks, and when he finally got under the pallet he had to back up and approach again to center the load. He felt something cold drop from his armpit and roll down his ribs.

"Don't show off, now," she said. When he had the skid down he could have taken what she needed and put it back on the shelf, but he could feel her shifting behind him, so he drove her and twelve hundred pounds of paper back to the lip of the dock where her car waited. By the time they got there you could hear the battery running down, though the charge should have lasted the rest of the week.

"Sounds low on something."

"Battery." He was out of breath for no reason. Maybe the batteries were shot.

"Maybe I just have that effect on things." He smiled at her, wishing he'd thought of it. Then he looked for something to open the box with.

The girl from the BMV shook her head. "You don't have a pocketknife?" Jelonnek looked up.

"I thought all men had a pocketknife," she said. "And a dog." Then she laughed and touched his arm and he ripped apart the tape with his fingernails.

He took one out and gave it to her. Was there anything else? She held the shiny square package.

"Most fun I've had since I started here," she said. "All that for this."

"It wasn't just for that," he said, and surprised himself once again. He wondered who else she might show him he was, in that light of her dark that lit him alone, and while he wondered he might have considered that she was about to leave, that if he was going to ask her now was the time, and then it didn't matter because she asked him instead.

"It's the end of the world."

"How's it going? Hey, what?"

"How's it going. He doesn't know how's it going. You live in a cave or you just smell like it? It's on every channel."

"Who are you talking to?"

"Not guilty, man. Not fucking guilty."

"You mean L.A? I heard something."

"Not just L.A.: San Francisco, Seattle, New York. I think I heard something about Atlanta."

"What about it?"

"You didn't know? You can't drink beer and watch TV at the same time?"

"I'm watching a tape."

"Not anymore you're not. They just hit a car with a Marlboro sign. It's your duty to watch this shit."

"Is it here?"

"Oh, man. They're dragging him out of his car...beating the shit outta this guy."

"White guy?"

"Yeah, no...Mexican...he's getting away. Jesus, he left his old lady by the car."

"Not here?"

"Not here. Nothing's happening here yet, I haven't heard anything. Probably just a matter of time. I mean we're fifty-fifty here."

"Where are the cops?"

"You know what Code 3 is?"

"Code 3?"

"Not guilty. You believe that?"

"Yeah, I heard."

"I know the guy's a piece of shit but Jesus Christ."

"Yeah, hey…congratulations."

"Congratulations. Congratulations for?"

"On you and…"

"On me and."

"Well goddamn."

"You don't even know her name."

"I just met her the once. Jewish girl, right?"

"Asshole. Like you can tell."

"Fuck you."

"Fuck you first. Thanks anyway."

"Do you know when?"

"Cop just drove right by. Code 3."

"You set a date?"

"Yeah, I don't know. We might have to postpone it if civilization comes to an end. Fucking animals, right off his neck."

"What?"

"They took this Jap's camera…The old man's supposed to be there."

"What?"

"The old man."

"You're kidding."

"Would I shit you? Mention was made."

"What about Florida?"

"You believe that shit?"

"Why would he lie?"

"He lied about Disneyland."

"Let me call you back."

"Birmingham. Las Vegas. Man, I gotta go. This is history."

"Alright. So you don't have a date."

"Why don't you give me a date?"

"For what?"

"For you know what. She's a good woman."

"Who said she wasn't?"

"She stuck by you."

"I didn't ask her to."

"Now that just makes me want to bend somebody up."

"What? Let me get going."

"They're surrounding the station. Goddamn police chief's away at a fundraiser."

"Call me back."

"I hope he raises a lot of funds. Didn't ask her to."

You could hear him shaking his head over the phone. Jelonnek hung up and took the quart out of the freezer. He'd have to start over. In the living room the girl he lived with was watching them surround the police station. They were yelling, "No peace, no justice!" Shouldn't it have been the other way around? Jelonnek rewound his tape. A car on it's side, a guy trying to push it over the rest of the way. Finally he gave up and just set it on fire. The mob at the station looked angry, but everyone else seemed to be having the time of their lives. Jelonnek changed the channel. Dan Rather. *Three's Company*. He changed the channel and a man with a bloody face was on all fours, next to a truck, carefully pawing the air like he couldn't see.

The tape clicked.

"Let me finish this," he said. He wore the jersey with Number Nineteen's number on it.

"The Game?" she said, on the couch, making something.

The Game. The first half always a disaster. Kansas City going eighty yards on the opening drive, litter blowing across the field like they were playing in a ghost town. Then they'd recovered a fumble on the ensuing kickoff and scored again. Nineteen got them within field goal range, but the Chiefs ran a punt back in the second quarter and it was 21-3 at the half. Jelonnek loved watching them dig themselves a hole now, knowing what was going to happen, but back when the game was actually played he'd screamed and thrown things till the neighbors pounded and the girl he lived with had left and gone to her sister's. He'd knocked over the TV, gouged his temples with his nails till they bled. Now he was entitled to enjoy it. He'd paid his dues.

AT&T, the answer people—he'd forgotten to take out the commercials.

By halftime the quart was empty and Jelonnek was that much braver. He switched off the tape and announced he was going to the store.

The anchorman says, "Three alarms per minute." Frederick's of Hollywood was on fire. She didn't want him to go, they were dragging people out of cars. He had work tomorrow.

There'd been no reports. "They're all on the east side anyway," Jelonnek said. He said he'd take the tracks. You can't live fear, he slurred.

Behind their building was a parking garage where you had to pay twenty-five dollars a month for a space, and behind the garage were the railroad tracks. Jelonnek didn't walk much but he liked the tracks. They led in a long curve to the street that ran past 7-Eleven, and as you followed them everything turned; backyards, garages, clotheslines, buckled rust of a three-foot swimming pool. Kids came here to sniff things out of bags. Jelonnek didn't see anyone now but once something big rustled the weeds at the edge of the gravel bed. The sun was behind and below him.

Nobody had believed in Number Nineteen at first, least of all Jelonnek. A thirteenth-round pick, rangy, slow-footed—a sitting duck in the pocket, they said. No deep ball, and that awkward sidearm! His first year he was third-string, his second year League MVP. He'd proven them wrong, though Jelonnek didn't remember being wrong. Number Nineteen was a chessplayer, magician, surgeon. Could read coverages like reading minds, change a play at the line as if he would alter the future. Who needed muscle when you had eyes that saw the entire field in an instant, where everyone was and would be? Just find the holes in space and the ball would reappear where the receiver was headed all along, his entire life leading to that moment. He'd set an all-time record for completions without a pick his third year—the year he'd taken them to the conference final. The Game. Not that Jelonnek fully understood the nuances of the sport; in truth he wasn't sure of the difference between a cornerback and a safety, a nickel defense and a dime. He only knew that Number Nineteen had taken them to Kansas City, one step from New Orleans. That everything was different forever afterwards.

Jelonnek left the tracks.

When he pushed through the door at 7-Eleven, he didn't at first know he'd hit anyone. Then he saw a kid who might have been seven years old standing by the comic book rack, holding his head. "That's right," a man said. "I told him not to stand there." Big guy, long hair and a beard, leather jacket. Standing at the counter. "Fool me once, shame on you."

The kid trembled, struggled with himself, you could already see the bump between his fingers. Jelonnek went to the cooler. A guy with a copy of *Hustler* stood there watching and said, "Said the same thing to me."

Jelonnek grabbed a forty. It slipped out of his hand and shattered on the floor. Nobody seemed to notice. He took this as a sign and took a twelve-pack to the checkout.

"Any trouble?" the biker asked the clerk.

"Quiet as a rat pissin on cotton."

"Closing up early?"

"Not a chance," the clerk said. He glanced behind the counter like he was making sure something was still there. "I knew this was coming."

"I hear that," the biker said.

Jelonnek mentioned the broken bottle but the clerk waved it off. "Probably not the last one I'll see."

The kid still wasn't crying. Jelonnek opened the door carefully. He hurried back along the tracks, didn't want to miss the second-half kickoff. Then he stumbled and realized he wasn't going to miss anything, that the game wouldn't start till he pushed the button. He slowed and pulled a can out of the carton, opened it one-handed. Now he liked the tracks that much more. Close to where he lived they straightened and you could see to the vanishing point, beyond the smoke and fire. Jelonnek belched. The distance felt like a promise. The sun was gone but its light remained; he wanted to keep it there. He dropped the empty can and opened another, opened his throat and emptied another one into it, arching his back, as if he would dissolve whatever it was that kept him from getting together with that light.

The girl he lived with wrapped her arms around him as soon as he got in the kitchen. She was crying, they'd dropped a brick on someone's head, kicked him while they danced…it was hard to make her out.

"This weighs a ton," he said.

In the living room Los Angeles was burning in fifteen hundred places. A man ran out of a store so laden with furs he looked like some huge misshapen bear. Again they showed the man on his hands and knees, next to his truck on his hands and knees, blind with his own blood, groping the air. This time they showed it from a helicopter, as if to make it new. Jelonnek pushed the button.

In the living room it is January again, the comeback is on. The front four finally show up, and the ground game, muscling the ball inside, but mostly it is Number Nineteen. Number Nineteen, just twenty-four in good-guy white, crossing himself on the sideline, rangy, slow, taking the snap with one leg splayed out so as not to trip over his own linemen, freezing the deep men and even the camera with play action (how could he still have the ball?), spreading the field, beating the crowd noise with a silent count. Twelve for twelve in the third quarter, *Hewlett-Packard: the people who never stop asking what if.* Then the left tackle sprains his right knee and the pocket starts to collapse. Number Nineteen takes hit after hit, hobbles back to the line with a separated shoulder, hairline fracture, three cracked ribs, his whites dirty but pure with grace, shouting his colors and numbers into the late sun, setting a playoff record for yardage—not that he ever cared about records, and because he didn't. Finally, one last posession, a one-score game, no timeouts, no huddle (On the ball! On the ball!), throwing for the long shadows—corners, fades, and outs—driving into night at the end of the field, to fourth and goal, last play in regulation, hitting Eighty-eight on a slant for the tie and getting hit one more time, blindsided just as he released the ball, going down and staying down, the sound of bone snapping through the crowd roar of national television, the sound of the announcer on national television saying, "The game becomes unkind," and it was that piece of magnetic tape, that stretch of history that Jelonnek replayed over and over, click and whir, click and again, till the tears came and the girl he lived with would roll her eyes and sigh.

But tonight she was the one crying. Into the phone. In the kitchen.

Number Nineteen would not join them in the afterlife of overtime, would not return to the game. It would be said he never did. The voices he'd proven wrong spoke again, saying *Gun-shy*, saying *Diminishing skills*, but this time Jelonnek would not be one of them. He'd erased that final episode of the Game, the toss of the coin and sudden death. There was no end now, no clock, only the static and snow of what might be. The past is never complete. You just rewind it while you get another beer, then start over again.

The girl Jelonnek lived with asked him what he was doing.

He wasn't sure. He couldn't see her. Something he hadn't done before. He couldn't taste or smell, he'd had enough. They were in the way. His neck hurt from holding his head just so. He tried to move them with his tongue. Maybe there was a better way. Something he didn't usually do.

It scratched, she said. She wasn't cooperating. He was doing all the work, but didn't he want it that way?

What was he doing? she asked. She really didn't seem to know. He passed out. He passed out with his face in her cunt and as if seeing it there saw the house he grew up in, the bleak fortress of hate it had become. Fenced, curtained, overgrown, painted a dull green even his dreams could not refine. A car drove by out front. A man was pitched out of the car, bleeding. His leg had been cut off at the knee. They threw his hat out after him but kept his leg. The man got up on one foot and Jelonnek asked him if there was anything he could do. His voice was thin, weak, like he really didn't mean to be heard. The man didn't answer. He put his hat back on and hopped off toward the store at the corner as if this were remedy enough.

The old man had sold the house to the people across the street. They weren't going to live there, they would rent it out. It was said they were doing this to prevent a certain element from moving in.

Jelonnek had taken the girl he lived with there just before the old man sold it, when he'd announced he was leaving. At first they sat in the kitchen. "You know about the Siegfried Line?" the old man kept asking her. He kept touching her arm. His hands were claws, his hair synthetic fiber, brand-new. The old one had been made of actual human hair, Asian or Indian, but they stripped it before they dyed it and it wound up looking faker than the fake. Beneath this gaudy fiction the curve of his skull had broadened, his spine had settled, barrel-trunk thickened, legs now skinny and hairless. His hands were claws. They got away from him sometimes, emphatically tapping words like nails into the tabletop, touching her arm.

They'd mixed mortar and dug trenches for the Germans, fired the turret gun of a tank for the British. Worked in a bayonet factory.

"She don't know what's the Siegfried Line." The old man grinned at Jelonnek with satisfaction. With mortar, cinderblock, barbed wire. Escape.

There was an aura of permanent flatulence about him. Grease stains on the kitchen walls. He washed dishes in cold water, never turned on a light before sundown.

"Ar*try*tis," the old man said, and told them he was retiring to Florida after thirty years of cold-rolling steel, thirty winters in this notch of the Rust Belt. The sun would straighten his hands; they'd unfolded the brochures. They'd knocked down bearing walls, raised the roof and added rooms till no one seeing the house from the street could believe the space inside. Laid the red deep-pile in the living room, tore down a garage and built another one, planted pear trees, apple trees, plum trees in the backyard. Built a go-cart and a crossbow at Christmas when money was short or he was just reluctant to part with it, slaughtered the rabbits his children thought were pets.

They'd use whatever was handy. Board, pipe, hose, strap. Themselves.

"But just think if I was a Jew."

He was born Catholic but a bomber crashed into the morning Mass his parents were attending on the first day of the invasion. Religion, he told her, touching her, was as useless to him as professional sports. Or art. His brother had been a painter. One of his oils hung in the living room: a boy and girl gathering mushrooms in a forest. Wolves lurking. Across the room the sun always setting, a blazing orange wallpaper mural hung by the hands that had installed the imitation fireplace, devised tinfoil armatures to simulate the crackle of burning logs, anchored the chandelier so securely in the ceiling it had supported the weight of his wife when she hung herself from it.

She was a small woman. When he spoke Polish he was still talking to her.

It was too cold to go outside. The old man could barely read or write. He lived alone.

"You know about Monte Cassino?" he said. He asked Jelonnek again what it was called when you chased Black Velvet with beer.

"How about let's have a boilermaker?" he said, and they went back into his kitchen. The bottle came out then, the cans, the photo album with the yellowing pictures and their quaint scalloped borders. The old man leaked stories, tears, gas; he couldn't help himself. It was nothing Jelonnek hadn't smelled before. He knew the stories that made the pictures and were made by them, and the old man would tell it till he was wet-eyed and wordless, then resolved with yet another shot, another chaser, what passed for a happy ending, and this was the only part he and Jelonnek still shared.

Monte Cassino. Mussolini hanging upside-down with his mistress. Wrecked fuselage of a German dive bomber—they had whistles in the wings to terrify. Some of them hand-tinted, the old man and his brother in red berets. They'd crossed the ocean together but Jelonnek's uncle had stayed up north to pursue painting and an early death from alcohol poisoning. He was still twenty-seven, had left Jelonnek nothing but his first name.

The picture had slipped under the table, and then things got tricky. Jelonnek on his hands and knees. He hit his head. He wasn't sure how he'd ended up alone. He must have crawled under the table to retrieve the picture of his uncle. Unless it was the real estate brochure, the booklet on synthetic fiber. He looked for her legs. He remembered kind of liking it where he was, but not whether he'd hit his head crawling under, or getting out of there when he heard the girl he lived with scream.

He ran upstairs. The sun porch was a narrow box of afternoon light. The heat was off but it wasn't cold.

"Why something has to happened?" The old man sounded like he really wanted to know, but why was he standing so far from her? The wig slightly askew, the part aimed off at an angle as if to divert.

Jelonnek's voice throbbed in his skull.

"The sun just felt so good," she said. "All these windows."

The old man put the bottle on a sill. That sound a corner of liquor makes. The light in the rest of the room the same color.

"He just startled me. I just didn't hear him coming."

"See? She even says."

Jelonnek touched his scalp where the pain was, feeling for a bump or a cut. He felt both.

"So what the big deal is about?" The old man produced glasses out of nowhere. "What's about a boilermaker?"

"Oh my God," she said. Something trickled down Jelonnek's temple.

"What you did to yourself?" the old man said.

Synthetic fiber, the booklet said, though lacking the body and tensile strength of pure Caucasian, is not only cheaper and more durable, but also colorfast; protected from excessive moisture, light, and other agents of time, its subtle shades and natural tints will neither blend nor fade.

"Is there any iodine?" the girl who lived with Jelonnek said.

◆　◆　◆

Then she was no longer asking him what he was doing, but "What the hell did you do?"

He lifted his head, tried to pull himself up. She put her foot in his chest. He felt himself pushed up, back and out, tried to grab her ankle but was already falling backward off the bed, landing hard and loud on the floor in front of the headboard while the guy downstairs yelled and she pounded down the hall to the bathroom to clean his retched up dreams out from inside her.

When he finally called the girl from the Bureau of Motor Vehicles, she seemed almost not to remember asking him to in the first place.

"I'd love to," she said anyway. She asked him where they were going. "Any place you want," he said, partly out of deference, partly because he wasn't sure where there was to go downtown. She asked him if he liked Greek. She and her coworkers would order gyros from a place near Fourteenth.

"It's not far," she said, "and it's not expensive."

Money, Jelonnek said, was no object.

"That's so sweet," the girl from the BMV said again.

He picked her up in front of the BMV at twenty-nine minutes past twelve. She wore a cardigan over a black turtleneck. They drove in silence at first but this was only to be expected. Then Jelonnek thought to ask about *him*—there was no singing that name—and when he explained who he meant she laughed in a qualified way, said, "Oh, he's not so bad. Not as bad as he's had it," and he wondered if she was of that nature that tries to see only the good in others, but not how he might suffer that appraisal. She asked if she could listen to the radio. Of course she could, and she tuned it to a station Jelonnek, who thought of himself as a rock-and-roller, never listened to.

There was a parking lot next to the restaurant but Jelonnek didn't want to pay, he wanted to demonstrate competence, some kind of principle. The only space was a block away. It looked like a tight fit but he got within a foot of the curb on the first try. He felt a bead of sweat drip from his armpit again.

"Close enough for government work," the girl from the BMV said. Jelonnek said something modest. The girl from the BMV said she hated parking downtown, and he asked her what she drove as they walked to the Pantheon, a foot apart.

A guy wearing earmuffs in May stepped out of a doorway and said, "Anthony and Cleopatra." Then he asked for a quarter.

Inside just a few tables were taken, but somehow Jelonnek hadn't counted on anyone else. A man met them at the door with an accent. He sat them in a booth and gave them menus. Another man poured their water. His shirt was very white and so were the napkins, the tablecloth was red and so was her mouth. The room was dimly lit. She took off her sweater and the turtleneck was sleeveless; dark upon dark within dark, and she was the core. The waiter asked if they wanted anything from the bar. He sounded harsh, but it was a harsh accent. Jelonnek looked at the girl from the BMV and she said water was fine.

"Feel free though," she said, but just water was fine for Jelonnek too. Maybe later, when things loosened up. But would he want that on his breath when he was dropping her off, as he leaned toward her lips?

"Separate check?" the waiter asked.

"I'll get it it," Jelonnek said, a little loud, and he looked at the girl from the BMV. She was looking at the menu.

"The braised octopus is good," she said. She asked the waiter for a lemon.

"Really?" Jelonnek said. He hadn't counted on the octopus either. His face felt hot. He drank some water. He kept his menu low because his hands were shaking slightly, and he could feel his stomach. He couldn't tell if it was empty or not empty enough.

They spoke haltingly after the waiter left, each topic consisting of a single question and answer. "So," Jelonnek kept saying.

She asked him what sign he was.

"You believe in that?" he said.

She shrugged. "I believe in conversation."

"I don't believe in that stuff," he said.

"Let me guess," she said. She guessed right but Jelonnek didn't tell her. She wanted him to guess hers and then the waiter came back.

The girl from the BMV asked Jelonnek if he minded her getting the octopus.

"Anything you want," he said like they'd just come in the door, but she was done thanking him. Next time would be her treat. Jelonnek ordered a gyro. "*Yearo*," the waiter said like a rebuke and turned to leave and the girl from the BMV asked him again if she could have a slice of lemon for her water. The waiter swept up the glass and a small splash darkened the tablecloth. She watched him walk away.

"So," Jelonnek said, and asked her what she did at the BMV.

"Thought you'd never ask," she said, and smiled but didn't laugh. She sighed: took pictures, gave eye tests, "Ask people what kind of plates they want..." Jelonnek tried to stay with her but got distracted—the table across the aisle was filling up.

"'Heart of it All or Birthplace of Aviation?'"

"I thought that was someplace else."

"Orville Wright was born in Dayton."

"Sounds interesting," he said to whatever she'd said last.

"You're nice," she said, "but twenty hours a week is plenty."

"You're not full-time?"

"School I am. I don't want to take mug shots the rest of my life."

School. A future. Jelonnek hadn't counted on a future, only the drab now from which he would rescue her.

"That's a nice car for part-time," he said. He'd assumed she rode the bus.

"My daddy bought it for me." They had an agreement: he would buy her a car if she earned her own spending money, bought her own books. Jelonnek didn't want to ask what she was going to school for, or where she lived. Or what her father did.

"Daddy's an orthodontist," she said, light pouring from her mouth.

A busboy brought her water back, replacing it more carefully than it had been removed. The food arrived. The octopus was served with rice and came in some kind of red sauce. It was all chopped up but you could still see the chunks of tentacle, the suckers it would affix to prey. The gyro was wrapped in foil.

"Would you like more water for you?" the busboy asked. Jelonnek grinned. He watched the girl from the BMV fork a length of tentacle and put it in her mouth. He wondered how she'd come to like octopus.

"Nassau," she said. "Ever been to the Bahamas?"

"Not yet." Jelonnek had never left the country, and hadn't been out of state since he was a child and it was somebody else's idea. He put ketchup on his fries. The sandwich was enormous; you goddamn needed a third hand just to hold it, and the ability to unhinge your jaw like a snake. The girl from the BMV ate heartily. Jelonnek felt himself get fuller every time she swallowed.

"They shot a fireman in the face," a voice from the table across the aisle said. Jelonnek looked at the girl from the BMV.

"Can't we all get along?" A misquote.

"I'd like to see that missing thirteen seconds."

She smiled at him with her mouth closed. He heard a newspaper. "Four percent had no opinion. How could you have no opinion?"

"So," the girl from the BMV said, and Jelonnek asked her what she was taking up at school.

"Broadcast journalism," she said. "That's my heart." She raised her fork. "I'm the next Ramona Robinson." She laughed again in a qualified way and told him there was a piece of foil on his lip. "You've seen the newsletter?"

He nodded, scraped with a forefinger. *Dateline District*, or something. The guy from the mailroom brought it, and Jelonnek had even glanced at it in the bathroom.

"I write What's News With You," she said and Jelonnck shoved some fries in his mouth, took another bite of the impossible sandwich. Something fell out of it and landed on his knee. His tongue couldn't find its taste. He took a drink to dislodge it from his throat and she asked him if he had his degree.

"I'm working on something," he said. She looked up and smiled but not at him. Someone was coming to the table.

"You can run but you can't hide," he said loudly, a nice-looking guy maybe Jelonnek's age, wearing a nice dark suit with a silver tie; he could have been a stockbroker or someone folding sweaters at Brooks Brothers. They hugged. The girl from the BMV introduced him as a friend. He offered his hand, one of those tricky grips Jelonnek could never get right—he knew only one way—but the guy was friendlier than you would have expected. The ones with lighter skin often were.

It didn't take long. Jelonnek tried not to listen from behind his sandwich. There didn't seem to be anything serious between them but she sounded different now, there were inflections in her voice that hadn't been there before. They said things were bumpin, and killin, he called her girl, called her Ramona Robinson. His stickpin had tiny jewels on the ends.

High yellow, they called it.

"Let me leave you alone before your lunch attacks me," he said and she laughed in a way that wasn't qualified, a way Jelonnek hadn't been able to make her laugh. "Will I see you at the Zodiac?"

Maybe, she wasn't sure when, she was busy with school these days. They hugged again before he left, but this time it seemed more his idea. He whispered something quick in her hair.

"He's a friend," she told Jelonnek. Jelonnek asked her about the Zodiac. He did not want to be a friend.

"Just a club I go to sometimes."

"You like to dance?"

"God, yes."

He saw her dancing, moving away from him. He looked around the room as if to see where she'd gone.

She asked if he was looking for a waiter.

He told her about *Armageddon Zero.*

"Civilization as we know it," he said. He told her everything except that she was in it, that The First Woman was also The Last. He was saving it. She sounded impressed anyway, seemed genuinely to like it. She said it sounded like a great idea, and then she said, "One thing."

What one thing?

"Isn't it all different now?" she said.

"Different."

"It probably doesn't matter."

One thing what?

The missiles, the Cold War. She took another bite out of him. "What's the word I'm looking for?"

He didn't know what the word was but he didn't want her to find it. He could feel it churning around in his stomach.

But it didn't matter, she said, she said it was still a great idea. "Good luck." She was almost done. "So you like movies."

"They're okay."

"Just okay? What's your favorite movie?"

He shrugged catastrophically. The world with its billions teemed again.

"Go figure," she said.

"So you want to be a reporter," he said.

"Anchor," she said.

"You could be more than that," he said.

"You're nice."

"You look like an actress."

"You're so sweet," she said. "Will you still want me when I get braces?"

She wasn't interested in acting. She still liked writing articles, though. Had an idea for a new one in fact.

She asked Jelonnek if she could ask him something.

His stomach lurched. He hated when people said that before they asked you whatever it was. Like they had to prepare you.

"Go for it," he said.

About what had happened. The aftermath. She'd already talked to several employees throughout the district. Points of view.

"It was a mistake," he said. His stomach cramped again, a sharp edge, and this time it wouldn't go away.

"It wouldn't be a lot of questions," the girl from the BMV said. "We could do it over the phone."

Jelonnek stood. "I was asking directions."

"Are you alright? "

"Fifty billion dollars in damage," someone across the aisle said.

She said he looked pasty.

"I'm okay." He was already moving. "I'm...right back."

"Call that acceptable restraint?"

"Call that a human being?"

He stumbled into the kitchen instead of the men's room, had to ask where it was. Somebody was at the urinal but nobody was in the stall. Normally Jelonnek would have waited till the other guy left, but today he didn't care and didn't have much choice. When the first wave had passed he felt his hair sticking to his scalp and his shirt was damp. She looked like the news, not someone who read it. There was a window over the sink. His stomach convulsed again. When it stopped all he could do was look at the toilet paper roll. The bathroom was empty. He looked at the window. The First Woman's daddy was a dentist. What time was it?

It was his treat.

The next discharge was less turbulent, and the last just gas and noise. Finally, he tugged at the roll. He'd thought they'd hold hands on the way back to the car. There was shit on his finger.

Jelonnek completed his community service at a church called Our Lady of Good Counsel. On the list it was categorized as a charity. He started out the day running errands for the parish priest, bought him a new watch and a pair of black slacks at Value City. Father Bob wore thirty length, forty waist. He wanted a watch with hands. After that Jelonnek stapled the church newsletter with a woman who was on work release; she'd assaulted her ex-boyfriend's new girlfriend. Hadn't started it, she said, she'd never been in a fight in her life, but once she'd started swinging and clawing she discovered an aptitude that seemed to justify her existence. There was no going back. Bit a cop on the nose and kicked out the window of the patrol car. She wouldn't stop talking, and she had skin like a canteloupe.

They went down to a room in the basement and arranged chairs for bingo in rows of twelve. A reckless driver showed up. He and Jelonnek took the seats out of the church van and drove to someone's house to pick up a donation of baby furniture. They took turns behind the wheel. The baby had been stillborn and the store wouldn't take the furniture back. The husband was alone. Say hello to Father Bob, he said; he'd gone to grade school there. The school was adjacent to the church and there'd been construction in the playground. All that was left was a pile of wet sand and when they got back Jelonnek had to shovel the sand into a wheelbarrow and dump it at the edge of the playground. It took an hour and was the hardest work he'd ever done in his life, but he was glad to be away from the woman who'd assaulted her ex-boyfriend's new girlfriend in self-defense.

He saw her again in the church, where they finished the day sweeping and mopping. The reckless driver had disappeared— nearly half of them don't come back. Jelonnek was rinsing the floor of the apse when he backed into the Madonna and broke her thumb. The woman who was on work release rebuked him: "You know where you're going," and Jelonnek said he thought he was already there, and she his assigned torment, and she was walking slowly toward him, marshaling a reply, when Father Bob arrived to see how they were doing.

Jelonnek showed him the damage. The father saw the narrow loop of wire where the Virgin's thumb had been and looked deeply distressed, as if the rude armature of his faith had been exposed.

He took Jelonnek to the rectory, the nicest part of the church. The kitchen had brand-new appliances: a fridge with an icemaker, a Cuisinart, a microwave with a turntable. Jelonnek went into the living room. Leather furniture, a twenty-seven-inch TV, a VCR. The rector sat in an armchair watching basketball. He was a very old man all dressed in white and wore a round cap like the Pope. The white was going yellow and the old man smelled as though bathing were not a requirement of his office, but was very understanding about the Madonna.

"So many statues in the church," he said, "but only one Body." He asked Jelonnek if he was Catholic, and Jelonnek had to think about it. He didn't want to tell the rector about his father. The church his mother had taken him to was smaller and poorer than the one the rector presided over, but it was close by and anyone could worship there. The deacon drove a beer truck. Jelonnek had gone there till he was eighteen, but when you are eight you have no choice. You might even enjoy singing "Bringing in the Sheaves" and "How Great Thou Art." You might even think you want to.

Sunday school was conducted in the pews after the morning service. The teacher wore a pin-striped suit. He was a small man with big ears and his hairline peaked nearly between his eyebrows. His hair was so shiny it looked like plastic. No one knew what he really did for a living. No one knew, when he asked them, how a Roman swordsmith quenched a hot blade.

"Stuck it in the belly of a nigger," he said. Something to do with the presence of salt.

After services Jelonnek would set a fire behind the old factory next to the church. He wasn't trying to burn anything down, he was trying to bring something to life; things didn't just burn, they became fire, and the fire used him to make itself.

It felt like the miracle they only talked about in the pews.

His classmates duly impressed. Their giggling and cursing crackled with the flames, but once the bright orange appeared Jelonnek became part of it and didn't know anyone else was there. He even forgot about the girl he wanted to impress most of all, but she didn't forget him or what he'd done, and told Jelonnek's mother, who told his father, who used the one-by-four he'd set aside in the garage for offenses of such magnitude. Jelonnek missed two days of school but never started another fire, and this was one of the few beatings the old man gave him that actually served its purpose.

The girl had an Old Testament name, but Jelonnek couldn't remember what it was.

"Congregational," he said finally. The rector smiled and nodded like he had Jelonnek where he wanted him. He told Jelonnek he felt sorry for Protestants because they didn't get to eat the body of Christ, nor drink His blood.

The blender had thirty-one speeds.

```
Cut to Hunter's face and it's not a pretty
a burned mass of scars and veins.
```

SURVIVOR
(screaming)
No!

HUNTER
yes!

CUT TO

Rolling around the floor in deadly moral
combat crashing into things bleeding, the
survivor holds his own minus one hand an
eye but not for long.

SURVIVOR How can you do this to innocent
people?

HUNTER you mean you haven't figured it out
yet mr? I didn't catch your

sURVIVIR Just get it over with.

HUNTER Winner gets to be G—

SURVIVOT (interupt) get it over with!

To end his statement the hunter brings down
the blade as the survivor dives out of the
way at the last as the knife stabs the
control panel 12 thousand volts shoot ing
direcly into the hunters body.

```
HUNTER No!
SURVIVOR Yes!
SEXY COMPUTER WOMAN'S VOICE 87, 86, 85,
84(and counting)
```

"It's only a game."

"What? Now what?"

"I mean it's not the end of the world…Don't tell me I have to tell you."

"Tell me what?"

"You? Hey, don't behead the messenger."

"Don't do what?"

"Diminished skills, pal, diminished skills."

"Bullshit."

"Not today, bro, not hey! You knew it was coming."

"They trade him?"

"Like anybody wants his ass."

"He's cut?"

"Would I shit you?"

"He still has it."

"What he has they don't want it. Not after K.C."

"All he needs is a line."

"A new arm and a set of legs wouldn't hurt. Or give him some fuckin roller skates."

"Marino has a line."

"He's no Marino."

"He doesn't have to be."

"He's not even himself. Listen, it's only a game. Did I tell you we set a date?"

Jelonnek hung up and drove to the store. He went right to the newspaper rack and there it was, front page. He couldn't finish the article, stopped when he got to those two words, the words he couldn't repeat even to himself. He put the paper back and bought a case of Blatz instead.

He'd planned to go home and play Nintendo till the sun went down and came back up, but the tape was there. The Game was waiting. When he got to the building he kept going. He tore open the carton with one hand and opened a beer, with the other drove across bridges, across town into the neighborhood where he'd grown up, past the house he'd once lived in. It looked as it did in his dreams, all one color, even the trim, the curtains always drawn. There was a gate to the driveway now and a fence around the front yard. The flower beds that had lined the drive were gone and so were the trellises and the birdbath and the year-round Christmas lights that might have sprouted from the siding. An infant wearing only a t-shirt watched him balefully through the fence. A dog next to the infant wore an identical expression.

Jelonnek opened another one and turned, turned, wound himself around the block. When he passed the house again he looked up the driveway at the garage the old man had built, wondering if anything was still there. The lawnmowers, the barbecue, old tires, a tireless bike frame, the rabbit hutch made of plywood and chicken wire, tools, a table saw, a crumpled inflatable raft, a wading pool, fishing rods, the flag, bags of fertilizer, thick must of rust and mold, damp cardboard, boxes of what the basement and attic no longer had room for; everything but the car. A dirty blue canvas bag, hanging from a nail by its fading orange strap. The orange glowed in an earlier dark, scored his shoulder and numbed his arm. Cards on a metal ring. Twelve-year-old days, paperboy days. The papers that filled the sack came in bundles bound with baling wire. The ex-Marine rolled them out the back of his blue truck, said there was no such thing as an ex-Marine. Third time they don't answer, he said, cut them off. "They just want it for the TV book anyway." You punched their card when they paid. The bundles thudded, slapped the sidewalk at the corner six afternoons a week. The corner pointed at the high school across the street, at the kids coming out of detention. If you got there late the bundles would be torn open, the papers scattered, and if you got there early enough to try and stop them, they would teach you to try and stop them. Sometimes Jelonnek just watched from a distance, but he wouldn't do what Leon did.

"Them colored?" the old man asked.

"Like animals," the old man answered. He'd had children late in life. He'd always been old.

The wind took the papers apart and blew them further down the street. They flapped on lawns, rattled in bushes and branches as if submitting an opinion to the editor. Dogs would chase them down, bark at print flapping in trees as if commenting on some state of affairs. They ran in packs with their hindquarters curved to one side in the event of assault from the rear, and it wasn't just the news they were drawn to. Jelonnek carried a stick. The biggest one didn't run with the others, it had a name and a home, though it seemed not to want either. It shared a brown-shingled row house with a more or less obese woman and could not be allowed to escape. You were only to use the back door. She appeared there every Saturday, squinting over a cigarette, one hand finding quarters in the doughy palm of the other, saying, "Keep it" with the big black head clamped between her thighs. There were ashes on the coins. She was a good tipper.

She insisted on Mrs. though the only man Jelonnek ever saw on the premises was his father.

The dog only bit him once. (But Leon's teeth were small and rotten. He would pay for the paper. He was a baseball fan but could name only the pitcher. He cried easily. Wore his pants up to his chest, his top button buttoned, answered to a woman's voice in the depths of the house. She would be so mad. Four hours a day chasing shopping carts at Pick-N-Pay. Sometimes the kids out of detention blocked the way home. If he has no money he still pays. The manager started sending him home early so this wouldn't have to happen to him, a man in his forties. The truth was he didn't mind. She needed her coupons, her Ann Landers. He moved the change around in the palm of his hand like it would add up right then. He'd make up the difference. You wouldn't even feel his sharp little teeth, they'd shown him how.)

It didn't really hurt. Jelonnek had opened the door to collect the bill and it came pouring out from between her legs. A sharp pinch, not like something that had gone deep, and he shouted more out of surprise than pain. The dog trotted off, head down like its feelings were hurt. Jelonnek went the other way, deeper into the courtyard the row house tenants shared. He got behind the old fountain where the only water was the snow that had melted weeks ago. Dropped his pants to assess the injury. A small bloodless hole six inches above the knee. A blackness in there. He heard her calling its name.

There was one house where you folded the paper and put it in a rat trap nailed to the porch post.

It didn't come back.

The old man wore his hat to see the woman in the brown row house. The dusty porch creaked. "Bad joist," he murmured, but there was no going around back now. His lips were tight. He breathed through his nose when he was mad. You could hear her gasping or whimpering inside as she struggled with whatever was in the way.

"Did you see what your animal did to this boy?" She loomed in the threshold, her eyes wet and shiny. She'd changed into some sort of frock. Dark, velvety, and she'd applied the color of cherries to her lips and cheeks.

Jelonnek had changed into shorts so he could display the bite without having to drop his pants.

"He brought him home when he was a puppy," she said, "and he left the same day. All I could do was watch him get bigger. Now they're both gone."

"What's about the rabies?" the old man said.

"He's had all his shots." She swung the door open. You could smell the shabby darkness leaking out from behind her. The old man let it swallow him, went in to see the papers. Jelonnek had never been inside.

He said he'd wait in the car. The screen door banged shut on his burning face. In the Dodge he waited a long time, then dozed and dreamed of a great thirst, and a great fear of what he thirsted for. He woke to the slamming of the car door, a familiar smell.

The ex-Marine said, "They always come back."

The woman in the brown row house acted like nothing had ever happened. The orange strap frayed, faded. (The powder he'd found in the church basement was almost the same color.) Saturday was Saturday. The old man fixed her porch. The grass in the courtyard went uncut, the flagstones islands amid weeds. Jelonnek listened for the click of claws. He drank water all the time and he was always thirsty. Later, he knew, the sight of it would be like broken glass in his throat. Twenty-one shots in the belly with a needle ten inches long. If it wasn't too late. He found a plastic bowl in the garage. He kneaded the mixture till the orange went away—the ex-Marine told him how much. The meat was so cold it made your fingers numb.

There was a grapevine in the courtyard. Something green grew in the fountain. The alley between the row homes was where he listened the hardest. The porch was bright and new and so was the back door. Jelonnek held his breath when he opened it, but the rusty whine he braced for didn't happen. Other laments, thick and close.

"I had to tell them. I thought they just gonna be deport, we didn't know about the camps."

"You were just a kid, a human kid."

"They were in the basement. We didn't have no refrigerator, we keep stuff cold in the basement."

"Technically it's a boilermaker."

Jelonnek reached into his bag, into the portable darkness under the canvas flap. Felt the plastic with the cold softness inside. Water didn't hurt yet, but it didn't help.

Maybe he shouldn't have told anyone.

They had a corner meeting. Subscription drive, the ex-Marine said. Winner won four tickets to Disneyland.

The bars and clubs down in the Flats had acquired a certain reputation. Brawling, drug traffic, underage drinking, auto theft and vandalism, fire code violations, boating accidents, sexual assault, bouncers on parole for manslaughter. Fights often broke out on the dance floors and in the parking lots and in one altercation a young man had been stabbed through the eye with a ballpoint pen, sustaining brain damage that would confine him to a wheelchair and round-the-clock care for the rest of his life. His companion was simply killed. Next to a popular bar was a simple shrine reminiscent of the kind often seen on the freeway commemorating traffic fatalities: a wreath, ribbon, Polaroids. In this case the man in the picture had been urinating in the river, then fell and struck his head on the way down. His body was recovered a half-mile downstream, minus a leg presumably sheared off by an outboard propeller. But it was almost summer and it was the weekend and everyone generally had a good time, just letting off steam, just looking to get lucky down in the Flats, because this was a working town and they'd earned it and it was the weekend just before summer.

The club to whose guest list Jelonnek and the girl he lived with had been added was on the east bank of the river and had three floors. Dancing on the first floor, a restaurant on the second, and at the top a comedy club where a midget comedian would eat you alive, it was said, if you took a table near the stage. Like many other establishments in the Flats it was also equipped with dock facilities so that boaters could moor their craft and drink and dine and dance via the rear entrance. Out front you could feel the rhythm in the sidewalk, small detonations of bass under your shoes. People were dancing in line. Because Jelonnek and the girl he lived with were on the guest list, they didn't have to wait in line or pay the cover. On the way to the entrance she ran into some of her coworkers from the bank. They were not on the list. She introduced Jelonnek but he'd already met one of them the year before, at the Asset Recovery Christmas party. He didn't remember her name but he remembered how her breast had felt, cornering her in a conference room, empty hand over their heads pretending mistletoe. She'd splashed rum and coke in his face and kicked him in the groin, but at least she hadn't said anything to the girl he lived with.

They said they'd meet each other inside. On the Titanic, they said. A guy dressed like a doorman unhooked a velvet rope and they entered the music, its giant electronic heart. Jelonnek wondered how you got used to it, he wondered how you got used to the women. There were TV screens everywhere showing the same music video like a display in an appliance store. They headed for the bar, a big circle enameled in white so that it turned whatever color the lights were. It stood in the middle of the room like the hub of a wheel, everything else was dance floor. There was no place to sit and they waited for a bartender. They had to talk into each other's ears. After a while Jelonnek began to recognize the music. On the radio they were just songs, harmless and familiar, but here they'd mutated into something monstrous, like B-movie bugs afflicted with radiation.

Between songs was the din of conversation. Jelonnek wondered what they were talking about, laughing and shouting about over their drinks, the numbing murmur of what seemed to be a single unintelligible topic. The girl he lived with turned to him and Jelonnek felt words spray his ear. He saw the tube tops, the skirts, the fishnets, the jeans like another layer of skin, and nodded to whatever she'd said.

The bar changed color again. A bartender came, blonde and tanned and as handsome as any of the patrons. When Jelonnek found out what they wanted for a beer, he told her too bad the guy in Commercial Loans wasn't the one who poured the drinks. But he had two before he let her talk him into dancing. He'd studied everyone's arms and legs, their efficient way of having fun, and got out there and lifted his feet. They weighed a ton. His knees were stiff. He saw what some guy was doing with his hands and tried to imitate it. He still wasn't sure if he was dancing or pretending to.

Her eyes were closed. She'd made the dress herself. Jelonnek didn't know if she was moving with him or by herself, but she looked okay doing it. Women always looked okay dancing, no matter what you'd put on their shoulders.

Finally, it was over. People clapped and yelled. The guy in Commercial Loans said something from the deejay booth and they shouted back. The girl Jelonnek lived with was smiling. He leaned into it and she told him he danced like he was standing on flypaper. He went back to the bar. She followed him and there was a vacant stool and Jelonnek took it.

The girl he lived with told him she was going to look for her friends. He ordered another beer and a shot of whatever was cheapest. Then he made it a double, just to get even. Straight up. "Neat," the bartender said, and Jelonnek wondered if he was being mocked, for he had almost turned that corner where every remark must be examined for the possibility of insult. But the bartender poured a generous drink and almost at the first taste Jelonnek wasn't as mad anymore. It didn't even hurt as much to look at the girls. She wasn't back yet. He finished and ordered another and watched the dancers, envying the best of them because they had conquered sex. A song came on—you could almost call them that now—and the bartender said if you sang the words to the girl you were dancing with, you were sure to get lucky. Jelonnek didn't know the words, and sang no better than he danced.

The girl he lived with came back with people from the bank. Jelonnek gave her his seat. Somebody bought a round. They knew his name now and he knew some of theirs. He drank what they were drinking. They were all pressed together. They shot another round and went back out on the floor.

Either Jelonnek's dancing had improved or he no longer cared as much. The lasers made it more interesting anyway. Light turned into sheets of green liquid, shadows writhed in mid-air like liberated spirits. Then the strobe lights came on and space and time were not the same again. It made the girl Jelonnek lived with dizzy and when the music stopped they headed back to the bar. On the way she bumped into a stocky guy in a baseball jacket whose beer sloshed over the rim of his glass. She said excuse me and kept going and didn't seem to notice him wiping his fingers on the skirt of the dress she'd made herself, or what the guy wearing the baseball jacket mouthed as he wiped his fingers on her dress like it was a towel in a lavatory. At least Jelonnek didn't think she'd noticed.

Back at the bar she asked if he was on the Titanic yet. Everyone took turns buying and in the abyss between rounds Jelonnek saw the baseball jacket and the mouth made ugly by its ugly words. What she didn't know shouldn't hurt him. He knew he didn't like baseball. Then somebody touched his shoulder and it was his turn. They still knew his name. They wanted to go back out on the floor but the liquor was doing what the light show did, only slower. Jelonnek said he would sit this one out. He was having trouble talking but he made them understand.

He couldn't finish his drinks. He had two of them now, in two hands, poured by two bartenders. He pushed off the bar like he was letting go of the life raft and went looking for a men's room. The next song. He knew the words to this one but they wouldn't do you any good. He pushed through a door. There were lines. There were the guys with stagefright holding everyone up. Someone got tired of waiting and aimed his dick in a trash can. You could hear retching in one of the stalls. Jungle drums pounded through the wall. A guy wearing a black t-shirt with the name of the club on it burst through the door. He had weightlifter arms and dragged away the guy pissing in the trash can.

"I told you they had cameras," someone said.

Then it was Jelonnek's turn. The toilet was full of puke but at least he got a stall; he was one of the guys who have trouble pissing to an audience.

He knew he wanted to get even for something but couldn't remember what it was. Out on the floor the scenery had changed again. A thick fog rolled in and pulsed as though with inner light. Everything was moving to the jungle beat. Jelonnek waded in. As long as you were dancing you were immune, but Jelonnek wasn't dancing. He tried to thread his way through, kept bumping into bodies and leaving a wake of shouts you couldn't hear. When he stopped the fog was up past his knees, you couldn't see the floor. He couldn't see the bar but he wasn't looking for it. Someone danced backward into him. She did it again and Jelonnek shoved as hard as he could and she fell and disappeared in the glowing mist. Someone shoved him back—or was it a punch? He wasn't sure but he stayed on his feet and turned and swung and though it wasn't a solid blow it was like he'd hit the whole crowd at once, the way they came back at him in a hard wave of arms and legs, swarming, tearing his shirt, clawing his back, knocking him down and piling on top of him so he felt instantly deflated, the fight gone out of him, concerned now only with the possibility of being buried alive.

Someone had him in a headlock. Jelonnek took five or six blows to the head and face before he even thought to cover up, and then they were pulled apart. It was just one other guy now and they faced each other still half-submerged in smoke, held apart by the guys in the club t-shirts. The music was still playing but it no longer came from the fog. The other guy asked him if he wanted to finish it outside. Jelonnek tasted blood and his nose felt like it was on sideways. Where was she? He waited till the bouncers repeated the question before he shook his head, so as to make it official.

They decided on the Calphalon; it would last forever. Jelonnek drove to Target. He took a shortcut through the park, drove past men standing in the middle of the river under shale cliffs, casting for whatever was running. It was still early and there would be plenty of parking. If it was late and they knew the parking lot was going to be crowded, the girl Jelonnek lived with would drive. He had a thing about parking lots.

Once a life-size cardboard likeness of Number Nineteen would meet you at the entrance, wearing a three-piece suit and holding a football, but now it was gone and in his place was a vending machine.

Inside the store was big and bright, the floor polished to the point of vertigo. It was early and empty and everything was red: the checkout stands, the shopping carts and baskets, the doors to the restrooms, the partitions between the urinals, the smocks the employees wore to help you in and this early they were still willing to give you the best hours of their lives.

Only the music was bad, but the girl Jelonnek lived with still sang along.

They took a cart because they were getting a whole set. The shopping carts at Target never seemed to squeak nor have that single defective wheel that spun around or wouldn't roll at all. There was a directory at the entrance, and big white signs hanging from the ceiling with big black letters, but they already knew where everything was: BED, BATH, ELECTRONICS. AUTOMOTIVE, OFFICE, ENTERTAINMENT. They split up, as they sometimes did. Jelonnek went to look at fishing rods, and there were video games you could try out and this early you didn't have to wait for some kid to finish. The girl Jelonnek lived with drifted past the colors of towels. Cayenne, Calm Violet, Dazzleberry. Indigo Wonder and Geometry Green.

She sang along.

They reunited in KITCHENWARE. The Calphalon cost a little more than they'd expected and Jelonnek wanted to go with the eight-piece set. The girl he lived with shook her head.

"He's your brother," she said, and hard-anodized aluminum was thirty percent harder than stainless steel. They use it in satellites and racing cars. Nothing stuck to it, and there was a lifetime warranty.

"Their marriage should last this long."

They got the ten-piece.

It was right under their window: "Damn goddamn thing."

It was nothing personal, she said, but you could hear it with the window closed.

"We have work tomorrow," she said.

He told her to tell him about it.

"I'll call the manager tomorrow," she said, and what would be the point? The manager was a voice on an answering machine with a long list of what he didn't do. And what would he do about the wind? It had blown warm and hard all week, knocked a tree down on an empty house, was seen blowing the hubcaps off a car. Traffic lights swung like silent bells, and at night it didn't stop.

"It's nothing personal," she said, her voice already slowing down. Her breath deepened, evened out, the soft rise and fall of her in the dark. A sound you could sleep to if it wasn't for the other one, down in the NO PARKING zone, bouncing, rattling, rolling.

Sometimes it stopped and you thought it was over. Then it started up again.

He swore.

She lifted her head. "Do you want me to go down and get it?"

It was the principle.

She told him to cover his head with his pillow, or try earplugs—they had work in the morning. But earplugs hurt, your heart beating in your head, and then he would worry about what he might not hear. It was too warm to close the window.

It was the idea.

After lunch Jelonnek called Human Resources again. He had questions. Human Resources said three months after you quit.

"You leaving us, Forms?"

"Just wondering."

"You could always quit and come back," she said. "It's been known to happen." She could name names.

He said he just wanted to know. He asked her which form was required for early disbursement and she laughed. He asked her what was funny.

"Do you know what ironic is, Forms?"

The bell rang. Jelonnek hung up without saying goodbye and ran to the side door. He stood there and didn't open it till the bell rang again. Then she wasn't there, but he was, the guy who sometimes came with her from the Bureau of Motor Vehicles. He was alone.

He looked at Jelonnek's face and said, "Looks like somebody been in the mix." Jelonnek looked at the order. It was small, he wouldn't need the ladder or the forklift. He didn't say he'd be right back but he was.

The guy from the BMV was sweating in his t-shirt. "No AC, huh?"

There was a fan in the office. "You get used to it," Jelonnek said.

"I don't think I could work here."

"I didn't know I was going anywhere."

"I'm just saying," the guy said.

"You'd work here."

"They pay?"

Jelonnek wasn't sure what the starting step was. He came up with a figure.

"That fan might have to get it then," the guy from the BMV said. "Shit." And he laughed. Jelonnek could not remember hearing this sound before. He put the order in a box.

It took twenty thousand years, the scientist on *60 Minutes* had said, to turn a black man white.

What was it? What was it about them? Over the arms and backs of chairs, over the footboard, hanging long and fluted from doorknobs, even layered now over the covers they slept under. Jelonnek often wondered what it was. Scattered on the floor like casualties in the bedroom, bathroom, every room. There seemed to be more of them every day, and when he was drinking Jelonnek could lose himself in them just looking at them. Cuffs, collars, legs and sleeves in the shape of what's lost or hoped for. Turmoil, surrender. If he drew, Jelonnek would think then, they would be his sole subject. He would draw you the truth of them. But he wasn't drinking now and he couldn't draw anything but stick figures.

He could hear it. Bouncing, rattling, rolling.

He got out of bed and took a pair of sweatpants from the back of a chair, the pair they both wore and had been wearing for so long neither could remember to whom they'd originally belonged. He put on the jersey that bore the number nineteen, he put it on inside out. A pair of slippers. She didn't wake up.

Down in the NO PARKING ZONE someone had once replaced the A with an O. Jelonnek stood at the edge for a while, watched it make noisy ragged circles in the same hot wind that had blown all day and most of the week. Dust too, and leaves and wrappers and a dirty flattened cup. Once, twice, it lapped near the yellow border and Jelonnek lunged halfheartedly, self-conscious, as if practicing, but it was even quicker and less predictable than it sounded. Then the wind picked it up and put it down so hard you had to wonder where anyone else was.

"I'm not God," the manager would say, and more power to him. He said he picked up the grounds as well as could be expected every day. Must have blown in off the street, he said, and walked away whistling and he was the best whistler Jelonnek had ever heard, more power.

Jelonnek moved to the middle of the zone. It circled him now like a satellite. When it slowed he stooped, reached, moved his feet. Felt watched. Someone up there in a window, invisible, rooting neither for one nor the other, seeing him bent over his small shuffling steps, hands close to the ground like it was them he was chasing, or some stray pet that cost a two hundred-dollar deposit to keep.

He lost the glint of its skin in the shadows.

It cartwheeled, end over end.

It stopped.

Jelonnek recognized the label. He reached through the silence around it and it was snatched away like a prank at the end of a string. He half-expected to hear laughter then and looked up at the windows. The wind pulled his clothes tighter. He saw nothing and looked up the rest of the way. Where were the Dippers? He'd had a book once. It showed you all the shapes the stars made if you knew how to look. Her winking eye, her head, the hero who gripped it by the hair. The triangle, the bearded king, the Tinted Hand.

Jelonnek had never learned how to look. He'd gotten it for Christmas and lost it. It said there was another kind of wind up there, pushing across the abyss. It moved worlds but was made of nothing, the book said, because nothing was not what you thought it was, and emptiness isn't empty. It is the womb.

He heard it. Something blew in his eye. He almost fell.

It lay and spun with its battered label like a compass needle in the middle of the world. Stood and turned like a top, pirouetted on its rim.

Jelonnek slowed, caught his breath. Tried to look a little less interested, even casual. Like he was out there for night air. Or meeting someone.

It rolled. He didn't stop.

T he Jews were not what Jelonnek had expected. They did not look or sound especially different, and if it weren't for the little caps you probably could not have picked them out of a crowd. Some of them had blonde hair. The little caps were in a basket on a table right where you walked into the living room. A sign above the basket said they were optional.

The rabbi was especially not what Jelonnek had expected. He was not old or bearded or wearing spectacles or a long black tunic. Though he wore one of the little caps, his hair was thick and wavy and styled to the side and back, and he was handsome and broad-shouldered after the fashion of a leading man in the action-romance film genre. As soon as he arrived, a small crowd of matrons gathered like middle-aged groupies around him and his hair, his tan, his grace and wit, his kindly eyes and his Italian double-breasted cashmere suit, and Jelonnek would not have known it was cashmere had he not heard the rabbi himself tell the old man, just as he had heard someone describe the house, with its steep gabled roof and dormers and exposed timbers and diamond pane windows, as being in the Tudor style. It stood on a serene, gated street where the houses were almost as old as the trees that shaded them, just a short drive from the art museum, children's musem, natural history museum, botanical gardens, the symphony hall where one of the finest orchestras in the world played; a stone's throw from the Play House, from the Institutes of Art and of Music, and from one of the finest privatet universities in the country if you wanted to be a doctor, lawyer, or engineer. The bride lived there with her parents and two small sons who called her by name and a cat who'd never been outside. Her father was a pornographer. The living room had been cleared of its customary furniture and filled with folding chairs and two colors of flowers. Jelonnek recognized the pink ones as roses and the girl he lived with told him the little white ones were baby's-breath. In the front of the room were four tall wooden posts with a cloth canopy stretched over the top. Next to this structure the old man stood with the rabbi, both his hair and his suit woven of synthetic fiber.

"Did I see you on the TV?" the old man said.

He had. Shortly after the outbreak of the Gulf War, the rabbi had appeared on the *Mor ning Exchange* with a Muslim clergyman to excoriate the firebombing of a local Arab grocer. After the wedding he would officiate a circumcision. Later that year he would scale a peak in the Andes with his friend the biochemist.

"You must be very proud," the rabbi said. His tie was made of silk.

"I used to be Catholic," the old man said.

The girl Jelonnek lived with left the Calphalon in the foyer with the other gifts. The bride was nowhere to be seen—Jelonnek had met her just the once. He saw his brother wearing one of the little caps.

"Covers my bald spot," his brother said, and punched Jelonnek in the chest. "It stands for what's between us and God." He told Jelonnek what the little caps were called, he explained the wedding canopy, then he told Jelonnek why he wasn't the best man. It hadn't occurred to Jelonnek to wonder, he wasn't sure what this tradition called for, but his brother's explanation made such complete sense he never had a chance to feel excluded or offended, and really he was relieved not to have to get up in front of people anyway.

But why didn't they just take them off, then?

"You want to be in charge of the music?" Jelonnek's brother led Jelonnek toward the back of the living room. They ran into the bride's parents on the way. The woman was small and nervous. "In an hour we'll be almost related," she said to Jelonnek, then resumed telling someone about a bladder infection. The pornographer looked like he'd been born skeptical. He released Jelonnek's hand and said, "What do you do?"

"Forms," Jelonnek began.

"That's it?"

"I work for the state."

"You work for the state. So what are you, the secret police?"

"I pull orders," Jelonnek said, "I work alone," and he thought this guy you might pick out of the crowd. He was said to be opening a new store, to replace the one that had just burned to the ground. The lone fatality had been found in a private viewing booth with his penis in his hand, shoes melted to the floor.

There was a stereo with a cassette player in the back of the room. "When I give you the signal," Jelonnek's brother said, like they were blowing a bridge. There would be another signal for the silence.

Jelonnek's brother left him sitting with the music. When the girl he lived with joined him, he showed her the button he'd been given to push and asked that she not let him forget. They watched the room fill. Mostly everyone looked dressed for church, some with portions of thigh and breast disclosed as if to impart a certain status. They didn't know anyone. They still hadn't seen the bride and the girl Jelonnek lived with said something about bad luck.

It was the first Sunday of summer.

"Sulfa," the bride's mother said. Two small boys kept running in and out. The pornographer grabbed one by the arm and whispered gently to him. The boy took it with the gravity of a death threat, his whole fist in his mouth. The room was almost full. The rabbi looked at his watch.

Jelonnek's sister was one of the last to arrive. Jelonnek didn't see much of her either these days. He was fairly sure she was in real estate, showing houses, and she looked like she was dressed for work. She was wearing sunglasses and chewing gum and so was the guy she was with. The guy she was with had red hair and wore a black silk jacket that came to his waist. He kept his hands in his pockets. When he turned to be introduced there was a colorful dragon embroidered on his back, an inscription in Chinese, perhaps, perhaps what the dragon was saying. He took a hand out of his pocket to shake, then put it back.

There were vacant seats in front of Jelonnek and the girl he lived with. His sister approached, boyfriend in tow. She saw her brother and her eyebrows rose slightly. Jelonnek took a breath. A stiff and perfunctory embrace, no warmth wasted, no love lost, the blood accidents of birth notwithstanding. She introduced her boyfriend and he brought out his hand again. He had the whitest teeth you ever saw and seemed to be always smiling. His eyes were another story; when he took off his sunglasses it was like he'd left them on.

"You don't look like a George," the girl Jelonnek lived with said.

"My middle name," George said, and Jelonnek thought maybe he wasn't smiling, maybe his mouth was just made that way. He asked George what his first name was.

"I'd tell you but then I'd have to kill you," George said, and Jelonnek's sister expelled a laugh so hysterical only hers was possible.

The girl Jelonnek lived with asked about the back of the jacket. Some kind of martial arts thing, not kung fu but something like it, three or four words Jelonnek could not have repeated.

The girl he lived with giggled. "Does that come with rice?"

"Keeps me in shape," George said. He put his glasses back on, took his hands from his pockets and made a quick Bruce Lee motion with them. The sleeves of his jacket snapped like a flag in the wind.

"You should think about it."

Jelonnek's brother was coming. "Where's Pop?" his sister said. The old man was gone. So was the rabbi. Jelonnek's brother nodded and went out the back door. Jelonnek waited for his sister and her boyfriend to sit, then pressed the switch. The music was familiar, they used it in a wine commercial. Conversation ebbed as in a theater at the dimming of the lights. Then there were just the violins and the candles burning on a small table at the front of the room. There were three candles and the tall one in the middle was unlit. A man in the front row aimed a video camera.

The rabbi appeared. He stood beneath the canopy and faced the audience. The back door opened. An elderly couple helped each other up the aisle alongside the seats. Grandparents, Jelonnek figured, though he wasn't sure whose till he saw the pornographer in the old woman's face. They sat in the front row. The old man came in alone.

The children, the best man, the groom, the best woman. The bride's parents came in last, walked halfway up the aisle and stopped. The bride came down the stairs. She wore a big white hat with a net over her face, a white jacket over a dark flowered dress. She met her parents in the aisle and they embraced, but she walked alone to the groom. They entered the huppah. The parents sat. The rabbi nodded but Jelonnek missed the signal. The girl he lived with reached behind him and then you could hear the birds outside and basketball in a distant driveway, everything you couldn't hear before the music. It was Sunday.

The rabbi said, "Welcome family and friends.

Jelonnek's sister reached into her purse and removed a piece of tissue. She spat her gum into it, then held it under her boyfriend's chin. She wadded up the tissue and put it back in her purse.

Someone's baby threatened to cry. The rabbi spoke in a language Jelonnek had never heard, harsh cracked sounds from the throat of the desert. In English he spoke of loved ones who could not be here today but would be rejoicing with them if they could, and asked that they be remembered in a moment of silence. The infant continued to complain, and though it did not break into outright bawling, the rabbi glared in its direction till it was taken from the room and the moment could complete itself.

The boys fidgeted and were acknowledged, as were the traditions of the bride and those of the groom. None of the latter were observed. "'Your people shall be my people,' the rabbi said, 'and your God my God.'" He explained the huppah. He told them what love was, and was not, and what it did and didn't do.

"'If I give away all I posess, and if I deliver my body to be burned,'" the rabbi said, and was without love, he said, he was nothing, and said so without benefit of text or microphone, his empty hands clasped in front of him, looking at the audience as if they comprised a single eye and he would stare it down.

The mother returned with her baby, who remained quiet for the duration of the ceremony.

"Blessed be," the rabbi said.

"Blessed be," the rabbi said.

"Praise and thanks," the rabbi said.

"We praise you," the rabbi said.

The serpent rippled and writhed, Jelonnek smelled a fart. He thought he'd counted only six blessings—wasn't seven the magic number? George put his arm around his sister's shoulders. Jelonnek felt something brush the back of his neck; a breeze was billowing the curtains behind him. The candles guttered but did not go out. The yard behind the house darkened and so did the living room, and though the room brightened again and the breeze subsided, the rabbi did not.

He held aloft a cup. He blessed the wine in Hebrew and English, then he blessed the nuptials and bride and groom drank from the cup as he held it.

"Will you," the rabbi said.

"We will," they said. The rings appeared as unaccountably as the wine. The rabbi told Jelonnek's brother what to say when he placed the ring on his bride's finger, and so instructed the bride in her turn. He blessed the marriage. Bride and groom each took one of the burning candles and together lit the central flame. The rabbi spoke of symbols. He displayed the wedding contract, a yellow sheet of parchment written in both languages. From where Jelonnek sat he could see only the bold downstrokes of the ancient script, as if the document were as old, and the undersigned betrothed in antiquity.

The pornographer nodded with his arms folded. George yawned. There was a fly in the room. The yawn was infectious and though Jelonnek wasn't bored, he covered his mouth. The old man's hand went to his nose.

After the pronouncement husband and wife kissed. The fly buzzed around the room.

Down the street the sons of Abraham were shouting, and the daughters of Judah danced. A jet plane tore the sky above Jerusalem.

In the end a used light bub was wrapped in a towel and placed on the floor. The rabbi explained. He sang a short verse in Hebrew, his voice as lovely as his hair. Jelonnek's brother put his foot on the glass.

In the backyard the old man was dancing with a ten year-old girl. The band played "Wipeout" on a gazebo. The old man pumped his arms vigorously and twisted his trunk, his grim face shiny with sweat. The girl laughed. The band were friends of the groom; he'd known them since high school and had once been a member, but had sold his guitar and enrolled in computer school. Someone came and got the girl. The old man danced as though she were still there.

The breeze had died. The yard was big and decked with streamers and garlands and balloons, and the sun was just getting behind the trees. Jelonnek could see the spiderwebs shining between them, and the gnats that hung in the air like a green mist. It was still warm. The best man asked him what he did.

It was not the first time Jelonnek had been asked that, but for the first time he answered by way of his Armageddon.

The best man nodded. He was in the insurance business. He was one of the friends Jelonnek's brother had acquired through his fiancee, and he was going to help Jelonnek's brother find a job in the firm after he graduated from computer school. Hearing this again, it again made almost perfect sense to Jelonnek, who was still grateful not to have to stand and face yet another jury.

"Are you using a computer?" the best man asked him. Jelonnek said well there was one in the office, and this was the last word he got in edgewise for the remainder of the conversation. He listened. He didn't mind hearing all about them, about RAM and ROM and bytes and hard drives, the impending literacy on which his future was predicated, though he found what the best man's wife was talking about to be more interesting. She was the best woman, some kind of nurse or medical worker, and she stood next to the wedding cake with its tiers and columns and absent wedges, waving a fork, telling the girl Jelonnek lived with about the Red Cross, the Peace Corps. She told her about some remote village in Africa or maybe South America where people trained monkeys to eat lice from the heads of their children.

She was active in the community. The song ended. The starlings screamed in the trees.

The band was taking a break. The old man looked stranded in silence, out of his element, then got himself another glass of champagne—there was only champagne—and wandered around till he found his daughter talking to the rabbi with lipstick on her teeth.

The guests retreated, the starlings took over the yard. When another bird came around they chased it away, and when someone's cat got too close four of them circled her like fighter planes harrying a warship. They meowed.

The bride hated the birds. She hated them the way she hated the bats that had twice gotten in the house, the raccoons that knocked over the garbage, the skunks that sometimes kept you from your own front door. They were being overrun; Jelonnek had heard her say as much though he hadn't spoken to her. Her voice carried. He'd tried to hug her at the receiving line, as he thought he was supposed to, but her back had stiffened and she'd touched his shoulder not to accept the embrace, but to fend it discreetly off.

Skunks killed rats, she'd said, but rats didn't give you rabies.

"You of all the people should understand," the old man said. He had the rabbi to himself, his eyes already brimming. He frisked himself for a handkerchief and the rabbi got a napkin from one of the caterers. The old man blew his nose and said there is no God.

The rabbi's kindly eyes once-overed the wig, the polyester, the suede loafers, and he quoted from Proverbs.

"Energy," the old man said, energy was the immutable force of the universe. It said so on *Nova*. He asked the rabbi if he watched *Nova*. He asked the rabbi if he watched *Sanford and Son*, or *The Dukes of Hazzard*.

"I understand you're good with your hands," the rabbi said.

"Were you on the TV?" the old man said.

"It's very possible," the rabbi said. "Do you by chance know anything about roofing?"

"I can barely hold a hammer."

"Too bad," the rabbi said, "union labor is just…" He looked at his watch. Another ceremony, a cutting, the excision of something else that gets between man and God. The bride's father wrote him a check for three hundred dollars. Before he left he collected all the yarmulkes he'd brought and put them in his basket, except for the one George was wearing. George was wearing it as he talked to Jelonnek's brother, though he wasn't just talking, he was demonstrating, narrating with fists and legs, punching, kicking, demolishing the air. Jelonnek's brother waited till this reenactment was over, the opponent subdued, then said something and walked over to say something else to his former bandmates, who took their time returning to the stage.

"Of all the people," the old man told the pornographer.

"Mega, giga, terra," the best man said, each word superseding the previous, and Jelonnek was still listening to what the best woman was telling the girl he lived with. She wanted to go to Bosnia, but for reasons Jelonnek couldn't hear the Red Cross wouldn't send her there. Somalia was her second choice.

"I've got my fingers crossed," she said, and asked where the bride was. They'd known each other since kindergarten.

Someone popped a balloon.

The bride was in the patio, poking under the eaves with a barbecue fork. Pulling out twigs, leaves, dead grass, the makings of a nest. The band plugged back in. She stopped. Looked at something on the tines. Shook it discreetly off to the patio floor. A cat came out of nowhere, picked it up in its jaws and ran off. The children chased the cat, screaming. The music started up again, the guests danced with a second wind between the long tables. The caterers were packing up the dinner buffet—the pornographer had opted for the three-hour Elegance Package, champagne only—but still dessert remained.

"What camp did you say?" The pornographer had to raise his voice. He sat at the end of a table with a small group of friends. They were not dissimilar to the old man in dress and demeanor, and sat dipping crisp brown turnovers in mustard.

"You heard about the Siegfried Line?" the old man yelled.

"That was labor," one of them said. "You didn't have it so bad."

Jelonnek felt someone standing next to him. He expected it to be the girl he lived with but it was his sister. She hadn't taken her sunglasses off all day.

"Do me a favor?" she said.

"I'll try," Jelonnek said.

"You'll try." She held up her car keys. "Can you drive a stick?"

Jelonnek couldn't drive a stick.

"Go with him anyway."

"Who?"

George was standing behind her with his hands in his pockets. Maybe he was listening, maybe not. He nodded his head to the music, or to something.

"He's out of cigarettes."

"Why don't you go? I don't know this neighborhood…"

"So get to know each other. I just don't want him to go by himself."

Jelonnek looked around. The music had gotten faster, the guitarist was playing a clarinet. Two chairs sat in the middle of the yard and the Jews had formed a circle around them. Jelonnek couldn't see who sat in the chairs but the girl he lived with was in the circle of dancers. He asked his sister to tell her where he'd gone. George had already left. He was near the end of the block when Jelonnek caught up with him. When they crossed the street a car was coming and in this situation there are two kinds of people: one walks a little faster, while the other makes a point of taking his time. Jelonnek broke into a trot.

His sister leased a shiny black Datsun with two doors. George started the engine and opened the sunroof before letting Jelonnek in. Then he u-turned smoothly out of the space and made a right at the corner without stopping. They headed down a four-lane road toward where the day was melting into dusk. George worked the stick. The pattern. They drove a full minute before Jelonnek asked him where they were going.

"I'd tell you but then I'd have to kill you," George said. He asked Jelonnek what he drove.

The father of the girl Jelonnek lived with had given her a nine-year-old Plymout Reliant just before he died.

George's chin went up and down. "I had a Duster once." Something had happened to his smile. He turned the music up. "You like that?"

"It's okay," Jelonnek said, though he didn't.

"It's okay," George said. "I like it," he said. "I like their music."

They pulled into the parking lot of a drugstore. "Don't get any ideas," George said and left it in neutral, running. When he came back there was a bag under his arm and he was peeling open a pack of Newports, trailing wrappers. Behind the wheel he pulled a brown quart bottle out of the bag and stuck it between Jelonnek's thighs.

"You're welcome," he said. Looking in the mirror, cutting the wheel.

"What's that for?" Jelonnek said.

"You know what to do with it."

"Back at the house…"

"You can drink that shit? Tastes like candy to me."

They waited on the apron for traffic to pass, no signal. "It's a right," Jelonnek said.

George looked at him. "You don't drive a stick?"

"Why?"

"You look like you can." George made a left, away from the wedding, the night rolling up behind them.

"Where are you going?" Jelonnek said.

"The long way," George said. "Just till we finish these. I just don't like crowds."

Neither did Jelonnek, but he'd told his sister. But the air coming through the sunroof felt good and the beer was cold between his legs. The signal was green, the light the sun had left behind another kind of permission. The bride's hand, gently pushing. Jelonnek raised the bottle and the beer did what it was supposed to do.

George raised his own, swallowed deliberately in low gear. He took off his sunglasses and left on the yarmulke. Jelonnek lit one. The light at the intersection was yellow, then red. They took the turn wide, barely slowing. The tires squealed softly and Jelonnek grabbed the door handle.

"Jesus," he said.

"Write me a ticket," George said. He dropped his cigarette out the window, meteoric trail of orange sparks. The street was lined with fast food and used car lots.

"No offense," George said.

"No offense about what?"

"Back at the house," George said. "What I said."

"What did you say?"

"To your girlfriend."

"What did you say to her?" Jelonnek wasn't sure he wanted to know.

"About working out. I didn't mean anything by it."

Jelonnek sort of remembered. He tried to figure out which way he should have taken it.

"That your girlfriend or what?"

"We live together."

"Live together." George turned on the headlights. "She dropped twenty pounds she'd be fine."

Jelonnek's mouth was full.

"Twenty, twenty-five."

Jelonnek swallowed and said, "What's that to you?" It came out with a small belch.

"Lighten up," George said. "It's a compliment." He took another long swig. "You're welcome."

They swerved around a pothole you'd need a tow truck to escape. Passed Mr. Hero and Waterbed Emporium and in between was a billboard with a twenty-foot bottle of malt liquor. The streetlights were on. A shrimp and chicken joint with a hand-lettered sign, an after-hours spot that was just somebody's house with neon in the window. They stopped at a red light behind a white Thunderbird. The light changed but the car lingered. George pressed the horn; it bleated like some scared animal. The car rolled forward and somebody on the passenger side showed them her middle finger. George spun the wheel and the engine growled. He shifted twice and Jelonnek felt the car push, a sudden wind in his face. They moved up alongside and ahead and then George spun the wheel the other way and they were in front so fast they seemed to have moved completely sideways. George said something and stomped the brake. Jelonnek didn't quite hit his head on the dashboard.

He heard tires shrieking and wasn't sure whose, but the horn definitely came from behind them. George added his own. There should have been an impact but instead came a woman's voice. George stuck his head up through the sunroof. He looked into their headlights and raised the bottle. The Thunderbird backed up and swerved around them, trailing hysterical epithets of skin color and cocksucking.

"We like your music!" George yelled, and fell back into his seat like he'd been dropped from the sky. They were moving again. Jelonnek's beer was foaming.

"Let's go," he said.

"We're going."

"I mean back."

"Finish your beer."

"It's almost dark."

"Almost."

Jelonnek had to piss. "I thought you didn't know your way around."

George lit up another one. "That what she told you?"

"Sort of."

"She tell you anything else?"

Jelonnek thought. "What else is there?"

"Lucasville."

Jelonnek repeated the name. He wasn't sure he believed it, or that it mattered if he did. He pretended.

"What's in Lucasville?"

"Three and a-half with good behavior." George held the filter between his teeth. He made a dry kissing sound every time he pulled it out. "Wanna know what for?"

Jelonnek thought again. "No."

George laughed. "You get high?"

"I'm good."

"You're good." George laughed. "I'm not."

"Where we going?"

"It ain't the art museum." The address numbers dwindled like some kind of countdown. They passed a boarded-up school with a small group perched on the front steps like they were waiting for it to reopen. Everyone behind a tiny orange dot. George stopped at a light and signaled a turn. He was careful about certain things. Jelonnek could just see the name of the street; he'd heard of it but had been never been down it. He read the name, spoke it the way he'd heard it spoken, and George said, "It's a long walk back." He touched the stick. "I'm the only friend you got about now."

They turned. The street was dark and narrow and they passed under a railway trestle, black iron so festooned with scribble it almost glowed.

"Just relax," George said. "It's like with dogs. Don't show any fear and they leave you alone."

He seemed sincerely curious: "You're not a pussy, are you?"

It didn't matter. They weren't just dogs. Dogs don't drag you out of your car and dance on your face pussy or not. Jelonnek had beer left. He said he had to piss.

"That's the spirit," George said. He held his bottle out the window, let the spit drain out, then smashed it on the street.

"Marvel taz," he said.

The first one was a kid standing near the corner beside a funeral home. Funeral homes were the best-kept properties in the neighborhood. "Hello," George said. He turned and pulled over across the street. The kid walked up in a t-shirt and jeans and a shiny cloth tied around his head with string. He had one pant leg rolled up. They'd seen others dressed almost exactly the same way, as though in uniform. He kept looking around. George assumed his imitation blackness, called the kid bruh. The kid looked at Jelonnek and to George said, "What's wrong with your partner?"

"Nothing," George said. "He was born that way."

"He look like a cop."

"Don't we all?"

"Askew me?" the kid said.

"It ain't a thing," George imitated. "He's one of us."

The kid made a sound. "Y'all ain't none of us," he said and backed away. George jerked the stick. "Son of a bitch," he said, and Jelonnek wasn't sure who he meant.

They took turns pissing in the bottle.

The next guy who came out of the darkness was older and willing to do business, but all he had to sell were bootleg videotapes, a Walkman, a watch that almost said Rolex on its face. He wouldn't let you hold anything. He wore an old pinstriped suit and carried a briefcase and Jelonnek wondered why they just didn't move on. George held the bottle between his legs and unscrewed the cap.

"Y'all like a do-it movie?" the guy said. "I'll hook you up." George jerked the bottle half out the window and popped the clutch. The spatter of liquid and they pulled away, left the guy screaming. Jelonnek expected something to hit the car but there were only words, then nothing. George worked the side streets. They were all one-way and he weaved from one to the other. He had no use for stop signs—they didn't, so why should he? They crept through a tight brick alley, bushes brushing the car and the spine of the road humped so they felt it scraping the muffler the whole time. Jelonnek stopped wondering if George knew where he was going. His door was locked, his window open two inches.

"Never saw so many dead ends till I drove around with you," George said, like some country song he'd just made up. A bunch of kids shooting baskets at a portable hoop under the streetlights. He scattered them with his bleating horn, yelling out the window, "Do you know where your parents are?"

He put the cap back on the bottle.

They saw a kid with no shirt on in front of a barber shop. He threw up his arms and they stopped. George kept his feet on the clutch and brake. The kid was very young and wore boxer shorts with his pants halfway down his ass. He was so young he let George inspect the contents of the bag but kept his hands close. They talked about buds and quarters. George called him my man and asked how much. He asked the kid if he had any matches, and the kid reached down and handed a pack through the window.

"You can walk with those," he said.

"Can you throw me some papers?" George said. The kid reached down again and George let out the clutch. The car lurched but they couldn't pull away fast enough and the kid grabbed onto the side mirror and reached inside. George gave it gas, then the brake. The mirror broke off and so did the kid with his handful of George's hair, somersaulting on the sidewalk in fast motion like a pratfall in a silent movie. "Fuckin bagboy," George said and put them back in gear. Shifted twice, his hand on his scalp, steering with one knee. A red light was coming and he shifted up again and there was a car in the intersection. Jelonnek put his hands on the dashboard but didn't close his eyes. Two horns in a single bitter chord. George yelled something. Jelonnek looked back and saw taillights. When he turned around they were passing back under the trestle with its pale mysterious text. The bright opening of a main street up ahead, and George was slowing them down. "Wasn't for this stick it would've been a lot easier," he said, but not how. He made a right with all due caution, and once again displayed the courtesy of a turn signal.

"We'll say we had a little accident," George said. At first Jelonnek didn't recognize the street at night, coming back the other way, then he did; it was where the girl in the Thunderbird had flipped them off. Where George paid back.

"Here." George took something out of his pocket. "Roll one up."

"I don't do that."

George sighed, a hiss. "No wonder you don't look right. Close your window." He rolled one one-handed as he drove.

"Somebody clipped off the mirror and we went after him but we couldn't catch him." He finished and Jelonnek opened the window halfway. Someone yelled. There wasn't much traffic but there were women out. One of them yelled and waved. For a second Jelonnek almost forgot he wasn't alone. They passed a furniture store. It was closed for the night and there were two of them out front. One was sitting. George said hello again and slowed and Jelonnek asked him what he was doing. George stopped and backed up.

"Goddamnit," Jelonnek said.

"Shut up," George said, and Jelonnek wouldn't till he got a closer look. They were both dark but the one who stood wasn't ugly. She did most of the talking.

"Hey handsomes," she said. "Wanna get up to no good?"

She asked them where they were going.

"Wanna go to a party?" George said. The ugly one didn't say anything. She was the right color and nothing else but skinny. She wore a long t-shirt to her knees and a pair of sandals. Jelonnek wouldn't have looked at her twice, and once was by accident.

Nothing to get arrested for.

The other one was dressed for the occasion and called him by the color of his eyes. She called herself a name that sounded fake, like a porn star, and except for the bulge that birth imparts to the belly, she almost looked like one. Close enough, anyway, to let you forget certain things, like that bulge, and the people waiting for you somewhere, the music over, the long tables cleared, streamers hanging slack and windless. Close enough to let you put your hand on the door latch and pull, and silence your better judgement, and wasn't that what you wanted in the first place?

He liked the way she looked at him. She looked at him with her mouth.

"Take your pick," George said. "They're all the same to me."

Jelonnek stood on the sidewalk in front of a furniture store closed on a warm Sunday night while she got in the car, then squeezed in next to her. The backseat was too small, it was just the right size. "Somebody fuck your pussy into early retirement?" she called to the ugly one, who stood with some effort, unfolding one limb at a time like they had all night. She got up front and shut the door. The one next to Jelonnek observed the formality of a handshake. Then she squeezed his balls and said, "Where the action is?"

"Wherever you drop your panties," the ugly one murmured.

"Where can we get some privacy?" George said.

"So it's like that," the one with a name like a porn star sang. "Go on back how you came then." Her nose was pierced, a tiny metal bead above one nostril. "Let's burn one on the way—we know you holdin." George seemed to enjoy this remark and U-turned carefully, and Jelonnek started to wish he hadn't gotten out of the car. Then he felt her hand again and it wasn't a mistake anymore.

She asked what kind of good time they were looking for.

"What aren't we looking for," George said.

"Where you get that little hat?" the ugly one said.

"You can go around the world for thirty-five," the one with a name like a porn star said. She ran down a short list of options.

George pushed in the lighter and spoke into the mirror. "Sound good to you?"

"Good," Jelonnek said. "Sure." He wasn't sure at this point what going around the world meant, or half-and-half, or even how much money he had. He only knew where her hand was. The lighter popped.

"He's the boss," George said.

"So you say," the ugly one said.

George left it in low and held the lighter to his face. He hit it hard and passed it back to the woman with a name like a porn star. She wasn't shy in this way either, and for all Jelonnek cared she could have finished it. When she gave it to him he turned away and brought it near his lips. Then he passed it over the seat and George said, "Excuse me" and took it before the ugly one could.

"Hey now," she said.

"This ain't what you want," George said.

"Ita do for now."

"You got a fake name too?" George said.

"Then I can smoke?"

"Just call her Littlebit," the one next to Jelonnek said. "She's a country girl."

"And you so proper."

"I know what she is," George said. He hit it twice more and then gave it to her: "All yours." When it came back to him, Jelonnek waved it away.

"Where is this place?" he said.

"It's comin," the one next to him said. The light was red.

The ugly one looked down at her feet. "Y'all got beer."

"Go for it," George said.

She picked it up. "It's hot." You could hear it slosh thick and foamy; it sounded like what it was.

"Tastes better that way," George said.

"I'm good," the ugly one said. The light turned green.

"You're good," George said. He moved the stick. "We know what you want."

"So you say."

"That's why your teeth are falling out, rock star."

The ugly one looked at him. "What I do to you?"

"That's why your face is flat as your ass."

"Listen at him," the one next to Jelonnek said. "He playin or what?"

"I'm playing," George said.

"Yeah," Jelonnek said. "He doesn't mean anything."

"I don't mean anything," George said.

"Ain't this it?" the ugly one said.

"Make a left right here," the one next to Jelonnek said.

A newly paved street with small businesses and factories on either side. The one next to Jelonnek read the sign on a print shop. "What *litho* mean?" she asked, and nobody answered till the ugly one shrugged and said, "They job." One building bright with a late shift, maybe double time on Sunday, door and windows open to the sight and scream of machinery but not a living thing to be seen. They bumped over railroad tracks past a body shop. Something growled murderously from the other side of a roll door and hurled itself against it. Freeway lights in the distance, but they weren't going that far.

Another turn, another, like they were spiraling into the center of something. A sign on a pole, the rough stretch it called a street resembling one only in that it was longer than wide, the yellow strip in the middle drawn by a kid with a crayon. To the right a field covered with brown weeds and litter, the rusting frame of a stripped Cadillac, a castoff easy chair still waiting for its occupant to come back from the kitchen. On the other side a ruin of low walls and foundations, so thick with spraypaint they might have been made of words, cement floors in aftermath cracked with weeds, sinking back into earth. People had worked here.

"Here," the woman next to Jelonnek said and George cut the wheel one more time. They went down a ramp to the loading dock of a building that no longer stood, glass and dead branches crackling under the wheels. The ramp was steep and embanked so that nobody would see you unless they were looking for you.

"Don't even the wineheads come here," she said. George turned off the lights but left the engine running. He pulled the parking brake. They sat there.

"We need to see some," the ugly one said kind of shyly.

"Right," George said. He went in and out of his pocket. The ugly one looked down and said, "I got a kid." Jelonnek couldn't see what she was talking to over the seat. He didn't see the gun till George hit her in the mouth with it. It was silver and not very big and his one thought was why hadn't he used it before. Then he wilted. She never made a sound.

"This one's on you," George said.

The woman with a name like a porn star was looking for a door but there weren't any in the back. She crawled over Jelonnek's lap like she might find one on his side. The woman up front couldn't get hers to open. George grabbed her arm, pulled her close and slapped her with his handful of metal. The other one made a sound like she was the one he'd hit, and then she was. She moaned and fell against Jelonnek and tried to dig herself in behind him. Like he could save anyone.

"Don't," she said. "Okay," she said. "I got one, too." Her hand up by the side of her face. "My purse."

"Fuck your purse." George sounded mad, like they'd done something he was getting even for. Jelonnek heard the tear of a zipper. George tried to grab the ugly one by the hair but it was cut too close to her scalp, so he grabbed her neck, pressed the barrel against her skull and pulled her down to him.

"You wanna date me?" he said. "You wanna date?"

"My teeth," she said.

"You won't need em for this," he said. Then he turned his head and swung his arm into the back. Light glanced off the gun from somewhere and it got bigger. "The fuck are you waiting for?" he said, and sounded like him against everyone.

The girl in the back leaned down. She had to do all the work but she couldn't do everything. Jelonnek felt the wet wound of her mouth and pretended it was just spit. Nothing helped. It wasn't even there.

"When you're done I got something you can wash it down with," George said. The ugly one grunted. The other one lifted her head briefly and said, "Baby you got to give me something to work with here."

The dock lit up. Jelonnek thought George had turned on the headlights but the glow was moving and they were hit from behind with a hard thump and somehow never heard another car. They rammed the low wall and everyone lurched forward but there were rubber bumpers fastened to the dock and only one headlight broke. One of the women screamed. The back window didn't break but popped out of its frame in a single piece and bounced off the trunk to the ground, still intact.

"Is it Peewee?" the one next to Jelonnek yelled. George looked for the gun. "Pewee!" she yelled and she was scrambling out the hole where the back window had been while Jelonnek was zipping up his pants to save his life and the woman up front looking for the latch to her door.

A deep angry voice boomed from the light: "Fuck off the car!" and George turned and straightened his arm. The flash at the end of it had a shout of its own and was so loud everything afterward was distant and muted. The other car pulled away and to the side with her still screaming on its hood. The woman up front reached through the window to open the door from the outside but George was already backing up, past the light now glaring at them from the right, and Jelonnek heard two shots that felt like someone hitting the side of the Datsun with a hammer. The voice was still yelling her off the hood, off the goddamn hood, and maybe that was what bought them some time.

They backed up off the ramp and across the street that was barely there and bumped over the brown field still in reverse, past the abandoned wreck and the empty recliner facing them like it would seat their audience, swinging in a wide arc till they were looking the way they'd come. George shifted and spun, his arm and the wheel blurred together, and Jelonnek turned his head. Here they came. The Datsun sped up in jerky increments, the sound of the engine rising the same way, Jelonnek hitting his head twice on the ceiling but George staying on the field till they got to the street heading away from the railroad tracks. The woman up front yelling let her out this motherfucker and George too busy to hit her so he just yelled, "Jump bitch!" and she lunged half out the window and then all the way back in before a telephone pole could take her head off.

A stop sign, a yellow light, a screaming wide left. A green sign with an arrow. They took it but no freeway, just another sign and they followed that arrow as well. They heard a horn and tires somewhere behind them but no crash and nobody looked. Across a bridge over the Innerbelt and there was a sign at the next light that would get them on it. George took the ONLY lane. Up ahead was a car across the intersection and this time the arrow glowed.

He took the turn leaning on the horn like he couldn't admit he had the right of way. At the bottom of the ramp they were in fourth gear and the sign said MERGE. There wasn't much room to but George used all of it and Jelonnek felt his body move in an unprecedented way, slanting across three lanes to fifth gear and the passing lane, heard the Dopplered outrage of yet another near miss. He kept waiting for the road to straighten but the Innerbelt was one long curve, bridges swinging overhead, the embankments faced with high retaining walls so that there was a hollow feel like being in a tunnel. The wind was warm and hard and as loud as the engine. It tore through the hole where the back window had been, stung their eyes and took their breath and words and when George wanted to know if he'd lost them, Jelonnek had to read his lips.

He couldn't be sure. He saw something but the curve kept taking it back. Then the woman up front said with a clarity that didn't seem possible, "He ain't gonna lose *you*," and George's arm swung out fast and urgent like he could beat it back into her mouth.

The interchange was coming. He went around a truck. They saw three tiers of highway, signs and numbers promising three roads and two cities. George picked one and veered back across lanes and for that time Jelonnek couldn't feel the air and felt weightless and in a vacuum. They took the loop at seventy and he hung onto the door handle across the seat. When they straightened out they were heading south and within two miles it was a mistake—construction, one lane, guardrail on one side and orange barrels on the other, oncoming lights beyond. The paving had been stripped and what remained was gray and rough and metallic-sounding, you felt it in the roots of your teeth. They sped up and the sound became a strange hum, a spectral chorus entombed in rebar and cement.

George yelled. Jelonnek couldn't hear but he understood. Lights in the stretch behind them, gaining slowly but still too far away to be sure. The ones ahead were red and coming much faster. A smell blew in the car like rotten eggs and the glow of blast furnaces, the west side works, rose from the valley along the highway. A blue flame burned high in the night, torchlike, and the narrow flue atop which it flared was not visible so that it might have burned a hole from the other side of the dark.

George blew his horn at the Ford in front. They were right on top of it but it wouldn't budge. His shoulder twitched and they slipped through a gap in the barrels so fast there wasn't time to think it could not be done. No one was coming. He passed the Ford and then back through the barrels. This time he clipped one with a dull slap and then scraped the barrier on the other side, lost the other mirror in a burst of shrieking sparks you could smell and Jelonnek felt one burn his cheek. The Ford took an exit and the set of lights behind it were much closer. George swore. There wasn't another gear to use but the engine sounded like it would tear itself apart making one. Jelonnek couldn't stop looking at the lights. They had a sound now, a low growl, and they weren't more than twenty yards back when they started flashing, then stayed bright, merged into a single brilliance, and George struck his mirror down and hit the woman next to him one more time just for being right.

Slumped in her seat, head to one side, she barely seemed to notice.

The sign said corporation limit.

The airport now, blue runway lights but no planes, and George was yelling something about that nigger's engine. Jelonnek heard something else and when it registered as a gunshot he lay down on his seat. He heard another, felt a blow to the trunk and tried to squeeze behind the front seats, curved over the hump of the transmission. The wind found its way here too, scoured his skin like it would reshape him, the road spinning past a hundred miles an hour a foot from his face. The gears churned in his gut. Something struck the car again, much bigger than a bullet. He heard it then, or thought he did, a murmured incantation coming maybe through the front seat, and whether it was the woman on the other side of it, or some lie of the wind, the engine, even the silk serpent, it would have to do. He would have settled for a cop, but he let it pray for them.

There was another blow and the inside of the car brightened. They were turning and this was it, end of the ride, and they turned again, then again in a way that seemed controlled and Jelonnek hit the door with the top of his head, struggled up to see. The road was wide with four lanes and George was using all of them, careening from shoulder to shoulder, nothing but trees on either side swinging toward them and away, sickening and exhilarating, lights atop high poles in the grass median so the whole stretch was as bright as Monday night football and you could see how big the other car was, starburst of cracks in its windshield, and the van that wouldn't let it pass till they rammed it and ran it onto the shoulder. George stopped weaving and used the horn. Another sound, not quite a gunshot, more of a crack to it, then a rattle important enough to make Jelonnek look and he saw the hood of the big car billowing straight up in the air like a mainsail. He shouted in George's ear, looked again and they were already dropping back, high beams swinging from one side of the road to the other and then completely around and Jelonnek was no longer wishing for a cop, just trying to tell if they were rolling, if they'd wracked up.

He spoke in George's ear again and George nodded. He thought he saw their lights where the median should be. Then the road dipped and he lost them. George stopped nodding. He fixed the mirror and started chewing his gum again, glanced at the woman next to him, who remained as indifferent to this turn of events as she had been to the last blow.

He still wore the yarmulke. The road darkened again. They passed under the turnpike.

Jelonnek kept looking. They stayed on the freeway another ten minutes, entered the next county doing ninety or so. George slowed when he saw police lights—ahead, not behind. They passed a state trooper administering a field sobriety test, a woman standing on the shoulder in a frenzy of colored lights like a performance artist, arms spread out, her mouth moving. They stayed in fourth gear. They saw motel signs, an exit, but George drove on and Jelonnek asked for the last time that night, "Where are we going?"

"Next one," George said, and was true to his word. A rest stop, water tower, blank billboard advertising all possibility and then nothing but a jagged blackness of trees. Then a high glowing sign perched on two high narrow legs. The sign said K Mart and they swung onto the ramp. The sound of the engine wound down, down and Jelonnek felt the speed leaving his body back to front like a fever breaking. The roar in his ears subsided but not completely. His skin felt burnished and numb. The woman up front shifted slightly, a child stirring in its sleep just as you're pulling into the driveway after a long ride home.

A blinking red light at the foot of the ramp. George didn't fully stop, stopping wasn't quite possible. There was no store but another sign that told them where it was. An arrow pointed left, down the state road. George turned that way but they weren't going shopping. He pulled up on the dirt shoulder under the overpass and said, "Take that off." He sounded like he always did, like he was picking up where he'd left off. Nothing changed him. He didn't need the gun. She pulled the shirt over her head and nothing else because there was nothing else but what was on her feet.

A yellow light came from somewhere, flashing slow.

"Them too," he said, and this time he needed it. "Shoes," he said and you heard her feet shuffling on the floor.

"Bye," he said.

She still had trouble with the door. A click when George unlocked it from his side and she practically fell out like he'd booted her. Jelonnek glimpsed her skinny shapeless ass, which he wouldn't have looked at twice, heard the dull slap of her feet on the ground. The light faded and when it came back she was gone. The door was open.

"If we had the time," George said wearily, "I swear to God." He was looking down at the bottle. "Get your ass up front," he said. "Get the damn door."

Jelonnek was already pushing the seatback forward. He put one foot on the ground, emerged, then the other. He shut the door but stood on the other side of it. As easy as that. As easy as standing on one side of a door and not the other.

"What're you?" George said. "You can piss at the rest stop."

Jelonnek took a step back. "Bye," he said. His legs felt stiff and unsteady, like they'd just been given to him.

"Get in."

"Go ahead."

George looked around. "Be that way," he said then and almost sounded hurt. Jelonnek might have expected more of an argument but the Datsun pulled away as easy as that. It slowed under three yellow lights flashing just beyond the bridge. The bottle shattered and George turned hard there and went back up onto the freeway, the engine climbing again, fading. The light came in and out like a tide. It showed Jelonnek the strip of dirt on which he stood, a guardrail, and on the other side a bed of gravel from which rose the columns that supported the overpass. They were flat and wide and behind one you could be invisible to every angle from the street, but Jelonnek didn't know. He thought he heard the last of the engine. Crickets. He didn't see where else she could have gone, but he didn't move. Then a car was coming and there was nowhere else to go.

It came down the same exit and turned his way. Jelonnek waited behind the first column. It was cool and damp and vibrated with something big passing overhead. He looked to the road. A pickup truck. There was a dog in the bed and probably everyone drove one around here. Then it was gone and there were three columns to go. The yellow light showed you how many but not what was behind them; he would have to see for himself and he moved from one to the next like a thief in a temple, terrified of stumbling upon her in some pocket of shadow. If he had to find her, he didn't want to find her here.

He came out on the grass under the moon and crossed the other ramp. There was no sidewalk on the state route. The yellow light faded behind him but the moon was everywhere. He stopped at a corner. Another road crossed his path, a county road said so on a sign that was almost easy to read. To one side it headed north, back toward town maybe; before him it ran past some kind of construction site, a wide lot of brown-gray earth and equipment. A big machine squatted there on caterpillar treads and Jelonnek crossed the street carefully. Backhoe, front-loader, whatever it was, it had silvery legs jutting from its sides, a long boomlike contraption projecting from the rear, in front a double-jawed scoop that had been left poised high in the air, a gaping silhouette. Teeth.

Behind it were the beginnings of a building, flanked by mounds of dirt like an excavated ruin. A gas station maybe, maybe a Taco Bell. Three walls and no roof, a back and two sides, one unfinished so that its edge rose in cinderblock steps like a stairway to the moon, or from it. Half the enclosed space moonlit, the rest in black shadow. To Jelonnek it looked as good a place as any, but he didn't speak or get any closer. Instead he walked slowly around it, the dirt soft and moist-feeling under his shoes, thinking Denny's or Dunkin Donuts, but all he saw were stacks of pipe, rolls of wire or fencing, a padlocked portable john that he stepped behind when he heard a car out on the street. When the way was clear he came back around to the opening between the walls. He was sure now, but from where had he gotten the idea that his circle had made the structure as complete as it needed to be?

He stood close but didn't go inside the slanting edge of shadow a foot from his shoe. It was a pit. He listened and maybe he heard something, a scraping, a drawing of breath.

He spoke the only name he knew for her; he'd forgotten the one of the woman who'd given it.

"Are you there?" He waited, and then he said, "I can try to get you some clothes."

Something. Choked off. Sob or retch, something.

"I couldn't do anything," he said.

"The gun," he said.

Littlebit. He felt wrong saying it, like he wasn't meant to. He waited for an answer, though he wasn't ready for one.

A square hole where a window would go.

"I'll try to get you some clothes," he said. "I think there's a store not far." He said it in motion.

Jelonnek went the way the arrow had pointed. There was still no sidewalk and he wished a cloud would cover the moon. A car passed him from behind. He hadn't even heard it, and another was coming the other way. So what, he was just a guy walking, but when the headlights hit him full on he felt like a convict in striped pajamas. Next time he'd dive in the ditch if he had to. He passed one of those green metal boxes that have to do with phones or electricity. Its high-voltage hum. The road climbed. At the top a big red K began to emerge and so did the nimbus of the next car. Jelonnek didn't need the ditch; there were trees and bushes close to the road and he ran in and crouched and waited.

A police car, moving slow. It had different markings than what he was used to, and he couldn't tell if they were looking for something or just taking their time, but weren't they always looking? He wasn't sure he felt guilty of anything, but they would look for that too. Jelonnek thought about the last time he'd sat in a police vehicle. Something cracked under his foot when he stood. He went back to the road, shielding his face from branches, and got there without seeing another car.

The store was closed. The parking lot could have been measured in acres and was almost empty, the lights inside dim. Jelonnek could have sworn he'd been in one at three in the morning once, but that must have been Christmas, or some blue-light occasion. A kind of dumpster at the edge. The shopping carts merged in a great gleaming chain between the entrances. When Jelonnek was a kid his brother had bolted a four-by-four to the bumper of an old Catalina. They'd driven around a parking lot just like this one, demolishing stray carts. He looked for a phone and didn't see one. Maybe at the store or the other end of the lot, but Jelonnek had no change and who would he call collect? He thought of his brother again, and then his brother disappeared.

He wondered if the dumpster was not a dumpster. It was about fifty yards in and the wrong shape and color. Closer up something was printed on the front. It wasn't as easy to read now and Jelonnek had almost to get his face right up to it before he could make out the word DONATIONS. At the top was a drawer like what you drop your mail into. The box was so stuffed the drawer was half open, and when Jelonnek reached in his hand felt softness and looseness, coarseness and silk, legs, arms, collars, hems, as if entangled in the convolutions of a single manifold garment.

Another car. Jelonnek swung around to the side of the box but kept his hand in it. He thought about cops and was in a hurry again, but managed to sort out a pullover sweater and a pair of shorts. He rolled them in a tight bundle under his arm and then cut short across a field next to the lot. There was no need to ask himself what it was about them.

He ran and walked and ran back to the site. The moon was almost straight overhead now and the wedge of shadow between the walls had retreated to one corner. He had to go deeper within the enclosure now and did so carefully; she might not be where he thought she was. There were rocks on the ground just big enough.

Littlebit. It sounded better when you were out of breath, but he got no answer.

"Here," he said. "Sorry…I couldn't find any shoes."

He put the bundle down at the edge of the black. He looked out the window and backed away, almost to the earth-moving machine, heard the rush of tires again out on the state route. He crouched behind the treads, dried mud caked on rubber. You could smell it. The car turned their way and kept going. Jelonnek went back in and without getting close could see the clothes were gone.

He thought he heard the sweater crackle in the shadow. "I could try to get a cab," he said, "but I have to get to a phone."

"I could call the police," he said.

"Naw." Jelonnek nodded, but to himself. He didn't think she'd want the police, he only wanted to make her speak.

"Alright," he said.

"It was motels off the highway." She sounded like her mouth was numb, the way you sound after the dentist, but she was right. He remembered the signs. He looked back over his shoulder to the county road. It seemed to parallel the freeway.

"Alright," he said, "okay. I can try to take this street back around there. If they'll let me use the phone—"

"I ain't stayin here."

"What?" he said.

"I can't stay here." It sounded painful to say.

"It might be better if you wait."

"It might be but I ain't."

He wanted her to, but he didn't blame her. He wanted to get going. "Alright," he said, and he waited.

"Go ahead with yourself," she said.

Jelonnek started off. He stopped just beyond the walls and looked back. "Go ahead." Louder, but he still couldn't see her. When he got to the corner he looked back again and saw a slight lumpy figure standing next to the machine, under its raised jaw.

The county road had few lights and still no sidewalk. Sometimes there was no shoulder either, and they had to walk on the edge of the road or in the ditch. For a while Jelonnek wondered about her feet. When he looked back she was at least twenty steps behind, but still he had the feeling it was he who was being led. When he stopped so did she. They never spoke. They heard crickets and sometimes frogs and other sounds that were less familiar. The first houses were big and far apart and set back from the road so you wouldn't have seen them if it weren't for their lights. One had its own gas pump, and a small carousel. Another fronted by a large pond with a diving board and capsized row boat, and when the moon shone in its center it was a vast liquid eye full of stars. The next was small and close to the road, a light on the porch but not in the windows. When they passed they heard a low growl and the rattle of a chain but saw nothing. The sulphur of a skunk, clouds of mosquitoes, Jelonnek heard her slapping at herself. The road bent, rose and fell past long stretches of open fields, a grade school, an old barn utterly abandoned and overgrown to the top of its stone silo, a cemetery impeccably groomed like a golf course with gleaming headstones and a Civil War monument. A country club, wide and low and mostly windows, filled with light and empty except for a man in a white shirt spreading a red tablecloth. One car in the parking lot and two deer who clattered off at their approach.

Took them two hours. Jelonnek wondered if they'd lost the freeway; he could neither hear it nor see its lights. On the opposite horizon a row of blinking red columns, the kind only ever seen from a distance. When headlights approached they hid in groves or crouched in tall grass or simply walked off the road and hoped to be out of range. Once there was nowhere to go and the driver, coming from behind, slowed to a walking pace. Jelonnek braced for a voice or worse, but when the car moved on he was too tired to be anything else. He stopped looking behind. They passed a turkey farm. An oppossum crossed the road in front of them, regarded them with her pale wise face, a litter of young clinging to her fur like they'd issued from it whole. Jelonnek heard a grunt of dismay behind him, but he'd stopped looking back. Not ten steps further an animal that had not survived the crossing, raw meat and fur flattened to the yellow line like the welcome mat of our era. And, as things sometimes arrange themselves, a veterinarian's office exactly on the other side of the street.

Two hours. Finally there was a sidewalk and the junction was in sight. An apartment complex sprang up on both sides of the road, so big it took almost ten minutes to pass. Jelonnek heard her feet on the slabs. Someone shouting from the buildings. When they reached the corner he looked left and saw Bob Evans, the freeway, the motel sign in front of it. He started walking, but the open brightness of the street unnerved him and he broke into a trot, not slowing till he reached the motel parking lot. He looked back once and went to the office.

The chimes on the door made a pretty sound. The light closed in like a trap. The room smelled like spicy food, and a sign said the phone was for office use only. A man wearing a turban pushed through a beaded curtain behind the desk. He looked at Jelonnek as though every possible reason for his presence had been taken into account. Jelonnek tried anyway. The man with the turban pointed at the sign.

"It's an emergency," Jelonnek said.

"Everyone says it. You ran? Someone is hurt?"

"I just want to call a cab."

"There are phones in the rooms," the manager said. "We have the hourly."

Jelonnek went back outside. Across the lot was a swimming pool with a fence around it. She stood between the fence and the parked cars. The pool was empty. The moon was low and didn't show much of her face, but Jelonnek still didn't look. He asked her what she wanted to do.

"Lay in the bed."

"What about a hospital?"

"They'll put me away."

He thought about it. "I could still call a cab."

"Cab or a room, one. I'm like to fall out." She seemed to be holding herself up with the fence. Jelonnek started to ask where a cab would take her, and realized he couldn't answer that question himself. The rooms were cheap, a place to wait. They were tired. Everything else was complicated.

He went back to the office and did a lot of writing. The key came chained to a hunk of plastic too big to put in your pocket. Outside he waved it at the pool and kept going. The room was six doors down. He unlocked the door and went inside without looking back.

A double bed. Brown carpet. Sparkling wallpaper and plastic curtains. The TV on wheels. Jungle life watercolor over the bed.

He'd given them names he could no longer remember. Once in the spring he saw his father carrying one of them around the back of the garage. A long squirming whiteness, a hammer in his other hand. By the time Jelonnek got there, the workshop door had shut. The blood looked black in the grass. A tapping drew him to the window. He looked inside, where the old man had made a go-cart and crossbow to save money at Christmas, given broken toys and appliances second lives. It was nailed spread-eagle and upside-down to the workshop door. The old man's hands prayed and blood gushed over them as they pushed gently into the opening they'd made, came back into this world cupped and full, as they were the first time he'd held it, hairless and nameless, now nameless once again. A vessel burst and something clear spattered the glass. Through it you could hear the skin coming off, the faint hiss like pulling tape. He cut off the head with his pocketknife. His bare scalp gleamed. The hammer hung on a nail by the curve of its claw, innocent of blood.

(Tapping draws him to the door. The body spread-eagle and upside-down, not quite dead. The Hunter skins him anyway.)

Independence Day, the shiny trunk dripping from the spit. The meat sweet and stringy. The old man, drunk by noon, had hung the flag bottom up as well. The phone kept ringing, a woman's voice: "We have a boy in the war."

A star in the window.

There were two other motels at the intersection. A gas station, a bank. The bank didn't have a cash machine and opened at ten. Jelonnek went to Bob Evans in the early light, sat alone at the counter. She couldn't eat, but he could, and he ordered the Sunrise Special.

From the room he called his supervisor and told him he'd be late.

The Forms Coordinator told him she'd called. Jelonnek asked what she'd said.

"Call her at work," the Forms Coordinator said. "Sounded a little rattled to me."

Jelonnek went to the office to ask when checkout was. The smell was the same but the man in the turban had been replaced by a woman with a sarong and a red dot on her forehead. You could hear *Regis and Kathie Lee* coming through the beaded curtain. Jelonnek asked her about the hourly rate, and where the bus stop was. She said it was down the street, but not that it was nearly a mile away. Jelonnek walked into the sun. He had to run the last block or so because the bus was coming. All the windows were open. He sat in the back and dozed; he'd slept fitfully on the floor. In the intervals they'd talked. A guy on the bus was telling some woman about raising pheasants.

"Chinese pheasants, ring-necked pheasants..." Every time the doors opened Jelonnek snapped out of it. The driver told someone to put out a cigarette.

If the girl he lived with had gone to work, how bad could things be?

She had perfect attendance.

In an hour they'd lurched their way downtown. Getting off the bus, Jelonnek would have forgotten his transfer if the driver hadn't said here, and waved it at him without looking. He walked across the Square. Everyone looked remote because nothing had happened to them. The bus stop was across the street from the Justice Center and that too stood at another remove. The local was almost empty. The driver talked about walleye fishing, but Jelonnek wasn't sure who he was talking to. He sat near the door; it was a short ride home.

Littlebit didn't say home. She said, "Where I stay at."

He went around back, through the parking lot. The car was there but of course it was; the girl he lived with always took the bus to work. A van, men in white overalls standing on ladders, painting the window trim. He listened at the door before he went in. The apartment was so neat it scared him. The dishes had been done and all the clothes picked up, like someone else lived there. Jelonnek was thirsty. A sheet of paper on the fridge said CALL ME in five-inch letters. There was a pitcher of iced tea inside and Jelonnek poured a glass. There were messages on the machine and he pushed the button. His sister's voice sounded small and strained, like she was lying down. It wanted to know where he was. It was so worried about him. It said George was okay.

"He told us all about it," she said. Her voice wanted Jelonnek to call the police and tell them everything that had happened. Everything would be okay—it just wanted to know he was alright.

The next one was his brother. The rest went unheard.

He drained the glass and poured the rest of the pitcher into it. He picked up the receiver and put it back down. He thought about changing his clothes but didn't. He drank the rest of the tea, got in the car and drove to work.

He hadn't quite made up his mind why he was going to work. There seemed to be several possible reasons but he had yet to pick one. He kept glancing in the mirror, as if expecting to see the big car and its flashing brights. Peewee. She seemed as afraid of him as she was of the police. He was affiliated with some outfit that called itself a tribe, which in turn had some larger affiliation, and when Jelonnek asked what that was, dropping names like Crips and Bloods because they were all he knew, she'd made a face and simply said, "They nation."

She had this cousin.

Jelonnek drove along the tracks. He approached the warehouse from the direction opposite the way you would come if you were coming from District, from the Department of Transportation or the Public Utilities Commission. If you needed an Affidavit of Lost Document. He could see the fence and the parking lot and what was in it about a hundred feet before he got there.

He saw a car he didn't recognize. The Forms Coordinator was supposed to come and open the place up when Jelonnek was late or sick, but that didn't look to Jelonnek like the Forms Coordinator's car. Unless he'd bought a new one.

Littlebit's cousin was a musician. Guitar or drums, she wasn't sure, but whatever it was he played it all the way across the country. She wasn't sure exactly where but he was two hours away from the ocean. There was a postcard where she stayed at.

Jelonnek turned up a side street he'd never had reason to take before. He found himself in a neighborhood he didn't know, Polish street names where Poles no longer lived, old frame houses and a Puerto Rican social hall, then an enormous church of yellow-gray stone with onion-shaped domes for spires. A saint whose name he couldn't pronounce. Then he wasn't lost anymore and headed back to the apartment. He parked halfway up the block. Just a few cars left in the lot and they were all unmarked. The painters were taking a break. No one waiting for him on the steps or at the door but maybe they were inside. The apartment looked stranger every time he saw it. He found a suitcase and opened it on the bed. The phone rang and he jumped like someone had tapped him on the shoulder. He didn't answer it. Someone was leaving a message. There was a button you could push and listen to the message that was being left, but Jelonnek didn't push it. He decided he didn't want to be seen leaving with a suitcase and put it back and stuffed some clothes in a grocery bag. He pulled the note off the fridge, turned it over and held a pen over the blank side. The plastic flower rolling on the floor. The rattle of the ladders getting longer. He left it blank. Got a pair of slippers that belonged to the girl he lived with and stuffed them in the bag. *Armageddon Zero.* The typewriter from the warehouse. Heard the super whistling as he swept the back steps and went out the front.

It was almost noon. Jelonnek got in his car and drove to a bank machine. Then he headed back to the motel. It was still getting warmer but the air was dry and the clouds were moving away from each other. He took the same freeway he'd been on the night before but didn't recognize it.

The TV was on loud when Jelonnek got back, he could hear it through the door. The room next to theirs was open, a cleaning cart parked in front of it. Jelonnek went in.

She was watching *The Young and the Restless* prone on the bed, her head at the foot, the screen a foot from her face. There was a pillow under her chest. She didn't look up.

"That Porta Rican lady steady knockin," she said. "I keep telling her do not disturb. They ain't gave us a sign."

She'd taken the liner out of the trash can, filled it with ice and pressed it to her face. It lay on the bed next to her, darkening the sheet around it. The swelling around her mouth and eye hadn't gone down, the crack in the side of her head was ragged, pink-edged, dark and clotted. It wasn't bleeding but looked like it might need stitches. Jelonnek wondered about her nose.

"It don't feel broke."

"What if it is?"

"Then it be broke." No doctors. She looked at the screen. "I might could use a dentist down the line." She was missing a front tooth but he couldn't remember if she already had been. Before George.

"Thank you," someone on TV said, "thank you, oh thank you, thank you."

Jelonnek turned down the volume. "Let's go to the store."

"I can't walk."

"I brought you some slippers."

"You bring some feet to go with em?" But she tried them on. "They small. I'm size nine."

"They'll get you to the car," Jelonnek said. "We should let them clean the room."

He'd parked right at their door. The cleaning cart had moved down a room. Littlebit walked delicately, wincing, like someone trying to be very quiet. The sweater and shorts were starting to look like they'd belonged to her all along.

When she was in the car he went to the office. He heard a TV or radio blaring on the other side of the beads. He wondered if there'd been anything on the news, but whatever they were watching or listening to was in another language. He bought two more hours.

They drove to Kmart. Jelonnek was relieved she couldn't come in the store; he said he'd find a pair that fit.

"*Size nine,*" she said, "men's. And Band-Aids." And Salem Lights. The *National Enquirer* too, if he remembered.

Inside the air conditioners roared from the ceiling, fans as wide as jet engines. The floors were clean and the merchandise neatly organized. Not like in the city. Jelonnek bought her a pair of rubber sandals and a small first aid kit. He spent ten minutes looking for road maps, kept forgetting what he was looking for, and finally had to ask someone. Jelonnek hated to ask.

Rand McNally, the whole country.

In line he looked at tabloids, compared their outlandish predicaments to his own. He grabbed a toothbrush. Outside the heat was a relief; the cold of the store was starting to feel like a punishment. He passed a newspaper box, stopped and made himself go back and buy a paper.

"I'm hongry," Littlebit announced in the car. "Is you hongry?"

"Can you chew?" Jelonnek said.

"I'll chew a milkshake," she said. "I'm good on one side." Jelonnek wasn't hungry. They found a McDonald's, pulled up at the window and went back to the motel. The beds had been made and what was left of the ice pack was in the sink. Littlebit turned the TV back on. Jelonnek made himself look at the paper while she tried out the milkshake. There was nothing on the front page.

"Metro," she advised. She didn't sound interested. She couldn't use the straw so she pried off the lid and let the contents slide into her mouth. It sounded like it hurt. Jelonnek saw pink. He scanned pages till he got to the obituaries. He relaxed a little but it had been late last night—probably too late for the morning edition.

Littlebit left the milkshake on top of the TV and took the first aid kit into the bathroom. She left the door open and ran water. Jelonnek heard her suck air through her teeth, a muffled groan. Then she said, "You got a woman?"

"Why?" Hadn't they talked about it last night?

"Who belong to them slippers?"

"Someone I live with."

"Y'all common law?"

"Didn't I tell you last night?" She made a sound but Jelonnek couldn't tell if it was what he'd said or the peroxide. He asked her about her cousin, what kind of musician he was.

"Don't start me lyin." She came out of the bathroom. "Some kinda jazz, I guess."

"California, you think?"

She sat on the bed. "It say on the postcard. What kinda music you like?"

He glanced at her. "We have until two."

She grunted, then bent over and sniffed between her legs. "That ain't gonna get it," she said and went back into the bathroom.

Jelonnek heard water running again. He unfolded the map and covered half the bed with it. It was white where they were but took on color as you headed west, green and brown and yellow. He heard water and saw it running blue-veined in the mountains that wrinkled up out of the flatness like you were seeing them from space. The interstates were thick and red and even if he wasn't sure where they were going, Jelonnek knew how to get them out of the white. He'd never driven through mountains.

He had trouble folding it up. When she came out he asked her if she was ready and she held up a finger. She wanted to wait till the commercial. To see what Todd and Margaret were going to do.

"They fin to connect." Jelonnek went to the office and checked out. The woman in the sarong wished him a nice day. When he came back he said they had to go and Littlebit said, "I'm waitin on you." She left the milkshake on the TV.

They didn't speak again till they were close to the city. Littlebit asked if the radio was broken.

"It works," Jelonnek said, but he left it off. "Why do you call him Peewee?"

"Cause he big as what."

"What if he's waiting for you?"

"He don't know where I stay." She touched her bandage. "It's a small world up in there, though. If I run into him, so do you."

"I don't see it. You didn't do anything."

"I got in the car—he one a them cold niggers. There you go."

She was pointing at the exit. It took them past the post office, past a high school for unwed mothers, and then there were blocks of housing projects.

"You live here?" Jelonnek said.

"It's been a while," she said. "I just need to say goodbye to someone."

"We don't have time for this."

"It won't take but a minute," she said. "But if you can't."

They pulled into a dusty lot and drove slowly past a series of low brick buildings like barracks, and behind them Jelonnek glimpsed a playground and laundry lines and barbecue grills and more buildings in what looked like a random arrangement. "You run in there you gone," Littlebit said. "Po-leeces never find you." Each building had a stoop. Each stoop was occupied and nothing was lost on its occupants. They ran over a kid's tennis shoe in the middle of the lot and parked in front of one of the buildings.

Littlebit said, "Is you holdin?"

He looked at her. "Holding what?"

"I just need ten."

"It costs ten bucks to say goodbye?"

"I owe this old boy more than that," she said. "He been lettin it ride and I might not see him again."

"But if you can't," she said.

He found two fives. When she got out of the car she still looked like she was walking on glass but a little faster now. Jelonnek stopped looking when she got to the stoop.

"The hell wrong with you?" someone said. He couldn't tell if someone knew her or was just asking. He didn't hear her answer.

"Check this shit out," someone else said, and Jelonnek looked ahead, looked in the rear view mirror. Kids riding by on bikes. All the windows rolled up but his, down about an inch. She'd left her door unlocked. He reached over without looking and pressed the button. He heard laughter, but maybe they were laughing anyway. Voices flaring up in anger, or maybe they just talked that way. He heard reggae, and Jelonnek, who thought of himself as a rock-and-roller, hated reggae a little less than rap; at least they could sing, though the beat made no sense to his body.

A young guy got up from the stoop and walked to the car. He had muscles and no shirt and wore a bucket hat and a chain around his neck, his pants hanging off his underwear like the kid last night. There was a word for it. He asked Jelonnek if he was alright.

Jelonnek said he was.

"You need anything?"

"I'm alright," Jelonnek said.

"Everything cool?"

It was, Jelonnek said.

"It don't look cool," the young guy said. "You dyin like a dog in there to me—you need to drop that window. Get you some air."

Jelonnek rolled the window down another inch and said he was fine in there. He couldn't hear them anymore on the stoop.

"The hell you doin here then?" the young guy said.

"Just waiting on someone," Jelonnek said.

"You waitin on that old girl?" the young guy said. "She strollin for you?"

Jelonnek thought he knew what he meant but pretended not to. He said they were friends.

"She ain't got but one friend."

He was doing her a favor.

"Then she do you a favor. That how it go?"

"I don't know," Jelonnek said.

"That fuckin skeezer in there doin somebody a favor right now. You know that?"

Jelonnek shrugged.

"Can't speak?"

He spoke, said what he thought he should.

"Excuse me?"

Jelonnek said what he'd said.

"You need to talk up—or drop this fuckin glass for I can hear you."

"It's broke."

"Well ain't that a bitch," the young guy said. "I can break it some more if you want. Not a thing."

"I like it the way it is."

"I know you do," the young guy said and stared at the side of his head. The audience was silent. People walked by, pushing their faces at him. Jelonnek didn't know what to expect next, but it wasn't laughter; laughter coming out of that moment, like a chicken hatching a monkey.

"Well alright," the young guy said. You couldn't see who was laughing. "It's all good." He looked around. "It's all good then?"

Jelonnek thought of the young guy's head popping like soft fruit under the tires of his car, muscles twitching uselessly. He spoke without listening to himself.

"Well alright then," the young guy said. "You need anything I'm right over there." Earnestly, as if there were no request he could not accommodate. He did something with his hand and walked back toward the stoop. He looked back once but Jelonnek pretended not to see; he wondered how long it had been. It occurred to him she might be setting him up in some way. He remembered the light, the angry voice behind it. They never saw it coming. The engine was running, all he had to do was back out and keep going.

He had another visitor. This one was wearing a shirt but it barely covered his potbelly. He had wild gray hair and a young face, and all he wanted was change.

"I got you covered," he said, and Jelonnek gave him a quarter.

"Is that enough?" the man said. Jelonnek shrugged. The man shrugged too, then took off his shirt and started wiping the windshield with it. Littlebit was tapping on the window. Jelonnek let her in and the man went away. "Give him a dollar," she said, "and hea take off his pants and start dancing." She said it like some kind of good news, and she gave him directions the same way. Her eyes were darker and shinier. Jelonnek asked her what a strawberry was. "Something you eat baby," she said, and rolled down the window. On the way out she spoke to a man like she knew him, though he looked at her like she didn't. The bandage was loose, flapped against her head every time she moved. It wasn't five minutes away, but she filled every second with her new self.

A two-story wooden house on a corner, shedding its paint like dead skin and then shedding the primer beneath. The house next to it had three or four colors of shingle siding in a kind of patchwork, and these were the only two buildings on the block. A sign said the rest of it was for lease. Two old men sat on the porch of the first house with a dog, passing between them a transparent liquid in a glass jar without a label.

"That's Grampy," she said, gesturing vaguely as if either man qualified. "I stay with him sometime."

The driveway was a strip of dirt between the two houses and seemed to serve both of them. It was narrow and Littlebit couldn't open her door all the way.

"Your bandage," Jelonnek said.

Him waiting in the car while she went inside somewhere on some half-explained errand; this seemed to establish the tenor of their relationship. In his side mirror

Jelonnek saw one of the old men working his way up the driveway. He had one hand on the house, and in the other held the glass jar. Jelonnek wondered what it would be this time.

"Whatchya know good?" the old man said. He reached into the window and his hand felt the way the side of the house looked. Jelonnek felt like he was holding him up. "I see your car corner a little rough."

"How's that?" Jelonnek said.

"Could be a tie rod on that side. Or stabilizer, one."

"I'll keep it in mind," Jelonnek said. "I don't think we'll have time to take it in, though."

"Better just drive in a straight line, then."

It took Jelonnek a second. Then he laughed and the old man raised the jar. "Ever had corn liquor?"

"No."

"Better start slow then." Jelonnek raised the jar to his mouth and felt the vapor in his nostrils, then his throat. It was all fire going down, you could barely tell it was liquid. When he could he said, "That regular or unleaded?" suddenly elevated to the limit of his wit.

"You can prime your carburetor with it," the old man said seriously. "Y'all goin to see my nephew?"

"If we can find him."

"He couldn't find anybody to listen to his noise back here," the old man said, "and I don't know that he found anybody out there." He turned his head. "Look out."

Littlebit had changed into a flowered print dress that had not been ironed. Her head was wrapped in a scarf. A bulging plastic garbage bag was slung over her shoulder, and Jelonnek thought she was taking out the trash before he realized this was her luggage. She prodded before her a girl of ten or eleven who wore a bathing suit and tennis shoes and had her thumb in her mouth. In her other hand a Barbie doll whose skin was not quite as dark as her own. She opened the back door and banged it against the side of the house.

"Am I goin to the beach?" the girl said. "I can't swim but I can float."

Jelonnek stared at her. The old man was looking at their tires.

"Get in," Littlebit said, and when the girl was seated put the bag in next to her. "This Miss D."

"Who beat up my ma's face?" the girl demanded.

Littlebit got in next to Jelonnek with something in her hand. "Baby, he tryin to be right."

"He gonna be my daddy?" the girl said. She sounded fairly bemused at the prospect. "I never had a white daddy."

"Quit now," Littlebit said and showed Jelonnek the postcard.

The buildings of a city at night, two mountains in the background and a large white moon between them. There was no phone number, and it wasn't California.

"One a them a volcano," Littlebit said. "Can we leave the old guy some change?"

"They moon bigger over there," Miss D said.

"We need to get gas," Jelonnek said. There was no message on the postcard.

It was tricky backing out of the driveway. The old man insisted on guiding them and Jelonnek scraped the side of the house trying not to hit him. Miss D waved, a stiff little gesture like she was wiping something off the window. She started saying goodbye. She said goodbye to the old man in the driveway, then the driveway, then the house, the porch, the dog, but not the neighbor sitting on the porch.

"He always tryin to grab on me," she said. "Lady ate a spider today and thew up." They pulled away and she kept finding things to say goodbye to till Littlebit made her stop.

She put her thumb back in her mouth like a plug.

They passed a bank with a drive-through machine. Jelonnek pulled in though he hadn't planned to. That morning he'd left just over a hundred dollars in the account; now he took the rest. Miss D wanted ice cream. "Just sit," Littlebit said, and this established another trend. Her good mood had turned. Jelonnek bought the girl an Eskimo pie at the gas station, and a quart of beer and a bottle of aspirin for Littlebit. Somehow he had no taste for it. The gas tank had a leak and you could only fill it two-thirds full, but at least they were beating rush hour. They drove past the post office again. Jelonnek got them under the green signs.

"This car raggedy," Miss D said. "Why the radio ain't on?"

"It's his car and he don't want it on."

"In a while," Jelonnek said.

They got on the freeway Jelonnek usually took home. When they passed the exit he would have taken he didn't feel anything; he was done feeling things for a while. He saw her every time he looked in the mirror. They took the turnpike. Jelonnek turned on the radio, looked at the speedometer. Everything came and went with a number.

An hour and a-half later they drove past a billboard announcing the home of the second highest roller coaster in the world. It was as far west as any of them had ever been. Littlebit was still nursing her beer. To the north they could see the silhouette of a ferris wheel, a small spoked circle that for a while rolled along the horizon with them.

"Can I ride the Mean Streak?" Miss Dee said.

Jelonnek said nothing. They kept going.

"You said," the girl said to Littlebit.

"I said maybe," Littlebit said. They kept going. "We already ridin, baby. Maybe in a little minute I'll put your hair in French braids." She nursed the beer.

"Promise?" the girl said.

NIGGER HEAVEN

INT. LAZARUS CHAMBER

A xxxxx burst of steam tube#10 slowly
starts to open. The SURVIVOR collapses at
the control panel exausted by his ordeal
the charred remains of the HUNTER next
to him…The lid of the tube opens slowly
SURVIVOR crawls painfuly on his belly
towards the tube with barely enough strenth.
With only one hand left. Tube is all the
way open but we are LOW ANGLE to see if
anyones inside The SURVIVOR keeps crawling
crawling with his blood stump…almoot there
crawling A DARK HAND comes weakly out of
the tube he gets there and reaches for the
HAND with the one he has left This takes
all he's got reaching…DARK HAND reaching
when they touch FREEZEFRAME HOLD SHOT for
all time.

FADE OUT.

THE END

He was falling in Iowa. When he landed he woke up and he was
still in Iowa. His stomach felt like he was still falling. It was pitch
dark. All he could see were the glowing red digits of the clock radio:
3:15. He waited for something else to show itself but nothing did.
He remembered stuffing a towel in the crack under the door, the
night clerk saying something about the curtains. He remembered

there was a place where you could stand in four states at once. Or was it three? Or were they cities?

She was the first. There'd been no other.

Miss D chuckled somewhere. Littlebit snored. He could hear them, sleeping one sleep on the other bed.

The night clerk said the curtains were lightproof; people on business trips liked them. Miss D slept in her bathing suit. Jelonnek turned over and closed his eyes. His stomach kept sinking and he thought of everything he was falling from. Technically, he was still employed. He opened his eyes and turned over, saw another minute had passed, only a minute, glowing in the same void that had swallowed them. He wondered what time it was for the girl he lived with—technically, she was still the girl he lived with. He closed his eyes and opened them. The night elapsed one red second at a time. Then he heard Littlebit's urgent whisper: "D! D!" waking her up because she'd wet the bed.

At McDonald's if you bought the kid's breakfast meal they gave you a toy figure from some cartoon movie. Littlebit seemed to want something that wasn't on the board; she settled for orange juice and made Miss D say thank you. Miss D repeated it till she said it loudly in Jelonnek's ear and he felt like throwing his coffee in her face. Then they were back on 80 and he felt better. The sun was well up behind them but wasn't yet hot and turned the grassland a bright billiard green. When the green rolled the highway rose and fell with it, the crossroads over which they passed rippling north and south. Jelonnek finished his coffee. Miss D sucked her thumb. Sometimes there were fields of wildflowers, yellow and white and pink and lavender, and other times just dirt with the grass stacked aside in round bales like rolls of carpet. They passed the birthplace of Herbert Hoover. Miss D missed her dog.

"Well you gettin a cousin," Littlebit said.

"Does he have a dog?"

"Don't start me lyin."

"If he your cousin he can be mine too?"

"Am I talkin to move my lips? I been told you."

"Is you on vacation?" Miss D asked Jelonnek. To exhaust one question was to bring on the next topic without segue, but she knew better than to ask about the beach again.

"He don't have a job," Littlebit said. "He don't have a job to be on vacation from."

Miss D wondered what he did for money.

"He got some comin," Littlebit said.

"How much?"

"Hea let us know."

"So we on vacation but you ain't," Miss D said to Jelonnek. "Why your friend make her face all swole?"

"Leave him drive, baby." There was nothing but corn now.

"Why he don't speak to me?"

"He wasn't my friend," Jelonnek said.

"He's nobody's friend," Littlebit said.

"Why you go around with him then?"

"Leave him alone," Littlebit said, "he carryin us." But she spoke without effort or emotion, head in hand, words leaking through her fingers.

It was hot enough now to roll the windows all the way down and turn up the radio. If Miss D had any more questions they either couldn't hear them in the warm rush of air, or she took the answers from her brown-skinned doll. When no one was looking she dropped bits of litter out the window and watched them. The corn crop was young, the stalks green and low and the soil between the rows black and brown. They passed the town where the washing machine had been invented.

Past noon the sky turned gray but didn't rain. A modest skyline developed ahead and they stopped to eat in Des Moines. A family restaurant. Walking across the parking lot, Miss D held her mother's hand. She tried to take Jelonnek's and he pulled it away and walked behind.

"I don't think I like you anymore," Miss D said. She turned to Littlebit. "He through."

It was crowded in the family restaurant and they had to wait to be seated. Littlebit and Miss D sat on a bench while Jelonnek stood, his face hot. He tried not to look at anyone. They should have got something to go but he was as sick of being in the car as they were.

The hostess looked at them uncertainly and asked how many.

"Two," Miss D said.

"Smoking," Littlebit said. The scarf covered her head but there was still her mouth and eye. The hostess led them to a booth, Jelonnek trailing. She called Miss D sweetheart and gave her a kid's menu and four crayons. She didn't look at Littlebit.

"I want a pig's foot," Miss D said. She scribbled furiously.

"They don't have it," Littlebit said. "I want a shoulder sandwich and they ain't got that either."

Everyone ordered cheeseburgers. Littlebit chewed with one side of her mouth, slowly, a look of great concentration on her face. Miss D ate with far less caution and looked at Jelonnek like she liked him again, her smile full of food. He wished he had the map. He didn't need it right this minute but he needed something else to look at; he could have sworn heads kept turning in the corner of his eye. The next time somebody did that he was going to look dead back at them. He might even say something.

Littlebit watched him. "Let em look," she said finally. "Let em cut they eyes."

Miss D ate everything and she was still hungry. Jelonnek let her order a sundae and after that they would start saving money. Littlebit smoked with the same side of her face she used to eat. She covered the other side with her hand. The waitress cleared the table and Miss D asked Jelonnek how old he was.

"I don't know," he said.

"Don't you ever say yes or no?"

"I don't know."

Miss D looked at her mother. "Is he playin?"

"I ain't in it."

"You look old," Miss D told Jelonnek.

"I hardly slept," he said to Littlebit.

"Your eyes look old," Miss D said.

"D," her mother said.

"Your hair look old.

"Your face look old.

"Your skin look old."

"But I know who my father is," Jelonnek announced in the middle of the family restaurant. Let them turn their heads to that. Miss D looked at Littlebit and sucked her thumb till dessert came. Jelonnek didn't look at anyone.

The restaurant was located in a strip mall next to a drugstore. Jelonnek walked ahead putting his wallet back. He took it out again at the drugstore and they bought Miss D barrettes in two colors, a pair of cheap sunglasses with orange frames. She wanted a Walkman but Littlebit got her a comic book and a coloring book instead. Jelonnek asked if she wasn't a little old for coloring books.

"She don't think so," Littlebit said.

"Is she slow?"

"I wish she'd slow down some more." Then she said, "She asked me the same a you."

He bought a can of shaving cream and a razor. Littlebit was out of cigarettes and it was cheaper just to buy a carton. She halfheartedly wanted another quart but she hadn't finished the last one. He bought her a deck of cards.

They stopped for gas. A guy filling up his tank at the opposite island kept looking at them. Jelonnek got back in the car and Miss D said, "What's he starin at?"

Littlebit had a smile that was like shrugging with your face. "Must think he the only nigger in town."

They left Des Moines and smelled cow shit all the way to the state line. Jelonnek didn't realize they'd crossed it till they were passing Omaha. Then traffic thinned and the speed limit went up ten miles. It was hot. The sky was white and all glare, the trees on the roadside windless. Some kids staring from the back of a station wagon; Littlebit stuck out her tongue. License plates from six different states, bumper stickers. IAMTHEI and IF YOU CAN READ THIS GET OFF MY ASS. The minor outrages of overtaking and passing, being overtaken and passed. Aftermath on the shoulder: burned out road flares around a puddle of glass. Insect splatter on the windshield: some yellow, some clear as spit, some red like they were made only of blood.

They passed somebody moving a whole house. Shreds of blown tires like roadkill. They passed a U-Haul truck and Littlebit said she'd come up from Alabama in one of those.

"Huntsville," she said. "I was a country girl."

"How was that?" Jelonnek said.

"I don't know, I couldn't see."

"It was dark?"

"In the back it was. Wasn't no windows, just furniture and cousins."

"How many?"

"Twelve us," she said. "Like snakes."

Lincoln. Aurora. Grand Island. Kearney. Hayfields, fields of sunflowers, patchwork of green and gold, farmhouses, round silver outbuildings with conical roofs, the proverbial red barn. Corporate farms the size of airfields, fractured rainbows in the mist from the sprinklers. They crossed a river and drove alongside. Miss D napped. Signs invited them up and down crossroads, to points of interest, to caves and tombs and gaps and passes, to wax museums, Indian burial grounds and the site of the Plum Creek Massacre. Littlebit looked for a radio station and it was mostly country-and-western, talk, religion. Souls were saved on the air; drunks, debauchers, addicts, abusers and the abused; forgiven, baptized, redeemed by an ordained disc jockey, their voices dissolving in static as if already ascending to their reward.

"It's too bored to sleep," Miss D said, and the distance stretched out behind them. In Nebraska you just got farther away, not closer, just kept pushing, and Jelonnek heard the engine a different way, heard rattles and overtones he hoped had always been there and just gone unnoticed. He felt a cramp in his ankle. He asked Littlebit if she drove and she didn't, so he drove for stretches with his left foot, hoping he wouldn't have to find the brake in a hurry.

A windmill in a field of orange grain. Miss D said if you looked at it right you could see the waves in it, rolling from one end to the other. A pasture with one gray horse outcast from a herd of brown, facing away. At the rest stop they unfolded backs and limbs, unpeeled skin from seats and clothes from skin, relieved themselves in all ways. Almost got used to walking again. Behind the facility there was a Scenic View but Littlebit wasn't interested: "Ain't we been seein it?" Jelonnek went to the platform anyway and Miss D followed him.

A prairie with wagon ruts five feet deep. "Ain't but a ditch," Miss D said, and they went back to the car.

They ate supper in the town where Buffalo Bill was born. Pizza Hut. Some of the men wore feed caps and drank beer, and Miss D looked at their hats and Jelonnek watched them drink beer. After the pizza they passed a feedlot on a hillside, a mile of fencing and heads of cattle dipped in troughs. Miss D swore one looked right at her. The smell was bottomless, the blizzard of flies so heavy they ran out of fluid cleaning them off the windshield. Men in red-stained labcoats like mad scientists having a smoke outside the slaughterhouse. When they stopped at the next gas station they were miles away but they could still smell it. There were still the flies.

Mountain Time. Ogallala. Wheat. The highway rose and the land turned the same brown as the map, flat-topped hills on either side, crested bluffs like dunes half made of rock. The windshield filled with more sky than earth, then more of either than the eye could contain: they were going down, everything before them again ready or not. They leveled out and the sun was low in front of them, round and almost red. It moved from one side of the car to the other and once got almost behind them, and Miss D marveled at how this could be.

"That sun knocks me out," she said, and so Jelonnek told her he could make it do what he wanted. When he saw a bend coming he told her where he would make the sun go, and to her amazement it went there, then to the next position he predicted, and the one after that. Though she didn't quite believe he had this power, she didn't quite understand it either, and when the sun finally disappeared for good she told him to call it back; he said he would let it rest and she was happy to call him a liar.

They played with the moon the same way but still couldn't get out of Nebraska. It wasn't late but the truckers were reminding everyone the road had been built for them, and Jelonnek was feeling the sleep he hadn't gotten the night before. He saw a motel on a billboard and took the exit. Two double beds and one wall all brick, but there was a pool and, tired as he was, Jelonnek changed into shorts in the bathroom and said he'd be back. There would be solitude under the surface.

"Would you take her," Littlebit said, "for she can get that damn suit wet? I would but..." She waved a hand in front of her face and said he had big pretty legs.

Clouds had gathered. Jelonnek thought he heard thunder, but maybe it came from the trucks on the interstate. Miss D followed him. He told her to stay in the shallow end and not to bother him. There was a Japanese family between them. The water was warm and filled with blue light, but Miss D spent five minutes lowering herself in. The family stayed huddled in the middle, then left when it started to drizzle. The water falling on them was cooler than the water in the pool. Miss D roamed her depth, arms outstretched as if looking for her lower half. Jelonnek drifted in the low gravity at the other end, washing the wheel from his hands. Light came in slow flashes that lit the clouds from inside, yellow and white, benign, something that wouldn't hurt you if you weren't afraid. They stayed in the pool. Jelonnek went under. He saw her legs vaguely at the far end, rising into the flickering sheet of the surface. When he came up for air he heard Littlebit yelling at Miss D to get out before she got electrocuted to death.

Jelonnek quit his job from Cheyenne. First they ate lunch in a Chinese restaurant, a dark room with burgundy wallpaper. Nobody used chopsticks. Jelonnek had a Chinese beer. The waiter barely spoke English and Miss D had to cover her mouth. She ordered egg foo yung because she liked saying it, but it sounded better than it tasted and she wanted to try what everyone else was having. Jelonnek said no and had another beer, then another; it tasted like Miller. Miss D traded with her mother, who seemed indifferent to food and hadn't eaten a full meal since they'd left.

Jelonnek went to the men's room. When he came back Littlebit leaned forward and whispered, "That guy over there was talkin shit."

Only one other table was occupied: on the other side of the room a man in a cowboy hat sat with two women.

Littlebit mouthed a word without making a sound.

"You heard that from here?" Jelonnek kept his voice low.

"I'll hear it across town."

Miss D nodded. "Are you gonna hurt his feelings?"

"I'd have to hear it myself."

"Let's just go," Littlebit said.

"Can you fight, Jelonny?" Miss D said. "You ain't a punk, is you?"

"Don't call me that."

"Don't call you which one?"

"Don't call him outta his name," Littlebit said. "Let's go."

Jelonnek stiffed the waiter just in case some kind of response was in order. Outside it was like a spring morning on a summer afternoon; they'd never seen a place the way the sun showed them this one. Jelonnek wasn't sure it wasn't the beer, but the air was pure as if it had no substance and you could see from the bus depot at one end to the library at the other, a mile off. Along the way were stores, old Victorian mansions, a Catholic cathedral, the gold dome of the Capitol building, the perfect light perfecting everything it touched.

"It look like Sunday here," Miss D observed. She was easier to take in t-shirt and shorts, but when Littlebit had opened the bag of clothes in the trunk, a roach had crawled out and headed back for the motel.

A horse-drawn carriage went by. Hardly anyone else was around.

They wandered into a gift shop. Miss D looked at books that talked when you opened them, and Jelonnek looked for stationery. Littlebit couldn't see why you just couldn't send a postcard, and Jelonnek said you couldn't do something like this on just a postcard, but Littlebit still didn't see what difference did it make as long as it had your name on the bottom, and some of them you didn't need a stamp for, so Jelonnek picked one with a picture of Devil's Tower. He'd seen a film where people had gathered there and been spirited away by a giant UFO. Littlebit grabbed one of Old Faithful and said, "Let me get this for Grampy."

"You folks finding everything?" the old woman at the counter said. They had to buy a pen.

Jelonnek quit his job outside in the ideal air, the card pressed up against the wall of the shop, squeezing it all in, To Whom It May Concern and effective immediately, printing his name at the bottom and signing it under that. He'd known what to say all along. Then he gave the pen to Littlebit, who scrawled on the back of Old Faithful and passed it to Miss D, who laboriously wrote her name and drew a face. They dropped the cards in a mailbox and went back to the car, Jelonnek still tasting the Chinese beer. You said it *ching dow*.

They passed an oil refinery, a shiny complex of pipes and tubes and rails like an industrial amusement park without visitors. Then a power station, a field of pylons with arms outstretched in giant metal cruciform, and Miss D asked if there would be cactus. A tree grew out of a rock in the middle of the highway. Sheep and cattle grazed behind wire fences as they had in Nebraska, but this was what Nebraska becomes. They seemed to be going up. The early hills were outside Littlebit's window, bare on one side, forested on the other, and you couldn't tell if she was looking at them or just facing that way. Then a bust of Abraham Lincoln perched on a stone pedestal fifty feet high, and what passed for a city in the rear view mirror before they realized they'd driven by it.

The grass thinned out and the livestock dwindled but still they blurred past miles of fencing, as though distance and silence were subject to ownership like everything else. To look into it was to receive nothing in return but wind. Low mountains to the north, the long velvety hills closer in with the shadows of clouds curving up and over and whose private property were they? Sometimes the brown and tan plain was hatched with dirt roads but no vehicle used them, and there was not a single cactus but always now the silvery green clumps that seemed to have replaced the grass. Words appeared in Jelonnek's mind, *sage* and *gulch*, words he vaguely knew and thought of as Western words, but he didn't know if they were Wyoming words, and maybe if you knew what to call things you would feel less lonely, or maybe the words just got in the way and only if you lost the right ones would you find yourself in the distance.

Littlebit was sullen. Jelonnek might have preferred her this way if she hadn't kept shifting in her seat like it was changing shape on her. If he hadn't seen the little glass tube, its brown burnt edge. He thought her face was becoming itself again, her nose and jaw, but maybe he'd just gotten used to it. She lit another cigarette and they crossed the Great Divide.

No more fences, just the steppe and the sage and gray-white rock. Just white clouds with gray bellies in a blue that stayed hard down to the edge and looked as dry as the land. No mountains. An oil field that looked abandoned, and then they saw the hammerheaded pumps nodding and it still looked abandoned. They crossed the Divide again somehow and stopped at a truck stop, a shoebox of a building with a long wooden awning and a propane tank the size of a submarine. A hot wind blew dust around the lot and a row of semis were parked in precise slanted parallel though the lot was unmarked. The crowd inside was small but raucous, and though the jukebox rocked and rolled Jelonnek felt it had nothing to do with him. Maybe there were words for that too. A woman in her forties, or maybe having arrived there in her thirties, sat on a truck driver's lap wearing green stretch pants and a pink leopardskin top. If anything was going to happen it would happen here. But everyone was in a friendly mood and the woman in pink and green laughed when she asked what she could get them and Littlebit said nothing legal. She gave Miss D a pinwheel when they paid for their cheeseburgers. There was a souvenir stand and Jelonnek bought a pair of sunglasses for three ninety-nine and filled the tank two-thirds full.

Miss D held the pinwheel out the window. It spun with a clicking sound and worked better than the sunglasses, which turned the sun into a discrete white disk and everything else into silhouettes. Jelonnek took them off and to the north the horizon serrated again, white-capped and transluscent blue. Gas wells, telephone lines, railroad tracks, no towns. The road swung near a passenger train and for a while they rode along with it. Someone held a squirming infant up to the landscape, its eyes bulging at Jelonnek. Then it veered away and disappeared behind a ridge and the wind took the pinwheel from Miss D's hand. She begged to go back for it. Jelonnek said nothing and drove on, and Littlebit said they couldn't turn around, they would get her another one, but Miss D didn't want another one and wished she'd never had the first, and carried on till Littlebit said in a voice louder than any Jelonnek had heard her use, "Then shut up fore I snatch you baldheaded!" The baby still looking at him.

No houses but tiny windowless huts atop bluffs or at the roadside, arrayed with antennas as though relaying signals through which the desolation spoke and listened. A herd of wild horses covered in red dust. Littlebit tried to show them to Miss D but she folded her arms and hated them like she hated the pinwheel for losing itself.

Twenty minutes before Rock Springs they entered a construction zone, and twenty became ninety. One lane, a camper in front of them, a line of cars behind and again the orange-and-white-striped barrels. Jelonnek glanced at Littlebit. Her eyelid twitched.

She tried to nap and Miss D didn't have to try. When they came out the sun was gone and it was already cooling off. They drove through town. Jelonnek turned on the lights. Everything around them gray and fading, early stars but no moon. Miss D woke up and wondered out loud where it was.

"We drivin on it," Littlebit said.

"You a lie."

"I ain't."

"Where it's at?" Miss D asked Jelonnek. They entered a tunnel and the radio was all static and this was the only answer she got. The tunnel boomed and echoed, bright and white-tiled, and Jelonnek drove with his shoulders slumped as if under the weight of the mountain above them. They came out on the side of a rocky slope. There was a town below them and a river they didn't see till they saw the lights of the town again, standing on its head. They curved away and there were no more lights then but those of other travelers.

It came down. Faint outcroppings of earth against the blue curtain of dusk and Jelonnek thought they would have at least that. Then these were gone and there was only what they could see at the corner of their eye, and this too was taken and still night fell, and stole and fell, till there was only the ragged patch of light in front of them through which the distance poured, and it seemed this would be encroached as well, then the headlights, the dashboard, and finally even the faculty of sight so that nothing would be left to them but motion and darkness.

"Where am I?" Miss D said. A sign said ninety miles to Little America.

The stars were gone. The windshield was smeared with grime and insects and all you could see was your own reflection in the dashboard glow. They overtook a truck driving with a blown tire, sparks trailing the rim, the shriek of metal and pungent sickening breath of it as they passed. Twice they saw things off the road, far away in the dark, strange configurations of lights whose origins they made a game of guessing at: "UFO," Miss D said, and Jelonnek thought a plant or refinery, Littlebit some government shit or a town. Then they were almost blinded by the high-beams of an oncoming car and Jelonnek flashed his own and beeped the horn, to which the other driver responded exactly in kind as if they'd encountered only themselves.

For a while there was no one in front or behind. The sound of the road changed to a sort of close rush and Jelonnek thought he smelled something green. The sound opened up again and Littlebit smelled something else.

"Like fish," Miss D said.

Now Jelonnek noticed it, too, and it got stronger and it wasn't fish. He looked at the temperature gauge for the first time since they'd left and said, "Damn."

"Damn what?" Littlebit said.

"Running hot."

"How to cool it off then?"

"I don't know."

"Well damn then."

The needle was at the end of its arc and now you could see steam curling over the hood in the headlights. The dashboard went all red like everything going wrong at once. The engine quit. The steering wheel went stiff and Miss D asked why it was so quiet. They slowed. Jelonnek shifted to neutral and turned the key and there was only the futile grinding of the starter. A car from nowhere beeped and went around them. They started to pick up speed. Vapor flattened against the windshield, raised drops on the glass. They kept going faster and Miss D said, "Is it on?" and Littlebit answered, "Just till we run outta hill."

Coasting, they got up over sixty and when they started to bottom out Jelonnek turned the key again. Still that pointless sound, and now he could hear it wearing the battery down. He used what momentum was left to pull them off the road. Rumbling and crackling of the tires, two on the shoulder and two in the dirt beside it. Dry bushes and patches of tall white grass in the headlights. They stopped. Jelonnek turned off the headlights and turned on the flashers. They sat and listened to the metallic click and the hiss of steam.

"Is it still Wyomee?" Miss D asked.

"Yeah it is," Littlebit said.

"Wyomee gettin old," Miss D concluded, and Littlebit agreed. "Wyomee broke us down. Ain't you gonna throw up the lid?" she said to Jelonnek.

"In a minute," he said, and looked around for something that would cover his hand. A semi hurtled by, rocked them with its passage. There were napkins from Dairy Queen. Under the dash he found the lever that popped the hood.

Outside it was almost cold and Jelonnek felt the steam turn to water on his face. It sounded like it could go for hours. He heard a pissing sound under the car. He stood under more stars than he'd ever ignored in his life and raised the hood. Groping for the stand that propped it he burned his hand and swore, but no one called from the car to ask what was the matter.

He stepped back, not knowing what else he could do. A car coming from the way they were going, passing, slowing but not stopping. Jelonnek felt himself fading in a dim red behind them. The dark opened briefly in their headlights, dirt and rock, then closed again. The endless sibilation. Something flew over his head with a kind of soft scream. He looked up and Jesus Christ couldn't ignore the stars any longer.

In the car they rolled up the windows and waited while the hissing subsided. Then there was the tick of cooling metal, the sound of the hazard lights, the strident counterpoint of the crickets. Another car passed. Jelonnek tried the engine.

"I'll bet this old car thirsty," Miss D said. Jelonnek didn't say anything till Littlebit said, "Well?"

"Must need water," he said, "antifreeze," and wondered what the girl he'd lived with would have done.

Gas, air, spark.

"Is we gonna hitchhike?" Miss D asked.

"Ain't nobody pickin up your black ass."

"Somebody'll stop," Jelonnek said.

"Po-leece," Littlebit said.

"When it gets light," Jelonnek said. "I'll start walking…probably just needs water."

Miss D had to go to the bathroom. Jelonnek swore.

"Listen at you. Like you dealin with it." Littlebit waited. "Well come on then." There was no flashlight but she had her lighter.

"Is it snakes?" Miss D asked.

"If it is they just as scared as you."

"I ain't gonna bite em."

"We'll stay close to the car."

"Ma," Miss D said.

"*Child.*"

They went and from behind the wheel Jelonnek listened to the muted exchange of complaint and rebuke. He thought about the girl he lived with and the girl from the Bureau of Motor Vehicles and about Forms and Number Nineteen and other things he'd left behind; they came to him unbidden and in no particular order. Littlebit's cousin and *Armageddon Zero*, and though he'd brought the manuscript with him, that too seemed out of his grasp. The ticks of the engine grew further apart like their clock was running down.

They got back in the car and lay down together across the backseat. Miss D said she was cold.

"Best I can do," Littlebit said. "You should be keepin me warm, big as you is."

"This car smell."

"Who you tellin?"

"Listen...."

"Sound like a coyote."

"Sound like just like TV. What they holler about?"

"The moon, I guess."

"It ain't no moon."

"Then he callin it up."

"How many stars you think it is?"

"How many questions you gonna ask me?"

"Is it gonna be falling stars?"

"What I say?"

"I know what I'ma wish for."

"...wish you off my last nerve."

When they were asleep or at least quiet Jelonnek leaned his back against the door and stretched his legs across the front seat. A truck went by; each one felt like the last. He slid down just enough to see the sky through the windshield, just in case there were comets or meteors or whatever else the night might send them to see. He kept closing his eyes and opening them like he might be missing something. He opened them and the inside of the car was throbbing with color, red and blue and a steady bright white. He sat up and another light was shining in his face through the window. It tapped on the glass. Jelonnek shielded his eyes and rolled down the window. Glint of a metal star and then a face in a wide-brimmed hat swung down and asked politely why they were pulled over there.

"Radiator." Jelonnek had to repeat it. "We stalled," he said then. "It won't start."

License and registration please. Like one word. Jelonnek looked in the glove compartment and the trooper played the flashlight beam all around the car.

"Who's in the back?" he said.

Jelonnek couldn't find the registration. He took the license from his wallet and handed it to the trooper. "We're just traveling together."

"You pick them up somewhere?" A mild voice with no twang or drawl.

"We just know each other. That's her daughter."

The trooper was big. When he stood straight his belt buckle was at Jelonnek's eye level and he filled the window like a wall in khaki. "Please stay in the vehicle, sir," he said in his mild voice.

They heard a car door shut behind them. "That's a whole lotta motherfucker," Littlebit said.

"Just pretend you're sleeping," Jelonnek said.

"Think I ain't?" She asked him whose car it was. "You or your woman's?"

"Both, kind of."

"Whose name on it?"

He thought. "Hers."

"Hope she ain't call it in stole." Jelonnek didn't say anything.

"Hope he don't start callin around either," she said.

"You have ID?" Jelonnek said.

"I got two-three but they fake."

The trooper took his time. They could hear his radio. Cars passed and maybe they heard something scampering in the dark beyond the road. Miss D slept on. There was so much glare from the lights they didn't see his approach, nor hear it; he was just there. He gave Jelonnek back his license and said, "Could you wake up the woman in the back, sir?"

Sir. It was a different word in the trooper's mouth, it meant someone who had to do whatever you told him to. Jelonnek sighed. "We've been driving for a day straight," he said. "I was hoping they could…you know?"

"Just the woman, sir."

It was hard rousing her, and Jelonnek wondered if she really had gone back to sleep.

She sat up in the glare with one eye. "What?"

The trooper stared at her with the flashlight. "What happened to your face, ma'am?"

Littlebit shrugged. "Guess I favor my father. That light don't help."

"I'm talking about your mouth, your eye. Have you been in a fight?"

"I had a accident."

"What kind of accident?"

Littlebit shrugged again. She fixed her scarf.

"You don't know what kind of accident you had?" Maybe, Jelonnek thought, they trained the drawl out of you.

"I get drunk," Littlebit said. "I forget."

The trooper swung the light back to Jelonnek. "Where are you headed, sir?" Jelonnek remembered the city on the postcard and Littlebit added, "Seein my cousin." The trooper said, "Let the driver answer, ma'am" and Littlebit muttered and the trooper said, "Excuse me ma'am?" and Littlebit said, "I ain't speak" and the trooper said, "You said something" and Littlebit said, "Just to myself" and the trooper said, "Do you have any identification ma'am?" and Littlebit said she sure didn't and the trooper asked her to step out of the car.

Miss D moaned and stirred but didn't wake.

"Step out of the car, please," the trooper said again.

"What I do?"

"Just do what he says!" Jelonnek wasn't sure who he was angry at. The trooper told him to stay out if it, sir, in his mild relentless way, reached through the window and unlocked the back door and opened it. Littlebit got out and Jelonnek didn't look to see if she was helped. The trooper closed the door and told her to put her hands on the car. Miss D said something in her sleep and laughed. The trooper shined the light on her like it would show him what she was dreaming. Then he said, "This way, ma'am" and this time Jelonnek heard two doors slam shut.

He thought it was starting to get light when they came back. Littlebit got in the back with Miss D again but didn't lie down or say anything. The trooper wrote Jelonnek a ticket. Jelonnek signed it but didn't find out what it was for. The trooper told him to try and start the car and this time the engine turned over but stalled immediately.

The trooper said, "Alright step out of the vehicle sir."

The beginning of the sky to the east. The badge on the trooper's hat had wings. He held the flashlight while Jelonnek twisted off the radiator cap and aimed the beam into the hole. Jelonnek shivered. A car passed. The trooper went to his cruiser and came back with a plastic jug of water. He emptied it into the radiator and the engine ran. He told Jelonnek to drive slowly with his flashers going, he would follow them to the next junction where Jelonnek was to exit and head for a town just north of the interstate. There was a garage there.

When they took the exit the hills to the north and south were already taking shape. Across the road at the bottom of the ramp were the ghostly outbuildings of an abandoned mine. A few miles up a federal highway they were just starting to overheat when they

179

saw the town. It consisted of a single unpaved street beside a single long wooden building divided into a service station, general store, motel, cafe, post office, and a video rental store. A small trailer park behind the building. A sign bore the name of the town, its population and elevation, and the latter far exceeded the former. No one was around.

The sign at the gas station said CLOSED and not even the occupant of the doghouse showed itself when they pulled into the lot. There was steam again but this time not as much. Jelonnek got out and lifted the hood and almost right away saw a thin jet of water spurting from a crack in the radiator hose. He left the hood up and got back in the car. Littlebit hadn't spoken since she'd come back from the cruiser.

"So what'd he do?" Jelonnek asked.

"Nothin," she said. "That ain't even the question."

"What is?"

"I can't speak on it."

The sun rose. Miss D woke up. Littlebit told her to go back to sleep but she might as well have told the sun to go back down. A white-bearded old man in an engineer's cap and overalls came toward them, glanced at their license plate and said, "I bet you folks didn't come to feed the dog." He glanced inside. "Nope."

Jelonnek told him what the problem was. The old man went into the garage and came back with a length of red rubber. Jelonnek stood and watched him take off the cracked hose, line it up with the red one and saw off a matching length with his pocketknife.

"Lucky it's not the water pump," the old man said. "Or therm-o-state." He might have had to get parts in Evanston then, and it could take some days, yep. He finished clamping on the hose and said fifteen dollars unless there was something else, and there was antifreeze, gas, wiper fluid. Jelonnek checked the oil himself, and he remembered to run the engine before checking the transmission fluid, the way the girl he'd lived with had done it. He washed the windows, left the rest of the car coated with dust. Miss D wrote something in it. She was hungry. He bought her a bag of chips and a pint of orange juice, and the dog was just creeping out of its doghouse when Jelonnek drove them back down the road to 80. When Littlebit spoke it was not to him. They passed Little America.

Out of the red canyons 80 became 84 and they drove past the Great Salt Lake. To the east a mountain range rose into the clouds and there were whole towns splattered under the rocky pleated foothills like pieces in a board game. The lake was long and blue. There were boats and jet skis and beaches and islands, some the familiar reddish brown, others so pale and bright it hurt to look and the air rippled over them like some old movie slipping into a dream state.

It had been a while since Miss D asked if they were going to the beach.

Littlebit shook her head. "It ain't nothing but salt."

"What that do?"

"You don't want to know."

"It's people in it."

"They boatin. Ain't nobody gettin wet."

Miss D thought. "Will it turn us white?"

"Worse than that," Littlebit said. "Pink."

Jelonnek turned on the radio. Miss D asked if there were sharks.

"Mormons," he said.

"Say who?" Miss D said.

"That's they religion," Littlebit said. "The mens can have all the wives they want."

Miss D was scandalized. "Even the reverend?"

"I don't think they do that anymore," Jelonnek said.

"That's what I heard," Littlebit said.

"So if we lived here," Miss D said, "he could marry both us."

"Theya put him under the jail." Littlebit said. "He ain't no Morman. He already got one anyway."

"Do he?"

"No he don't," Jelonnek said.

"Who to believe?"

"They common law," Littlebit said.

"I don't think I like her," Miss D said.

"She ain't did nothin to you," Littlebit said.

"Could we just?" Jelonnek said.

"If he quit his job," Miss D said, "he can quit her."

"True that," Littlebit said, "but true this: just cause you went away doesn't mean you gone."

They left the lake behind and conversation with it. Jelonnek thought maybe they'd fallen asleep but he didn't look. The mountains veered away except for one to the east that looked like it belonged in a motion picture logo. Perched on a ledge over a creek, the fuselage of an airliner reborn as a bar called The Crash Landing. They drove past bleached rock and cinnamon-colored hills rounded into domes, through a stretch of high desert scrub into the next state. It was hot, his left arm was sunburned and the left side of his face red like the symptom of an inner divide. The radio crackled. They were low on gas and coasted down into a broad green valley of farms, miles of irrigation pipe. Jelonnek looked for potatoes, all the potatoes, like they'd be heaped in drifts and mounds from the edge of the road on, but saw fields of yellow flowers with long leaves like vines, and a sign directing them to where the stuntman of renown had tried to jump a fifteen hundred-yard canyon with a rocket-powered motorcycle.

The needle was below E when they pulled into a patch of dirt from which sprouted a pair of ancient red gas pumps with rounded tops and shoulders, one of them canted like a tombstone. A low white wooden building with a single window, a pickup truck parked near the door with a bumper sticker that read I SUPPORT THE TROOPS. Miss D had to use the bathroom and she followed Jelonnek inside.

A man stood at the counter talking to the proprietor. The toilet was in the back, an alcove covered with a shower curtain. Jelonnek let her go first. When he was done he went to the counter and asked for ten, unleaded. Miss D wanted ice cream and he let her get something out of the freezer. She left tearing off the wrapper and the other man at the counter said, "You need to put up a sign against pets in the store."

"Anything else, sir?" the proprietor asked. Jelonnek gave him a twenty.

"At least it's housebroken," the other man said. He was short and slender, white-haired and hard, dressed all in denim and smoking a cigarette with his hands in his pockets. The ash was two inches long.

"Don't see none of him in her," he drawled around the cigarette. "Our blood don't have a chance against their's—if it's already watered down."

"I'm thinking I should oil the lot," the proprietor said. "Keep the dust down."

"Suit yourself," the other man said. "People having sex with monkeys," he said. "That's how AIDS got started."

The proprietor gave Jelonnek a ten. "Eskimo Pie's on me," he said.

Outside the wind had picked up and the pump ran slow. Jelonnek kept looking at the store. He looked the other way and saw a shack he hadn't noticed before, purporting to be a tavern. Two Indians came out and walked toward him wearing black hats. One of them held a gas can. The wind blew their hair around and something got in Jelonnek's eye. He cleared it and heard something and looked at a tree at the edge of the lot. It was full of crows like a black fruit grown beaks and wings and talons.

That afternoon they crossed a bridge and a sign said YOU ARE LEAVING at one end and WELCOME at the other. The road twisted and fell toward a river in an orange canyon that looked like it had been colored once by a late sun and left that way. At the bottom the rock filled with pockets of blue shadow but the river sustained an emerald pure and remote like looking at someone beautiful who does not look back. A ranger's truck parked on the bank as if to guard it. They drove alongside the river and saw no one fishing or camping. Then they left the canyon and the emerald behind, drove through high brown hills with supple curves that made your hands almost tingle for the shape of them. It started raining.

Drops wriggling up the windshield, then it was over. North and west and north. Littlebit on her knees facing the other way, putting beads in Miss D's hair. Sitting with her feet on the dash, knees apart, letting the car blow wind up her crotch. They ate as they rode, played Go Fish and Crazy Eights. Signs warned of deer and elk, dust storms, tumbleweeds, falling rock. How many miles to the city on the postcard. Runaway truck ramps dug into the sides of cliffs and hills, steep and short and looking like anybody going fast enough would either crash into the bottom or clear the top and take flight. Ranches, reservoirs, towns they never saw, just white letters on green. Same clothes for four days sweat-stuck to the seats, smell of food wrappers, gasoline, armpits, the ashtray, and maybe Miss D had wet the backseat. The beads clacked when she spoke. They stopped answering her questions and she stopped asking them, napped with her thumb in her mouth. Then it was too dark to see anything and they were in the mountains again without knowing it.

The car lost speed and made a rattling sound. Littlebit said, "This thing won't pull a hill?" and Jelonnek said, "Next time we'll take yours" and dropped it in low. Something took hold and he turned into the slow lane. They rode like this for at least twenty minutes, climbing and turning, everybody passing them like it was something personal and on either side nothing but trees; some you saw in the headlights and the rest you just smelled, pitch and pine. When they reached the top the transmission was smoking. Jelonnek put it in neutral and coasted down the other side toward the lights at the bottom. They got up around ninety, touching brakes on the turns, Littlebit riding with both hands on the dashboard and Miss D sleeping through all the wind and gravity.

A sign at the bottom said they could be there before morning. They turned west for good and pulled into the next rest stop. Jelonnek made sure Miss D was still asleep and said this was where they would spend the last night. Littlebit said nothing; she was looking past him, out his window. The space next to them was empty and in the space after that was a big shiny red car with white wall tires and gold wire spokes. A young man leaned against it, shirt open, a thick chain around his neck that matched the spokes. He smoked and waited for you to look at him.

Jelonnek pissed squinting in the bright tile of the men's room. When he came out Littlebit was talking to the guy by the red car. Jelonnek threw away the garbage, got back behind the wheel and rolled up the window. Littlebit came over and he rolled it down again.

"You got twenty?"

He saw her getting into the state trooper's car the night before and said, "Ten." She went away and came back.

"Alright then," she said, but he didn't have any tens and gave her what she'd asked for in the first place. She came back again and said she had to get into her bag. Jelonnek opened the trunk for her and got back in the car. He heard her back there, looking. Then the trunk closed and she walked into the building holding a purse. Jelonnek hadn't seen her with a purse before. She went into the brightness where the maps and vending machines were, and then you couldn't see her at all. The red car was gone. The picnic benches were empty. Jelonnek closed his eyes, Miss D breathing.

◆ ◆ ◆

In the morning the sound of a river woke them and they drove along it on their way to town. Next to the freeway the gorge was covered with evergreens and there were railroad tracks between the car and the trees. The cliffs on the other side were tall and bare. The river was wide as a lake and had waves like a sea, and for a while a big white bird kept pace with them, the edge of its wing at eye level as though they'd become airborne. They passed a dam and saw a sailboat, then a cabin cruiser, then people fishing and water-skiing and kayaking, and someone in scuba gear tumbled backward into the river and disappeared. Now the tracks were below them. The Bridge of the Gods was made by man and cost a dime to walk across. The gorge walls opened ahead and through the gap in the distance they saw a cloud, and then Jelonnek realized it was a white peak and the mountain beneath it seemed to have shaped itself from the sky. He wondered if it was the one in the postcard. The gorge closed up again and the next time they saw the mountain it was much bigger and right at their shoulder. Above and below them a town and another dam with locks and houseboats and someone doing a somersault with a sailboard. Cliffs poked through the trees above the road and sometimes there were waterfalls frozen in the moving glimpse from the car. The trees began to get between them and the water. For a while the river was visible in streaming flashes of sunlight and green, then it was gone.

They stopped at a gas station and Jelonnek bought a map. He had to be reminded you didn't pump your own gas here. Moving again, they saw the buildings. The road bent and the buildings went away, then came back bigger. Houses appeared, small and close together, neighborhoods, factories, billboards, and it wasn't as pretty now but the the mountain stayed in the mirror for good. The exits came more frequently, roads merging and diverging, traffic thickening, the cars closer. Overpasses bore the names of unfamiliar streets and districts. You could see the faces of the drivers now and they were different than the ones on the interstates; they were the faces who lived here.

A sign said DOWNTOWN. The freeway ended and another curved sharply south. They were alongside another river, smaller and dirty-looking, and the biggest buildings were on the other side. Jelonnek wasn't sure how to get there and then he didn't have a choice; the lane they were in swung onto a bridge. The ramp at the other end made a complete circle down to the street and it seemed you could take your hands off the wheel and the city would just keep drawing you in. The signal was green. Jelonnek wished it hadn't been, that they could have stood still for just the length of a light.

"I guess we here, baby," Littlebit said.

"Well I see some buildings," Miss D said. "Do a river have a beach?"

The city center was a grid of neat square blocks and all the streets were one-way. Like driving on a circuit board. The traffic lights were on poles on the corners and Jelonnek ran one and had to slam on brakes at another.

"Where is you going?" Littlebit asked.

He really didn't know; it felt like traffic was chasing them. "I think I'm looking for a place to park."

"How come this don't feel like nothin?" Miss D said.

They saw a blue brick building and over the entrance was a giant copper statue of a goddess with a trident. "Don't mess with that heifer," Littlebit said, and then a bus leaned on the horn behind them because there were streets where cars weren't supposed to go.

They drove around another ten minutes before they spotted someone leaving a space near an art museum. They crawled from the car like hatchlings from a broken egg. Jelonnek almost agreed with Miss D but it felt like less than nothing; the slant of the sidewalk, the breeze, the light, the faces, the names of the streets, all part of the same mistake.

He looked at the parking meter. It said you didn't have to pay on weekends and after a while they were able to sort out the days to Friday. Jelonnek dug for change. It was well past noon and Miss D was hungry. No one else was but there was nothing else to do and they walked, their legs not quite their own, getting the air under their clothes. There were coffee shops and a cafe nearby, crowded with students and their backpacks, but they were looking for something they knew. They wandered a couple of blocks and Miss D said, "There go Mickey D's." So they went inside and stood in line and the first words anybody said to them in this strange new place were: "Would you like to try one of our Value Meals today?"

They ate in a booth and Jelonnek unfolded the map. Littlebit had a milkshake.

"We in a hurry?" she said. Jelonnek looked at her.

"We just goin straight to him?" she said.

The city was divided into quarters. "Where else do you want to go?"

"I know where I want to go," Miss D said.

"Somewhere for we can clean up," Littlebit said. "Relax a little minute."

"Money's low," Jelonnek said. He studied the back of the map. "You don't look so bad."

"Yeah she do," Miss D said.

"How you gonna look in a minute you don't quit?"

Jelonnek was looking at Littlebit in a way he hadn't. A way he usually didn't look at anyone.

She gave it back. "You pressed?"

"You never called him."

She stopped looking. "I never said I did."

"You let me think so."

"You let you think so."

189

The postcard was in the car but Jelonnek remembered the name of the street. He found it on the back of the map, then the front. Northeast. He folded the map so the street was showing.

"He fittin to leave us?" Miss D said. She chewed on a French fry, hanging on to one end like it was licorice.

"Don't start me lyin," Littlebit said. "Ax him." Miss D asked for an apple pie instead.

Outside they looked up to the west, at the line of green hills rising over downtown. There were houses looking back down at them from up there, haphazardly planted, some on stilts, and you couldn't tell how anybody got to or from them.

"Folks put a house anywhere," Littlebit observed.

Miss D asked, "Is that where my cousin is?"

"I don't think so," Jelonnek said.

"Good, cause I ain't stayin up there. Y'all crazy up there."

They drove back toward the dirty brown river. The city was clean and well-kept and there were modern inscrutable sculpures and drinking fountains on the corners, street guides in bright green uniforms and hats who provided information and directions, and more vagrants than they'd ever seen. Miss D looked at their beards and thick outdoor skin and marveled that almost all of them were white.

They crossed another bridge. The streets on the other side were wider and busy and there was a mall and a sports arena and a convention center made of tinted green glass with tall spires like a place of worship. Jelonnek pulled over by the mall to check the map again. A group of teenagers crossed the street in front of them.

Miss D said, "It's more of us over here, Ma."

Littlebit shrugged. "Don't make me no nevermind. How many you need?"

They found it, a small brick apartment building on a short numbered street lined with bungalows and cottages, some painted bright colors and bearing ornately carved facades and smaller than the houses they were used to back home. Or was it just back East now?

They parked across the street with the engine running. Littlebit kept looking at the address on the card. "Y'all comin?" she said.

"I think it should be just you." Jelonnek said.

"I wanna come," Miss D said.

"Stay here now."

They watched her cross the street and try the front door. It was locked. There was a small sign next to the door and she pressed a button under the sign. Jelonnek turned his head. Then Miss D said, "Who she talkin to?" and he looked. The door was slanted open but they couldn't see who Littlebit was talking to. It closed and she walked back across the street and got in the car and said, "He gone."

"What do you mean?" Jelonnek said.

"What I say? He don't stay there no more."

"Who you was talkin to then?" Miss D said.

"A old white lady."

"Does she know where he went?" Jelonnek asked but he already knew the answer. He asked Littlebit how old the postcard was.

"I ain't had it but a year."

"Is our vacation over now," Miss D said, "or started?"

Jelonnek looked in the mirror. Miss D stared back and said, "Why you look at me so ugly?"

He looked away. "Just suck your thumb," he said.

T he motel stood at the edge of the city center, near the foot of the West Hills. During the day the manager was an old guy with a white mustache who told them that summer would be hot but not as hot as they were used to, and dry. He told them about the rain. He told them where the zoo was, and Chinatown, and to stay out of Old Town, which was right next to Chinatown. At night it was a college kid who sat over an open textbook, the phone pressed to his ear.

The room was on the second floor. Two doubles. There was no pool but they had cable and air. They were new to cable and spent most of the first day watching MTV and public access, the road still moving under them like a treadmill. There were no movie channels, you had to pay extra for a movie. Miss D giggled at a Korean soap opera.

Jelonnek looked in the phone book, but if there was a number it wasn't listed.

"If I could call long distance," Littlebit said.

"Are we still in the United States?" Miss D asked.

You could see the mountain from the bathroom. There was a small square window in there and when you sat on the toilet you could see the top half of the mountain, its white peak against the blue sky, and nothing else.

At night a man went past their window carrying a red and white lunch pail. He was small and walked as though one side of his body were dead weight. He had a room on the second floor.

In the morning Jelonnek went to the office and paid for another day. They had a weekly rate but Jelonnek declined; they weren't going to be here that long. You just had to lay low for a while, till things blew over.

He went to Dunkin Donuts across the street and bought a dozen, glazed. Miss D ate four of them and watched cartoons. Somebody knocked and said in a Russian accent, "Room to clean." They sent her away and left before she came back, drove around town getting no more lost than they already were. Miss D asked the question that had by default become the slogan of their situation, which was such that Jelonnek was almost beyond annoyance.

"Maybe tomorrow," he said, because he'd never been to the ocean, and because he figured they'd reached the end of the line and might as well look into the pit.

They wound up in a vast park on the other side of the hills. The zoo was there, and so were a Vietnam veterans memorial and tennis courts and twenty miles of trails. There was a rose garden with five hundred kinds of roses and a Japanese garden with tiny waterfalls and bridges and a pond of big orange fish that went for anything you dropped in the water. Miss D watched them eat her spit. The trail was shady and cool and they made way for joggers wearing bright chemical colors. The trees had small placards nailed to their bark and on the placards were the names of the trees. English first, below that Latin or Greek. Miss D moved ahead like an advance scout, tree to tree, reading off the names with no little difficulty, and anything that wasn't fir or pine was news to Jelonnek. There was one she couldn't read at all. Its bark was ringed with black and white stripes and Miss D said, "I'ma call that a *zebrawood*," and Jelonnek thought it a good name in spite of himself, and he remembered that Adam had named the animals, but who had done so for the flowers and trees?

Littlebit strolled behind, taking her time and muttering.

The trail led to a clearing on top of a hill where there was an old carousel and an ice cream cart. A friendly kid with a shaved head and pierced ears operated both. Jelonnek wouldn't buy Miss D a popsicle, then changed his mind, and then they each got on a horse. Littlebit sat on a bench. Miss D invited her to join them and Littlebit said, "Is you mad? Feel like I just got off one."

The kid turned the carousel by pumping a long wooden lever. The buildings of the city and the mountain spun by, then Littlebit on the bench. Jelonnek kept expecting the bench to go by empty on the next pass, but it didn't happen.

After the park they bought fast food and took it back to the motel and paid for a movie. You called the office and they added it to your bill. They sat and lay on the beds with the lights off and the air conditioning on, while before them played out the story of an murderous android from the future who comes to the present to kill the boy who will otherwise grow up to…Jelonnek wished he'd thought of that too though it was a sequel whose plot was identical to its predecessor, only more expensive. He thought about *Armageddon Zero*, still locked in the trunk of the car. He thought about money, how he could feel them running out of it. It semed to be something that was always happening, even just sitting there, like a slow leak, a meter running somewhere.

He went to the office and the kid glanced up from an histology manual. Jelonnek asked if there were any copies of yesterday's paper lying around. All that was left was the entertainment section but that was what he wanted. He took it back to the room and Littlebit was on the phone.

"He the quiet type," she said to someone. "What time it is over there?"

"I wanna call somebody," Miss D said. Jelonnek looked at her. He'd already made a call of his own.

"You ain't never lied," Littlebit said. "Yuppies, Japs and dykes. They bums dress better than we do."

Jelonnek opened the paper and pored over the music listings the way he had the White Pages. He'd heard her voice on the answering machine and hung up.

"Did he…hell no…"

Miss D whispered in her mother's ear.

"Be easy then," Littlebit said. "Miss D wanna bother you." Jelonnek reached over and pressed the cradle button before she could, and Littlebit almost slammed the receiver down on his finger.

"Goddamn you tight," she said.

"Is you tight, Jelonny?" Miss D said.

"Yeah he is," Littlebit said. "He too cheap to sweat."

Then she said she didn't mean it. She said she was playing.

Jelonnek sat by the window. "Find anything out?"

She hadn't found out her cousin's phone number or address, but whoever she'd spoken with had told her something about Sunday night. If it was true. If it was true, maybe it was just as well they could no longer afford to go back.

He watched them play Old Maid.

Later the man with the red and white lunch pail limped past the window. Jelonnek peeked through the curtain. One arm was short and had fleshy nubs at the ends like rudimentary fingers.

Littlebit had trouble sleeping, Jelonnek could hear it. Early in the morning he found her sprawled on the bathroom floor because the tiles were cold.

"Don't feel good?" he said.

"Sure damn don't."

"What's the matter?"

"I need twenty dollars."

"Make it ten," Jelonnek said.

"I'm cheap. I'm cheap and this is the last time," he said.

He remembered why the day manager had told them not to go into Old Town, so they told Miss D they'd be back with breakfast and hung the sign on the door. They drove through the gate to Chinatown. The gate had five roofs and marble columns and was guarded by two lions, one male and one female. There were restaurants and red lampposts, cherry trees, the street signs in two languages. Then Old Town, which was what it said it was. Buildings that looked like they should have had horses tied out front, and some of these had been converted into galleries, shops, or office space. One was being demolished and only the facade was left, like the set of the last western.

They drove around blocks. The streets were in alphabetical order and some people crossed them slowly, without looking. Jelonnek beeped at one of them, a white-haired woman in a baseball cap, who stopped and turned and looked at them, a bag in each hand.

"She'll suck your dick for ten cents," she said, and spat on the windshield.

"I'll do better than that," Littlebit said. "Now run that bitch over." Jelonnek ran the wipers.

A shelter, train depot, comedy club, a titty bar with a man in a velour tracksuit standing out front, looking at pedestrians and drivers in a certain solicitous way.

"Him?" Jelonnek said.

"Look for a white one," Littlebit said.

They saw him on a block where one whole side had been razed, pacing before mounds of rubble. Skinny, long baggy shorts, wifebeater. Jelonnek pulled over, looking around. The guy came near and leaned in Littlebit's window. Jelonnek didn't look at him; he could barely hear what they said. He passed the bill across the seat. The guy took it and opened his mouth and something dropped from it into Littlebit's lap. Jelonnek drove carefully away listening for sirens. He told Littlebit after that she was done.

"Sure damn am," she said.

"This was the last one."

"I mean."

They passed a laundromat and he said they should wash clothes soon.

"I'm sayin," she said.

◆ ◆ ◆

They took the sheet from one of the beds. Filled the trash can with store brand soda and cheap beer and ice, then covered it with the plastic the ice came in. They bought fried chicken and biscuits on the way.

Heading west there were more tree-covered mountains and sometimes they had strange-looking bald patches where the trees had been cleared away. Miss D asked which were mountains and which were hills, and she asked about the chicken. She wore her bathing suit for the first time since Nebraska. When the grades got steep Jelonnek drove in low gear as he had the night before they got into town, and if there was only one lane traffic would stack up behind him like he was leading a pilgrimage. Once he pulled onto the shoulder and let them pass, and they read license plates. Out here people expressed themselves through their license plates.

After two hours or so they saw a sign and turned off the highway. A narrow road twisted through a rain forest so dense Jelonnek had to turn on the lights. Ferns brushed the car. The road led to a parking lot on top of a cliff. A brink. Shorebirds cried overhead and when they got out of the car it was rock and trees and then just water and sky. The air heavy with a living smell. Miss D forgot about the chicken. A trail zigzagged down the face of the cliff and she forgot to be afraid of heights. When they got to the bottom she ran to the water's edge and waited for them, Jelonnek with the trash can and the sheet folded over his shoulder, Littlebit carrying the food. The waves kept chasing Miss D back toward them.

They took off their shoes and held down the corners of the sheet with them. The sand was soft and not too hot, then damp and smooth and firm as a floor where the waves came in. Up close the blue was almost gray. Littlebit stayed just out of reach, wearing a dark sleeveless dress that dropped off her shoulders like it was still on the hanger. Rumble-rush of the breakers, the water so cold it made the bones of your feet and ankles ache, and Miss D screamed in pain and joy. Your feet sank in mud and the surf rushed back out as hard as it came in, wanting to pull your legs out from under you. Jelonnek threw out his arms. Miss D screamed. The ocean withdrew in layers, hissing white foam subsiding to cloudy brown, and then sheet upon lucid sheet shed one after the other like leaves of a liquid text unveiling its conclusion: the sand, smoothed to a shiny unbroken slickness in which for a moment everything was reflected.

"Jelonny we standin on the sky!" Miss D yelled.

They got as used to it as they were going to get, and still you couldn't do anything but wade. No one was in deeper than waist-high except the dogs, and even the guys with surfboards wore wetsuits. Miss D remembered to be hungry. They went back to the sheet where the breeze had flipped one corner and half-covered it with sand. The ice had melted but the pop was cold enough and so was the beer. Sometimes you could feel the ocean lightly on your face and Miss D said it felt like she was growing freckles.

Everything was far away from everything else. Behind them the bluffs fell away to dunes and beach grass, refreshment stands and beachfront property. In between a row of striped tents where you could change your clothes. A group of teenagers picnicked on a blanket nearby, in the shadow of a smoldering log. One of them kept throwing bits of hotdog into the air, and a big white bird would swoop in and catch it before it landed.

"You see that shit?" Littlebit said. She threw her bones in the sand and lay down on the sheet with an arm over her face.

"You good, Ma?"

"Good as I get."

"Can I bury you?"

"You do it might be for good."

The gulls cried through the surf.

Jelonnek looked down the beach, where everything became vague and misted. A couple of big rocks rose out of the water there, and one of them looked to be the size of an office building. Jelonnek finished his beer and got up and headed that way. Littlebit stayed where she was but Miss D followed. He'd had two beers and didn't stop her. People flew kites, sat under umbrellas. Fat man watching a nine-inch TV on his belly. A gang of kids were building a fortress as if preparing for an invasion from the sea. Seagulls hovered over a big scaly carcass as if tethered to it and there were shells aand polished stones and dead jellyfish to avoid, transparent blobs with tendrils going yellow and brown in the sun.

They passed two women in broom skirts holding hands, one of them saying, "It's an angry coast." Miss D wanted to know why two women were holding hands, and Jelonnek said he didn't know. She asked him if they could and he said they couldn't.

It was farther than he'd thought. The rock was much bigger now but still gray in the mist, like it had yet to become real. You could see the birds flocking on and around it like bees at a hive, and there were big green patches of grass or moss. They sloshed through clear shallows between sand bars and came to a stretch of boulders covered with tiny black mussels. You had to watch your step because the boulders were slick and in between them lived another kind of life, bulbous dark-green gourds that opened like a chorus of mouths when the tide came in, closed when it went back out. Jelonnek showed them to Miss D and she touched one. It opened up and she screamed and ran back up the beach. Jelonnek slipped, gashed his knee. He looked down and saw blood. Then the ocean took it away and he swore with the sting of saltwater.

When they got back to the sheet Littlebit was sitting up with her hands behind her and a cigarette in her lips: "Ready to raise?" Jelonnek's arms and legs were pink. Miss D drank another pop and seemed to have forgotten all about the boulders and the terrible green things that lived among them. They let her wade a little while longer, then dumped the water out of the trash can and stuffed the sheet into it. There were a couple of beers left for the road. On the way back up the bluff Miss D said goodbye to the waves and the sand and the birds, and Littlebit told her to watch where she was going. Jelonnek kept looking back. Sand met water met sky like the seams of the world, and the world got bigger the higher they climbed.

At the top Littlebit pointed. On a cluster of rocks maybe a hundred yards offshore, sea lions had gathered. Miss D couldn't see them for the life of her but said goodbye anyway, waving with that stiff little gesture like she was leaving home again.

Two men came to the motel in a taxi. They took a room on the second floor at the corner of the building. Jelonnek and Littlebit watched from the window. The two men wore loud, outdated clothes that looked like they'd been purchased new, and one had a ponytail. When Jelonnek turned from the window, Littlebit had her face at Miss D's crotch.

"Why you smell my privacy?" Miss D said.

"Cause you nasty. Now go do good with that rag like I showed you."

Miss D slammed the bathroom door saying something. "Maybe you should go in with her," Jelonnek said.

"Maybe I'll go for a walk," Littlebit said.

"Where to?"

"Gimme the rent," she said.

"What rent?"

"For the room. You been paid it?"

"We got time."

"Give it here," Littlebit said. "I'll take care a it."

"That's alright," Jelonnek said. He was looking in the Yellow Pages. "I'll get it on my way out."

"You don't trust me?"

"I got an errand to run."

"Then go ahead with yourself."

The old guy was in the office, a lump in his cheek. Jelonnek asked about the weekly rate. He didn't have enough cash so he tried his credit card. He'd used it up on the road but he tried it anyway. The old guy came back and said, "Better contact your bank." Jelonnek paid for another day and headed downtown. On his way through the parking lot he looked up. The man with the ponytail looked back from the second floor balcony, picking his nose.

The girl at the temporary employment agency said they weren't taking applications at this time. She was very nice and gave Jelonnek a key to the bathroom down the hall. He returned the key and took the elevator down to the lobby. He asked the security guard there if they were hiring. The guard didn't know but he told Jelonnek where he could go to find out.

It was bright and warm on the street. Jelonnek walked past an old courthouse, crossed the street to a square where a pole bristling with signs told you your exact distance from thirty other places to be, five blocks over or Guadalajara. At the corner a bronze statue of a businessman with an umbrella. The square was sunken like an amphitheater and Jelonnek crossed to the other side, through skateboarders and office workers and past a recess where people spoke and listened to their echoes. The bricks under his feet had names written on them; you could buy a brick for a hundred dollars. Young people sat on the steps or leaned against the walls asking for money. "Wanna look in my box?" one of them asked Jelonnek. On his lap was a cigar box, and next to him sat a pretty girl with a smudged face. They were much younger than the bums Jelonnek was used to.

"Okay," he said. The girl opened the lid and an eye painted on the inside of the box stared back up at him.

"Cost you a quarter," the kid said. Jelonnek told him he was crazy and got going.

"I can sing you a song," the kid said.

"Have a better day," the girl yelled, six thousand, seven hundred and twenty-eight miles from Timbuktu.

The next kid had a guitar with about three strings that made a dry buzzing sound like an insect in a jar. A case was open on the ground and a sign propped against the lid requested donations with which the owner would acquire lessons and strings and become a proper musician. A spattering of change shone in the lid and there were even bills, but Jelonnek didn't add to it.

A man outside Starbucks kept asking people for the precise amount of a dollar thirty-seven. He would follow you a little ways.

But everyone else you saw was nice-looking and they drove nice cars and wore carefully chosen clothes. At the corner Jelonnek took a drink from a fountain and the water was cold and tasted of some deep dark place.

He explained his situation at the security firm. They told him things were slow right now, but they let him fill out a six-page application and said they'd call him if anything turned up. They even let him watch a training video. He sat at a tiny desk in a small dark room with two other people. The video took a humorous slant; a vastly corpulent guard eating a turkey leg at his post, snoring in oblivion while a pair of intruders cleaned out the premises. Only Jelonnek laughed.

When he got back to the motel Littlebit wasn't there. Miss D lay on the bed watching *The Real World*, the playing cards spread out before her.

"She gone for a walk."

"Where to?"

"Don't start me lyin. Can you play Old Maid with me?"

Jelonnek looked out the window. Later they heard a door slam from the other end of the building. Littlebit came in with a look on her face like she'd discovered something amazing and was about to share it with them. They'd seen this look before.

"Where you been, ma?"

"Around the world." She lay on top of Miss D and kissed her.

"Your mouth smell," Miss D said.

"I love you too."

Miss D looked at her. "Your eyes bugged."

"I love you too," Littlebit said. She looked at Jelonnek and loved him as well, then loved everything in the room for the next five minutes or so. She put a cigarette in her mouth but didn't light it. She picked up the remote and clicked it at the TV with such finality that every channel she changed was a world that ceased to exist. She clicked it around the room in a sort of experimental way, then aimed it at Jelonnek, said, "Smile," and threw it against the wall over his head and locked herself in the bathroom.

In the evening Jelonnek went back to the office. The young guy was there leaning over his book, this time the bulge in his lower lip. Everyone here chewed, it seemed; Jelonnek had even seen women.

"Those two guys that checked in today," Jelonnek said. He said the room number and the night manager spat into the same coffee can the day manager used.

"I think they're up to something," Jelonnek said. "Selling dope or something."

"What do you want me to do about it?" The day manager looked at his book.

"Well," Jelonnek said. "I think…the police?"

"Can you prove anything?"

Jelonnek wanted to press the night manager's face into the book so he couldn't breathe, into histology or calculus till he never breathed again. Instead he went to the store across the street and bought the cheapest twelve-pack in the cooler. When Littlebit saw it she said, "I thought we ain't had the money."

"We," he said. A piece of the remote cracked under his foot. "It cost four bucks." He needed ice. He took the bucket down to the machine under the stairs and filled it. There was a room next to the machine. The door opened and a woman stood there for him. Jelonnek saw flat sagging breasts, veins, stretch marks, a belly under a belly. He couldn't look at her face. He backed away with the ice as if she might drag him inside and went up the stairs. The door slammed shut.

He sat in a chair and drank beer and smoked. Littlebit asked for one. "You had yours," he said.

"Naw she ain't," Miss D said.

"Shut up," he said.

"You ain't my daddy," she said.

"Won't be the last time you say that," Jelonnek said.

He watched TV and drank, and after they went to sleep he was still watching TV and drinking. The show on public access consisted of a naked man sitting on the floor with his legs crossed, meditating. The beer was bitter. Jelonnek had to press the buttons on top of the TV since the remote was broken, and each time he passed the public access channel the naked man was still meditating. The beer was bitter but he got used to it and drank every can before he felt like going to sleep. He was still sleeping in the chair when another taxi came and brought visitors to the two men in the corner room.

They stopped buying fast food. They went to the store across the street, and while Jelonnek bought a loaf of bread Littlebit shoved a pack of baloney into her purse.

They filled the ice bucket and put the baloney on top.

Later they told Miss D they were going to play a game.

"Like hide-and-seek but it ain't," Littlebit said. Miss D and Jelonnek were to go hide somewhere. If Littlebit couldn't find them, there would be a surprise.

Miss D was dubious. "I wanna hide with you, Ma."

"Next time," Jelonnek said.

"I don't know."

"Well you playin anyway." Littlebit stood at the window, barefoot, wearing that long t-shirt. She kept looking past the curtain. The man with the red and white lunch pail pulled in every night around this time and limped past their window.

"What if he keeps going?" Jelonnek said.

"He ready," Littlebit said. "He more ready as you."

Miss D said, "What kinda surprise?"

Littlebit looked out the window once more and covered her eyes. "One, two…"

Jelonnek gestured at Miss D and moved quickly to the bathroom. She seemed to have forgotten her misgivings. They went inside the bathroom and Jelonnek shut the door. Light from the street came through the small window but it was too dark to see the mountain.

"Get in the tub," he said. Then he drew the curtain over the window and stood in the tub with her. He drew the shower curtain but not all the way.

"I can still see," Miss D whispered with a kind of disappointment. They crouched and Jelonnek told her not to say another word. He was practically begging.

The door rattled. Jelonnek felt Miss D stiffen next to him. It rattled again and they heard the room door shut. A muffled conversation.

"Who that?" Miss D whispered.

Jelonnek hushed her, then said, "TV." They could hear traffic outside. Littlebit's voice got louder: "Ain't nobody in there." The bathroom door opened and the room brightened and Miss D shut her eyes like it would make her invisible. The door closed but not all the way. Somebody sat or lay on the bed. The TV got louder and that was all they heard till Littlebit moaned.

Miss D stiffened again. Another moan. A succession of harsh grunts and Miss D said, "Ma." She was still whispering like she didn't want to break the rules, but she was standing too and Jelonnek lunged and grabbed what he could. They fell back against the wall with Miss D against his chest, and Jelonnek was sure they could hear it over the TV. He covered Miss D's mouth and she bit his hand. Her hair was thick and dry and he pulled it till she stopped.

The man out in the room said something. He said it like he was talking in his sleep. It was hot behind the shower curtain and Jelonnek smelled Miss D. He was sweating. He kept one hand in her hair and one tight over her mouth. The breath from her nostrils was hot. Snot and tears. If Littlebit got into trouble she would call his name, that was part of the game too.

T hey had enough to buy another day now, but when Jelonnek
went to the office the old guy wouldn't take his money.

"You know why," he said. "Or should I call the authorities and
have them explain it to you?"

Jelonnek went back to the room. "I ain't mad," Littlebit said.
"This place tired anyway. We got the car."

"The car don't have cable," Miss D said.

"Ain't shit on no way. I ain't mad."

Authorities, the old guy had said. Like mere police wouldn't do.

"Let me hold mine," Littlebit said to Jelonnek. "I earned it."

He held out his empty hand. "Call us even."

"Well fuck it then," and she dropped her arm. "I ain't mad."

They finished the bologna for breakfast and drove downtown.
Littlebit suggested the blood bank but the line was halfway down
the block. They drove on. Either you find a way or time does the
killing, and they wound up at the library. The children's room was
on the first floor. There was a bronze tree there and in its trunk were
carved animals and musical instruments and fairy tale characters.
You weren't allowed to climb it, but the more you touched it the
shinier it got. On the third floor Littlebit found a carrel where you
could put on headphones and listen to music, and Jelonnek sat
in a stuffed chair on the second, glaring at magazines. When he
looked up Miss D stood before him with fifteen books in her arms
culled from every department, a fair survey of human thought and
endeavor. He told her she could look at them but they couldn't
take any out because they didn't have a library card.

She rolled her eyes. "You fired." He still had her teethmarks in
his hand.

On the way out they passed a small child sitting on the wide
front steps, flipping excitedly through a book meant for adults.
Repeating the same phrase over and over as though it comprised

the whole of the text: "Gimmesome gimmesome! Whatsamatter whatsamatter?"

They ate once more that day, Polish Boys with everything from a cart downtown, then decided to cross the river. Waited twenty motionless minutes in traffic for a drawbridge to close, then u-turned and went to the zoo in the park instead. Going to the zoo did not mean paying its admission, it meant walking the hills above it, looking for vantage points from which to see the animals. They smelled more than they saw but they heard an elephant and the trail was alive with small brown lizards. They watched people play tennis and there was a puppet show in the amphitheater till evening: Pinocchio becomes a boy, though not a man. They used the restrooms and sat in the car while it got dark. They sat in the car till a ranger or whatever he was came and told them the park was closed.

"This place tired anyway," Littlebit said.

The gas tank was slightly more than a quarter full. They drove around till they found a spot in Old Town, an unlit street behind a brewery and that was what it smelled like.

"We need to find a place," Jelonnek said.

"This ain't a place?" Littlebit said.

"For you and…"

"This ain't that?"

"You know what I mean."

"Think I don't? You want us gone for you can have it all to yourself."

"Have what?"

"What you got comin." She spat out the window. "So it's like that."

"Don't put words in my mouth."

"I don't have to. It ain't no big puzzle."

"I'm just saying for a while. I just think it would be easier."

"It ain't. You ever been to one? Left my teeth in one, and with kids? Not in this life. I'll sleep in a car any day, till it get cold or you put us out, one."

The front seats reclined. Miss D slept in the back with her thumb in her mouth.

In the morning Jelonnek counted what they had left though he knew the sum by heart. They were as glad to leave the car as they'd been to get to it, and they wandered the edge of Old Town till they found the blood bank. The line was much shorter now but when they got inside a woman told them they couldn't use an out-of-state ID.

"They don't take outta-state blood?" Littlebit said. Miss D was hungry. They walked on, passed a small art gallery. They had no interest in the exhibit but a sign said there were free refreshments inside.

It was crowded. Small rooms with white walls, polished wood floors. The paintings on the walls were no bigger than snapshots; you had to put your eyes almost right up to them to make them out. Jelonnek waited for a woman to finish looking at one so he could take his turn. Her face was almost touching it. "You know what his problem is?" she was saying to somebody, or to herself. "He's too happy."

"I roomed with him," someone else said. "I watched him work."

"What's his process?"

"He wore earplugs. Uses a toothbrush."

Littlebit stood behind Jelonnek. "Where the food at?" Her low scrape of a voice.

There was a doorway and another room, smaller than the first. There were fewer pictures on the walls and in a corner a card table with cheese and crackers and some kind of punch. On the other side of the room a large book open on a white countertop. A very

209

pretty young woman stood behind the book and said, "Do you have any questions?"

"If we don't like your pictures can we still eat?" Miss D said.

"What ain't to like?" Littlebit said.

Jelonnek looked at the book with his mouth full. It contained a list of the paintings and, next to each picture, a price. The prices seemed to him inversely proportional to the size of the work, but what did he know about art? Somebody liked them; according to the book a fair number had already been sold.

"Are you sure you don't have any more questions?" the young woman said to them on their way out.

They headed uptown. The weather was sunny and mildly warm but had been for so long it seemed fake, an official smile. Now it belonged to everyone else—like money, a place to sleep, a place to squat in private. They passed the square Jelonnek had walked through two days before. Next to the statue of the man offering an umbrella, a man stood on a newspaper box, identically posed, but in his other hand he held a large cup into which passersby occasionally dropped change. He never moved. Littlebit and Miss D took turns looking back at him as they reached the corner and crossed the street. Then Littlebit looked at Jelonnek and said, "Y'all tickle me sometime."

They went to the library again, but only to use the restrooms. When they came out they heard drums. The sound was far away but you could tell there were a lot of them and that they were having trouble staying together. Maybe they didn't want to. The drums got louder as they walked, and they couldn't tell if they were being drawn to them or heading that way anyway, or anywhere at all.

They found themselves near the spot where they'd parked upon arriving. A row of long grassy blocks stretched from the art museum to the university, with benches and shade, fountains and statues. *Farewell to Orpheus* and *Rebecca at the Well*. The drumming was much louder now and it came from the middle block, where there was a sunken round with rings of steps and a platform in the center. The players sat or knelt on the platform, some with actual congas or tom-toms or timbales, others beating on trash cans, coffee cans, an inverted kettle, the platform itself or their own bodies. An audience had gathered on the steps and some were dancing, and at the edge of the round a crazed-looking old man with wild gray hair and a beard presumed to conduct this racket with a stick he'd found in the grass.

Jelonnek and Littlebit and Miss D took a bench and looked at the people in the park blocks; those on lunch hour, between classes, or passing some other, indeterminate interval. A one-legged man went by pushing a grocery cart, using a crutch devised from a boat oar with one end thrust into a tennis ball. There were young people with bright-colored hair and chains and clothes covered with handwritten slogans, their faces and bodies pierced with metal in unlikely places as with implements of torture. They were loud and foulmouthed, called each other Wolf and Bam-Bam and you couldn't tell if they had nowhere else to go or were just pretending they didn't.

"That ain't me," Miss D said. Littlebit answered but you couldn't hear it over the drumming.

They saw a group of long-bearded men identically attired in camouflage and boots like renegade infantry, squatting amid a jumble of bedrolls and enormous backpacks from which hung pots and pans, a portable latrine, lanterns, a collapsed bamboo fishing rod, a camouflage guitar. The biggest dog you ever saw with an American flag scarfed around its neck. Nearby a dirty-faced family almost as heavily burdened, and with the added weight of three children, two in a stroller fashioned from a shopping cart, one in a papoose on its mother's back. And then those with nothing but themselves.

On the sidewalk a skinny kid with no shirt went from car to car, sticking his arm in windows left cracked open against the heat.

A gray-headed woman in baggy clothes came near them. She looked fondly at Miss D and asked in a loud voice if she could embrace her. Miss D slid closer to her mother, and Littlebit told the woman, "Go ahead with yourself."

"You people need anything?" the woman fairly shouted.

"Not no fleas," Littlebit said.

"Sit tight," the woman said in her loud voice. "Wagon's on its way." And she went off to converse with an elm on the tree lawn.

They didn't know what she meant till a battered Volkswagen minibus pulled up beside the block and the drumming abruptly stopped as though its purpose was fulfilled. Two men and a woman got out of the minibus carrying something toward the round. The musicians dispersed and a propane camp stove was placed on the platform. The woman fired up the grill while the men returned to the minibus and came back with bags of hotdog buns and plastic spoons, paper plates and cups, a ten-gallon beverage dispenser. They shaped the gathering crowd into two passable lines while smoke drifted through the trees. Beans simmering in an iron stock pot. Within fifteen minutes plates were passed to the people in the blocks, along with cups of green Kool-Aid, and it was the last meal Jelonnek and Littlebit and Miss D ate for the rest of that day.

They sat on the bench with their food in their laps. "We need a plan," Jelonnek said.

"Who you tellin?" Littlebit said.

"I plan to kill me another hotdog," Miss D said.

"I'm listening," Littlebit said. She listened for a while but no plan was forthcoming, only the sound of chewing, people sucking their teeth and fingers. Then she said, "This shit hurt my mouth."

The men in fatigues got a plate for their dog. The kid reaching into cars on the sidewalk got his arm stuck and yelled for help.

When they got back to the car there was a parking ticket under the wiper blade and the antenna had been broken off. They spent another night there anyway, Jelonnek dreaming of someone coming at him with the broken aerial. In the morning Littlebit and Miss D were still sleeping while he walked to Burger King to take a piss. When he got there his back still ached from another night in a car behind a brewery, and a security guard inside told him the restrooms were for customers only. Jelonnek bought a small coffee. In the men's room he looked at someone in the mirror, at his hair, his eyes, his wrinkled shirt. A thick roughness growing on his teeth. He fixed what he could and left the cup on a urinal.

In the car Littlebit was stretched out in the back and Miss D was behind the wheel pretending to drive. Jelonnek told her to move over and open the window, let the smell out.

She told him a man had come by and said some things. He wanted to know her name.

"I was sleep," Littlebit murmured. Her hand covered her eyes.

"My stomach hurt," Miss D said.

"Caught herself eatin on the toothpaste," Littlebit said.

Miss D grunted and Jelonnek started the car. He drove around downtown, then parked in a spot a block south of Chinatown because there was no meter. They drifted uptown till they came to an indoor mall and went inside. The mall had a curved glass roof and four levels. You could take the escalators or a glass elevator and on the ground floor there were fountains filled with blue marbles. Shafts of light leaned in from the ceiling and they shuffled through them past The Sharper Image and J. Crew and Eddie Bauer and Godiva Chocolates. They didn't go inside. They used the restrooms and then sat in the food court, smelling pizza and MacDonald's and something Middle Eastern. Around them people sat and ate and made their noise, and when they got up they often left things unfinished, drinks and French fries, sandwiches and platters, and some sullen kid in a fast food uniform would come and clear it away. Littlebit tapped Jelonnek's arm and pointed. He followed her to a table where they sat for a while, till she stood and picked up a tray and took it to the trash bin, motioned for him to do the same. They put the trays on the bin and walked out with a baked potato, something Chinese with chicken and rice, most of a salad, a large drink cup rattling with half-melted ice. They didn't lift anything to their mouths till they were back on the street. Someone else's food, someone else's mouth. Miss D ate the chicken and left the rice, then drank from the cup until her stomach stopped hurting, kept drinking till it started hurting again.

They walked to the river, Jelonnek trying to think. At night move the car, maybe just outside the city, find a place where they wouldn't be ticketed or approached, and then. And then. He thought about calling back East again but didn't seem able to give himself permission. As if some principle he could not define were at stake.

Gimmesome gimmesome. Whatsamatter whatsamatter?

They crossed the street under a bridge and entered the park by the river. Between the street and the riverbank was a monument dedicated to some nineteenth-century battleship and they sat in the grass in its shade while people strolled by. A time capsule had been buried beneath them, not to be opened till the three hundredth anniversary of the Declaration of Independence. There were boats on the river. After a while Jelonnek and Miss D heard Littlebit say from a distance, "Here it go," and looked around because they hadn't even noticed she was gone.

She was on the sidewalk, looking at a bright pink flyer on a telephone pole. "Hey now," she said. "Here they go."

The flyer bore the name of a venue on the southeast side, and the name of a group that was playing there Friday and Saturday night. All ages.

"That's him?" Jelonnek said.

"Yeah it is."

"I don't see his name."

"He don't play alone, that's what they call theyself. No matter who he play with, they call theyself that."

"What do he play?" Miss D asked.

"I'm regular tellin you."

"Do I like jazz?"

"You don't have to," Littlebit said. "It might save your life anyway."

They asked somebody what day it was, then left the river. They didn't mind walking so much now and went back to the park blocks where they'd been fed the day before. They sat on a bench where someone had left a newspaper behind. Miss D looked at the comics and Littlebit helped her read them and find where to laugh. There were no drums today and they watched four kids playing a game in which a small beanbag was kicked from foot to foot. After a while they realized the van with the hotdogs and beans wasn't coming. By now they knew you could ride the bus for free almost anywhere downtown, and took one back near Chinatown where they'd parked the car. There was another ticket on the windshield and a man sleeping on the hood with a blue Civil War cap over his face, a sign around his neck requesting a lift back to Oakland. When they got in the car Jelonnek tried without success to wake him with the horn, so he backed carefully out of the space and headed down the street to the next corner, where his passenger woke just as they slowed for the light, rolling off the hood like he was using public transportation. The ticket could not be dislodged as easily and Jelonnek turned and crossed the drawbridge with it flapping on the windshield.

It was flatter on the southeast side of the river, the neighborhoods older. Humble. There were strip malls, discount furniture stores, industrial parkways, and it reminded them a bit more of where they'd come from, except for the mountain jutting into the eastern sky and the guy they saw waiting for a bus, shirtless, his vest, hat and boots all made of snakeskin. A knife in a holster on his hip.

There was still a little left in the tank.

They went to a drive-through where it was buy one, get one free. "Just water to drink," Jelonnek said, and the voice on the intercom said he'd have to charge them a quarter. They found a playground that had public bathrooms where they would eat and wait till evening. Jelonnek sat on a swing. Miss D took one end of the seesaw and her mother sat motionless on the other, just ballast, still holding the pink flyer. Boys were playing basketball and Miss D joined three or four kids on the monkey bars. Later they washed up as well as they could in the bathrooms and brushed their teeth with hot water because there was no toothpaste left.

They changed clothes out of the trunk of the car. Jelonnek counted.

The pink flyer said nine but it was Friday night and by the time they found parking it was twenty minutes past. The club was three blocks away, one corner of an old building next to a tattoo parlor with a kid out front covered in ink, a living mural that smoked and stared back like what of it? The music had started. A guy sat at a table just inside the door with a box of change and a stamp pad. Jelonnek asked how much and the guy said, "Sliding scale," then had to explain what that meant. Jelonnek gave him a nickel and held out his wrist.

Three white guys stood on a small stage playing saxophone, bass, and drums.

"That ain't my cousin," Miss D said, louder than she had to. Littlebit looked at the name on the flyer, then the sign over the door.

They took a wobbly table in the back. You could smell incense and there were lit candles on the tables and every other flat surface. Along the dark-painted walls were stuffed armchairs and other pieces of mismatched living room furniture. You could smell them through the incense. A guy with a knit cap and a long coat asleep on an old sofa. A waitress approached. She wore black lipstick and had a very pale face.

"Who playin?" Littlebit asked.

"Opening act," the waitress said. "I forget the name." She sounded like she had candy in her mouth, then you saw a piece of metal shining in her tongue.

"Do that hurt?" Miss D said.

"Not anymore."

Littlebit held up the flyer. "We here to see him."

"That's my cousin," Miss D said.

"They're next," the waitress said, and asked if she could get them anything from the kitchen. She recommended the gardenburger.

"How much is a beer?" Jelonnek asked.

"We don't serve alcohol."

"We're fine, then."

The waitress pointed to a sign. "You're going to have to order something."

Littlebit looked at the bum on the couch. "I'll have what he havin."

Nothing on the menu had meat in it, but Miss D was always hungry and they could afford a basket of French fries. Jelonnek returned the menu and said they would drink water.

The trio's set consisted of just five or six numbers but the songs, if you could call them that, were long and loose and random-seeming; you could tap your foot but there really wasn't a beat you could follow, especially if you were a rock-and-roller and Jelonnek supposed he still thought of himself as one. There was a piano onstage but it was covered. Each player took turns soloing. Some solos elicited more applause than others, and Jelonnek wondered what everyone knew that he didn't.

He leaned toward Miss D and asked her what she thought.

"They just messin around," she said. "I could do that. Can I get a pop?"

A man walked in carrying a guitar in a case. Then came a man carrying round dark luggage followed by a tall figure in a hat with yet another shape on a handle, this one a long rectangle. Littlebit tapped Miss D's arm and pointed. They whispered to each other.

The fourth musician entered. They set their instruments down in the corner across the room from the stage, went out the door and came back in carrying cymbals, stands, an amplifier top and bottom. Coils of cable. They moved stealthily, like intruders who have broken in to bring you something. They made two more trips and the last time just two of the men returned and stayed with the equipment; the others didn't reappear till the trio had closed its set and started packing up.

Jelonnek looked at Littlebit. "Which one?"

"With that stingy brim." Only one of them wore a hat.

"Does he know you?"

"Used to."

"Is he famous?" Miss D said.

"Compared to us." Littlebit shrugged. "I don't hear nobody hollerin..."

They watched the band set up, plug things in. They and the other players seemed to have little to say to each other. The man who'd entered last opened what looked like an ordinary briefcase. There was a glint of gold light on his face and he took out a saxophone, smaller and shinier than the one the trio had used. Jelonnek went to the bathroom. The toilet was clean but the walls layered dark with scribbling. He took his time. There was no fan so the window above the sink was open and you couldn't see what it opened on. Jelonnek splashed cold water on his face.

When he came back the fries were almost gone and the band was tuning up. The trio were gone and so were some of their audience. The new one trickled in from the dark. Jelonnek kept looking at Littlebit but she didn't look back. He folded a napkin and shoved it under the table leg.

The quartet finished tuning up and sat at the bar that didn't serve alcohol. One of them argued softly with the soundman. The instruments left in repose on stage: the chrome of the sax and the brass of the cymbals and the lacquered finish of the guitar, bouncing light off each other as if given to exchange even in silence.

"This bored," Miss D said. The waitress poured them some more water and asked if she could get them anything else. Jelonnek asked what they owed.

"You're just gonna surprise him?" he said to Littlebit.

"I'll let him play a minute first."

"I wanna play piano," Miss D said, the way she wanted to try everyone's meal.

There was four dollars and change left.

The lights went out. Just the candles now and the light on stage and they sat in an undefined flickering space, the walls gone as if they could not contain what was about to come. Somebody whistled. You could have counted the hands clapping but they meant it. The musicians stepped into the brightness and started tuning up again. First the guitar and saxophone. The drummer blurred a pair of mallets over the cymbals and the sound spread out in sheets. Jelonnek thought of the surf coming in and not going back out, but dissolving and coming in again. He felt something in his groin, felt it before he heard it. The air bulged against his head. He saw the bass player's fingers move and it was like a magician finding his card behind your ear.

It was slow, they weren't just tuning up. The drummer soothed his snare with a brush. The sax and guitar kept sharing the melody like two men in love with the same woman, and no matter what you thought yourself to be you couldn't blame them. Near the end the man with the fedora took a solo. He played a lot of notes that seemed to Jelonnek to have nothing to do with the rest of the song, but everyone else thought they were the right ones and let him know it. Again Jelonnek wondered. The bass player closed his eyes like he didn't want to see where he was going, and the long neck of his instrument, fretless and unmarked, looked designed to get him lost.

"Say it, brother, say it," someone yelled from the tables, and Miss D put her hand over her mouth.

The guitar and the saxophone took up the melody one more time, said goodbye with it, and everyone clapped except for the bum who remained asleep on the sofa. Littlebit's cousin thanked them and pronounced the names of the musicians. He seemed to be the leader, though Jelonnek hadn't thought a bass player could be a leader. He told them the name of the song.

"That's the one we use to pull a crowd," he said. "Now here's where we chase them out."

"Somebody's got to do it," somebody said, and the bum snored. Littlbit shook her head.

Things started out well enough. One-two-three-four and the guitar played chords even Jelonnek recognized and it made him want a beer again. Then the rhythm section started counting in some higher mathematics. The drummer stopped being so kind to his cymbals, the guitar dropped out and the saxophone stepped up. It was smaller than the one the opening act had used, and it climbed higher and seemed to contain more notes. Even that was alright for a while, but then the guy blowing into it started making mistakes. Jelonnek was almost embarrassed for him till he realized he was doing it on purpose, blowing more into the horn than it could handle, yawping and screaking and mewling like some deformed creature giving birth to greater deformity. Miss D's hands covered her ears, Jelonnek felt gooseflesh in places he never had before. It was up to the guitarist to put things back together again, but he had forgotten how to play as well and reentered the noise from the wrong side like running a light at rush hour. The bum woke up and started clapping and Miss D laughed with her hands still over her ears.

Nobody left. Littlebit's elbow was on the table, her hand on her face like a bandage.

She listened with one eye. The candles vibrated. Jelonnek took the change off the table and stood. Everyone looked like they'd stumbled in by accident. Miss D moved her mouth at him but only the music came out. He shoved a dollar at her and headed for the bathroom.

The door was locked. It was just the drums while he waited, falling down the stairs and back up again, the air filled with the shards of cymbals. A woman came out. Jelonnek went in and locked the door. He stood over the toilet and nothing happened but he washed his hands anyway. The writing on the wall was as dense as the music. He looked at the window. There was hardly any less of the music in here, but that square of night looked different from this end of it. Someone shouted out in the room; the bass, guitar and sax were back in it now, each a planet of its own. Jelonnek stood on the toilet and opened the window the rest of the way. It didn't help much. He supposed he could have used the front door, but the dark in the window was the one he wanted. He felt it on his face. He grabbed the sill and lifted a knee.

Someone was shouting—was the piano coming to life? He tried to get a leg through the opening but it was just too tight, and he ended up sticking his head out, then his shoulders, wriggling through snakelike till his arms were free and his hands pushing blindly down in front of him to break his fall.

INT. LAZARUS CHAMBER

A triumphnt burst of steam the last tube
starts to open slowly. The SURVIVOR
collapses at the control panel siezed
by a terrible head ache. The lid of the
tube slowly opens SURVIVOR on all fours.
Suddenly the pain is better The Survivor
looks up with a look in his eyes. We almost
don't recgonize his face with no emotion.
The tube is open we don't see whose inside.
The Survivor looks at the chared remains
of the Hunter the crossbow next to him.
He picks it up and stands up. He looks at
the open tube and back at the crossbow not
just once. He slowly starts an evil smile.
FREEZE. We hear that evil WHISTLE FREEZE.

                              FADE OUT.

            THE END?

S am Thirteen, in shades of blue. Shirt, pants, tie, epaulets. Everything itched. A hat like a real cop and a plastic silver badge pinned to his chest. A jacket for when nights were cool. Sam One was a voice who spoke to him from his lapel, called him every hour on the hour. He told Sam One everything was 10-12. Everything was always 10-12, and Sam One would say, "10-4."

Sam One called him about a lady who needed an escort to her car. Instead of making circles he could walk in a straight line for a while. He waited for her in the south concourse. The escalators had ground to a halt for the night. She came carefully down the grooved risers wearing heels, a dark business suit with a skirt and tie. He wasn't sure exactly what she did but it had something to do with contracts, something international. She was gray-haired but he had to stop staring at her legs. She had a cigar.

She apologized for parking two blocks away, but what the garage was charging was a crime. At least it wasn't raining, she said. He agreed; it was okay to talk with them, Sam One had said, you just had to let them lead. She mentioned skinheads she'd seen hanging around the plaza, drinking beer on the picnic benches. Relieving themselves. Surely he'd noticed them on his rounds?

He kept five feet back while she opened her door. Sam One said don't crowd them. It seemed she could have afforded indoor parking, but maybe she had principles as well. He read her plates like they might be written there.

"Bimmer," she said.

"Pardon?"

"Beemer's a motorcycle," she said.

The next time he saw her she told him about the guy in the south stairwell. You weren't supposed to get sleepers till the weather got bad, but she'd almost had to step over him. And the smell! The third time he let something slip about his movie. She told him about her son doing rewrites in L.A. Additional dialogue. He'd almost saved enough to relocate, concentrate on something serious.

"All the young people are thinking Prague," she said, and she asked him if he knew where Prague was. He started heading back before she had her key in the lock. She chuckled good-naturedly: "So be that way." He expected to get written up but he didn't, and after that he didn't see her again.

Back on the wand tour. At checkpoints he waved his access card over a blinking red dot; this was how they knew he'd been where he was supposed to be. Sam One called to ask him about the sleeper. Jelonnek told him the stairs were 10-12 when he'd checked. At five-fifty an hour, everything was always going to be 10-12.

Sam One sounded skeptical: "Must be the other south stairwell." He called the next night to say he was still getting complaints.

"What do you want me to do?" Jelonnek said into his lapel. "Just wake him up?"

"No, give him a continental breakfast."

"Then what?"

"I'm sending backup. What's your 20?"

Sam Seven would have done it for free. He was a natural, if there is such a thing. He'd had a stick and spray when Jelonnek started, had since graduated to a gun and handcuffs. He had his guard card, Power To Arrest, permits for three calibers. He'd served as an MP in the Gulf, and was a born leader. He was qualified to engage.

He took over and led the way to the stairwell. "10-30, Thirteen." He opened the door.

"Jesus," they both said and tried not to breathe. You could have cut it with a knife.

Sam Seven said, "Let's boost him."

Jelonnek asked how.

"I'll grab his legs."

"You sure about that?"

"The feet are what you want to watch out for." You couldn't see his hands anyway; he was curled up under the risers facing the wall, an old trenchcoat for a blanket. Jelonnek suggested they try and rouse him first. Sam Seven frowned, then prodded the sleeper with his boot. The snoring stopped, then started again.

"Be my guest," Seven said. Jelonnek hesitated, held his nose and brought his face within a foot of where an ear should be. The sleeper twitched and that was all.

Sam Seven rolled his eyes. "How it's done," he said. He bent down and his voice boomed like a shotgun in the stairwell. The blanket heaved. Both hands moved so fast they blurred and you saw blood before you saw the knife. 10-0.

The Turks gave him a bad time but the port was better anyway. At the port Jelonnek sat in a yellow wooden shack the size of a phone booth, and there was the dry dock and the sheds and a lagoon with ducks and the great blue heron. The shack had a plastic window and a heat lamp for light because out here the summer nights were sometimes cold. Just before dark Jelonnek would open a can of pork and beans and pour it on a plate. He bent the lamp over it and within an hour the beans were hot. He wore a hardhat with a badge.

The shack stood at the foot of a gangway. The crew at the other end were under quarantine and were not permitted to leave the ship, with the exception of the second mate, who periodically came ashore to look at the waterline. If anyone else tried Jelonnek was to alert the gate and record the incident in the logbook. You had to write everything in the logbook, they'd give you a rash about it. Every thirty minutes he left the shack to walk the length of the ship, not exactly sure what he was supposed to be looking for. The bow was inscribed with strange markings and pointed to the dry dock at the end of the pier, to the ocean a hundred miles west. In the dry dock was the revelation of a whole ship in the air, its hull, keel, and propellers, torches dripping sparks from the scaffolding, the shouts of workers and the clank of the crane and the amplified voice of its operator. You couldn't see the welders but one of them was a woman.

Out here they called second shift swing. The stange markings said *Sofia*.

The lagoon was on the other side of the pier and in it Jelonnek saw the great blue heron, standing as still as a tree near the piling. The thin stalks of its legs, the S of its neck, its long pointed bill. Sometimes it would bend suddenly and take something out of the water, but usually it remained motionless, and when Jelonnek came back hours later it was exactly as he'd left it, keeping a different vigil in a dark all its own. It frightened easily; a movement a hundred feet away would send it flying off, its wings prehistorically wide, beating slowly and impossibly like some futile early flying contraption. Once Jelonnek saw two birds no bigger than sparrows chasing it over the Turkish ship, the heron making an awful cowardly braying, its pursuers with black feathers and slashes of red above their wings as if in the uniform of a totalitarian regime.

Sometimes he sopped bread in his beans, and if there was any left he'd feed the ducks. When you fed the ducks the whole population of the lagoon would come at you in a wedge, and it seemed they would keep coming even after you ran out of bread. The males had a white band around their necks and all the color. Sometimes people tried to fish in the lagoon and Jelonnek told them they couldn't, entered it into the log in his yellow shack. In his green folder in the yellow shack he tried to find an ending, but every time he found one another door would open. Someone made bird sounds over the radio. They couldn't figure out who it was but Jelonnek thought he knew.

The Turks would give him a rash from the other end of the gangway. They made strange gestures at him, as incomprehensible as their language, and found in this activity a savage entertainment that was only enhanced by repetition. Jelonnek had made the mistake of responding only once, but they seemed to have him where they wanted him then and never let him forget it.

You teach me English with you. Teach you something back. Sometimes things hit the shack.

"They are zero," the second mate said, pointing to his head. He'd come down the gangway to check whatever it was he checked. Jelonnek asked him why the crew were under quarantine, if they were sick, and the second mate nodded, "Yes sick, so sick," because he hated them as he hated the sea, though Jelonnek wasn't sure which hatred depended on which. The second mate looked to be in his early twenties. He was from Ankara, where his father was a doctor, and he'd become a sailor to avoid becoming his father. *Ankara.* He said it like the only word for that which cannot be reclaimed.

Jelonnek told him where he was from, and it only sounded like where he was from.

"Then you are alone, and we are alone," the second mate said. He gestured at the ship. "You could come on to drink. We drink to your home, to my. To go home, each one, we have a drink." Jelonnek told him he couldn't leave his post. He liked the second mate but suppose the crew were laying for him. Suppose they beat him senseless and he woke in the middle of some ocean at their mercy, pressed into who knew what kind of service. Or maybe the second mate would slip something in his drink.

Maybe he had other things on his mind.

Jelonnek told him he could lose his job.

In the lagoon he saw a beaver swim by with a catfish in its mouth. The catfish had a white belly and was as long as the beaver, and the lagoon was full of carp as long as your arm. Navy ships came in for repairs, all the same gray with or without guns, and their crews would leave in the evening and come back at night drunk and stumbling and sometimes Jelonnek would run into them on the way to his car.

At night he'd see the big paddle-wheel boat out on the river beyond the berths, all lit up with its cargo of tourists, hear the megaphone voice of the captain telling the sightseers what it was they were seeing.

You couldn't see the mountain from the shipyard. Sleeping at your post meant immediate termination.

You heard pigeons over the open channel, seagulls. They hadn't found out who it was, but Jelonnek suspected one of the rovers, the one who liked to talk about the birds, who'd told him what the great blue heron was and how its bill turned yellow and its plumes grew long in the mating season, who once stole one of the duck eggs, bit a hole in the end and sucked the yolk out. Who had a scar on his cheek where, he said, a hen had objected to this thievery. The rovers didn't have a shack or a post but made rounds for eight hours, and each rover walked twelve miles a night. Jelonnek liked the rover who liked birds but he wouldn't have traded places with him, nor any of them, nor with the other guards at the other shacks and posts, where crew and labor came and went and you had to check ID's and lunch pails and toolboxes, because most of them were drug addicts or ex-cons and not to be trusted and that's why you were there in the first place.

Tonight we come, the Turks yelled. *America is fuck tonight.* They played rap music in their own language.

An elderly woman wearing the same uniform as Jelonnek brought her knitting to the shack every midnight, wincing at the smell, and Jelonnek walked the better part of a mile back to where his car sat hidden, leaking oil. On the way he'd pass the aircraft carrier berthed at the south pier. Word was they were going to turn it into a shopping mall. Behind the fence on the opposite side were the sheds, huge, corrugated, big enough to house the ships you'd see in dry dock with room to close the doors. Jelonnek didn't know what they kept in there and if you asked someone the answer was always: "Everything."

Two nights before the Turks were scheduled to leave, the dispatcher at the gate radioed Jelonnek and told him his relief had called off tonight. They wanted to know if he would work a double. Jelonnek said 10-4 and a fog came in off the river. It filled the dry dock and rolled up the pier, and when Jelonnek looked at the Turkish ship it was already fading. He wrote in the log that a fog had come in. He looked out the window and the ship was gone and most of the gangway. He looked at his other pages in the green folder, at the words he'd typed on them and the words he'd scribbled over those words. His eyelids were heavy. There was nothing out the window now but a shifting paleness filled with sound; everything was close but nothing was there. He nodded off. Snapped out of it. He dozed off again and didn't wake up till he heard the field supervisor knocking on the window.

The roommate was a short-order cook. Jelonnek found out what else he was by accident, but looking back how was he to know? You couldn't tell by his voice. They lived in a complex of green clapboard buildings in a little valley below the highway. The valley was filled with evergreens and you could step over the stream that ran through the middle of it. In the stream there were crayfish under the rocks. As was often the case on that side of town, the buildings didn't really seem to belong there, and the driveway up out of the complex was so steep and long Jelonnek's car would barely make it in first gear. The bus stop was a mile away.

They shared a two-bedroom apartment, though it didn't feel like sharing. When Jelonnek worked he worked all kinds of hours and weekends, and his roommate often went out so sometimes they'd see each other for just hours at a time, or not at all for a day or two, and this was just as well since there were things Jelonnek should have been told when he'd responded to the ad. Looking back he realized there'd been certain signs, strange questions he'd been asked from which he was apparently expected to infer the unspoken, but the roommate did not act or sound like one of them, and he'd been very understanding about Jelonnek's situation and when you have been sleeping in your car certain things are bound to be overlooked. The plant manager sent him home early for not having steel-toed boots; he'd walked in on them in the living room. Afterward the roommate was more discreet about guests, and when he gave parties Jelonnek, though invited, would go to a movie or lock his door, and slept with earplugs now because their bedrooms shared a wall. He'd wondered what else might pass through it. He knew they didn't all automatically have it, and the roommate looked healthy enough, was in fact tall and tanned and in better shape than Jelonnek, and though he was older he looked younger, but they said you could have it for years and not know it. He was sure you couldn't catch it just being in the same room with somebody, but didn't they say the germ could mutate? He didn't know much about the tenant he'd replaced, but he was sure he slept in the same room and figured he was probably one too. If he'd died of it, he could have left it behind in some dormant form, in the walls, the mattress, the floor. Jelonnek scrubbed every square inch with a sponge and Lysol, wearing a mask, and called the hotline he'd seen on a billboard. They told him of course you couldn't take chances, but they also told him the ways in which they were certain you couldn't catch it and Jelonnek hung up somewhat relieved, especially about the toilet (though he continued to take precautions), and about the food because his roommate was really a terrific cook and often made more than he needed and invited Jelonnek to help himself, though Jelonnek still bought his own groceries as agreed, and paid half the electric and half the cable.

They had ESPN. Number Nineteen was talking to Dallas.

But what if he cut his finger?

The kids in the complex were out of school for the summer, and their parents seemed to have taken a separate vacation. The kids liked playing by the creek hunting for crayfish and driving their Big Wheels, and when they drove their Big Wheels the plastic tire in front sounded like it was cracking the asphalt. You started hearing that sound in the morning, and it didn't stop till dark. One of the boys liked to hit the side of the building with a stick. You had to go out and tell him to stop, and later the skinny guy who lived two units away might come knocking on your door, wearing a muscle shirt, asking you if you had a problem. Twice he had been taken away in handcuffs by the police, shouting things over his shoulder to a woman you otherwise never saw, whose belly was a little bigger the second time around. A day or two later he was ferried home on the handlebars of a bike driven by a man who could have been his twin. Jelonnek wondered why the manager never threw them out. She was a big-boned, athletic blonde girl who drove a jeep with a bumper sticker that commanded: QUESTION AUTHORITY. A lot of people out here displayed that bumper sticker, or the one that said KILL YOUR TELEVISION, and others concerned with the preservation of salmon and old growth and the spotted owl, and they drove new cars and had high cheekbones and car phones and when they spoke they enunciated with a clarity that was almost painful. All the women were Nordic blondes and athletic-looking like the manager, and Jelonnek knew they wouldn't give you the time of day or night because out here people literally wouldn't give it to you: once he'd stood in line at Safeway thinking he might be late for an assignment. He hadn't seen a clock (there seemed to be a scarcity of those in town) and had asked the man ahead of him if he had the time, and the man had started to straighten his arm as if to expose his watch, then seemed to have a second thought and dropped his arm and said, "Who does?" and Jelonnek was sure he'd seen a silver band under his sleeve.

Two-fifty a month. Rent was due on the fifth. After midnight the mail slot at the office was padlocked.

There was a sauna and a pool. The pool was filled with splashing and screaming during the day, and sometimes there were mixers with free hotdogs and beer for a dollar. Jelonnek went to one once, and left after two beers. Later he realized he should have said something about a girlfriend back East, that people must have made certain assumptions, but the roommate was handsome in a rugged way and a terrific cook and did not have a sibilant voice or use certain gestures—unless he was giving a party and his friends were over, and even then Jelonnek would wonder which behavior was the act, and for whom—and even though he might have said something he didn't feel up to the trouble of correcting this impression, and so he would wait at night till everyone left and the water was flat and still, and he would float on his back in the warm glow under stars rimmed by the jagged crowns of trees, listen to the distant coming and going of Interstate 5, and then it didn't matter what he was or was thought to be, as long as he wasn't sleeping in his car and got to see the bright dissolving streak of a meteor before the pool closed, hear the bats sending signals overhead, finding their way.

He woke up behind the wheel. They were standing outside the window, both of them. He couldn't see them but he knew who it was. Tried to drive away but somehow couldn't manage the ignition. He had to wake up again and he was in the pool at night, treading water.

You didn't have to take lunch if you didn't want to, but every break he went out and knelt in front of his car. He saw a drop. He counted till he saw another one. How many to a quart? he wondered. He tried to judge the size of the puddle. He slid a fresh piece of cardboard under the oil pan.

Back at the table was the half-fold, the two inserts, the reply coupon, the keychain. 9x12 manila. Piecework. The more you stuffed, the more you made. Seven-thirty in the morning to four in the afternoon. Sixty drops an hour. Back at the table were the punk rockers, the lady who listened to self-improvement tapes on her Walkman, the guy with the accent and the green rubber gloves.

It is pronounced Spo-*can*. The guy who ran the power shears met his wife there. He said she wasn't good-looking but she could cook and had once been a professional bowler. Power shears, press brake, slip rollers, he knew his way around the shop. Jelonnek handled stock for him. 16-gauge, galvanized. Electric eyes kept the die from coming down on your hands when they were on the work bed, but there were ways, the guy who ran the power shears told Jelonnek. Thirty-five-ton horror stories.

"It don't stop for anyone," the guy who ran the power shears said.

They'd made control panels for the space shuttle. Those were precision days, but now…look who was running the drillpress. His hands made Jelonnek think of his father. He said they needed help in shipping, someone to band skids, drive the forklift. Jelonnek said he wasn't looking for anything permanent right now and the guy who ran the power shears was quiet for a while. When he'd warmed up again he pointed out the drillpress operator and asked Jelonnek if he could tell what she was.

"What do you mean?" Jelonnek said.

The guy who ran the power shears shook his head. Nothing shook his head like a mixed marriage. Or uninsured drivers. There was this show on cable, he said.

"Me too," Jelonnek said. He hadn't paid on his premium since he'd gotten here, but he sure liked watching people who knew their way around the shop. There is even a right way to use a broom.

The day he got the letter about his Personal Retirement Fund, Jelonnek signed the form and put it in the return envelope. (Retirement, like he was sixty-five.) The return envelope was addressed to the state capitol back East. Ninety days, he knew, but not whether that meant ninety days from the date of termination, or after they received the form. They would let him know.

The mailboxes were on top of the hill next to the manager's office and the three-bedroom apartments. As he climbed the hill things came to him. At the top of the hill you could see the mountain. Jelonnek caught his breath, then went back down the hill to the apartment without mailing the letter. He tore open the envelope, changed his address on the form. He drove to the post office and rented a post office box. Driving back he felt better, but still things came. It came to him to report another change of address to the agency, start picking up his checks at the office. He'd say he was living in a motel again, the one with the mountain in the bathroom window, where they'd stayed before they became he. Now he felt a lot better, though it seemed something always found its way to him.

He hadn't done floorwork for a long time, but apparently it was a skill he couldn't shake. The hospital was quiet at night. There was no boss to speak of once they left the maintenance office, and the three of them took turns riding the scrubber, damp-mopping, waxing and sealing. The illegals came to work in a loud red Volkswagen with the engine sticking out the back. They called it *tortuga*, not Beetle. Once a week they waxed Central Supply, and you had to be careful of the green tanks. The ones filled with nitrous oxide made you feel drunk, but it wore off fast and there was only a brief headache. The others contained something like helium, and the illegals would take a hit from the silver nozzle and it was like Donald Duck telling you to fuck your mother in Spanish.

Once a week they would wax the pathology lab on the eighth floor. The view was something, inside and out. From the windows you could see the Cascades to the east, and on the shelves were jars of organs, fetuses, tissue, God knew. There was a white bucket in the back of the room. The illegals tried to get Jelonnek to crack off the lid and look inside, but he wouldn't.

They played Frisbee with the buffer pads, and someone decided they needed supervision. One of the illegals was let go and they got a lead man in his place, a kid whose father knew the Chief Administrator. There was no more taking turns. The kid rode the scrubber like an officer driving a jeep, and he was bossy but no leader. He had a degree and a handheld video game. Jelonnek wasn't sure what his degree was in because the kid had designed his own major, and told you so as if life were a matter of choosing the right template. He listened to reggae and hardcore and called everyone G, wore baggy clothes and a baseball cap turned around on his head. He wanted to go into the music business. Then he wanted to open a club, or produce movies. His father was in carpeting, went on fishing trips to Alaska with the Chief Administrator. He spent more time at the green tanks than anyone.

"My way or the highway", he said, and slouched on the scrubber like it was a recreational vehicle. "Your way is the doorway." He made circles in the middle of the hallway.

235

In the end Jelonnek took him up on it. Later he wasn't sure exactly how it had happened. He couldn't remember exactly what it was the kid had wanted him to do, only that he'd wanted him to go somewhere and get something from there, and Jelonnek had started walking in the opposite direction.

"Going down the road?" the kid whose father knew the Chief Administrator said, but Jelonnek really wasn't sure where he was going. The kid bent down over a green tank.

"Be that way," he said, helium-voiced, and Jelonnek wondered where he'd heard that before. The illegal waved in Spanish.

He found himself in the pathology lab on the eighth floor. The door was open and a fan was on, but the floor had dried. The white bucket in the back of the room. The mountains were invisible in the dark, and in the bucket was half of a man's head, split down the middle. The cross section of the brain like a cauliflower, his mouth wrinkled and embittered.

"It wasn't anybody's fault," the woman at the agency said. "It was probably just a misunderstanding."

Jelonnek spoke into the phone: what else did she have?

"Ever done quality control?" She gave him a job number and told him who to ask for. He went to an eyeglass factory and inspected frames. If you found a bubble you scoured it off with sandpaper and acetone. The girl next to him drank something with ginseng in it, said it gives you energy when you move. It tasted like root beer to Jelonnek. She tried on all the frames that came down the line. There were no lenses in them.

She said she was going to a protest over the weekend. She was going to chain herself to a tree.

He asked her questions. She kept saying, "What?"

Twelve-hour shifts, sixteen days running. He stood at a urinal, nodding off. One of the engineers came in and washed his hands and stood next to him. The engineer finished first and washed his hands again. On his way out he said, "Don't they have bathrooms in Membrane?"

Jelonnek pushed through the door with wet hands and walked through the Doghouse to Membrane. He put on his goggles and gloves. The accummulator was floating, they were changing product. They'd started him on the coater but the smell had made him sick so they'd put him in mixing with a big Indian named Junior. Junior wore headphones and a sideline cap with a Redskins logo. He had a thick braided cable of hair that hung down most of his back when he took the cap off, and a .22 shoved down the front of his pants; sometimes in Membrane you saw rats eating the compound.

The compound came in hundred-pound sacks. It was white like flour when you dumped it in the hopper, but when it got to the coater at three hundred degrees it was thick and black like tar. If it got on the floor it hardened and shone like black glass and you took a scraper, heated it red-hot with a torch and chipped it off.

Jelonnek asked what was in it.

Junior said, "Horseshit and hay."

His fingers cramped from pinching the ends of the bags. Cold water helped. The air was always filled with a white mist and you'd have to clean off your goggles. If you didn't clean them right they filmed over and everyone in the room was transfixed with spires of light.

"Two guys walk in a bar," Junior said.

The accummulator dropped and the horn went off. Everything stopped; there was a problem in windup. The tweaker couldn't keep up and they sent Jelonnek to help out. In windup the product came off the accummulator in rolls five feet long and heavier than the sacks in mixing. The ejector kicked them off the mandrel onto the shuttle, but the shuttle was down and they had to stack the rolls on pallets by hand. While they waited for start-up Junior napped on the forklift and the tweaker soaped the mandrel with a brush. You could tell he was a tweaker by the way his face twitched. He showed Jelonnek the buttons: cycle start, cycle stop, float, drive, continuous. E-stop.

Someone yelled, "Wind it up!" from the coater. Sometimes the rolls didn't wind evenly, formed a lip at the edge, and the tweaker tapped the edge of the roll with his hand to keep it flush. "Two guys walk into a bar," Jelonnek said and the tweaker twitched his eyes at him. His fingers got under the product and his hand began to wind up with the roll in a way that the human wrist is not meant to turn. He screamed E-stop but it happened very fast and by the time Jelonnek found the big red button he'd already heard a sound not like one stick cracking but a bundle of them. It was the only sound the tweaker made.

After they cut him out with an electric hand saw they put a new chain in the shuttle. They put Jelonnek back on the mixer and brought in a guy from the Doghouse to cover windup.

It came on after midnight on the public access channel. They tried to make it look like a regular talk show. A host sat behind a desk and he had guests who sat in an armchair next to the desk. Jelonnek could tell he was wearing a toupee, though it was darker than his father's. He also wore some kind of khaki uniform with an armband. He made a living as a TV repairman, and hadn't filed a tax return in seven years.

He introduced tonight's guest as an anthropologist. The guest wore glasses and a bow tie and said *caucasoid* and *negroid* the way, Jelonnek supposed, an anthropologist would. He had two skulls with him and he put them on the desk. He used a pair of calipers.

"Cranial capacity," he said.

The host said they were taking a break. When they returned, he said, they would talk about Ruby Ridge, and Jelonnek wasn't sure if that was a person or a place. Instead of a commercial, they showed some footage that looked like it had been shot from a helicopter. Jelonnek had already seen it. He'd already seen the guy dragged out of his truck at the intersection, the burning cars and broken glass and bodies, the two men rolling a floor-model TV on a skateboard. The difference now was that the commentary of reporters and anchors had been replaced by singing, a male chorus performing some kind of anthem, something to march to. It sounded German.

Jelonnek's roommate was in his room with someone, at one end of the transaction or the other, but he'd left beer in the fridge. Jelonnek promised himself he'd replace it; you couldn't catch it from drinking their beer. He watched a skinhead wedding. Civil rights demonstrators blown across a street like leaves by firehoses. Jelonnek wondered how the firemen felt, if it was like fighting just another kind of fire. The song was kind of catchy.

The host never came back. Instead they showed amateur video footage. At first it looks like a fishing or hunting trip, but the men wear armbands over their camouflage and a lot of them carry M-16's. They shoot cardboard targets shaped like people and execute drills with varying degrees of proficiency. They gut a deer you didn't see them kill. They fish, casting upstream for shad near a waterfall. You knew they were casting for shad because somebody says so, though the audio is intermittent and of poor quality.

A fetus spills out when they dress out the deer. More fishing. The guns make a muffled firecracker bang but the targets disintegrate.

At night they burn a cross. They stand in a circle around it with their right arms raised, holding beers. One of them explains

239

that this was how the clans signalled each other in the Scottish Highlands. He sounds drunk. Two guys start wrestling.

Daylight again. They form another circle and a helicopter lands in the middle. A rugged middle-aged man emerges wearing fatigues and a beret. He has served in Special Forces in Vietnam, speaks four languages, is a fifth-degree black belt, has made a fortune in real estate. He demonstrates self-defense techniques and the proper maintenance of automatic weapons. He lectures on how to resist taxation by declaring sovereign citizenship and invoking alloidial property rights. He speaks at length though the quality of the audio sometimes renders him unintelligible.

They will obey the law unless it opposes God or common sense. He is not a racist—his granddaughter is half-Chinese for heaven's sake.

A narrator we haven't heard before says the ex-Green Beret has been named Aryan of the Year.

He talks about fishing and hunting and history. Eat what you kill, he says, but personally he always throws them back. He ties his own flies. He names the plants and shows them which ones you can eat and how to prepare them. He knows and loves nature, you can tell, and Jelonnek wished he knew how to know it and love it half as well.

He looks around and says, "This country is the palm of God's hand."

"The palm of God's hand," Jelonnek said.

A triumphant burst of steam

Silence is the only answer

With a triumphent burst of steam

```
The crossbow is gone

SURVIVOR: Who's there?

Silence is no answer.

SURVIVOR(louder) Where are you?

The crossbow is gone. Again the WOMAN S
LAUGHTER one more time. SERIES OF SHOTS the
empty chambers the passages of the instalat
ion made of rock and metal. tube#10
```

"We're sure it wasn't your fault," the woman at the agency said. They were as forgiving as an impoverished church. "You'll ask for Dan," she said and Jelonnek covered a football field with sheets of plywood, wearing jersey gloves. He forgot why. Scraped birdshit off stadium seats with a bucket, sponge, and putty knife. Then he asked for Steve, who controlled a stutter by starting every sentence with a drawn-out "ah" like a doctor was looking down his throat, who put Jelonnek in a room where they replaced the air every six seconds, where everyone was dressed in hooded white bunny suits and walked through an air shower and wore face masks like minimum-wage surgeons. Loaded microchip wafers onto a carrier with a vacuum wand, took them to the acid bath, the gas cloud, the gold evaporator. Looked through German microscopes and Japanese X-ray scanners. A micron is a hundredth as wide as a human hair. The plant was surrounded by farm country, and they call it a campus.

"They didn't say why," the woman on the phone said. The dark-skinned girl in the gowning room. He'd only asked her name, but the way she'd stormed off.

"It's slow," the woman at the agency said, and Jelonnek was almost out of gas money. He was about to ask his roommate for a little time, a little slack, when the phone rang and she sent him to a place where they called bottle caps tamper-evident closures.

"I usually get those by the gross," the guy who did stand-up on weekends said. He said it to everyone but Jelonnek could barely hear him. The mold clamp opened and dumped bottle caps onto a belt that took them to the collection hopper. They sorted out the bad ones. You could barely hear your own voice but everyone was talking. There was always a line and always a belt, and everyone was always talking, about coupons and TV shows and exes, and there was one guy who kept insisting his late brother was a dead ringer for Tom Cruise. He would show a picture to anyone who stood still long enough for it.

At the end of the night he asked Jelonnek for a ride downtown.

In the car he chewed gum and took out the picture. Jelonnek conceded the resemblance but he was a coarse, asymmetrical version, a discarded prototype. Someone who might make a career out of almost looking like someone.

He'd set himself on fire and jumped off a bridge.

"Was something on his mind?" Jelonnek asked.

"He was in training," the guy said. "He was going to be a stunt man."

It was a local bridge. "Why didn't he go to Hollywood?"

"He was a pioneer." He shoved another stick of gum into his smile. Where did it all go? "He figured you didn't just have to do movies, there's grand openings, sporting events, expos. Fly a hang glider into a stadium at halftime, you know? You know Evel Knievel had his own comic book?"

It wasn't really a question.

He'd landed on the boat that was supposed to pick him up. Jelonnek didn't ask who was at the rudder, he told him what was in the green folder instead.

"Oh, I got a script," the brother said. More of a treatment, really, but that was for Tom's eyes only. Tom was coming to town this fall to shoot on location. The plan was to get a job as an extra on the set, then get in Tom's face with the picture as soon as he shows up. Pitch him the idea while he is momentarily stunned by the sight of his virtual twin. It was a biopic about the would-be stunt man with Tom, naturally, up for the lead. The surviving brother, the guy Jelonnek would some day tell his grandchildren he had dropped off at the Jack London Hotel, would play himself.

"Bet your family's proud," Jelonnek said.

His passenger didn't answer. Jelonnek glanced sideways and he was looking at the road, his smile mostly gone, chewing slow. He didn't speak again till they got downtown and he opened the door.

"Mom's not up to much," he said softly. "I'm all there is."

S he began every other sentence with the words "My professor." She believed that all human endeavor, even art, presupposed law and economics. She had long yellow hair that she sometimes wore in braids, and she'd graduated from high school when she was fifteen. She told Jelonnek about elasticity of demand. She had no breasts to speak of.

The ex-organizer, on the other hand, was beyond sex. His pocket always ran low. He moved in a jerky uncentered way like a marionette, and he looked twenty years past the age he claimed. Won bets showing his ID to prove it. He ate chocolate bars and potato chips all day, but he looked like you could lift him with one hand.

She needed a ride home.

When a pocket dropped the collator shut off. The operator wanted to make books and let them know it. A parts catalog. The ex-organizer fell behind for good. Jelonnek didn't need them cramming any more hours into his day. Fake it, he said, and he would take up the slack.

"What do you think I've been doing?" the ex-organizer said. Slack was all he had left. He was gone for days, came back minus a kidney that weighed twelve pounds. Coughed less when he smoked. He looked clean but he smelled like garbage all the time, smelled like he was dying. He leaned on you when he told you about his dog and Jelonnek started to itch. He thought the ex-organizer had given him fleas, then found out it was scabies. The Cambodians were running a pool on how long he would live. Jelonnek gave him six months but knew he wouldn't be around to collect.

He asked her if she was a commie. She laughed and said there was no such thing as surplus value. The ex-organizer gave him literature. Jelonnek gave it to the guy who did standup on weekends, who gave it to the libertarian, who gave it to the guy who'd come back from a smokery in Juneau, who gave it to his wife, a squat, pretty-faced Eskimo who never spoke and worked only at her husband's side.

Job openings were posted in the shipping office. Jelonnek heard the plant manager on the phone. "Don't send any more you-know-whos," he told the woman at the agency.

A box held thirty books: four stacks of five the short way, two the long way. Their hands touched sometimes while they packed. She invited him to her twentieth birthday party. "You'll get to see me drunk," she said. It always surprised him when she laughed. She had no chest to speak of, but the way the other guys looked at him.

She was so pale.

The libertarian showed up in Continental bluecoat; he was wearing it to court to fight a traffic ticket. They relegated the ex-organizer to the baling room, where you slowly drowned in paper dust. He kept letting it back up; the trimmer jammed, the binder would stop. Too much downtime, they announced, and took one of their breaks away—there was only so much busywork. Everything started running faster but the clock.

"Give us our break," the comedian yelled. "State law says—" The machine swallowed his words. He wasn't trying to be funny, but he only sounded defeated and his work was shoddy to begin with. Jelonnek took up his slack too, and now he was feeding three pockets and keeping an eye on them while he moved skids with the hand jack. They never dropped, not one. You had to earn things.

They offered him the job but he said he wasn't looking for anything permanent.

At lunch she sat near him but not next to him with a book called *Leviathan* on her lap, her yellow hair dipping in the gutter. Notes. A sketch pad and a charcoal stick. She showed him drawings of machines and faces, of workers waiting, eight people doing one thing. She flipped pages and said her goal was to purge them of all sentimentality. She looked pretty good at it to Jelonnek, but what did he know about art?

Her hair came undone stacking off the trimmer. It didn't touch Jelonnek's arm, but he thought he felt it crackle. The plant manager came over and grabbed a handful, held it near the blade and said look what could happen. She piled it on top of her head and fastened it there. Jelonnek looked at a young woman gathering her hair behind her head, arms bowed out, pin in her teeth, and might have wondered in his way if this too were a sentimentality she would expunge.

She showed him a drawing of a horse. She had four of them. Her father had taken the car and half the house, left her the horses and his wife. They rode the bus to the stables. She showed Jelonnek a bruise where one of them had bitten her. She'd punched it in the face. She wouldn't hesitate to use her crop if one of them got sentimental about jumping a rail, and the way she talked about it bubbled in your blood.

She spent her breaks on the phone and came back with wet eyes, unable to speak. She stood near, inviting consolation and maybe what it might lead to, but Jelonnek kept his hands in his pockets.

"Your mother?" he said.

He got a notice in the mail. He wasn't sure if the date on the notice was when they would mail it or when he was supposed to receive it, but he went back to the post office on that day anyway. He parked a block from the building and walked towards it like maybe he was on his way somewhere else. He didn't see any police cars but they would probably be unmarked. But of course he didn't really think they'd be there.

He went through the front doors, the lobby, past the line where people were being waited on. Around the corner was the long hall with all the boxes lining the walls like drawers in a morgue. A man and a woman were talking. Jelonnek pretended to look at stamps in a display case till they left. The hall seemed longer with them gone. There were three sizes of boxes, and the ones just big enough to hold letters were near the end. Jelonnek had trouble getting the key into his. The box was empty. The box was some kind of trap and he'd fallen into it. He would have gone to the restroom then, looked for another window, but the post office had no public facilities. He looked at the stamp display again, Kittyhawk and George Washington Carver. He heard the clock, stopped breathing and headed for the door. A man walked in. Jelonnek felt light in the head and knees as the man walked toward him, but when he was outside heading for his car he looked back only once. Sitting behind the wheel he had to wait for his hands to stop shaking.

The next day he drove past first and there was a police car out front. He kept going but maybe it was just coincidence.

She'd cut all her hair off. On the way to the car at night she apologized for the other day. "The soap opera," she said, and grabbed the door handle before he could; she didn't believe in chivalry either. Jelonnek shrugged, he was just driving her home so she didn't get her bones jumped. They pulled up at a modest townhouse in an old neighborhood now favored by young professionals. A bum was sleeping on the lawn with his hand in his pants. Jelonnek walked her to her door. She asked him if he wanted to see her English riding trophy. Her best drawings were inside.

"So's she," he said.

Horses are prey animals, she'd told him. They don't move in straight lines. In the wild it is the mare who leads the herd to water.

"I'm tired," he said. She was so pale. If you looked closely there were little blonde hairs on her face.

They don't learn from pressure, they learn from release.

The next day summer was over. She was leaving in a couple of ways: she was quitting at the end of the week, then she was taking the semester off to travel. She was thinking maybe Alaska, sign on a floating processor as a deckhand, a roe sorter. Or sell her horses for a handful of plane tickets and a passport, leave him to stitch coupon books for Safeway.

Or she could trade them for a pair of tits, he told her.

"How about we get you a pair?" she said.

He advised her to start riding one of her ponies to the job. He worked through his break, took lunch alone. She walked past and tore a drawing out of her pad, dropped it half-crumpled in his lap. He threw it away without looking at it. At night he saw what was left of her yellow hair in the parking lot and kept going. It wasn't anybody's fault.

On his last assignment it took all of them to drag it out. Unfolding it released an ancient smell. Insects. It was caked with mud and pale stains that could have been another kind of life. They kept unfolding it away from each other. No one remembered how big it was supposed to be. You could hear water moving inside. The edge was somewhere under there, its length or width. Feel for the grommets, they were told.

It had no color.

There would be additional seating once the field was covered. Squeaky folding chairs, rusty and dry to touch, thirty dollars to sit in and watch a country singer. If you worked that night you could watch the show for free. They had to separate the singles from the doubles, the one-arms from the two-arms. The supervisors conferred. One of them unfolded a sheet on his clipboard.

It wouldn't stop, it sounded like something was stirring beneath it. Under the stadium lights it was the terrain of a primordial planet. The water formed pools.

The supervisor studied the master plan.

When Jelonnek opened his box there was a slip of paper inside. It said he had a certified letter. It said he would have to sign for it at the counter. 'That was how they were doing it.

He walked back up the long hall, turned the corner and got in line. There was a separate line for express mail and no one was in it. The clerk looked at him over the tops of her glasses. Jelonnek gave her the notice. He started to explain but she turned and went somewhere. He tried not to look at the people in the other line but he couldn't help it. No one seemed interested in him; maybe the clerk had gone to get someone who was. Of course she hadn't but maybe that's what was taking so long.

She was gone a while. She came back holding a brown envelope with a signature card attached. She would need to see some identification; she pronounced every syllable.

Jelonnek showed her his driver's license.

She frowned. "Spelling's different."

"Different?" he said.

She showed him from a distance, hanging onto the envelope with both hands. There were two l's.

"Now what?"

"We'll have to see." She was that kind of government worker who assumes all the authority of her employer. "Let me see."

She left again with the envelope and his license. Jelonnek looked at the other line, then the clock: the post office closed in less than fifteen minutes. He could leave, come back tomorrow. Maybe a different clerk would let it ride. She came back with the notice he'd found in his box. He signed his name and printed it. The pen was chained to the counter. The clerk returned his license, then held the envelope down on the counter and Jelonnek signed where she told him to. She tore off the card where it was perforated and gave the envelope to Jelonnek. There was a window in it and he saw his name on a green card. It looked like a computer had printed it, and there were little rectangular holes punched in the card. It was a check. You couldn't see the amount under the brown paper, but Jelonnek knew what it was.

A voice from a loudspeaker said the post office was closing in ten minutes. The envelope didn't feel like anything, but Jelonnek felt different holding it. Like he should give something in return. He felt the clerk standing there like she was waiting for him to look at her.

"Does anyone need stamps only?" she said loudly.

He fed another page to the fire. The door was locked. His roommate knocked. Come on out and have a beer, his voice said. They were cooking out.

"You live here too," he said.

Jelonnek took another page out of the green folder. The folder was battered and wrinkled and had white cracks in places. He could hear music, voices, the incessant beat. The page blackened and ignited, curled up into a little black flower that glowed at the edges. A little black fist.

He knew the guest of honor wasn't dancing—he could barely stand. The words darkened and dissolved. Black flurries drifted up out of the trash can. The guest of honor had a collapsed face, and when he spoke his tongue looked furry. Jelonnek had put the can by the window, atop the dresser, but the smoke made his eyes tear and he fanned it with the green folder. He hated the beat but he could have used a beer. He wondered if men were kissing. Tasting other men's skin. He wondered if later he'd hear them in his roommate's room, on the other side of the wall to which he'd taped a poster of Number Nineteen.

The folder was almost empty now. He lived there too. He fed the fire and his eyes burned. Something was smoldering on the floor. He stamped it out and there was a black spot on the carpet. A flaming corner of paper drifted out of the can and landed on his pillow. Jelonnek batted it with his hands. He coughed, wished he'd thought to buy some beer.

You could just hear the smoke alarm over the music. His roommate was pounding at the door, yelling that he smelled smoke, and if everything was okay.

Littlebit's cousin was opening for a singer from San Francisco. Except for movies, it was the first time Jelonnek had gone out since he'd been here. This time the club was downtown. It was bigger than the other one and inside had brick walls and fake Greek pillars. Admission was twelve dollars but they served real drinks. Jelonnek arrived in the aftermath and sat at the bar while the band broke down. The bartender was still shaking his head. Littlebit's cousin thanked everyone for being there.

"For every sound you made or didn't make on behalf of every sound we made or didn't make." He said the headliners would be on shortly and the applause was scattered and wary, like they weren't quite sure they were out of danger.

"I was pouring drinks on the house just to keep em from walking out," the bartender said.

"Like hell you were," the guy on the next stool said.

"Practically. There weren't any notes in it."

"I heard Cecil in it," the guy on the next stool said. He sounded a little drunk. "You like Cecil?"

Jelonnek ordered a beer. The tables were filling. He drank another one and went to the men's room. When he came out the band were gathered loosely at one end of the bar. He weaved through the thickening crowd and the pillars and sat down next to

Littlebit's cousin. They were talking. It was like listening to people who knew a lot about sports or cars or politics, except the subject was Bartok and West Africa, ragas and pitch intervals, loosening up the vibe and flying on it while staying conceptually strong. Other musicians they called by first name. Jelonnek waited for the bartender. He kept glancing their way, and finally Littlebit's cousin glanced back and Jelonnek said, "I like your sound."

He was drinking something clear with ice. "I thought I heard someone clapping," he said. He tilted his head toward the band. "I guess that makes five of us."

"At least he didn't call it music," one of them said.

"Is it jazz?" Jelonnek said.

Littlebit's cousin had a beard and you couldn't tell if he was smiling. "I like this question," he said. "What's jazz again?"

"You hate jazz," somebody in the band said helpfully.

Jelonnek wasn't sure if he should apologize.

"I think we're kidding," Littlebit's cousin said. "If folks don't know what to call it, we must be doing something right. Call it music to wash dishes by," he said, "call it what you hear. The sound of democracy." One of them laughed. "Do you play?"

Jelonnek was flattered. "I'm not a musician."

"Neither are they." Littlebit's cousin tilted his head toward the band again. "But do you play?"

"I just listen," Jelonnek said.

"What to?"

He shrugged. "Rock-and-roll?"

"I'm all for it." Littlebit's cousin nodded. "Only women should sing rock-and-roll," he said. "Preferably in German, or Japanese." He mentioned some names Jelonnek didn't know, and so wasn't sure if they'd moved on to another subject. The bartender came. Jelonnek ordered a shot and a beer and started a tab. He asked Littlebit's cousin what he was drinking.

"Water," Littlebit's cousin said; he had to get up for work in the morning. Jelonnek asked him what he did.

"I try to play music," he said. "I drink water and I don't eat meat. In the morning I go sit in a cubicle—something to do with the insurance business."

Jelonnek asked him if he had a cousin.

Littlebit's cousin stared at him. "Littlewho?"

Jelonnek repeated it and Littlebit's cousin repeated it back and said, "I don't know anybody by that name."

It was the only name Jelonnek had. "You have a cousin here though, right?" he said. "I think I know her."

"You think you know somebody," Littlebit's cousin said. "That's good for you. I got all kinds of family I don't know. You probably do too."

"Maybe she said something about me."

Littlebit's cousin drank his water. "Maybe you should say something about you," he said.

"Who the hell are you?" he said.

Jelonnek swallowed some beer and started with the night of his brother's wedding. He omitted certain particulars—he'd sort of rehearsed. He ended at the club where they didn't serve alcohol. He couldn't remember the name of the club but he remembered which side of the river it was on. The trio, the candles.

He remembered what night it was.

"This is an interesting story." Littlebit's cousin spoke slowly. "You sure you didn't leave anything out?"

"I've come into some money," Jelonnek said.

"You think somebody wants your money?"

"Sometimes people can use a little help."

Now you could tell he was smiling through his beard. "You're gonna help somebody," Littlebit's cousin said. "You been hiding in the can all this time? Or you just swim from toilet to toilet?"

The crowd was bigger and louder now and Jelonnek had to raise his voice. "Do you know where she is?" he said. "Is she staying with you?"

Littlebit's cousin asked him if he ate meat. Jelonnek looked at him.

"It's hard to talk to people who eat meat," Littlebit's cousin said. "They're not who they should be. You know you don't really digest it, it just rots in your stomach. I haven't had any in twelve years. I drink water."

"I adjust claims for a living," he said, "but a living ain't a life, is it?"

Jelonnek asked him what he meant.

"Just more noise." He raised his glass. "If you have to ask."

"Can I give you my number?" Jelonnek said. "If you see her?" He reached for the slip of paper in his pocket.

"What do you all think?" Littlebit's cousin said, but he'd turned and was facing the drums, saxophone, and guitar. "Should we add keyboards?"

"You hate keyboards," the guitar said.

"But should we add them?"

They started talking again, and Littlebit's cousin kept his back to him. Now you couldn't tell if they were talking music or the American League playoffs. The club kept filling up. Jelonnek saw an empty stool at the other end of the bar. He finished his drink and left the slip of paper next to the glass of water. The stool was still empty, and he got up and took it. When he looked back there were no seats left.

"Find one you like yet?" the bartender said. Jelonnek nodded and ordered. It was kind of a relief, really, and what if she'd actually been there? He was just here to see the singer now. She came on accompanied by bass and piano, percussion but no drums. She sang a Beatles song. Jelonnek recognized the lyrics only; the melody she seemed to make up as she went along. It wasn't so bad if you didn't try to follow her. She sang something that made him think of snake charmers and men in turbans, then she sang that she'd remember April. The pianist played with his back to the room. Jelonnek watched the folds in his shirt ripple like a sea. The crowd went nuts, standing room only, and he wondered again what they knew that he didn't, or if they were just faking it, and then he was done wondering for good.

Autumn was slow and drawn-out and took place mainly in two colors: yellow, then brown. If you wanted more than that you could go to a park that had a fall color tour, a trail along which had been planted trees that turned the colors you might expect if you were from back East. A fall within the fall, and the names of the trees nailed to their trunks on little wooden placards.

Jelonnek didn't know what to call the tree in the middle of the front yard, but it had a short thick trunk and spreading upright boughs, and its leaves fell like big yellow hands. The trees near the curb were tall and slender with small purple leaves that shriveled but didn't change color and clung obstinately to their branches. The big yellow ones fell with a soft click. They turned brown and curled up in the grass, but Jelonnek liked the front lawn ankle-deep in them and had no intention of raking till the property manager called. The property manager said the owner had driven by, as he did on occasion, and thought Jelonnek should get up the leaves before the rain started.

Some of them turned brown before they fell, or didn't fall at all, but it took a long time, leaf to leaf, tree to tree, like some slow invisible conflagration, the turning of a great wheel.

The Welcome Wagon lady gave them a Welcome Wagon Packet. Her Honda leaked oil, left a rainbow in the carport.

The street turned once and ended in a sort of bulge so you could turn your car around without having to use anyone's driveway. Maybe that was why the property manager said cul-de-sac instead of dead end. The house was on the corner. You couldn't see it from the state road, though, unless you were looking for it. Jelonnek had driven by before and hadn't noticed it till they put the sign out. You wouldn't notice the house from the state road because of its color and the trees on the front lawn, because of the thicket in the side yard, and because of the tall picket fence between the side yard and the road, overgrown with vines and weeds and brambles.

Jelonnek wondered if the property manager would call about the overgrowth in the side yard, but after the leaves they only called about the grass. He knew he was supposed to cut it, but he didn't have a lawnmower and thought if he put it off till the cold weather, the grass might stop growing. Then they called and said the owner had driven by. Jelonnek saw an ad in the paper and bought a used push mower for fifteen dollars. The old woman he bought it from said she'd just sharpened the blades herself. Once he'd started Jelonnek didn't mind cutting the grass, and in a way even enjoyed it, but he didn't know what to do about the flowers. He didn't know what to call them but they were big and bright and burst from tall bushes in front of the windows to Miss D's room, and in the backyard at the edge of the gully. It seemed a terrrible responsibility had been foisted upon them, the fragrance, the brightness, the red and white and purple, and Littlebit said they should call the property manager. The girl on the phone said they knew a very reasonable landscaper. Do the best you can, she'd said, and Jelonnek found a spigot. He bought a length of hose and used it daily, even tried his hand at weeding, but this was all he knew and the flowers faded, shriveled, dropped like heads hung in mockery of his shame. Jelonnek consoled himself by thinking maybe it would have happened anyway, what with the cold weather coming, and tried to make up for it by cutting the grass once a week.

The Welcome Wagon Packet contained a newsletter, a map of the vicinity, a coupon booklet, a pack of tissues, and a raffle ticket. Raffles were held once a month at the Welcome Wagon Club socials. They were called doings in the newsletter. Jelonnek kept the tissues.

The landscapers took care of the lawn next door. They used leaf blowers and a riding mower and kept the grass a shade of green you could see in the dark. You saw the landscapers there more often than you saw the man who lived there, who pulled up every couple of weeks or so in a gleaming white New Yorker. He was a nice-looking man with white hair and a tie, and he'd get out of the car holding his jacket and a suitcase. A day or two later he would leave as he'd arrived. There was no fence between them, just a tree and a few shrubs to mark the property line, a border which words never crossed.

The Plymouth could not always be relied upon, so every weekend a van came for Littlebit and Miss D. The name of a church was hand-lettered on the side of the van. It usually came on Sundays, but sometimes it came on Saturday while Jelonnek was cutting the grass and they would be gone all weekend. Besides church there were picnics and sleepovers and

Jelonnek was invited along. He was invited to church, but didn't think he was up to all that hollering and hand-waving. Littlebit said it was Baptists who did that, but football season was just starting and that was as far as it would go.

Otherwise, people didn't seem to go to church as much out here. Some went to ashrams, though Jelonnek had yet to find out what those were.

He saw another classified ad in the newspaper and bought a used washer and dryer. He saw an ad and bought Miss D a bike. She rode it in circles across the street, in the parking lot of the business that repaired typewriters and other office machines. The building faced the state road, and the school bus stopped in front of it in the morning and in the afternoon. The school held Miss D back because of her reading. Three other kids waited at the bus stop with her. Two of them were brother and sister and lived down the street. Sometimes they came over and played—they could play on the front steps but said they weren't allowed in the house. The house had two front steps but no porch. A dishwasher, a fireplace. Littlebit did the laundry.

Once there was a dead cat in the parking lot of the business that repaired office machines.

The newspaper came in the mailbox at the foot of the driveway. The front page was in color. The mailbox was dull silver with a rounded top, had a lid in front and a rusty metal flag and was fastened atop a square wood post. Most of the mail they found in it wasn't theirs; the previous tenants hadn't left a forwarding address. Utility bills, canceled checks, credit card bills, credit card offers, final notices, a letter from the Clerk of Courts, brochures describing programs for troubled children, a summons, and, as if to stem the tide of bad news, colorful envelopes guaranteeing the recipients they had all but won great sums of money, an all-expenses-paid Carribean cruise. Jelonnek would periodically rubber-band a stack of this correspondence, scribble a note to the effect that the addressee no longer lived there, and put it back in the mailbox and swing up the flag. The bundle would disappear but was soon replaced, and after a while they just started throwing it away.

At first Miss D liked playing with the mailbox. She'd put something in it and say she was mailing it to herself. Then she'd raise the flag and take it out. Once she opened it and it was crawling with termites. They were an inch long, with pale segmented bodies and pincer-like mandibles. She ran to her room and shut the door and never went near the mailbox again. Her bedroom door was hollow; you could tell by the hole about a foot from the bottom. It looked to have been kicked. There was a chain on the door, but for some reason it was on the outside. Jelonnek was going to remove it but Littlebit said, "Well you know you never know."

The property manager took care of the door. They promised to take care of the shed but so far nothing had been done. The shed was in the corner of the backyard, at the end of the picket fence. Its walls leaned, there was a hole in the roof, the door dragged on the floor and wouldn't open more than a third of the way. Just a small window for light, and it was full of spider webs and leaves and pine cones and was so musty you could hardly breathe. Coffee cans on the floor filled with used motor oil.

Miss D wasn't allowed near the shed. You'd have thought the property manager would have given its removal some priority, what with a child on the premises and especially after Jelonnek had paid a year's rent in advance. They said they were taking bids. Behind the shed, below the backyard was a gully with a trickle of water at the bottom. A drainpipe emptied into the stream. There was supposed to be a park on the other side of the gully but all you saw were trees. Sometimes you faintly heard children yelling and dogs barking, but you never saw them. You heard the traffic on the state road, on its way to groceries or video, Chinese food or imported furniture.

There were spiders all over the property.

It was hard getting used to Number Nineteen in that strange uniform. He stood on the sideline wearing a baseball cap. They hadn't let him keep his number either, they made him wear eighteen, so Jelonnek was wearing it for him. He was wearing a baseball cap too, and starting over in a new city just like Number Nineteen was. The only difference was that Jelonnek had a beer in his hand instead of a football.

The reception was bad.

Someone was at the door.

It was still the first quarter and they'd already shown him twice. They wouldn't have done that for just some second-stringer; even wearing eighteen he was still Number Nineteen. Even wearing the sideline cap he was still a starter, a playmaker, could still call signals in the NFL. But Aikman was playing well, and Jelonnek half-seriously wished he'd said something to Littlebit before the van had taken her and Miss D away, had half-seriously asked her to put in a word for Number Nineteen. Not that he wanted to see Aikman hurt—it would be enough if he started throwing picks. But how many would it take before Nineteen got the nod, and who was at the door? Maybe one of the kids from down the street, looking for Miss D, but it didn't sound like a kid.

He didn't want to answer it. He finished the beer and got up.

Not a kid, a man. Middle-age mustache and glasses, one foot on the bottom step. Asking if Carl still lived there.

Jelonnek recognized the name from all the mail. "No," he said. Then he wished he could say more. There always seemed to be more to say, but Jelonnek rarely knew what it was.

"I would have tried calling," the man said, "but he hasn't had a phone for a while." He was tall and wore shorts and knee-socks, was holding what looked like a check. "He did some work for me a while back…Did he leave a forwarding?"

"I wish," Jelonnek said. "We keep getting his mail."

"That right?"

Jelonnek nodded. The man tilted his head and his eyes were obliterated in twin reflections.

"Well," he said then, "you gotta love this weather." He looked at the shrubs in front of Miss D's bedroom window. "What happened to the azalea?"

"What kind of work did he do?" Jelonnek said. "Carl."

The man made a face. "Same kind you need."

Jelonnek looked at him. "I'll show you," the man said, and went to a corner of the front lawn near the neighbor's driveway. Jelonnek followed. The man planted his foot, put some weight on it. The grass and soil sank and rose like a sponge. "Feel that," he said, and Jelonnek put his foot where the man's had been. It made him a little queasy.

"Now tell me you don't have em," the man looking for Carl said. Jelonnek didn't tell him anything. He was right about the weather though, though usually Jelonnek didn't give the weather much thought.

"It's a problem," the man said. "My whole yard was ready to cave in, front and back. I don't want to tell you what the landscapers were asking."

"I'll bet," Jelonnek said. "I see them next door."

"See? They're everywhere."

"I mean landscapers."

"All they use is repellent. Chases them away but they come right back."

"Well sure."

"Sound waves too, but that's no better. Traps," the man said. "That's the way to go. He uses traps, and he's the best there is. It ain't as easy as it sounds."

"Carl you mean," Jelonnek said. He heard faint cheering from the living room.

"Placement," the man said. "You don't just drop em in the first hole you see."

"Scissor traps. He says those are the most humane—not that I give a shit."

Jelonnek thought of how he hated the Cowboys' colors, the star on the side of the helmet. America's team. "Have you tried the property manager?" he said. "Maybe they know where he went."

"Now there's an idea," the man said. "Would you happen to have their number?" Jelonnek knew it by heart. The man had a pen and took a scrap of paper from his wallet.

"It's just a hundred dollars," he said, and then lowered his voice. "But I think he could use the money."

"Well," Jelonnek said, "a hundred bucks."

"Problem with being jack-of-all-trades," the man said, "you think you're working for yourself, but who's writing the checks? I'll punch a clock any day."

Jelonnek wondered if the man who was looking for Carl would ask him what he did for a living.

"Yardwork, plumbing, mechanic, roofing..." He looked at the bushes where the flowers had been and lowered his voice again. "I think there was some kind of problem with the landlord."

"Yeah," Jelonnek said. "Well good luck finding him, then."

"They're not blind, you know."

"Who?" Jelonnek said.

"Not who, what," the man said. "Most people think they don't have eyes, but they do. They're just real tiny. He showed me."

"I don't think they work too well, though," he said.

"I guess not," Jelonnek said.

"The kid's bipolar," the man said.

Jelonnek waited. Someone went by walking a dog. "The kid."

"The son," the man said. "Carl's. Couldn't be left alone. He was supposed to be on medication but I don't think his parents believed in all that. I think the state was giving them a tough time." He stopped and looked around, looked at Jelonnek again. "Warm enough for you? I wonder what's taking the rain so long."

"Yeah." Jelonnek looked back at the front door. "Guess I'm getting back to the game there, then."

"Who's playing?"

"Dallas." The opponent didn't matter.

The man nodded. "Aikman's good," he said, "but I don't think they can do it without Smith."

Jelonnek nodded, backed away and slammed the door. He'd hoped the man might say something else.

◆ ◆ ◆

A tree with green nuts stood over the shed. A squirrel stood on the roof, eating the nuts from the tree. It stood on its hind legs, spinning one in its forepaws. Bits of green shell bounced off the roof of the shed to the grass, and you heard the click they made on the roof but not the sound they made in the grass.

Jelonnek watched from the kitchen windows while he did dishes with his hands. They had a dishwasher but Jelonnek didn't like the way it smelled. He liked doing dishes in the sink.

The house had two bedrooms. Littlebit slept in one and Miss D in the other. There was a half-finished attic that could have been turned into another bedroom, but Jelonnek was not his father. The sofa in the living room folded out, and that was where Jelonnek was sleeping when Littlebit woke him to ask as to the location of the appendix.

"What?" She was wearing an oversized sweatshirt and what there was of her hair was wound into tight little knots.

"You know where your appendis?"

He opened the other eye and said what again, though he'd heard her.

Littlebit cocked her head. "Hear that?"

It came out of thin air, a low, dry-throated moan that didn't sound like anyone Jelonnek knew. He knew it must be coming from Miss D's room, but for a second he thought it might be some animal trapped under the house.

He sat up. "What's wrong with her?"

"She hurtin," Littlebit said. "Her stomach in pain."

"Give her something."

"I give her some aspirin, but if it's her appendix it won't do no good. You know where it is?"

Jelonnek wasn't sure, except he knew it was low, on one side or the other. He remembered his sister's had burst when they were kids. She'd almost died, but first she'd had a terrible fever. He asked if Miss D had one.

"She don't feel hot."

"Does she have to throw up?"

"Naw. Go to the bathroom neither."

"Warm milk maybe," Jelonnek said. "Give the aspirin a chance."

"It's been had a chance," Littlebit said, but she went back to Miss D's room and closed the door. Jelonnek turned on the TV and lay back down. You could still hear that stranger's moan coming through the wall; it had risen slightly in pitch and came at almost regular intervals. He heard what might have been Littlebit praying and turned up the volume. Food poisoning, maybe. He tried to remember what they'd eaten, looked at the table where Miss D and Littlebit sometimes ate as if that would help. Behind it were the sliding glass doors that opened onto the backyard. There were vertical blinds but they hadn't closed them again and in the doors you could see yourself, half-dissolved in darkness.

The reception was bad. Out here you needed cable just to get the regular channels in. Because of the mountains.

Littlebit came back and said, "It's her stomach and her privacy." She picked up the phone. "I'ma call the prophet." At the church the van took her and Miss D to every weekend, the clergy were called prophets.

"What's that gonna do?" Jelonnek said.

"Or call the doctor, one."

"Warm milk," he said.

"She like to die in there."

He turned off the TV.

Littlebit put on the wig she wore to church and a pair of earrings. Miss D said it hurt too much to get dressed and they let her stay in her pajamas. She said it hurt too much to walk and Jelonnek carried her to the car; she was heavier than he thought she'd be.

Her eyes were shut and her thumb was in her mouth. On the way out to the carport Jelonnek bumped her head on the doorjamb and Littlebit covered the spot he'd bumped with her hand. Miss D was quiet. It was cold out. They got her in the backseat and she lay right down.

"If you had your license," Jelonnek said to Littlebit. She rode in the back.

The hospital where Jelonnek had once waxed floors was about fifteen minutes away, high in the West Hills. When people from around here said they were going up The Hill, that was what they meant. It was also a medical school. Miss D started up again. "Alright," Jelonnek said, "we're almost there," but he said it like he was saying shut up.

They twisted up the road in the dark. Signs directed them to the emergency room entrance. Jelonnek carried Miss D through a set of automatic doors and a security guard got them a wheelchair. Littlebit got behind it and Jelonnek went and parked the car. When he came back they were at the counter. Miss D had quieted. The receptionist was asking Littlebit questions, then typing the answers into her computer.

She looked uncertainly at Jelonnek. "Can I help you?"

"You been helpin him," Littlebit said.

"We'll pay cash," Jelonnek said. They paid for everything that way.

"We keeps money," Littlebit told her.

They sat and waited, Littlebit filling out a sheet on a clipboard. Jelonnek hadn't been in this part of the hospital before. Miss D was still quiet but she didn't know if she felt better. Littlebit liked the smell. Someone approached, a woman wearing a colorful tunic and a stethoscope around her neck. She spoke in a friendly and reassuring way and got behind the wheelchair. Littlebit followed. Jelonnek stayed behind in that nearly weightless state of something finally being taken off your hands. There was a month-old Newsweek on the seat next to him, a TV mounted high in a corner.

He waited. So did an Indian family eating fried chicken out of red and white boxes. Denim and braids and turquoise. He wondered if she was faking, then remembered how raw her throat had sounded. The automatic doors slid open and two cops walked in with a third man between them. He was small and young but the cops hung onto his arms as if he were capable of great mischief. There was a long gash on the side of his face that looked like it had been made with something more jagged than sharp. His flesh was dark but inside it was pink and had stopped bleeding. The man looked bored. He flirted with the receptionist.

"Let's have a seat," one of the cops said.

"I'm good to stand," the man said.

"Let's not get started," the cop said and they sat him away from everyone else. The Indians talked quietly.

Jelonnek saw Littlebit pushing Miss D back toward him. Miss D looked tired but not like she was in pain anymore. She looked like she did when the van dropped her off after some all-day outing. She had a balloon and a sucker.

"I can't tell you where he looked," she whispered to him.

He settled up at the counter while Littlebit pushed Miss D to the exit. All they'd done was look at her, but the bill was itemized like a supermarket receipt.

Miss D fell asleep almost as soon as the car was moving. "She like to get breasts," Littlebit said.

"What?" Jelonnek said.

"Got hair under her arms too."

"She's a kid."

"Not for long. It be that way sometime. Early. She probably fixin to get her period."

Jelonnek drove. "So those were…cramps?"

267

"Mm hm."

"Jesus." He didn't need this. "Anything else?"

"Doctor found some paper in her ear. Gave me something to put on her thumb." And she needed glasses.

When they got back they couldn't wake her up. Jelonnek had to carry her in, her body changing in his arms. They'd left the carport light on.

A woman came and installed their cable. She was tall and tanned and had frosted hair and a loud, friendly laugh. She looked like the outdoor type. You saw a lot of women like that out here but you didn't expect it to go any further. You didn't expect them to come to your house and put in your cable.

Jelonnek followed her around the house while she did what she did, and Littlebit followed Jelonnek, carrying her Bible. It seemed to make the cable woman nervous.

She had to drill a hole in the baseboard of the living room wall. She tied the cable to the back of an arrow and pushed it through the hole. Jelonnek wondered if she used the arrow for outdoor things like bowhunting or archery tournaments. He might have asked her but he didn't want Littlebit to get the wrong idea. Or was it the right one?

She cut her finger on the tip. He put it in his mouth and sucked the poison out. She stood behind him, showing him how to draw the bowstring, sticking her tongue in his ear.

Jelonnek gave the woman who installed their cable a Band-Aid and a glass of water. When she left they saw she'd forgotten her arrow. There was blood on the tip.

"Maybe she'll come back for it," Littlebit said.

"Maybe," Jelonnek said. He examined the remote.

"Bet youa like that," Littlebit said.

Jelonnek shrugged. He stood in front of the TV with the remote, changing channels.

"You likeded her?"

He stopped briefly on the local news. He was trying to find ESPN.

"Is you on bone?"

"What?"

"Is she your type?"

269

"I don't have one."

Littlebit made the sound she made when she was trying not to swear. "Like she invented pussy," she said. "Well I got one too."

"Alright," he said. He went through all the channels and started over.

"What is you lookin for?" she said. "Is you lookin for the naked channel?" She touched the remote. "Put that down then, I'll be that."

He didn't answer. There was no answer.

"Buy me some teeth," she said.

He reminded her of what had happened at the dentist's office.

"I get some teeth youa deal with me? For we can be natural?"

He didn't look at her. "Aren't there guys at church?"

"Why can't we be natural?"

"It is what it is."

"It ain't what it could be."

He looked at her, and with his arm made a sweeping gesture that encompassed the living room, the house, came back to the cable. Some kind of life.

"Ain't my premises," she said. "Ain't but a roof and some walls. Even when you look at me you don't look at me."

"You don't have to work," he said. "You live here for nothing."

"Ain't nothin for nothin. Let me pay my way."

He pushed a button he hadn't tried before and the TV screen dissolved in snow. He couldn't fix it. He sat down on the couch and Littlebit sat next to him.

"I don't lie to me about me," she said, and passed a hand over her face, her chest, her belly. She'd gained some weight since they'd moved into the house, but most of it seemed to have gone to her stomach, her neck. There was hair on her chin.

"All this blowed," she said, "but I got one too."

"I know I'm hard," she said, "but I ain't dry. Touch it." She took his hand and pulled it and he pulled it back. She rubbed her fingers between her legs, sniffed them and put her hand to his face.

"See?" He knocked it away like he was warding off a blow.

"Why you don't have a girlfriend, Jelonny?"

"Don't call me that."

"You like to pull on yourself? I'll do better than that."

He turned it off, turned it back on.

"You change up on me, Jelonny? You like the mens?" She touched his thigh. "You ain't a punk, is you?"

He told her to study her goddamn verses.

"Think I don't?" She kept one hand on the book, the other on his thigh. "You got big pretty lips, Jelonny. You look like you suck good pussy."

"You pray with that mouth?"

"I do all kinda things with it," she said. "Only one He give me." Her hand slid up and he grabbed it. "I'll suck yours if you suck mines. Don't need teeth for that."

He moved his leg. "Just let me figure this out. I'm asking you."

She licked her fingers. "I got some helluva ways, Jelonny."

He pushed buttons.

"I'll cook a nigger," she said.

They were going to do it right this time. This time they were going to stay all day at the beach, even though it was cold. They bought a cooler and filled it with ice and Coors and root beer. They had hotdogs and buns, potato salad and chips. They bought marshmallows and a quart of strawberries—Miss D liked strawberries. They had charcoal and lighter fluid and Jelonnek planned to have a big fire that night, near the waves, though he wasn't sure how to build one. They had a real beach blanket.

271

The car was in the carport. They put everything in the trunk and got in and shut the doors. Jelonnek started the engine but couldn't back the car out. The gearshift was stuck in park. He tried for ten minutes or so with all his might, but the lever might as well have been planted in stone. He started pounding on it. He pounded on it till something cracked.

It began to rain. Jelonnek spent the rest of the day in the house drinking all the beer.

The next time someone was at the door Littlebit answered it. "What you got I don't want?" was how she always answered the door. Jelonnek was trying to get a fire going. He heard her ask, "Why?" and he got up to see for himself.

A boy and girl, teenagers, stood under the awning. The girl stood on the bottom step in front of the boy. She had a loop of twine around her neck and hanging from it was a badge or ID card in a faded plastic pouch. They wore ponchos and light rain pelted the plastic.

"I think they sellin something," Littlebit said.

"Are you the head of the household, sir?" the girl asked. Her voice was clear and penetrating, like a tool you sharpened.

Jelonnek shrugged. "I don't know if we have that."

Littlebit mumbled. The girl extended her hand and told Jelonnek her name. She asked him how he was doing in her clear empty voice. Her hand was soft but her grip was strong and Jelonnek felt it around his cock, then felt his cock in her mouth and ass, spattering her ass and face and tits in the rain.

"I'm alright," he said.

"Me too," the girl said. She said she hadn't always been, though. A year ago you wouldn't have recognized her. She'd fled an abusive home and become a ward of the street, mired in a life of drugs, petty crime, and violence. A year ago her self-esteem was such that she couldn't talk to you the way she was talking to you now, couldn't even look you in the eye. She could only stare at the ground and mumble, and she stared at the ground and mumbled now so as to demonstrate. Then she lifted the card hanging from her neck in its plastic pouch. Her name and picture were on it, and the name of some organization or association which was hard to make out because the plastic was so yellowed and scratched.

"Thanks to them," she said, "this story has a happy ending." She had turned her life around thanks to them. They'd given her shelter, counseling, gotten her off drugs, enrolled her in night school so she could get her diploma. Given her direction, goals, purpose, and Jelonnek heard her begging him for more even though she wasn't his type either.

There was a van parked down the street.

"So how'm I doing?" she demanded suddenly and so brightly Jelonnek looked away. He looked at the boy behind her, who also had a string around his neck. The boy smiled shyly and looked at his shoes. He held a sheet of paper in his hand, also in plastic. A list.

"Shea look you in the eye now," Littlebit said. "What she need us for?"

The girl took a breath and said, "Well they're not done with me yet." Apparently this remarkable recovery wasn't the end of the story after all; the organization to which she already owed so much was sending her abroad to live and study for a year, but it depended on the cooperation of people like Jelonnek and Littlebit to make this next phase of her reinvention possible.

"Like she know what we like."

"Ma'am, we don't expect something for nothing," the girl said.

"Where are you going?" Jelonnek asked.

"Paris, France!" she announced happily, like everyone was invited.

"She goin all that way for she can look em in they eye, too?" Littlebit said.

"Believe me, ma'am," the girl said, "there's more to it than that."

"I mean. What she studyin on?"

"Foreign languages."

"I don't see it," Littlebit said. "His word is all the tongue you need."

You could hear the rain on the awning.

"Sir," the girl said, "you look kind of athletic. Do read *Sports Illustrated*?"

Sports Illustrated had called Number Nineteen a competent backup. Jelonnek shook his head.

"*Popular Mechanics*?"

"I guess you look mechanical too," Littlebit said.

"Ma'am?" Her voice didn't sound as empty now. "*Good Housekeeping*?"

"She need to quit callin me that. Sound like she sayin something else."

"We have *Essence* too," the girl said. "And *Jet*?"

Littlebit made the sound she made these days. "I don't read but one book."

"Sir?" the girl said, but she was still looking toward Littlebit. "Would you like to look at our list?"

The boy took a tentative step, proffered the list in its plastic sleeve. He had a bruise under his eye. There were drops of water on the plastic. Jelonnek looked at both sides of the sheet while the girl quoted the newsstand price of an issue of *Outdoor Life*, then compared it to the subscription rate.

Time. Forbes. Rolling Stone. She explained the point system. You needed twenty thousand points to go to Paris, France.

"Better keep knockin then. Maybe theya teach her to tell a better lie."

Jelonnek handed the list back, shaking his head. "I don't see anything." He put his hand on the edge of the door.

The girl held up her badge again. "Here's a number you can call if you have any doubts." The rain came harder, and so did her voice. "We'll wait while you call."

Jelonnek was still shaking his head. "Sorry." He started to close the door.

"Is the weather getting you down?"

"It ain't about the weather," Littlebit said.

"Ma'am," the girl said and Jelonnek finished closing the door. He went back to the fireplace. He'd bought firewood but couldn't seem to work the trick of the tinder. He had the impression that if he looked out the window they'd still be standing under the awning. Maybe he would get some of those chemically treated logs at the grocery store, the kind anyone could use. He got up and looked. They were gone, and so was the van. He wondered where the bruise had come from. The next day it was still raining and there was a dead rat in the mailbox.

The junkyard said they'd give Jelonnek twenty-five dollars for the car. They sent a tow truck in the morning. The driver was a friendly kid in dirty overalls and no shirt. He had pierced ears and a tattoo of a guitar on his shoulder and Jelonnek asked him if he played in a band.

"Nope," the driver said, "I tow cars. I get that though." He didn't know what an ashram was either. When he had the car hooked and hitched he reached behind his bib and pulled out a wad of damp greasy bills. He asked Jelonnek if singles were okay.

When the paper came Jelonnek looked in the classified section, in the category where people sold cars for a thousand dollars or less. *Looks bad, runs great. Lo mi.* The guy who answered the phone said it was his daughter's car. No beauty but reliable.

"Car's okay too." He laughed. He said it had good rubber, which must have meant tires.

Tomorrow, they agreed. Jelonnek stood on a chair in the kitchen and moved one of the ceiling tiles. They didn't have a bank account.

You had to take two buses, the first one downtown. Jelonnek went alone. Miss D was in school and Littlebit didn't want to go; she hadn't been downtown since she'd lived with her cousin and some white kid had Maced her on the library steps.

Jelonnek took the second bus to the north side. A woman got on with a guide dog. "Don't pet," she told everyone, "he's working." Her green eyes looked clear with sight but, she told someone, she had no depth perception and was therefore legally blind. Jelonnek wondered if she worked for the state as well, but it was time to ring the bell and he stepped off in a neighborhood of small houses with fences and big cars with union bumper stickers. He'd been given careful instructions. It was a long walk in a steady drizzle from the bus stop, and by the time Jelonnek got to the address he'd have bought anything just to be able to drive home.

The guy who'd answered the phone was waiting for him—he opened the door before Jelonnek could knock. They shook hands. The guy was wearing a company shirt like maybe he was on his lunch hour. His daughter was going to college and needed the money.

"Out front," he said.

It was an ugly box with two doors, one of them a different color than the rest of the car. The radio didn't work but it had a tape player. New brakes, the guy said. Plugs, fuel filter, tranny fluid. Low mileage unless the ododmeter had turned over, but Jelonnek didn't think of that. It was clean and hardly smelled and he wanted to drive it.

"Let me see if she's ready," the guy said. Jelonnek thought he was talking about the car but the guy invited him in the house. He waited in a small dark front room while the guy yelled up the stairs. On the mantel over the fireplace were dozens of pictures, dim family faces in rectangles. The house smelled like breakfast. *Wheel of Fortune* was on in another room, the volume low.

"She'll be down in a minute," the guy said. Jelonnek hadn't heard a response.

"Chicago," the guy said after a while.

"Chicago what?" Jelonnek said.

"Iowa."

"What about Iowa?"

"The way you talk. You're not from around here," the guy said.

Jelonnek didn't think he sounded any different than the guy himself but he told him he was from back East. That was as specific as he ever got.

"I figured. How do you like the wet stuff?"

Jelonnek thought. "I think I'm getting used to it."

"Either you do or—" The guy put his finger to his head and pulled the trigger. He smiled. "It'll go through spring, but last year it rained all June. Beats snow, you ask me."

There were worse things than rain. There were Mexican gangbangers moving into the neighborhood.

"It doesn't snow here?"

"Once or twice a year. When it does, look out. You can't get around without chains or studs."

"I've driven in snow before," Jelonnek said.

"Not like this you haven't."

His daughter came down the stairs. "Did you come to take away my baby?" She looked older than Jelonnek expected and wore a lot of makeup. The name of a softball team stitched on the back of her windbreaker. Her father got up.

She sat in the front. Jelonnek felt like he had when he took his driving test, like he might make mistakes. He headed down the street and started making right turns. You needed both hands to turn the wheel.

"Make a left," the father said in the back. "Check the alignment."

"Turn here at the crack house," his daughter said. Then she laughed.

"It's only a stop sign," her father said. Jelonnek hadn't seen it, he couldn't concentrate with them in the car. The father kept pointing out things in the way it handled, nuances Jelonnek was insensitive to but pretended to notice anyway. They told him how to get to the freeway.

"She's no beauty but she starts every morning," the daughter said. "She's got good rubber."

"A good work car," her father said, and he asked Jelonnek where he worked.

"Nowhere," Jelonnek said.

"You live at home?" the daughter said.

"I'm renting a house," he said.

"With what?" the father said.

Jelonnek wasn't sure how to respond. "I had this idea for a movie," he said then.

The father grunted. "You and everybody's grandmother. That pays the rent?"

"What's it about?" the daughter asked, and Jelonnek chose her question to answer.

"I like whatshisname," the father said. "The Terminator."

"I write poetry," the daughter said. She said *Star Wars* was her favorite movie. They got to the freeway ramp. The car didn't have a lot of pickup and Jelonnek had to cut somebody off. The other driver beeped and the daughter raised her middle finger and called him a douche bag.

"What do you expect with a four-banger?" the father said. Jelonnek didn't know what that was, but he didn't ask. He asked them if they knew what an ashram was.

"An ashram," the father said.

"Why do you ask? his daughter said.

"Like a guru or something, isn't it?" the father said. Jelonnek pictured a brown-skinned guy in a turban, a Nehru collar.

"No, stupidass," the daughter said. "The ashram is a place, not a person. Like a retreat. It's where you go to meditate."

"Do they believe in God?" Jelonnek said

"I think it's optional," the daughter said. "I had a girlfriend who went to one. Wore white all the time. She had these crystals. Do you live by yourself?"

"No," Jelonnek said.

"Married?"

"No."

"You can take this exit," the father said.

"Well what do you think?" the daughter said.

They wanted five hundred for it. Jelonnek told them he had four, cash. They settled on four twenty-five and he gave them the greasy singles. On the way home some kids in a mini-van pulled up alongside and ragged on his ugly car.

"Go fuck your mother," Jelonnek muttered.

They didn't hear it anymore. The ticking and tapping and drumming, on the roof, in the trees, on the grass, the cement. They didn't hear it against the windows, though inside the house they smelled it. The hiss of car tires on occasion became a shriek. At night you didn't hear it but in a different way, and sometimes when it came down harder you heard it till you got used to it, and then it was in you and part of that silence again. The downspout on the back of the house leaked. Water poured through a gap where it joined the gutter, and you could see the hole it was making in the ground. Sometimes it came down even when the sun was out, and once Miss D announced it was falling in the backyard but not in the front.

They no longer heard it falling on the carport, where the car sat as if for no other reason than to justify having a carport. Littlebit said pride was a sin, but Jelonnek was sure she thought it too ugly to be seen in. Miss D said the backseat hurt her behind. The backseat was narrow, little more than a shelf, and Miss D seemed to have more behind her these days anyway. She seemed to have more everywhere.

She'd grown quiet.

The weather did things to people. It got inside.

There was an article in the paper that came in the mailbox: the state in which they now lived had one of the highest suicide rates in the country. Sunlight deprivation, hormone deficiencies. Emotional imbalance and depression, fatigue and strange cravings. Some cases so severe the sufferers used lightboxes for an hour or so each day, dosing themselves with ultraviolet wavelengths the way other people take vitamin supplements.

Jelonnek didn't need a lightbox, he had beer. But it was good to know about just in case. Littlebit didn't need either; she liked the rain, said she felt His presence in it; the flood, the ark, His power withheld only by His promise. She said it sometimes felt like she'd been waiting all her life for it.

There was another article in the same section. A bigger one, about a volcano. Jelonnek hadn't been aware there was a volcano anywhere near them but there was, not a hundred miles to the north. Then something came back to him. He was just a year out of high school. Survivors said the sky turned pitch black. He remembered how it had been on every channel, like the President getting shot or the space shuttle exploding, only it was something that was supposed to happen in remote exotic places, Japan or South America, not here in this country, this day and age. Now it was just a couple of hours away.

"Don't you remember?" he asked Littlebit.

"Don't start me lyin'," she said.

They'd heard it in Canada. A plane had gone down. The article compared it to a thermonuclear bomb, measured it in megatons. It had only killed some fifty-odd people but thousands of big game animals and millions of fish and an incalculable number of small mammals. All the birds. The number of trees destroyed, the article said, could build eighty-five thousand three-bedroom homes. Twenty-one bodies had never been recovered.

Somebody's last words were: "Vancouver. Vancouver, this is it."

They broke it down into dollars and cents, property damage. Riot or earthquake, they always told you how much it was going to cost.

There were pictures. The volcano was white with snow and looked like a mountain with its top third sheared off. Arrows directed your sight to glaciers, the lava dome, the pumice plain. Puffs of cloud hung over it and there was an enormous gash in the wall of the crater, from which had issued the largest landslide in recorded history.

The cloud of ash and dust grew fifteen miles in fifteen minutes. In three days it crossed the country and particles of it are still orbiting the earth.

There were interviews. A woman operated a gift ship in which all the items were made of volcanic ash. People shared their memories: hit the winning run in a softball tournament with the black cloud billowing over center field. Conceived their third child and named her Ashlee. But the gist of the article was that the volcano was once again showing signs of life; seismic activity had been detected, and recently there'd been a series of small eruptions.

Experts were certain it was going to blow again, they just weren't sure when.

Jelonnek looked at the clouds again and realized they weren't just clouds. He showed the picture to Littlebit and Miss D.

"If you fell in it," Miss D said, "would you go down there?"

"You can say it if you ain't cursin," Littlebit said.

"Would you?"

"Some folks, I guess."

"Is it lava down there?"

"It's fire and darkness. The fire burns but it don't give light, and the dark so cold it hurt."

"Does that make sense?"

"It don't have to."

Volcanoes provide us with geothermal energy, valuable minerals, fertile soil and recreational opportunities.

They were supposed to get a break in the weather.

T he anchorman says, "In the interest of good taste."

The street reporter calls it a rental property. "A child," she says. "A man and a woman…who may or may not be husband and wife."

We can't see all the words. We see a man wearing a blue smock. Behind him are shelves of typewriters with little tags wired to them.

"I'm the first one in the door," he says. "I'm the last one out." Probably he was the first to see it. He called 911 and and started greasing carriage returns.

A sign in the window: "We dont speak to Reporters." Some of the neighbors do but nobody saw or heard anything. They stand in front doors and on porches, looking hastily dressed for an appearance. A woman still in her bathrobe: "We turn in early on a school night." Their next-door neighbor, she adds, is never home.

She says they seem like nice people. She says, "They keep to themselves."

You can see certain words, a name, crude figures, but the shots are composed so that other words are intimated in fragments, or missing entirely. The pace of the editing is rapid, like a movie trailer.

A boy and a girl pretend to wait for a school bus—the children of the woman in the bathrobe, perhaps. "A prank, like," the boy says. "Like trick or treat." We watch the girl watching him talk.

The car, the windows. Lines of rough grammar that bend around corners. Some of it is blurred, washed out, almost shimmers; they must have done something to the video.

"With the aid of digital technology," the anchorman says. "For those who might be offended."

"The owner could not be reached," the street reporter says. She conducts interviews in a trench coat, nodding emphatically. She is attractive but not glamorous; energetic, likeable, down to earth.

"Residents say this *has* to be the work of outsiders."

"Troublemakers," the man in the blue smock says. "What's that outfit up from California?" They've set up headquarters in the west suburbs. (We don't see him trying to think of the name, or saying that a Selectric has more than three thousand moving parts.)

"My kids play with their kid," the woman in the bathrobe says.

A police spokesman, a spokesman for an anti-bias group. A former skinhead whose face is a shadow.

"On condition of anonymity," the street reporter says.

(We don't see the girl at the bus stop imitating the dead cat in the parking lot: "His eyes were made of ants." Her tongue lolls in footage that will not be seen. She will not be heard describing the two women who live together at the turnaround, who could be mother and daughter but are not.)

The street reporter stands at the corner with her microphone, police cars and yellow tape behind her.

"Until that happens," she says.

"Back to you," she says. In the studio the anchorman shakes his head. On a brighter note, he says, it looks like the dry weather might be around for a couple of days. He turns to the staff meteorologist.

The man from Hate Crimes wanted to know if they were married. Littlebit asked what difference it made. He asked if they rented or owned.

"What difference do that make either?" she said.

"We're not married," Jelonnek said. He said, "Jelonnek

Everything is important, the man from Hate Crimes said, but they didn't have to answer anything they didn't want to. He wore a tie. His partner wore a turtleneck.

"Police report says there's a child," she said. Miss D was still at school.

"Should we have kept her home?" Jelonnek said. Her emphatic knocking, like she'd forgotten something. She forgot things sometimes.

"We can always talk to her another time," the man from Hate Crimes said; he did most of the talking. He didn't look like a cop. His partner was a young woman who watched him attentively while he spoke, as though she were in training. She wrote things down in pencil. They both wore windbreakers with the words SPECIAL UNIT printed on the back, and they had ID badges strung around their necks. Jelonnek wondered if they both carried guns.

Littlebit wouldn't let them use a tape recorder.

They sat at the table where Jelonnek and Littlebit and Miss D sometimes ate dinner, though not always together. Language and yellow tape surrounding them on four sides, words inverted on the other side of the glass. Hieroglyphic. They'd taken pictures. Everyone else was gone.

When did you become aware a crime had been committed?

The phone rang. It was the girl from the property manager; Jelonnek wasn't sure how they'd found out. She asked him if he and everyone else were okay. On behalf of the property manager she expressed concern, ourage, and sympathy, in that order. The owner was in Europe, she told him. They were insured.

"We're taking bids," she said. "We'll try to get a contractor out there today."

Littlebit had walked around the whole house and read every word. They'd covered every wall. She didn't say anything, just went back inside and called the Apostolic Faith Church (Body of Jesus Christ of the Newborn Asembly). She spoke with the prophet.

The woman from Hate Crimes smiled carefully when you looked at her. She made a mistake, corrected it, and Jelonnek felt the tip of her tongue on the eraser.

"Tomorrow at the latest," the property manager said.

Why do you think this incident happened?

The man from Hate Crimes asked about the neighbors. "Any arguments, harassment, verbal confrontation prior to this morning?" He asked if Miss D was having any problems at school.

"She behind is all," Littlebit said.

Jelonnek said the neighbors seemed okay.

"Somebody liked to mail us a rat one time."

Jelonnek told them about the kids who had tried to sell them a magazine subscription.

The woman from Hate Crimes scratched down the details, the man said they would pursue every possibility. He looked like a math teacher.

Studies have shown there to be five categories of perpetrator.

"This state's a hotbed," the man from Hate Crimes said. He recited the names of certain groups and asked Jelonnek and Littlebit if they'd heard of any of them.

"Christian what?" Littlebit said.

"Posse Comitatus," the man from Hate Crimes said, and named the names. One was familiar and Jelonnek remembered the TV repairman who'd hosted a public access show on cable. Another one, exotically foreign, belonged to a man who'd been beaten to death with a baseball bat on the northeast side.

"Ethiopian," the man from Hate Crimes said. "Don't even consider themselves black."

"Guess it ain't up to them," Littlebit said, and didn't say anything about the time she'd been Maced downtown.

But why hadn't they called the police themselves?

The show had apparently been canceled.

The phone rang again. The church wanted to know if there was anything they could do. The man from Hate Crimes nodded approvingly. Jelonnek saw him put his gun in Littlebit's mouth.

"Grass roots," he said. Organized resistance at the community level was the best deterrent. Neighborhood coalitions, block watches, rallies. The force had a civil rights officer who could get them in touch with certain groups. Advocates.

He used the word proactive, but Jelonnek didn't ask what that meant.

"So what brought you out here?" the man from Hate Crimes asked.

"Our business," Littlebit said.

Jelonnek sighed. "They're trying to help."

"They police," Littlebit said. "Can't help that."

The man from Hate Crimes stood. He was going to canvass the street, interview neighbors, see what anyone saw. His partner had some follow-up. He left his card and zipped his windbreaker.

"This kind of incident almost never repeats itself at the same location." He told them what their success rate was in apprehending perpetrators.

"Try to enjoy the sunshine while it lasts," he said.

"Let it rain," Littlebit said. "Wash they word away."

He saw himself out. The woman from Hate Crimes followed up. "Ever notice any large groups of youths, male or female, hanging out on or near the property?" she asked, and took Jelonnek between her breasts.

They would not take no for an answer.

The contractor didn't come on Thursday. Friday morning a man pulled up in a pickup truck, walked once around the house and drove off. Later the property manager called and said there was a problem with the original contractor, they were sending someone else out as soon as possible. They didn't say what the problem was.

Friday afternoon Jelonnek looked out the living room window and saw someone standing near the front of the house with a spray can. He went outside and recognized the young guy who lived down the street with a young woman and a baby. They drove a microbus with Grateful Dead bumper stickers. The young guy wore a red bandanna and was holding a bottle in the other hand. He put it down to tell Jelonnek his name. He said he sometimes painted houses in the summer—he said they'd be happy to help.

"Property manager's sending someone around," Jelonnek said.

The young guy nodded. He had a dust mask pulled down around his neck. He kept shaking the can, you could hear the bead rattling inside it. "Hope the weather holds up," he said. "You ever paint in the rain?"

"A guy come out this morning…" Jelonnek shrugged. "Now they're sending someone else by. What's that?"

The young guy popped the cap off and put on his mask. He was someone with a spray can once again. "Step back," he said, "this stuff'll blind you." He aimed the can at the siding and sprayed part of a word. The skin of the letter bubbled and hissed, bled down the wall as if disintegrating under its own terrible magic. It gave off a choking smell.

Littlebit looked out the door: "Amen."

It wasn't going to disappear, the young guy said behind the mask. You just wanted to fade it, back it down a little. Keep it from ghosting.

"I don't know," Jelonnek said. "The contractor—"

"It's up to you," the young guy said. It would just make their job easier—as long as they didn't wait too long. You can paint in the rain, he said, but nobody wants to.

"It's up to you," he said.

"Ain't nobody else doing anything," Littlebit said. "What they gonna say, put the words back on?"

The young guy went home and got a ladder. After you neutralized it you could just rinse it or wipe it off. The first can didn't go very far, and Jelonnek went with the young guy to Home Depot for more. He bought a mask. When they got back the contractor still hadn't shown but there were more visitors. They introduced themselves, though Jelonnek had met a couple of them the day before; they'd dropped by after the people from Hate Crimes left.

He heard their names again.

Tomorrow, they said, as if it had already been decided. They said they wouldn't take no for an answer—it wasn't just about painting a house. Jelonnek would rather have held out for professionals. You could just take it easy while someone else took care of it, you didn't even have to be there. (And wouldn't they expect him to help?) But the contractor still hadn't arrived and the people from Hate Crimes said you should get rid of it within twenty-four hours and they seemed to have made up their minds anyway.

He called the girl who managed the property and explained the situation. She just sounded relieved, and said they would pay for the paint.

Saturday it rained once, early, and there was intermittent sunshine the rest of the day. The young guy who'd brought the remover was the first to come back. He brought his wife and their baby, who had some kind of Indian name and was old enough to stand but couldn't yet walk. They had a bagful of rags and Jelonnek and the young guy went around the house wiping off the siding, getting rid of cobwebs and the gray shell of a wasp nest now writhing with small green caterpillars. Littlebit let the young guy's wife unfold a playpen in the living room. She told Miss D to keep an eye on the baby. Then she stood outside with her arms folded while the young guy's wife helped prep the siding.

The lady who lived next to the business that repaired office machines and had been on the news brought her husband and two children across the street. They brought baked beans and potato salad and chicken wings. The wife of the young guy had made chili with no meat in it.

"Do I like that?" Miss D said. From further down the street came an ex-biker who lived in a tiny one-bedroom house and gave people massages for a living. He rolled his own cigarettes, and thanked Jelonnek for having the only car on the street uglier than his own. Jelonnek had never seen him before yesterday.

They brought pails, brushes, rollers, trays and screens, a stepladder, extension ladder,

Doritos, store-brand cola, some kind of casserole. Drop cloths, sandpaper, putty knives, razor blades, tape. They wore caps and old clothes and everyone seemed to know what to do, even the kids. One coat today, they said, the finish tomorrow. If the weather held.

"Cross your fingers," the young guy said.

"I'd as soon put my hands together," Littlebit said. "Hea take care of the rest."

"I see He's not big on recycling," the ex-biker said. He was looking at the beer cans in the garbage. "You want your grandkids playing in a landfill?"

"The city'll pick it up for free," the young guy's wife said.

Littlebit looked at Jelonnek. "What that mean, some grandkids?"

The young guy masked off the windows.

They'd already bought the paint. Acrylic latex, specially made for cold weather, and the color almost matched. Jelonnek watched from the edge of the lawn. The young guy used a roller, working in diagonal strokes his wife filled in with a brush. You could tell she wasn't wearing a bra. "Jump in anytime," the ex-biker said. "It'll keep you warm." Littlebit went in and out of the house with her arms still folded. Someone stuck a brush in Jelonnek's hand. He hadn't painted a house since he'd briefly helped the old man years before. It hadn't gone well then and his skills hadn't improved with time. The husband of the woman who'd been on the news gave him some pointers. Follow the grain, stroke from dry to wet. He owned a small carpet-cleaning business of which he was sole employee, and he was soft-spoken and barely said anything he didn't have to. His wife filled his silence. She stayed home with the kids now, she told everyone, but once she'd managed a Red Lobster.

"Don't quit your day job," the ex-biker told Jelonnek. He was standing on the step-ladder with a cigarette in his lips, hand in pocket, painting under the eaves, completely balanced and relaxed, and Jelonnek looked on marveling that a man could do things beyond nature naturally, as if born to them, and wondered what he might be born to, and he wondered if that cigarette would ignite turpentine if he dumped a can of it over the ex-biker's head. But it was latex paint and there was no turpentine.

"Need some help?" Two women stood at the edge of the lawn wearing overalls. They were the women who lived at the cul-de-sac and could have been mother and daughter, but they were not. Littlebit turned her head and made one of her sounds.

"About time," the young guy said.

"It ain't," Littlebit said.

"We heard there was free food," the younger woman said, but they were holding a cooler between them. They were dressed identically.

"That's alright," Littlebit said. "We good." They looked at her. For once the woman who'd been on the news had nothing to say.

"The more the merrier," the young guy's wife said.

"It's her house," the older woman said.

"Yeah it is," Littlebit said. "We good. Thank you anyway."

The women lingered a while, then left. "Got something against them?" the ex-biker said.

"I ain't got nothing for em," Littlebit said.

Jelonnek loaded his brush.

They had the front and two sides done when someone said, "Who's hungry?" They ate outside and the wings and potato salad went first. Jelonnek didn't have any of the chili but the woman who'd been on the news couldn't say enough. She never could. Miss D tried it when no one was looking, made a face and went in the house.

"So how did you two meet?" the young guy's wife said.

"Kind of by accident," Jelonnek said.

"It wasn't no accident," Littlebit said. Miss D screamed and ran out of the house and they could hear the baby screaming as loud.

"He bit on my stomach!" she cried. The young guy and his wife went in the house and came out with the baby. The young guy's wife was carrying him and was terribly sorry but she looked angry, kept looking at something on the child's face.

His name was Algonquian for "He laughs," and Littlebit said, "He ain't laughin now."

The woman who'd been on camera and lived next to the business that serviced office machines asked how old Miss D was.

"You're kidding," she said, and Miss D took her thumb out of her mouth.

Then they sat in the living room and talked about things other than painting, because that wasn't really what it was about, was it? A faint, well-intentioned smell of sweat. There weren't enough chairs for everyone and the children sat on the floor. They discussed neighborhood watches with alternating shifts, petitioning the police to beef up patrols, also used the word proactive. They surmised who the culprits might be, and everyone agreed it could not have been anyone who lived on the street; kids in cars used the turnaround at night, it might be someone who'd brought in a typewriter for repair. The woman who'd been on the news kept looking around at the furniture, the TV, the carpet. She preferred to stand.

Jelonnek thought they might have come up the gully behind the house, but his mouth was full of baked beans. It was the best thing there and Littlebit agreed.

"Put her foot in it," she said.

The ex-biker went to his house to get a radio, and the young guy went with him. They were gone a while, and when they came back they seemed sluggish and glassy-eyed and Littlebit glared at the burnt smell of what they'd been up to.

They brought a football too, but didn't throw it.

After the break they painted to music and didn't talk much. The young guy's wife stayed in the house with the baby, and the young guy used the brush and the roller at the same time. Littlebit decided to help then and the lady who'd been on the news and had once managed a Red Lobster showed her what she was doing wrong.

"That's too much like work," Littlebit said. "I got my own way to go."

The radio had a tape player and Miss D put in a cassette. They started hearing one of the words that had been sprayed on the house, and Littlebit turned it off, took the cassette out and unspooled the tape with long jerks of her arm. Then she went back and dipped her roller in a tray.

The boy and girl who'd also been on the news said they were tired.

"You're painting the paint," their mother said. A cat prowled for scraps.

The ex-biker turned the radio back on. He and the young guy's wife moved together to it and Miss D covered her mouth at their graceless lurching. In the evening she was told to take off all her clothes in the bathroom, and Littlebit went in behind her with a rolled up TV guide and shut the door.

Sunday morning was gray but it still hadn't rained, and only the men returned to put on the second coat. Littlebit was in church with Miss D, ostensibly holding up the sky with prayer. They painted the trim the same color. Nobody brought anything to eat, and Jelonnek paid for pizza and beer. Littlebit and Miss D had still not returned when they rattled the ladders for the last time, folded up their drop cloths, cleaned off their brushes and wrapped them in paper. They would keep in touch (they were neighbors!) and everybody shook hands. Most of the beer was left and Jelonnek drank it after they'd gone, and he was passed out on the couch when Littlebit and Miss D came home with the prophet and two of his associates from the Apostolic Faith Church (Body of Jesus Christ of the Newborn Assembly). He slept through the prayers and the holding of hands and the blessing of the house, and did not wake up even when a drop of anointed oil was placed on his forehead.

The property manager called the following week. The owner had driven by. He had not approved the color so they couldn't take anything off the rent, nor would their insurance cover his vehicle. They reimbursed him for the paint. Jelonnek cashed the check and found a place that would paint your car for ninety-nine dollars.

The next president was elected. It rained hard through the holidays. There were no ice storms but it rained so hard there were mudslides in the West Hills. People lost their homes. The street reporter stood in the rain wearing her trench coat. "Back to you," she said and the house behind her suddenly lurched off like a ship at its launching.

Littlebit put a turkey in the oven for Thanksgiving. The little button that was supposed to let you know it was done never popped, and the object that emerged was shriveled and dessicated as a mummified infant. Nobody cooked anything for Christmas. Jelonnek looked in the phone book and all the Chinese restaurants were open, so they ordered takeout and ate quietly around the round table.

They had a real tree. Out here real trees were a dime a dozen, and they'd bought one for fifteen dollars. It had a sharp citric smell and all the presents under it were for Miss D. (The prophets frowned on gift-giving but made exceptions for children of a certain age.) Barbie dolls, a new bathing suit, rollerblades, an AM-FM CD player that also played cassette tapes, a David and Goliath video game. Miss D was very happy, and you could barely discern her disappointment that she hadn't gotten a TV, and that none of the dolls had blonde hair. She'd only wanted one, but on balance she was very grateful. Her mother saw to it.

She said she didn't believe in Santa Claus but Jelonnek didn't believe her. He asked Littlebit if Miss D wasn't too old for dolls.

"If she was she wouldn't ax for em," Littlebit said. "When she want clothes and books she'll ax for that. When she caught up to her body." But her body seemed to have pulled out of reach.

The church had had a special service on Christmas Eve. Jelonnek was invited but it was the last game of the season.

After New Year's the tree started to dry out and there were needles all over the living room. The city was sending a truck around. All you had to do was leave the tree out in front of your house and they would take it away for free. Jelonnek overslept and missed the pickup time. He ended up stuffing the tree into the shed behind the house, silver strands of tinsel still entwined in its branches as if grown there. After he shut the door as well as he could, he went and looked down the gully behind the yard. The creek at the bottom was wide with rain. He was sure they'd come up from down there.

In the second half of the conference final Aikman got kicked in the head and was slow getting to his feet. Number Nineteen took off his baseball cap, started warming up on the sideline. He'd grown a mustache. Aikman sucked oxygen. When they asked him his name he told them it was Thursday. Dallas punted. San Francisco scored, now down by fourteen. Number Nineteen hadn't thrown a pass all season and leave it to Summerall to say maybe this was the break the Niners were looking for. They knew he couldn't move, and when he took over they brought up the linebackers and went after him. Three and out.

Miss D chuckled: "He runs like Big Bird." Jelonnek sent her to her room and put the chain on the door. Littlebit had no use for sports.

Next series Number Nineteen beat the blitz three straight plays, found Harper in a seam for the last forty-five yards and the end zone in Dallas, Texas on national TV. The crowd was ecstatic but all you could hear was Jelonnek. He told Miss D she could come out but she stayed where she was. In the fourth quarter Number Nineteen led them downfield again, this time into field goal range and the Cowboys led by twenty-four. Even that prick Summerall was impressed, and Madden himself said there was no other quarterback he'd rather have in this situation. This is a former coach with two Super Bowl rings saying this to America.

Littlebit made her come out.

Number Nineteen finished the game, so technically you could say he'd won it, that he hadn't just managed a lead. You could say he'd gotten them to the Georgia Dome. Jelonnek hoped for more but Aikman had two weeks to remember his name and was ready to start in Atlanta. You didn't see Number Nineteen on the field again till the last series of the Super Bowl, when the Cowboys had already clinched the game and he was taking a knee just so he could get a ring. Not that he hadn't earned it. If it hadn't been for Number Nineteen they technically wouldn't have even gotten to Atlanta, and a week later he announced he was retiring to become partner in a telemarketing firm.

The school called about Miss D. Jelonnek said, "Hold on," and went down the hall. When Jelonnek picked up the phone and it was a teacher calling about Miss D, he always let Littlebit do the talking. He was nobody's father.

The teacher wanted to see them. She would talk to Littlebit alone but she preferred they both be present, even though Jelonnek insisted he was not a parent. He agreed to drive. Meetings had been arranged twice, and neither appointment kept. Once Littlebit had either forgotten or simply hadn't said anything. Or she'd told Miss D to go to the bathroom and take all her clothes off. The other time Jelonnek had overslept. He'd been having trouble getting to sleep lately, and the night before last he hadn't sleep at all. He felt like he'd had too much coffee too late in the day, but Jelonnek hardly ever drank coffee. Maybe the sofa had something to do with it. The sofa converted into a bed but Jelonnek didn't use it that way anymore. It was heavy and there was all that bother with the sheets, and sometimes something got stuck and you had to keep starting over till it properly unfolded. Something poked him through the mattress. Maybe it just needed oil; the old man probably could have fixed it. The old man could have turned the attic into a proper bedroom, but Jelonnek didn't have that. His father couldn't give him his arms or shoulders or his terrible wonderful hands, only the wrong half of his blood. All his mother gave him were her eyes.

Littlebit said she'd seen him from her bedroom window. She'd looked out to see if the rain had stopped and saw someone hanging around the shed.

"Who?" Jelonnek said.

"I don't know," she said. "He lookeded small."

"We get some pretty big raccoons back there."

"Well this one stand on two legs and wear a cowboy hat."

"A kid? A bum?"

"I don't know."

Jelonnek went to the kitchen and looked out the window over the sink. You couldn't tell if it was raining. The door to the shed was halfway open. It was always ajar but he couldn't tell if it was open now more than it usually was.

The previous tenant had left a golf club in the carport, some kind of iron. Jelonnek had never touched it before. He went around the side of the house into the backyard. The grass was wet and soft and hardly made a sound. It wasn't raining. Jelonnek thought he saw buds on the tree over the shed, but wasn't it too early for buds?

He stood at the door and listened. The golf club felt rusty. There was a small window in the door but you couldn't see anything through it. Jelonnek looked inside almost shyly, like it wasn't part of the property. It had always felt that way, like it was someone else's. Not even the landlord's.

Cans of motor oil and the Christmas tree. The needles were almost all brown now and half the branches bare. Smelled better in there anyway. Jelonnek backed out and looked to his left. A gap between the picket fence and the corner of the shed; had it been there before or had someone made it? Someone could come in off the road and leave the same way. He went around to the back of the shed. There was no one there either, but on the strip of ground above the gully was an empty pint of wine, a flattened Fritos bag, cigarette butts. The bottle had a rose on the label.

The pawnshop was downtown. It called itself a Jewelry and Loan but inside it was like a flea market: toasters, VCRs, golf clubs, furs, musical instruments. Unredeemed items. All the jewelry was under glass behind the counter, and there were bars on the windows.

The pawnbroker was a squat old guy with a Star of David around his neck. He sat on a high stool behind a counter. "Just gold or silver," he was telling someone through the window. "Didn't I talk to you on the phone?" He spoke with a drawl that didn't go with the star.

Jelonnek had never been in a pawnshop before but he knew a little. Years ago, working nights for the state, he'd waxed floors with a guy who had everything but his left nut in hock and might have tendered that as well had he found a taker. So Jelonnek knew you left things here as collateral and borrowed money off them. If you couldn't pay back the loan in time, whatever you'd left was up for sale. An unredeemed item.

The customer left. The pawnbroker flipped through a tabloid with a magnifying glass. "You got something for me?" he said "Or I got something for you?"

"I've never been in one of these places before," Jelonnek said.

"I can halfway tell," the pawnbroker said.

A chainsaw, ice skates, other things. The other things were locked in a case and Jelonnek asked if he could look at them.

"For?" the pawnbroker said.

"Where I live," Jelonnek said, "in my neighborhood…" He felt obliged to explain.

"Recreation? Protection?" The pawnbroker came through a door at the side of the counter.

"Vandalism…a rash of—"

"You're gonna shoot vandals. I'm all for you, but we got a waiting period in this state."

"For my home," Jelonnek said. There was a banjo hanging over his head.

The pawnbroker had keys, he pointed at something in the case. It was silver with an ivory handle and had a barrel the length of a ballpoint pen. It looked like a toy.

"Can I interest you?" the pawnbroker said.

"How do you tell?" Jelonnek said. "I mean, which one?"

The pawnbroker opened the case. "I don't do this for everyone."

"I appreciate it," Jelonnek said.

"I know you do." He made sure it was empty and gave it to Jelonnek. It didn't feel like a toy. Jelonnek wondered if someone had loved it.

"First one I've ever…"

"I can halfway tell," the pawnbroker said. "Go ahead," he said, "dry-fire it."

"What's that?"

"Click."

"Is the safety on?"

"No safety on a revolver. Just watch where you point it."

"It's empty, right?"

"It's bad luck. They're all loaded you ask me."

"Guns don't kill people," Jelonnek said.

"Right. People with guns do."

Jelonnek swung it around, his finger on the trigger. He aimed it at a saxophone, which was the same color but not as shiny.

"Okay Deadeye, you're done," the pawnbroker said. Jelonnek pulled the trigger. The click was almost painful but afterwards it didn't feel as heavy. He heard the clock, which didn't tick but hummed. A voice outside.

The waiting period was ten days, and there was a background check. The pawnbroker got behind the counter and sat on his high stool. Jelonnek filled out a form.

"Anything else?" Jelonnek said there wasn't, but when he came back to pick it up he bought the saxophone too.

"No waiting period on that?" he said.

"I make the jokes here," the pawnbroker said. "I'm joking."

Jelonnek drove home with the saxophone in its case on the seat next to him. Two kids in a pickup truck pulled up close alongside and rolled down a window.

"Is that a car or a doghouse?" one of them said.

"Go fuck your mother," Jelonnek said.

"What?" one of them said, and Jelonnek showed them the silver barrel.

If it wasn't the phone it was the door. A knock he wasn't sure he'd heard. Jelonnek started to open it, then dropped his hand from the knob and flattened himself next to the living room window. His forehead touched cold glass. He remembered being a paperboy calling to collect, his customers hiding behind furniture with just the TV on, curtains drawn, whispering in the dark that day the bill came due.

A yellow slicker, a woman's leg, another badge on a string. He just didn't want it to be someone he knew. Another solicitous neighbor. She knocked again and he opened the door.

Mousy, defeated, a librarian who has long stopped looking for quiet. She said good morning.

"Morning," Jelonnek said. "Are you with…?" He couldn't think of it.

"Department of Human Services." There'd been a complaint.

"They don't live here anymore," he said.

"I can't tell you what the complaint was or who phoned it in," she said. She smelled like an ashtray. She seemed to be trying to look inside the house. "I'd just like to talk for a few minutes. Can I come in?"

"We still get their mail sometimes," Jelonnek said. "Is this about…?"

"Can I come inside?" she said. "So we can talk?"

He still threw it away except for the license plate stickers. "Do I have to?"

She sighed. You couldn't tell if she was disappointed or relieved.

At first just knowing it was there was enough. He didn't tell anyone. He hid it above one of the ceiling tiles in the kitchen, the one with the water stain. Like planting a seed. As soon as it was out of sight it became the center of the house, just sort of took over. Everything else existed to be protected by it.

Littlebit twisted Miss D's hair in the living room, protected. She took two strands at a time and twisted them around each other. "Do this for your own self," she muttered, ""big as you is—be a woman soon."

"Do I wanna be a woman?"

"I hear that," Littlebit said, and sent Miss D to bed. CNN was on: Cossacks in Bosnia, a fire in Waco.

"When do you get to sleep?" she asked Jelonnek.

"When I get tired," he said.

"When do you get tired?"

"I just want to watch the news," Jelonnek said.

Littlebit went down the hall. She was saying something else but these days half of what she said was under her breath anyway, a subliminal prayer. Her door closed. She had a TV in her room, but no cable.

But the first night just knowing it was there was enough. Sitting there watching TV with the lights on and a gun embedded somewhere in the house felt like a form of action. Just sitting there with the blinds shut. Then getting up and opening them and turning off the lights in the living room.

The news channel never let up. War crimes. A rape camp, a death camp, prisoners forced to lick the buttocks and genitals of another prisoner. Bit off one of his testicles at gunpoint. The victims were Croats and Muslims but now they were fighting each other. It got loud. Jelonnek turned it down and changed the channel. He hadn't heard the word infomercial before they had cable. He was also partial to talk shows, and shows about science and nature, changed the channel till he saw a two-headed snake. He turned off the light in the kitchen and looked out the window.

It was loud again. Jelonnek kept turning it down. Eventually there was no sound at all, and the only light came from the screen. Jelonnek went down the hall. A faint shifting glow came from under Littlebit's door and he could hear someone being healed on the other side. You didn't need cable for that. He went back and sat in the living room.

He tried to make a pot of coffee in the dark.

Jelonnek drove Littlebit to the school but he wouldn't go in. He waited in the parking lot and dozed off, dreamed about the volcano. A patch of mist formed on the windshield in front of him.

Littlebit woke him up getting back in the car. "She missin days," she said.

"She's cutting school?"

"What I say?"

"They couldn't tell you that on the phone?"

"Too much like right, I guess." But there were other problems.

"I see her get on the bus," Jelonnek said.

"Well she gettin off somewhere else," Littlebit said. "Youa have to carry her."

"I can drive her."

"Truant officer step in after the fith time."

Missing assignments, fights, feminine hygiene.

"Put that chain on her door while she does her homework."

"We'll see."

A bunch of kids walked by, glanced in, kept going. Books, bags, the boys with their pants low on their hips. They spoke to each other, heads close as if in confidence.

"Everybody wanna look like they got a secret," Littlebit said.

"She startin to sound just like that," she said.

"Like what?"

"Proper."

Jelonnek liked doing the dishes. He watched his hands disappear into the suds and water. He made the water as hot as he could stand it; it smelled like lemon. He would let things soak for a while. He washed each knife, fork, and spoon one at a time, and when he rinsed them he rubbed them with his thumb and made sure he heard them shine.

They had a dishwasher but Jelonnek didn't like it. He didn't like the way it smelled.

He fell asleep doing the dishes and woke up. His hands were gone. He looked up out the window. The sun was in the backyard and the squirrel was back on the roof of the shed. The green nuts on the tree behind the shed hadn't grown back yet. Jelonnek heard his hands dissolving. The squirrel jumped off the roof. There was a trail of red drops in the grass where it landed. The trail curved from around the side of the shed to the door.

Someone covered his eyes.

He couldn't see. She was standing close behind him with her hands covering his eyes. The water was warm.

"Guess who," she said.

Jelonnek made his rounds every hour on the hour. His back against the house in the dark, sliding from corner to corner, the ivory in both hands next to his ear, the silver pointing up. The way he'd seen it done. The siding was wet but it wasn't raining. When it rained he wore his hardhat, the one he'd worn at the port.

Through the overgrowth in the side yard; weeds, rocks, ferns. His shoulder bumped the electric meter, a blister protruding from the wall. He stopped when he got to the corner. He peered around it with one eye, then stepped out decisively, feet planted, arms straight, pointing it with both hands. Sometimes he put one hand under the butt of the grip, the way he'd seen it done. Maybe he'd give them a warning shot first, but he had yet to buy bullets and the sight of it should be enough. You could see that shine in the dark.

Always them, and they. Never one, but two. Or three.

A guy made Molotov cocktails on public access. A stand-up comic saying, "Does the Pope shit in the woods?" A knife that never needed sharpening, it could slice tomatoes paper-thin or saw through steel pipe. A beer ad, but Jelonnek hadn't had a beer since the Super Bowl. He drank black coffee with sugar. Peed with the light off, gun in one hand, glancing out the bathroom window into the backyard.

He waited till they'd gone to bed.

On public access a gospel choir moving their mouths. He turned it up just a little. A Russian poet touring Serb positions. No electricity or water, Ukrainian Peacekeepers trading food on the black market for cars, TV sets and jewelry. A hippopotamus defecating underwater. How cosmic dust forms a star.

He made rounds, he didn't always hug the house. He went to the edge of the yard and looked down into the gully. It was a pit. He pointed the gun into it and pulled the trigger. One emptiness swallowing another. But he was sure they'd come up out of there—unless they'd come off the road. He had to do something about that gap in the fence.

There was a noise in the carport. He willed himself into silence—the element of surprise. Sometimes racoons got in the garbage. Had he locked the carport door? The door was locked but they might already be inside, making examples.

What if you tried to call 911 and the phone lines were cut?

But these people were basically cowards.

The President favored enforcing the no-fly zone. Four thousand shells a day. They'd been high school sweethearts, snipers shot them when they tried to leave the city. Each side blamed the other. They had lain in no man's land for four days but the U.N. would not help the families recover the bodies; it was a local issue. Jelonnek changed the channel. Los Angeles still holding its breath. A six-point approach policy, an eight-point plan, an eight-point declaration and fifteen cease-fires. Her arm across his back. Real-life footage, police extricating a burglar stuck in an air duct. Jelonnek almost knew a cop once. He'd shared his corner with a paperboy whose brother was one. A particular family moves into a house on a particular street. Someone throws a firebomb on the porch. The family moves out and doesn't come back. The other paperboy's brother the cop knows who did it. He and the other cops know but they pretend not to because they don't want that particular family living on that particular street any more than whoever firebombed the house does.

Back then they didn't call them hate crimes.

After the van left he opened the case in the living room and an old smell rose out. It lay in three pieces, dull metal embedded in red velvet. A strap with a hook at the end. Jelonnek pried the metal sections out of the velvet and put them together, hooked himself to it with the strap around his neck. He held it slanted across his body with one hand high and one low, and so far it felt like he was doing everything right. There was a place for your thumb. The mouthpiece was tapered black plastic with a slot at the tip, and Jelonnek forgot to wonder whose mouth had been on it before. He was a little afraid of what might happen when he put his to it and blew. It was like thinking about driving, and Jelonnek didn't like to drive much these days.

The keys made a clicking sound.

Jelonnek took a breath and tasted the mouthpiece. He blew and heard the air from inside him curving through the bent metal tube. He blew again and there was no music, only that low rushing sound. He kept pushing air through it, his mouth and tongue in a variety of positions, and each time the bell was silent. It tasted like it smelled.

He stopped, he was making himself dizzy. Had he purchased defective merchandise? He could call the pawnbroker but he knew all sales were final. Maybe he was doing something wrong; he could call a music store, ask for some pointers, but who would be open on Sunday?

Jelonnek didn't like the pawnbroker, but he trusted him.

He took the saxophone into the bathroom. The bathroom had a full-length mirror on the inside of the door, and Jelonnek locked the door and stood in front of it. He looked just like a musician wearing a saxophone; playing it would come from looking the part. He worked the keys and made them click. Looked at himself with a saxophone in his mouth. He leaned forward and back, then swung it to the side with one hand. He started to run in place, pumping his knees and snapping his fingers the way he'd seen it done.

When he got back from the store someone's car was parked in the driveway. It was big and silver-gray and the windows were tinted so that it looked like ten at night inside. Jelonnek pulled in behind it and went into the house with two bags of groceries. He put them on the counter in the kitchen and went into the living room.

Littlebit was sitting on the couch with a man in a suit. The TV was off, and they seemed to be engaged in earnest theological discussion. The man, who'd been quite comfortably reclined, leaned forward and stood as soon as Jelonnek came in the room. He was short and slender and his hair hung over his eyes in greasy curls. You couldn't tell how old he was—it was like that with them sometimes.

He put out a hand. Jelonnek hesitated, but it was just a regular shake.

"Are you the prophet?" he asked. There was a stain on the backrest where the man's head had been. He had long polished nails.

"I ain't the one," the man said, and shook his head regretfully. "Some of us deliver the news, and some just got to read the headlines."

"You get milk?" Littlebit asked.

He introduced himself, some kind of nickname. "I'm small but I'm scrappy," he said, explaining. His eyes were glassy and there was a scar under one of them.

"The van broke down," Littlebit said. "He carried us."

"We just conversatin," the man said.

"He can see," Littlebit said. "He ain't pressed."

"I don't know that," the man said. "Maybe he want me gone. You want me gone," he said to Jelonnek, "I'm in the wind."

"Why would I?" Jelonnek said.

The man looked at him, then doubled over in laughter you couldn't hear. "Why would you," he said, savoring some wit Jelonnek could not fathom. "What sign are you, player?"

"You get milk?" Littlebit said again.

He'd forgotten.

"Everybody thirsty for something," the man said. "Is he a Virgo?"

"I ain't with that," Littlebit said. "You shouldn't be either."

"You know you're daughter is an angel?" the man said.

"She's not my daughter," Jelonnek said.

"It's all good."

Jelonnek pointed his thumb behind him. "I'm gonna put some things away."

"I'd give you a hand but it's the Sabbath," the man said. "Just remember: God loves you whether you like it or not, and so do I." He sat back down. "I don't have any choice."

"Back to ending my sentence," Littlebit said. Jelonnek went back into the kitchen and put the groceries away. They spoke in lowered voices except when the man in the suit laughed. Jelonnek folded the bags. He forgot that he'd forgotten.

It lay under the Christmas tree in the shed with its legs straight out. Even its fur looked stiff. Half its tongue was gone and both eyes. The sockets were gray muck, seething with movement that was not tears. Tiny, white, squirming. The ones in the fur had wings. Jelonnek had a handkerchief tied over his face so the flies wouldn't get in his mouth.

Must have dragged itself in off the road. There was a gap. The rain must have washed the trail away, but it wasn't raining now.

If you breathed through your nose you would taste it.

Jelonnek shoved the gun down the front of his pants. He kept the flashlight trained on the dog and took the knife out of its holster. It had an eight-inch serrated blade and a compass in the butt of the haft. An unredeemed item. He crouched and poked the dog's neck with the tip of the blade. Sound and movement: death nursing its litter.

Must have gotten hit by a car and dragged itself in from the road. Unless someone had put it there. Like a warning, or a sign. Like a rat or a cat.

He backed out of the shed, pulled the door as far as it would go, and turned off the flashlight. He went and stood at the brink of the yard where the light over the back door of the house didn't reach. He looked down into the gully. Water whispering at the bottom of the pit. After a while he could even see it, or thought so; a certain pale strand, a glint where you didn't expect it. Sometimes you couldn't tell it was there.

Jelonnek holstered the knife and put down the flashlight. Took out the gun and pissed down the gully. He broke into a run toward the patio, felt the ground give under his shoe and fell in the wet grass, rolled over and got up on one knee, aiming the gun at the house of the neighbor who was never home. He swung around and covered the back door, the picket fence, the shed. He could hear the flies buzzing there and could still smell it like the origin of all decay. The ground gave, sank, the roof of a hollowing world.

He found the flashlight and jogged past the patio, rounded the corner and slowed along the side of the house. The bushes in front, from which all the color had sprouted when they'd first moved in. They were thick and taller than Jelonnek, and they'd kept all their leaves. He slipped behind them, clawed spiderwebs from his face. The leaves were wet.

310

The bedroom window, dark. You wouldn't know if someone was in there right now making an example of her. Cleansing.

He put the flashlight to the window and switched it on. The wall, posters of Whitney Houston and some twelve year-old rapper. He aimed down and saw her clothes on the floor in a path, the stained crotch of her underwear like she'd just stepped out of them. He could see the edge of her bed too, and he moved the light over and up till she was lying on her side with her pajama top rolled up to her neck. Jelonnek saw one round breast and its wide dark nipple, an eye looking back at him. He couldn't see her face.

He pressed himself against the house.

Somebody was at the front door.

"Somebody at the door," Littlebit said. Her voice was low.

"I heard," Jelonnek said. Then he said, "Your turn."

She stared at him. There was another knock and Jelonnek looked at the windows. The blinds were closed. They were white but when the sun shone against them they looked pink. He could try to peek through the slats but whoever it was might be waiting for that. He went into Miss D's room. The bushes out front almost covered the windows so he couldn't see who was at the door, or if there was a car in the driveway.

Again. Once it had been the mailman with a letter you had to sign for. They hadn't opened the door then, either, and the mailman left a notice saying they could pick it up at the post office. Or maybe it was a neighbor, a social worker, someone looking for a stray dog. They hadn't seen the neighbors for a while.

"Maybe it's your friend from church," he said.

"Might be the T.O." They were whispering now.

"Then why don't you talk to him?"

"Why don't you?"

"It's your kid."

"Then it's my business," Littlebit said and went down the hall to her room.

The knocking continued at a reasonable volume, at deliberate intervals, like some kind of Chinese torture. Jelonnek sat back down on the sofa. Let them. It was still early, no one had as much time as he did. Let them knock till their knuckles bled. He heard the TV going down the hall. Jerry or Jenny or Sally or Ricki.

Sunday the van didn't come so they went on a picnic. The sun had been out most of the week. They drove to Kentucky Fried Chicken, where you had your choice of two side dishes out of four, then stopped at a gas station to buy a quart of beer. They drove to the park. It wsn't very far and they could have walked there if it wasn't for the chicken and beer.

At the park all the picnic benches were taken, but they'd brought a blanket and spread it under a tree. The grass was almost dry. Littlebit nursed the beer, and Miss D froze whenever she saw a bee. They barely touched their mashed potatoes and gravy, so Jelonnek finished it for them—he liked it better than the chicken anyway. When he was done he got up and threw away his garbage, then went off looking for a place to take a leak.

"Where's he going?" he heard Miss D say.

"I don't know if he know," he heard Littlebit say.

He found a trailhead and entered the woods. The trees enclosed him in their world, dark and cool and unspoken, and he followed the trail and knew without looking back that everything behind him was gone. You could smell it. After he'd relieved himself he kept going in, pine needles and fallen blossoms underfoot. A jogger pounded past going the opposite way. Jelonnek heard birds. He heard a layered softness like static high in the branches and didn't know if it was air making sound from leaves or the other way

312

around. Something skittered across a patch of sunlight in front of him, too fast to tell what it was.

There was a sign on one of the trees. Jelonnek heard a dog barking. He left the trail and went into the brush till it got too thick, turned around and waited. A Great Dane the size of a pony trotted past, followed by three kids who sounded like ten and a man and a woman. Jelonnek wasn't sure he was out of sight but they went by without noticing him.

When he got back on the trail he looked at the sign on the tree and it said *Green ash*. Under that was its scientific name in scientific language, and under that a brief description. Something to edify. He moved on. The next one said *Yellow birch*, and there were more. For a while he read them. They said *Ponderosa pine* and *Turkish Hazel*, and they were about the size of a post card. They were fastened to the bark with a single nail and said *willow, aspen, silk*. Wooden, but not wood.

He stopped. Thought he'd heard something. He looked all around himself and the sounds spoke to his mind. *Phellodendron amurense* and *Smallflower tamarisk. Wild black cherry* and just a single nail. It came off easier than he thought it would. He'd only meant to take one but he took the next one he saw too, and the one after that. He stopped reading but he couldn't stop removing them. This made another sound. Tree to tree, *Dogwood* to *Madrone*—with its red bark and green flesh—looking around to see if anyone was there.

He came to one that wouldn't come off. He hadn't heard anyone for a while.

Jelonnek put his foot on the trunk and pulled with both hands. The nail gave and he fell backward clutching the sign, sitting. The trunk recoiled, shuddered, and here came God's big yellow hands, crashing softly down on his skull and shoulders.

The palm of God's hand is palmate. It is lobed and serrated, symmetrically veined as for the circulation of blood. It is shaped like a star, a tongue, a valentine, it is thick and shiny. Curls dryly back in upon itself at the edges, tapers and curves to a point: a claw with a single talon.

There was no more room in the palm of God's hand.

Someone was coming—he was sure of it this time. He took his armload of names back into the brush, found a tree wide enough to hide behind. This time when they'd passed he stayed where he was. He felt a burning sensation and looked down; he'd rubbed himself raw on its trunk.

Deeper in the woods nothing had a name, this must have been the way to go. It was getting late but the path is not always on the trail.

Behind him was now ahead of him. He saw something, what was left of a brightness, an openness, the edge of something. He pushed through thickets of branches that crackled and scratched his face, crushed a dead wet log under his foot, didn't see the thorns on a vine and it was like grabbing a handful of tacks. When he got to the edge of the gully his hands were empty. There was a stream at the bottom but he was breathing so hard he didn't hear it till he saw it. He stood and looked across. People lived on top of the other side; he saw yards, what looked like the back of a shed. It was late and he was out of breath. He sat on a rock, heard traffic somewhere.

Movement at the corner of his eye. A small, thin pale shape creeping across the ground.

Another, another, at the corner of his eye. He sensed motion all around him in these tiny pale components, the leaves and twigs crackled with it. There wasn't enough light left to tell quite what they were, but they were easier to see from the corner of your eye. He wondered if any of them had wings.

He shook the can. The rattle of the bead made him look around.

He stood at the side of the house that faced the neighbor who was never home. No windows here, nothing, just a blankness that seemed to glow at you. It was a mask, and Jelonnek knew what was behind it. If you put your ear to it you might hear it.

The moon big and low.

He popped the cap off the can and held it six inches from the wall. When he pressed the button there was a harsh sound, the exhalation of a long-held breath, and he stopped after a single upward stroke. Who would see? He pressed the button and wrote with his whole arm.

A diagonal slash down, then straight up again. He planted his feet, put his shoulder into the curve of the G.

He'd planned to cover the wall. He'd wanted to empty the can, but as soon as he started he realized that one word was enough. He rattled the bead again after the H. Was it one word or two? The paint hissed. You could almost see it in the dark.

J ust two of them in one car. No yellow tape this time, and they didn't take any pictures. They walked around the house. Jelonnek filled out another report.

"You know you've got some kind of dead animal in the shed back there?" one of them said.

"It's a dog," Jelonnek said.

"Used to be," the other one said.

"We won't cite you this time," his partner said, as if he might make a habit of it. They gave him a number to call so someone could come clear it out of there.

This time there were no reporters or cameras. If there was anything in the newspaper they didn't know about it; their subscription had been canceled.

The detective from Hate Crimes came alone. He took some Polaroids. They sat at the dining table with the gun somewhere in the house, protecting them. He didn't want any water. He asked some of the questions he'd asked them last time, then asked some new ones. Littlebit never said a word.

He had a folder. He compared the pictures he'd taken to the ones in the folder.

"To the trained eye," the detective said.

"You're the expert," Jelonnek said.

"My point is," the detective said. He said if it happened again the FBI might get involved. He said it like a threat.

He left Jelonnek another card. Jelonnek put it in his wallet on top of the other one while the detective went door to door again. Someone knocked. The stoner kid from down the street, the bandanna blue this time. Jelonnek thanked him and said he would take care of it himself. It was just one word.

The young guy said it wasn't just about painting.

Jelonnek thanked him. Two words, if you looked at it that way.

Later there was more knocking and the phone rang. The property manager. Jelonnek didn't want anyone's help. All he wanted anyone to do was see it.

The property manager reminded him that the grass was high.

The next day he got behind the push mower. The woman who'd been on the news came by when he was almost done.

"The second trial," she suggested. "The verdict must've pissed somebody off."

"Could be," Jelonnek said.

"The important thing is justice was done."

He thanked her.

"A marriage like yours is a brave thing," she said, "but not like it used to be, you wouldn't think."

"Thank you," Jelonnek said. The blades bit into the sidewalk. Sparks.

At night a small group stood in front of the lawn holding candles. Jelonnek peeked out between the slats of the closed blinds. He thought he knew who they were but the flickering flames made their faces strange. They were a small group but he felt surrounded.

When he switched on the light he saw it almost right away. It was covered with dust but not as much as everything else—the bags, the boxes, the Exercycle he'd found in Classifieds. He approached it carefully, crawling over the rafters on all fours, put his ear to it and heard nothing. The attic vent was small—no one could get in that way—but when Jelonnek brought it down and put it on the dining table, he spent at least twenty minutes just looking at it and listening to it. He walked in slow circles around the table, wondering if he should call the police. There was no lock on it. He picked it up, gave it a tentative shake. Put it down, turned his head away, held his breath and opened it.

He was alone.

At first he thought it might be the previous tenant's; he was a jack-of-all-trades, why not a musician as well? Tarnished gold, red velvet. You had to put it together. There was an instruction book and two reeds, tapered strips of wood in a wax paper sleeve. The book told you how to fasten the reed to the mouthpiece, what to call the metal clamp with which it was fastened.

"Ligature," Jelonnek read.

He thought of Littlebit's cousin. He didn't play the saxophone but maybe he had something to do with it. She wasn't around to ask. The man who drove her and Miss D to church had pulled up in the driveway in his big car. He hadn't come inside, just beeped the horn. They'd disappeared into the almost-black behind the windows and driven away to Cinco de Mayo. She called him her friend.

Jelonnek wasn't sure what day it was, but it wasn't Sunday.

There was something familiar about its weight. He tasted the wood. He tried to blow air through it but couldn't get past the mouthpiece. The bell sealed in its membrane of silence. He tried again. His lips and tongue buzzed.

Jelonnek looked at the book. You were supposed to wet the reed first. There was a word, French-looking, that meant the way you shaped your mouth around the mouthpiece.

He went into the bathroom and shut the door. He blew into the saxophone and something gave way and he went all the way through it. He heard something. It hurt to hear but it was his. He made another one. He watched himself make sounds in the mirror, using used-up air pulled out of his blood. They came from his shoulders and spine, he bent his waist to squeeze them out of himself. Sometimes they surprised him, seemed to break through from somewhere else—the door, the wall, the window—like answers to questions he didn't know he'd asked. He felt sparks jumping on the back of his neck.

Cinco de Mayo.

His face in the mirror was all red now. You didn't get as dizzy if you did it right, the horn didn't feel as heavy. The book showed you where to put your fingers. It showed you how to play "Mary Had a Little Lamb," but he'd left it in the other room.

Jelonnek closed his eyes and was surrounded by candles again. Maybe if he blew the right notes he could blow them out.

He hadn't slept all day, hadn't even dozed. Whenever he started to fall asleep, he'd see them moving in the corner of his eye. Tiny, pale, hundreds, maybe more. If you looked right at them you wouldn't see them, but you could hear them. They made a sound that kept you awake, so he hadn't slept. When it was dark he put on a pot of coffee and sat down in the living room. He closed his eyes. That was all he was going to do, just close his eyes till the coffee was ready, but the coffee didn't wake Jelonnek up, nor did the phone. The phone was ringing, but it was Littlebit who woke him.

"The phone," she said.

He looked at her. "When did you get back?"

She looked at him. "Please." Her eyes red and shiny.

It wouldn't stop. It was somewhere in the room. Littlebit told him where it was but she wouldn't answer it.

A woman's voice. A sergeant. A police sergeant with a woman's voice. Jelonnek told her she had the wrong number. She repeated the number and it was his but still the wrong one. He told her no one named Imogene lived there.

Littlebit grabbed the phone. "Who want Imogene?"

She said, "Why?" Jelonnek sat down.

"Who wanna know?" Littlebit said, and wanted to know why again.

"Sure you don't," she said. "She right here." She went to Miss D's room, opened the door and looked in. She came back.

"My baby," she said flatly to no one. She'd left the door open. Jelonnek went and looked inside.

"Please," Littlebit said, "she don't even drive." She looked at Jelonnek. "I know your car still there."

He went to the carport. He came back.

"She alright then?" Littlebit said. "Y'all gonna keep her?"

"You can keep her," she said.

"Where is it?" Jelonnek said.

"I need a ink pen," Littlebit said. She took down an address. When she hung up he asked her where the car was again.

"Tore up," she said. "Is it stealin if it's in the family?"

"It's wrecked?"

"Through. Other car too. Ain't nobody hurt though, she ain't hurt. Caught herself turning up the wrong-way street."

"Where was she headed?"

"She ain't say."

She hadn't gone a mile.

Jelonnek put his shoes on, looked for his keys; he kept forgetting she'd taken them. Littlebit called the man she called her friend but there was no answer, and the buses had stopped running. She told Jelonnek they weren't going anywhere and he took off his shoes. They sat on the sofa watching TV.

"I'm outdone," Littlebit said.

"At least she doesn't have school tomorrow," Jelonnek said.

"It's gon be me and her."

"At least nobody was hurt," he said. "Who's Imogene?"

"Just a name." She sat up. "We could call a cab."

"We could…I don't know how much is left." He didn't move.

The picture was bad. The mountains interfered with the reception and they only had four channels since the cable had been disconnected.

"Well then," Littlebit said, "ain't nobody hurt." And went back to bed.

There was wood in the furnace room. One-by-fours, one-by-eights. Jelonnek took an armload out to the backyard, nailed four or five boards across the gap between the fence and shed. Hammering the nails made him think of the old man, but he really didn't think anyone would come in off the road.

He could hear Littlebit through her bedroom window. The big car with the tinted windows was in the driveway.

"Like *that*," he heard the man who drove it say. He said it over and over.

Jelonnek took off his shirt. He'd bought fishing line and eyebolts. Tackle. The pawnbroker told him it might need a drop of oil. He wedged the stock in the crotch of the tree, put a milk crate under the barrel. He got behind it and looked through the sight at the shed. Put a brick on top of the crate. He pounded eyebolts into the boughs, put one in the trunk of the pine behind it. You drew the bowstring by turning a crank.

The squirrel watched him from the roof of the shed. Watched him thread the fishing line through the eyes and tie on a swivel. He had trouble with the knot, got mad and kicked the tree. A bird flew out.

Miss D had been released into their custody. The judge said, "A nurturing environment must exist in the home." He'd found the milk crate in the carport.

The sun was high and there were no clouds. The squirrel ate the green nuts from the tree behind the shed. The line was ten-pound test. Jelonnek walked backward along the edge of the gully, reeling it off its plastic spool, using a pen for a spindle. A court date had been set. He hammered one into the shed. The squirrel jumped off the roof and the flies woke up. He pulled the line as taut as he could, cut it and tied it off. He remembered the knot now, it was like a hangman's noose but small. There were not as many flies as before.

The pawnbroker said they were bolts, not arrows.

Littlebit yelled, "Stab it you black sonofabitch!"

Jelonnek stood at the edge of the yard with his back to the gully. The fishing line was just below his knee. The grass was high and there was a Barbie doll in it. There was Miss D's bike and a red ball and a sandal. Wrappers. He'd taken off the trigger guard. He took a step. The line was tight but nothing happened. He pushed into it with both legs and it broke without pulling the trigger. He thought of the old man—the old man would have measured. It was going to be harder than he thought, it was going to be trial and error.

The squirrel climbed back on the shed.

"It's been so long," Littlebit sobbed. "You just don't know."

"This is martial law," Jelonnek said. He sneezed. "A citizen's arrest."

It was mostly fur and bone. There didn't seem to be as many flies now, and either he'd gotten used to the smell or was smelling inside it. The Christmas tree was all brown but still had needles, and some of them fell soundlessly as Jelonnek stood there. Tinsel. A dead moth floating in oil.

"Zero rhymes with hero," he said. He crouched down, knife in one hand, gun in the other. He didn't need a flashlight; at the pawnshop he'd bought a lamp that strapped around his hardhat like a miner's. He didn't need a shirt. He poked it in the ribs with the blade. Something was moving underneath, something had made its nest.

He poked the long silver of the gun into its ear.

"In the name of." He felt the trigger. "I hereby." He squeezed and a cloud of flies erupted like they'd shot out of the barrel. Needles falling in fur. The flies roared and Jelonnek backed out of the shed. The light over the back door was burned out. He ran across the grass and dove into the side yard for cover. The hardhat flew off and tumbled ahead of him, the beam whirling like the spoke of a wheel. It came to rest pointing up into a tree.

The tree had sprouted big pink blossoms. They'd fallen off then and covered the ground, withered and faded, but the yard was full of their scent. Jelonnek crawled with crawling things through it toward the light, the knife in his teeth. The ground was cool. He dragged himself over leaves and sticks and rocks and trash thrown over the fence, trash thrown from the house, but didn't feel it in the same way he didn't smell the dog. Tampons and coffee grounds. They'd made a garden. When he reached the lamp he shut it off and put the hardhat back on his head. At the corner of the house he sat with his back to the siding, covered with dirt and sweat and faded pink petals, smelling like them and sweat and the inside of the shed and what he had not washed off himself in days. His breathing was the loudest sound in the night. A cat's eyes glowed blind in the driveway. Headlights. There was half a moon.

Zero equals hero, but where was the other half?

He put the knife back in its holster and stood and looked down the street, listened for approaching cars. Shoved the gun down the front of his pants, warming its hard cold. It softened. He crept around and got behind the bushes in front of the house.

One of the ceiling tiles in the kitchen was wrong. There was a gap. Had he not replaced it properly? He put a chair in the kitchen and stood on it, moved the tile and reached in the opening. Felt plastic. He opened the bag and counted it though you could see it all at once. A plastic bag from Safeway. He reached back in the opening and felt around but there was no more.

Out here they said sack instead of bag. He told Littlebit he was probably buying groceries for the last time.

"We spent that up good, didn't we?" she said. She said a word he hadn't heard her use in a long time. She'd lost weight in places; he hadn't noticed that either.

Something bumped the sofa. Jelonnek woke up and heard shouting. He opened his eyes. Miss D was standing over him, panting, looking toward the other end of the sofa where her mother was. Littlebit said something. He closed his eyes and opened them and they'd changed places. They were throwing dirty clothes at each other. He pulled something soft and foul off his face. They were gone. Jelonnek wasn't sure who was chasing whom, or if they were just playing around.

He had a blanket on. He could feel the gun, embedded.

The store was big. It was one of those places where you saved money and bagged your own groceries. Jelonnek found the ground beef but had trouble locating the bread aisle. A store manager looked at the look on his face and said, "Can I help you find something?"

"I'm good," Jelonnek said. Her name tag said she was an associate. She smiled at him, at his grass-stained jeans and the white plastic sticking out of his pocket.

He found the hamburger buns but the aisle was crowded and he couldn't do it. He walked around. In front of the magazine rack there were two kids looking at comic books. Jelonnek hid himself beside them, took out the bag that still smelled like money and stuffed the meat and buns inside it. He added an issue of Batman and headed for the Customer Service counter. On the way he passed the associate who'd offered to help him, tried to look like he was someone else.

He stood in line, working up his nerve. The exit was twenty feet away. He waited in line till someone had been helped, then someone else, then walked out the door. There was no shrill beep like you heard sometimes at Safeway. He walked down the sidewalk past the ATM, then started across the parking lot.

"Excuse me, sir," the associate said. She was stepping off the sidewalk behind him.

Jelonnek kept going, down an aisle between two rows of cars.

"Do you have a receipt?" she yelled.

"Yeah," he said hoarsely, not looking back. He walked faster. Ahead of him a guy was loading groceries into his trunk.

"Can I see your receipt?" She sounded like she wasn't used to walking fast. She sounded like she still wanted to help him.

The guy had taken an interest. He slammed the trunk lid and turned, his shoulders square. "What's the problem?" he said. He was big and his shirt said I DO ALL NUDE SCENES.

Jelonnek cut between two cars into the next aisle. The big guy emerged almost at the same time and came his way. Jelonnek headed back toward the store, not sure where this was going. He broke into a trot and heard the big guy say, "Don't make it worse for yourself, partner."

He almost ran into a car backing out. At the end of the aisle he turned and ran parallel with the sidewalk, full speed now. He could hear the big guy behind him, huffing and pounding. Someone beeped. He turned one more corner around the back of the store into a problem. The parking lot dead-ended. There were stacks of milk cartons and flattened boxes with lettuce stuck to them, a rotten smell. Two stock boys smoking.

"Grab him!" the big guy yelled. One of them muttered something but didn't move. Jelonnek kept running. There was a wall at the back of the back, a dumpster in front of it. He wasn't sure, but he thought the state road was on the other side. He'd be okay if he could get over the wall. He ran. The comic book fell out of the bag.

He woke up. Somebody was knocking at the door. The knock was familiar but he stayed on the couch. He didn't stay on the couch because he didn't want to answer the door, but because he didn't want to step on them without any shoes on. He wouldn't look at them but he could hear them, crackling softly like static electricity. Something eating something. Bubbling up through.

Littlebit said, "I got a pussy" and Jelonnek woke up on the couch. He heard a sound, then another, an animal grunt. He opened his eyes. She stood in front of the TV, holding the golf club high. The man who drove the big car with dark windows lay on the floor holding his face.

"It ain't like that," he said.

"It's like this," she said, stood more like a batter than a golfer. "I know what time it is."

"Ain't nothing happen."

"You wanted it to." She brought the club down. It made a sound like a whip, then like beating a rug when it hit him in the ribs.

"Bitch!" It knocked the word right out of him. "She's lyin."

"I got a pussy," Littlebit said and hit him once for each word. The iron flew out of her hands and bounced off the coffee table. She turned to get it and the man who drove the big car tripped her and got up and headed for the door. He wore a black shirt with a red tie. His mouth was bleeding. He picked up a tooth and left his hat and pushed through the door.

Littlebit followed him outside.

"You damn straight you wanna leave." She was out of breath but her voice was clear like she was still in the living room. Jelonnek heard the man say something.

"Fuck your pissass ride." Then metal hitting metal, so as to demonstrate. The car started, and you could hear her demonstrating as it backed down the driveway.

"Fuck is you lookin at?" she said. She came back in the house.

"Fuck they lookin at?" she said, and commenced beating his hat to death. "I got a pussy. Where she at?" She stomped through the living room with the club. Jelonnek heard her bang open the door to Miss D's room. He felt the gun in his pants but he couldn't move, like it might go off if he did.

"Where she at? I need to talk to her."

Miss D's hair was dry. So was her scalp. Jelonnek had expected them to be greasy but they weren't.

"Does that hurt?" he said.

It didn't, she said. He tried to gather two lengths of hair between his thumbs and forefingers. If you were braiding it was three strands, but Jelonnek wasn't trying to braid.

"Show me," he said.

"Ma," she said.

"Big as you is." Littlebit got up. "Youa gimme back some a them ass and titties, I keep doin your hair?" She pinched two strands and said, "Here" to Jelonnek. He squeezed them between his fingers right at the scalp and started to wind them around each other.

"Am I pulling it?" he said to Miss D.

"You're supposed to be," she said.

"Tighter," Littlebit said. Jelonnek pulled the strands apart at the top.

"Did that hurt?" he said. It was late. When he'd finished they sent her to bed and put the chain on her door.

"They ain't comin back," Littlebit said, smoking.

Jelonnek put a piece of brick on the book to hold it open.

"Come on," he said to Littlebit.

She shook her head. "I don't need no book," she said. "Where that golf stick?"

"It's just practice," he said.

"I ain't the one," she said. She looked at Miss D. "You wanna play boxing?"

Miss D got up and took off her glasses.

"It's just practice," Jelonnek said. "We'll take it slow."

It was hot out in the backyard and the sun was bright but Jelonnek kept his shirt on. The grass was tall in some places, burnt in others. Flies circled something in it. There was clover and crab grass and dandelions, and weeds where the flowers had been. If the phone hadn't been turned off they probably would have heard from the property manager by now. The book lay open on the steps.

"Here I go," Miss D said. She put up her guard and stepped in with one foot, looking so genuine and formidable that for a second Jelonnek almost forgot what he was doing. But in the book *uke* did not start out this way. *Uke's* feet were together and his arms were at his sides. Jelonnek corrected Miss D's stance and said, "Alright."

Littlebit seemed to be talking to herself: "Like I blacked out or something."

Miss D frowned, her hands in fists. One of them rose and swung toward Jelonnek's face, faster than he intended. He waved his hand in front of him and deflected her arm, but her knuckles still brushed his nose.

"Hey now," Littlebit said. Jelonnek followed through, straightened his arm across Miss D's shoulders, just above her chest. At the same time he stepped forward, behind her, and swept her back with his arm but something was wrong. She was supposed to trip and fall but she just stumbled backwards, her buttocks into his hip, arching her back beneath him in a maneuver for which there was no defense. She had a musky smell.

Littlebit laughed in her dry-throated way. Something cracking. The starlings tried to imitate her.

Jelonnek went back to the book. He saw now that he'd stepped in with the wrong foot. His nose stung.

"Okay," he said. "Again. A little slower."

"They not comin back," Littlebit said.

"Who?" Jelonnek said.

"A hundred," Jelonnek said.

"Forty," the pawnbroker said. He was wearing a cowboy hat.

"It's a nineteen-inch."

"I can see that. That's why I'm saying forty."

"I rode the bus with it." His arms were still sore.

"You want me to pay you for mileage?" the pawnbroker said. "That don't appreciate its value."

"It's got to be worth eighty."

"I'll say a hundred twenty," the pawnbroker said. "I loan a third of what I think I can get. I'm telling you up front the way I do business."

"I've given you enough of it," Jelonnek said.

"Nobody got robbed."

"I've been a good customer."

"So why stop now?"

"Fifty."

"Forty-five," the pawnbroker said. "Forty-five and I'll throw in a bar of soap. I'm smelling you through the bulletproof here."

Jelonnek made his inside round.

He turned on all the lights. He checked the spare room, the furnace room, climbed the wooden stairs into the ceiling, into the choking warmth of the attic. The bulb was burned out but he had the lamp on the hardhat. He turned his head slowly one way, then the other, lit up what he looked at. Old yellow newspapers, the dead skin of the past. He sighted down the barrel.

Jelonnek turned off all the lights except for the one in the hallway. He was trying to conserve his batteries.

He checked the bathroom, listened at doors. He saved Miss D's for last. His ear touched wood and he held his breath. Sometimes she talked in her sleep, but all he heard now was the song he couldn't get out of his head.

He took off the chain, turned the knob and pushed. The door made no sound. The slice of light he let into her room stretched into a path, grew till it led to her lying on her back, in his custody, one breast covered, the other looking back at him. Her face and arm were past the edge of the light where he couldn't see them as of some truncated ancient sculpture, but he knew by the bend of her elbow where her thumb was.

She slept the same way every night. They say if you sing it you won't hear it anymore.

The opening was just big enough to let him into the room. He put the gun in his pants but held on to the knife. He kept to the dark. At the edge of the bed he could see her breast heaving up at him, slowly, and he could hear her breathe now and he could smell her. Nothing came through the window. His shadow curved where she did. He took off the hardhat like a sign of respect.

Jelonnek knelt, lowered his head into his portion of light, put his mouth on her breast. She stopped breathing for a moment, then started again.

There were empty beer bottles in the side yard. Quart, forty-ounce, torpedo-shaped. People must have thrown them over the picket fence from the road. Some had the caps screwed back on, or Jelonnek would find them lying around.

He'd walked over a mile to the store. On the way back he stopped at a gas station. He'd stolen the kerosene but had to pay for the gas, filled the can the previous tenant had left. The previous tenant left dirty motor oil in the shed.

The sun was as incessant as the rain had been, the air dry and the nights cool. Jelonnek worked in the shade of the carport. He rinsed out the bottles and peeled off the labels. He mixed some of the motor oil with the kerosene; the guy on public access said it would help. Jelonnek didn't remember how, he'd only seen one installment before the cable had been disconnected, but they probably would have taken the show off anyway.

Was there anyone who didn't like that smell? Some of it spilled and the next time you looked it was gone.

The guy on public access said to leave a little air in the bottles. He had a kerchief tied around his face, and so did Jelonnek. Jelonnek screwed the caps back on, wiped off the bottles and let them dry.

Littlebit watched from the doorway. "You fittin to rob a bank?"

He'd stolen eight yards of bandage roll, something he hadn't seen on the public access program. He'd seen it in a war movie years ago, resistance fighters on roof tops, bombarding tanks in an occupied city. He wound the bandage around the bottles, completely wrapping them. It came with tape. The tape unpeeled with a hiss, a snake rearing in his head.

"What is you makin?" Littlebit said.

Jelonnek looked at her. "I put an ad up for the washer and dryer at the store." There was a bulletin board near the entrance. People sold things, advertised for roommates, offered rewards for lost pets.

"How they gonna call? The phone dead."

He shrugged, not looking at her. He'd left an address.

331

"Ain't nobody comin. Is that my scarf?"

He used all the tape. The box said it was flammable. It was done. He'd done a neater job than he'd thought himself capable of, but he was beyond satisfaction. He'd left a little air in each.

"She say she been havin this dream," Littlebit said. "Some man comin into her room...exetra.

"I don't remember my dreams," Jelonnek said through his mask.

"She sleep hard as what," Littlebit said. "What is you doin?"

"I'm done."

A pair of newlyweds from the west suburbs bought the washer and dryer. The wife was four months pregnant. They backed their pickup truck almost into the carport, and Jelonnek helped the husband load the dryer onto the bed. The washer wouldn't fit through the side door; they had to turn it sideways and the husband took a fitting off the back. He was handy.

They said they were looking for furniture.

"Come on in then," Littlebit said.

They hadn't taken the garbage out and the wife kept covering her mouth. "What's wrong with you?" Littlebit said.

"Morning sickness," the husband said. He sounded like he wasn't using his nose.

"Way past noon," Littlebit muttered.

The wife seemed reluctant—she wasn't sure there was room in the truck—but they bought the dining set, a lamp, two lawn chairs, the coffee table, and the microwave. Only the hard furniture. Littlebit brought out the fern from her room but they didn't want that either.

The husband asked if they were moving.

"Why?" Littlebit said.

"We just need the money," Jelonnek said.

"We ass out," Littlebit said.

The husband wrote something on a piece of paper and gave it to Jelonnek.

"We're hiring," he said. Jelonnek asked what they did there.

"I have no experience," he said.

"You start in setup," the husband said.

His wife asked to use the bathroom. They told her it was out of order and in a way it was. There was a bucket next to the toilet. If the man next door wasn't home, they would fill the bucket from a spigot on the side of his house and pour it in the tank so the toilet could flush. Otherwise they would fill it another way and dump it in the gully. Or the side yard.

The man next door was home so it was out of order.

"I could take a look at it," the husband offered.

"The property manager knows," Jelonnek said.

Miss D's door opened as far as the chain would allow. The wife jumped.

"It's a Taco Bell down the street," Littlebit said.

"I might save you some trouble," the husband said.

"Taco*time*," Miss D corrected. She'd used the toilet when you weren't supposed to.

"I'll be in the truck," the wife said.

The husband paid with cash and Jelonnek helped him load the truck. They beeped the horn when they left. Jelonnek couldn't remember what he'd done with the piece of paper the husband had given him.

"Morning-sick all damn day," Littlebit muttered.

Miss D pulled on the door, rattled the chain. "Can we eat lunch yet? My stomach hurts."

"For you can make another mess?" Littlebit said. "You ain't clean up the last one."

Jelonnek asked them what they wanted to eat.

"Whatever we can walk to," Littlebit said. "Maybe I'll put in a application."

"You always say that," Miss D said.

"You hear something?" Littlebit said.

"I made up a word," Miss D said. "Can I say it?"

"I can't hear a thing," Littlebit said.

The park was closed. Jelonnek didn't switch on the lamp till he was in the woods. The battery was dying but showed him what he needed to see, where not to put his feet. There was nothing to either side of the trail but sometimes he heard things: rustlings, strange cries in the trees you would only hear at night. A stick came to life and slithered away. The dirt looked yellow and gray and was covered with pine needles. The backpack was heavy. In it he might have heard them thudding gently against each other, maybe even the slosh of liquid, but his head was filled with the Fourth of July.

He'd only touched the big ones. The M-80's, the quarter-sticks. He would wait till the old man was too drunk to care what he was doing. He would light the fuse with a sparkler, cock his arm back, and wait till the fuse was almost gone. It drove everyone crazy but he never got hurt.

He was wearing Miss D's backpack. He was wearing number nineteen.

When he got to the point where you left the trail, he took the knife from its holster and started hacking at branches. He stumbled but didn't fall once. Heard the swishing and crackling of green and brown things, felt them grab, leave their colors on him. He saw the dead log and stepped over it. The light from his head was dim and orange now, dwindling to zero like everything else. That was how you knew it was time. When he got to the edge of the gully he stood there and let it die. He couldn't see the house. The stream was dry.

Down. Dirt, rock, roots, smell of moss and clay. A couple of feet from the bottom he lost his footing and slid the rest of the way on his backside, one hand keeping the hardhat on. The gully strewn with their garbage, their sewage, their blood and their piss. He stood and leaped across the stream bed, but the backpack was heavy and his back shoe sank in mud. He stopped, looked up and around with one foot heavier than the other. He didn't like the way it felt so he dipped the other one in and started up.

It was an easy climb—in a way coming down was harder—but the weight on his back made him stop at the top to catch his breath and listen. He smelled himself. Crickets, a frog down in the gully, his laboring lungs still climbing. Even the grass made a sound, and Jelonnek heard the stream that no longer ran and the needles still falling from Christmas and he looked up at everything in the night sky and heard that wind as well.

The house was quiet and dark, but breathing.

He got to his feet and took two steps. He didn't feel the fishing line but there was something, a slowing of his leg...He pulled harder and heard a loud twang to his left like the release of a heavy spring, and he tripped and fell on his face. The bottles clanked. On his knees he took off the backpack and groped inside. He was grateful for the bandages again.

Over his head: a dissolving streak of light. He hadn't been looking for a sign but he'd been sent one from beyond. He set the backpack down, took one out by the neck. The tape was so white it almost glowed in his hand. He held it the other way. Dug the lighter out of his pocket and thumbed the wheel, saw flame on the first try. He touched it to the tape.

Quarter-sticks, half-sticks, it drove them crazy. But he would wait longer than anyone else, and then it would leave a trail of sparks from his hand and explode in mid-air, because as far as Jelonnek was concerned that was the only way to do it. Blowing holes in the dark on Independence Day when he was a kid at the height of summer.

The tape flared, hissed and bubbled. Jelonnek approached the house, holding it like a torch. He saw it burning in the glass, the wall throbbing with shadows.

Jelonnek, in number nineteen, cocked his arm and threw the bottle at the glass doors in the back of the house. They broke with a dull simple sound, not what you'd expect, and he turned and walked back toward the backpack. A deeper sound then, a brief concentrated roar, glass shattering like it properly should and a yellow flash from behind throwing his shadow over the edge of the gully. Something like a handful of gravel pelted his back in a wave of heat.

He knelt and lit the next one, limped toward the corner of the house holding the backpack by the strap. He put it hard through her bedroom window but there was still the sound and feel of everything going slow and soft. He rounded the corner. At the side of the house, next to the neighbor who was almost never home, a thump like a blow against the inside of the wall. He slowed to light the last one but didn't stop. He didn't know why he was limping. He turned to face the bushes in front of the house and it was burning too fast, his hand was on fire. It crashed through the window but nothing happened. Too much tape, or it was wound too tight. He thought he heard a voice inside, though, and then the windows filled with light. He threw up his arms almost in time. A gust of heat, something whipping past his cheek—it didn't hurt but he felt something run down the side of his face. A bright orange cloud rolled out the windows and up into itself. Into black. The bushes were burning.

He crossed the lawn, the driveway, heard a door opening down the street. Soon there would be other sounds, other doors. At the other side of the house, next to the road, a sudden tearing in his leg stopped him. He reached down and felt the shaft of the bolt protruding from the side of his thigh. Feathers. A tree branch had snagged it. There didn't seem to be much blood, and it hadn't yet started to hurt.

He limped into the light and heat behind the house and stood and watched. Crackling and sparks. He hadn't realized how fast it would spread—it was curling up over the eaves, the shingles blistered, started to melt. It looked as though only the shed would survive. He still held the empty backpack, the lighter was in his pocket. He could hear them now. His face and hand hurt, his leg was starting to, but he wasn't finished yet.

A window burst with a scream.

Jelonnek started counting. Another window. The stars fading in the glare and smoke. He was going to count to five, but when he got to three he dropped the backpack and walked into the house.

He was cold. He couldn't see. He was wrapped in a wet sheet and when he moved it felt like he was lying on aluminum foil. They did things to him without him knowing it. He was wrapped in bandages that were wrapped in bandages. They put holes in the first layer and injected water with a syringe. He was confused but he was in no pain. He heard things but he wasn't worried about them. Pneumonia, that was one thing he heard. A lung filled with water was another. That couldn't have been good but it didn't feel like anything. Maybe they were talking about someone else's lung.

He was just cold. There was heat coming down on him from somewhere above but it didn't help.

"Where is he?"

"Ma'am."

"Who that?"

"Miss."

"That ain't him."

The rattle of paper on a clipboard. "That's him."

"Not no more it ain't."

"Your voice, ma'am."

"Well he ain't got ears."

"He can still—"

"His head…"

"His body is fighting infection."

"His *head*."

"Swelling is normal at this point."

"Normal."

"Are you a relative?"

"Common law. Ain't no hair on it."

"That's the least of his worries."

"Yeah he got worries."

"Would you happen to have his insurance information?"

One of them became a man: "Mr. Jello-neck."

"Jelonnek

"Mr...?"

"Sir."

"Can you hear me Mr. Jelonnek? I know you're..." A voice he once knew, but it kept fading in and out. "But this is very important."

"That's going to have to do."

"This is very important...How do you say it again?"

"Sir."

"Sergeant."

The hardhat had melted to his head. The jersey with the number nineteen had melted into his flesh in places. They had to operate to get it out, and they weren't sure they got it all.

They stapled the skin of the dead onto him, and the skin of pigs. It was too early to do any harvesting.

A complication arose during surgery. His blood wouldn't clot, he started to hemmorhage. He lost so much blood his heart stopped on the operating table. He was dead for two and a-half minutes before they brought him back. They didn't tell him.

He heard a scream from somewhere far away.

They drilled holes in the bones of his legs. They screwed bolts into the holes and clamped the bolts to the bed frame. He wasn't sure why, but it was important that he didn't move his legs. They itched like he'd never itched before. His arms were in troughs. They couldn't get the IV tube into them so they put the tube in his neck.

He could see. The nurses wore spacesuits. He couldn't stop seeing, couldn't close his eyes. They dripped saltwater into them, as if to supply him with tears.

Bottles and bags and tubes hung over him, and every day started with a needle in the stomach. Twice they gave him another shot to paralyze his heart; once it was beating two hundred times a minute. There were other numbers, rates and ratios: ninety-six over fifty, a hundred-twenty over fifty-seven, ninety-nine over forty. Like the scores of a test he kept having to take over.

His temperature was another number. They said it was too low but he was hot. He was hot but they said the heater over his bed had to stay on till his temperature returned to what they called normal. It made him thirsty. He was always thirsty and he itched and this could not be quantified. He asked someone in a spacesuit for something to drink. It was the first thing he said and his mouth was dry and his lips wouldn't come together to form certain sounds. Somehow she understood and asked him what he'd like.

"Gray jew," he said, and she surprised him again and filled a syringe with Hi C. Then she removed a tube and injected it into the hole between his mouth and eyes. He couldn't taste it but he thanked her. She told him not to talk if he didn't have to.

Then the nurses weren't wearing spacesuits anymore. There were still bottles and bags and tubes hanging over him but sometimes he heard a TV. The Secretary of State said they would deploy troops to Macedonia. He couldn't see it. He tried moving his head to take a look around but it gave him a terrific headache. He heard enough to know there were other people in the room with him. Not just personnel, but other patients. Roommates. He wasn't sure how many because some of them probably couldn't speak; he had trouble talking himself so mostly he just listened. In this way he was able to learn more things with numbers, like adding your age to the percentage of you that was burned to calculate the odds of your survival. You could almost do it in your head. Or words like debriding. He didn't think his lips could say it, and it was starting to seem he no longer had any.

He heard a scream from somewhere, closer. Another room but close, maybe just the other side of the wall.

"Debriding," someone said.

"Tub room," someone else said. Another new thing.

"They made him a mummy," Miss D said.

"Alright now," Littlebit said.

"How did you like being dead?"

"You gon find out for your own self you don't quit."

At first he thought they were nurses, some kind of personnel. They wore surgical gowns and caps and masks, and Littlebit's purse was in a plastic bag. They were all eyes. When they spoke the masks would move, but everything seemed to come from their eyes.

"I'm hot in here," Miss D said.

"It's good news and bad news," Littlebit said. There always was. Jelonnek saw that her forearm and hand were bandaged. He drifted off. When he came back she was saying they said his lung was inflated, but he didn't know if this was the good news or the bad.

"Was there a light?" Miss D said. "Did you hear a big voice?"

"Just you and your simpleass questions. You should be thankin him."

"He ain't save me," Miss D said.

"He was lookin to," Littlebit said, and this much he remembered. He itched.

"He didn't save you that good either."

"Good enough. You want me to put her out?"

He wanted something to drink.

"We were on the news," Miss D said.

"Paper too," Littlebit said.

"They didn't have our pictures in it though," Miss D said. "Why can't he speak?"

"What I say?"

Sometimes he couldn't see the masks moving and it was like he was hearing their thoughts. This frightened him.

Littlebit lowered her voice: "That cop been comin around."

"It's not polite to whisper," Miss D whispered.

"Steady sniffin, askin me what you tellin me. I told em we common law."

A big dog walked into the room and stood behind Littlebit and Miss D. It looked like the dog from the shed. Jelonnek wondered if the shed was still standing. Maybe it wasn't, and that was why the dog had left.

Miss D said something. He couldn't hear everything. The voices would fade, or he would.

"You believe that shit?" Littlebit said. "They out they mind."

"Did you shoot yourself with a arrow?"

She was an old woman who almost reminded him of his mother. She said she had a son who came and did things around the house, but Jelonnek never saw him. There was a rat trap nailed to the porch post. He would fold the paper and put it under the bale. You had to watch your fingers. She never tipped but she paid on time and once a week gave him a bag of stale candy. Some pieces looked like they'd been mouthed and put back in their wrappers, but because his mother might have looked like her if she'd gotten that old, he couldn't bring himself to throw it away. Maybe he was being tested.

The rope creaked, the chandelier turning slowly.

◆　◆　◆

"How many fingers am I holding up?" the attending staff surgeon said. It was impossible to tell because they kept multiplying and dissolving, and didn't look much like fingers in the first place.

"Side effect of the anesthetic," the surgeon said. "Special stuff. Due to the extent of your injuries."

He explained to Jelonnek the extent of his injuries, called them acquired deformities. Damaged dermis. Jelonnek found himself listening raptly while the attending staff surgeon discussed the nature of second and third degree burns, and then went on to explain the fourth degree, which category Jelonnek hadn't known existed.

They would have to remove the muscles from the left side of his chest.

"The good news," the attending staff surgeon said, "is that your white blood cells are looking better."

The bolt hadn't pierced the bone.

"Let me be frank," the surgeon said. He said that thanks to recent advances in emergency medicine, patients were capable of sustaining and surviving a greater degree of trauma than ever before. While this is all to the good…Jelonnek saw the dog from the shed come out from behind the attending staff surgeon and crawl under his bed.

"This is where I come in," the surgeon said, and he explained skin grafting, scar management, free flaps, dog ear flaps, five-flap Z-plasty, harvesting—how they removed a tiny skin sample on the operating table and cultured it in the laboratory, how in a couple of weeks it would be a hundred times its original size. How fragile it was. He explained artificial skin, described a little-known therapy in which live maggots were applied directly to wounds. How the maggots devoured dead and infected tissue, and how their movement and secretions promoted new growth.

"We should be grateful for Vietnam," the surgeon said. Great strides in the field had been made thanks to Vietnam. Thanks to napalm.

The kid who cried all the time had knocked over a candle. He cried so much they had to clear his breathing tubes so he wouldn't choke. His father had brought him in wrapped in a blanket. When they took the blanket off most of his skin came with it, so the father had donated some of his own.

The guy next to Jelonnek had been pruning back branches from the roof of his house. (Jelonnek assumed he wasn't a renter.) The clippers had touched a power line and burned his arms off to the elbows. Because his body was an usually good conductor, the rest of him had remained virtually unscathed.

"No more choking the chicken for me," he said cheerfully. He said it every chance he got.

The guy on the other side of Jelonnek had been cleaning the carpet in his apartment. He'd mixed some chemicals. The explosion had blown him out of his living room and into someone's backyard, so in addition to full-thickness burns over fifty percent of his body and the loss of his sight, he also had a broken back. The guy next to the guy on the other side of Jelonnek had fallen into a vat of molten steel. The nurses privately called him Ironside.

"In a strange twist," the anchorman said. The nurse changed the channel.

There were patients who were at least as badly off as Jelonnek and unable to speak, but the guy whose arms had been burned off took up everyone's slack. He told knock-knock jokes, flirted with the nurses, tearfully consoled the crying kid, had more visitors than anyone, said, "Doctor, will I be able to play the piano again?"

"Your right arm for both my ears," he said, and said he'd give you the skin off his back. His positive attitude was considered exemplary, his spirit indomitable, but he was starting to repeat his jokes now and to Jelonnek they'd become a complication of his own injuries, something else to survive, and the continual lament of the kid who'd knocked over a candle seemed the only possible response.

He'd made it to her room but she wasn't there. Perhaps she'd run away.

A couple of beds emptied. The guy whose propane stove had exploded got sent home in pressure garments. (You had to get all the detergent out when you washed them, or the itching would drive you back to the hospital.) The guy with the broken back left, too, though he didn't go home. First his kidneys shut down, then the rest of him. He was replaced by a young man who'd set himself on fire in protest, though no one knew what he was protesting.

In the tub room they used scissors and tweezers. They used staple removers like you see in an office. Jelonnek saw a mirror in the tub room. He hadn't wanted to, somebody must have left it there by accident. He thought it was a picture. It had no lips or nose but it moved and had his voice. A screaming mask. Maybe they'd done it on purpose. It made a kind of sense, considering everything else they did in the tub room.

But they hadn't seen him see, didn't know that he knew.

Every morning. The only good thing about it was being able to open his mouth and drink from the showerhead when they weren't looking. He was so thirsty.

Maybe they thought he was asleep. Then he realized it didn't matter. Something was covering his eyes. He could hear them. The covers were being lifted off of him.

"While he is no longer at death's door, he is still certainly on the premises." He recognized the accent of the attending staff surgeon, noting the flexion contracture of the popliteal fossa.

There were other voices, male and female, younger, asking questions. Someone doing something to the bandages.

"Isn't this the guy—?"

The doctor prognosed lip eversion, microstamia, distortion of the nares. He warned that lid elevation could be compromised by violation of the orbital septum.

He couldn't close his eyes. He couldn't see.

"Note the fusion of the genitalia to the femoral tissue," the attending staff surgeon said. "Apparently a lighter exploded in his pocket. While it may be possible to restore a degree of function…"

He lectured on capillary permeability and blood viscosity. Jelonnek learned, was learned from.

One was from the property manager. Another from the Apostolic Faith Church (Body of Jesus Christ of the Newborn Assembly), though Jelonnek wasn't sure Littlebit still attended. There was one from some lawyer who'd printed his phone number inside, and two from Jelonnek's family back east. He couldn't imagine how they'd found him.

Littlebit opened the one from his brother. She wasn't wearing a mask or gown, but some kind of fast food uniform and if he could have smelled she would have smelled like fried fish. The shelter for women and children had a job placement program.

"Long John Silver," she said. Her arm was no longer bandaged, but it hurt when she got near the vats and she had to wear a denim sleeve.

She liked the feel of the linen. Flowers were not permitted in the ward.

While Jelonnek was being burned alive, Littlebit read, his brother had turned himself into a Jew. They were sending their prayers, she read, and Jelonnek wondered if the prayers of Jews might be more effectual than those of other creeds; his predicament would not have seemed out of place in the Old Testament. He wondered if his brother had been circumcised. He'd heard that skin donors sometimes donated foreskin, glanced at the card as if a scrap were enclosed. But the guy who'd had his arms burned off had told him this, and maybe that was just his indomitable spirit and sense of humor, affirming life once again.

"Here go another one." It was from his sister. There was something inside and Littlebit palmed it and slipped it into her uniform. Then she was tired of reading cards and picked up the remote. She enjoyed watching TV in his room, and could easily pass an hour doing so without speaking. She also enjoyed the smell of things with alcohol in them, the cool white linen, the Salisbury steak, and generally seemed to be visiting the hospital as much as she was visiting Jelonnek, the way other people go to the mall or a park.

There was one from Miss D's classmates, but Miss D wasn't there. He tried to ask where she was but Littlebit thought he'd said something else.

"They ain't been by," she said. "But it's one outside your door."

He asked again.

"She ain't well," Littlebit said. "Thowin up like what." She clicked through soap operas. Paul and Nurse Sheila, Luke and Laura, Laura and Scottie. "She off her time, too. Act like she don't know what's wrong—think I don't?"

"I find out who she been dealin with," she said, "I'll stab a nigger in his sleep."

◆　◆　◆

They were nice till they made him move his arms. They said it was important that he bend his arms at the elbows, otherwise the joints would go solid. Jelonnek didn't like them when they did this. He knew they knew what they were talking about, they just didn't have to act like he had no choice. Wasn't there always a choice?

They wheeled him off to PT, miles away, fluorescent lights streaming like the broken line on a highway. They strapped him to the tilt table. They tilted the table in increments so his joints could get used to the weight of his body. They would tilt it, leave it in that position while they saw to someone else for a while, then tilt it some more. They did this till he was standing, still strapped to the table. He hung on to the rails while they unclamped the bolts in his legs and undid the straps. They took his arms. He couldn't have fallen if he'd wanted to.

They told him to walk. On the walls were posters of unlikely athletes, people playing basketball in wheelchairs, mentally retarded Olympians. Mottos and slogans of struggle and endurance.

NO PAIN NO GAIN.

He would have the world then.

JUST DO IT.

He did it. Moved his right foot half an inch. The session was over.

They'd moved him to his own room. There was a TV but they wouldn't give him the remote; they didn't want him watching the news. He didn't mind, at least he'd gotten away from the guy whose arms had burned off. He could not get away from the thirsting and itching. Then they took him off the morphine drip and it was all over him. It started in what was left of his fingers and toes, under the nails he no longer had, and worked its way up. It seemed to consist of discrete units, like carnivorous ants swarming just under his skin, and seemed to have a kind of rage in it. He felt on fire all over again, just under the skin. He started shaking. He heard a sound like a steam kettle whistle.

She gave him a shot of something with a nice name. Everything that took pain away had a name that was nice, like Demerol Elixir. Anything to do with the body made another sound. When you heard them say eschar or debride or hypertrophy, you knew it was bad news even if you didn't know what it meant.

The nurse who gave him the shot asked him how many fingers she was holding up. She showed him a business card and said the man whose name was on it wanted to visit with him. Jelonnek turned his head to the window. He had a view of the West Hills and if you stood you could see the river and the houseboats and the neighborhoods on the southeast side. The mountain. He hadn't been outside since he'd been admitted.

Metacarpophalangeal. A terrible language that seemed to cause the condition it referred to. You felt it in your throat and wanted to throw it up, though someone else had said it.

Someone said something else and it turned into a blood clot. His leg swelled up to the size of a fire hydrant and they had to downgrade his condition. They sounded disappointed, like he'd failed them. Like when he'd eaten tuna salad and thrown up on his grafts. Everyone was mad then except the attending staff surgeon, who certainly had a right to be.

"What's one more operation out of thirty?" he said.

An old man in a white shirt and red vest, a volunteer, came around with a basket of inspirational booklets. The guy who mopped the floor in the evenings barely spoke English. He whispered to himself in Spanish and made the sign of the cross. Jelonnek closed his eyes. He woke up and the bandages were red. He hit the button and she came and reassured him that he wasn't bleeding; the bandages were medicated. She laughed gently and said they couldn't afford to let him lose any more blood, he'd taken thirty-six pints already.

His family came to visit. All of them, even family he didn't know he had. They'd crossed oceans, they crowded the room. Even his mother. He asked the nurse who'd let them in without asking him first.

She held up fingers.

A visitor came to the ward. She was a survivor, not a victim. She was on a national tour. She was very pretty and wore a trench coat. When she took off the coat her skin from the neck down looked like melted cheese. She wore denim cutoffs and a halter top made of stars and stripes.

This was how she dressed for speaking engagements, she said. Auditoriums filled to capacity. This was how she dressed when she shopped for groceries, when she rode her Harley, when she sang the national anthem at semi-professional sporting events. It was how she'd always dressed. She took off her wig.

They weren't victims, they were survivors.

A jealous boyfriend had doused her with gasoline. Her breasts had burned off and from the neck down she looked like gum that has been chewed and spat out, but she'd kept up her figure. She went hang gliding and scuba-diving. She sang the national anthem right there in the ward.

The surgeon cut off Jelonnek's big toe and attached it to his hand so he would have an opposable thumb. He made Jelonnek a nose and planted it on his forehead. He said it would have to incubate there for a while.

Jelonnek wondered where they'd plant his new cock.

❖ ❖ ❖

The detective from Hate Crimes came with the detective from Arson. They were going to take turns. A videographer came with them. An orderly raised the bed into the sitting position and left. They shut the door. The camera was on a tripod. The videographer wasn't permitted to use a light so he raised the blinds. A small tent covered the nose on Jelonnek's forehead.

He had no fingerprints. His saxophone lay blackened, melted in a plastic bag in an evidence room.

The detective from Hate Crimes read something off a sheet of paper. It was similar to the rights you are informed of when you are under arrest, but Jelonnek wasn't under arrest. He was a person of interest.

"No," he said. "Yes."

The camera made no sound.

The detective from Arson sat on the other bed. He chewed gum and cleaned his glasses.

It starts with a name, date of birth, race, sex, social security number. The night in question, and before. We do not see who is asking the questions, only who is answering them. The camera makes no sound.

"No," he says, nodding. "No."

They gave him a shot and sang "Happy Birthday" to him.

He wouldn't have known if they hadn't told him. He'd forgotten all about it. He was handcuffed to a wheelchair and pushed into the unit rec room where they formed a circle around him.

All the nurses were there, and the nurse manager, the unit director, the resident, an orderly who'd been walking down the hall. Littlebit moved her lips but you couldn't hear her, the way some people sing in church. Miss D wasn't singing at all but most of the patients in the ward were, even a man who was in such condition he couldn't speak, who managed a low, unarticulated moan bent into a kind of melody.

He looked at her belly but he couldn't tell if it was still there.

The dog sang loudest of all.

Balloons, a card, party hats on burnt scalps, a cake without candles. The cop outside Jelonnek's door had two pieces. The resident did card tricks. The people standing in the back of the room where the dog was weren't doing anything. There were windows there but it was dark and the people standing there were silent and unclothed, a naked choir waiting for its cue. A jury that will sing its verdict. Jelonnek wondered if they were there at all, but he didn't ask. The resident told him to pick a card.

Miss D gave him the present, a box wrapped in shiny colorful paper. Jelonnek held it on his lap without opening it. It was wrapped so that all he had to do was lift off the lid, but the paper was so shiny and colorful it could have been empty for all he cared.

"Open it," they said, "open it," in a circle around him, and finally he did. He looked inside. Then he put the lid back on the box and it was perfect.

Eugene Marten is the author of
In the Blind, *Waste*, and *Layman's Report*.